THE MANE
SQUEEZE

The
Mane
Squeeze

Shelly
Laurenston

BRAVA

KENSINGTON PUBLISHING CORP.
www.kensingtonbooks.com

BRAVA BOOKS are published by

Kensington Publishing Corp.
119 West 40th Street
New York, NY 10018

All Kensington titles, imprints, and distributed lines are available at special quantity discounts for bulk purchases for sales promotions, premiums, fund-raising, educational, or institutional use. Special book excerpts or customized printings can also be created to fit specific needs. For details, write or phone the office of the Kensington special sales manager: Kensington Publishing Corp., 119 West 40th Street, New York, NY 10018, attn: Special Sales Department; phone 1-800-221-2647.

BRAVA and the B logo are Reg. U.S. Pat. & TM Off.

ISBN-13: 978-0-7582-3166-6
ISBN-10: 0-7582-3166-0

First Kensington Trade Paperback Printing: November 2009

10 9 8 7 6 5 4 3 2 1

Printed in the United States of America

PROLOGUE

As soon as the earrings and shoes came off, he knew it was a brawl.

A brawl he wanted no part of. Especially when he'd been trying to sneak out. And one of the hardest things for someone like him to do was sneak anywhere. Yet he couldn't walk away, he couldn't turn his back. This was his friend's wedding, and he wouldn't let a couple of cats ruin it because they couldn't hold their liquor or their predatory instinct to maul. But maybe, just maybe, if he defused this fast enough, he could still make it out without being caught. The key was to prevent an audience. No audience, no witnesses, and sneaking away could continue.

There. A goal. He liked goals.

And with that goal solidly in mind, Lachlan "Lock" MacRyrie walked through the trees surrounding the Long Island, New York, property that held his friend's wedding. He'd never been to a wedding at a castle before but it fit the style of the bride, who brought geekiness to a whole new level. In fact, she was the one who'd told him to go. Wait. That wasn't right. She didn't tell him to go. She'd told him to, "Make a break for it! Before the hounds of darkness come for you and destroy our plans to release our people from their enslavement! Go, Lachlan MacRyrie of the Clan MacRyrie. Go! And don't look back, my friend!" It would seem strange to those who didn't know her, but Lock knew it was simply Jessica Ward's way of saying, "Could you look more miserable? Just go already!"

He'd never been so grateful, although it wasn't Jess's fault he was having a miserable time. He did a little better at full-human events since he mostly received the "shock and awe" reaction. But among his own kind, the reaction was much less . . . welcoming.

Not exactly surprising, though, when the predators knew what he was. Knew that he could shift to a ten-foot, fifteen-hundred-pound, silver-tipped grizzly bear whenever the mood struck him. How did they know? Because from early childhood, shifter parents taught their cubs and pups to recognize a few things: the cackle of a hyena, the roar of a male lion, the howls of nearby wolves, and the scent of a grizzly. For the first three on that list, the directions were simple: "If you hear one of those and we're separated, call for me. Right away." But when it came to the grizzly, the directions were much more . . . specific: "When you catch that scent, go in the opposite direction. If you stumble across one, do *not* wake it up. If you do wake one up, pretend you're dead or climb into a tree. *High* into a tree. And if you get between a sow and her cubs—pray."

Tragically, Lock couldn't even argue that any of what the other breeds said was false, although it was perhaps blown a bit out of proportion.

In the end, though, none of that mattered, because he didn't like parties, detested weddings, and being trapped in this tux was annoying him beyond reason. Normally, to save his sanity, he wouldn't even attend something like this, but he couldn't miss Jess Ward's wedding. A more amazing woman, shifter, and friend a man could never hope to have, and that's why Lock was going to undertake the painful task of getting between two snarling females before they started tearing into each other. He was almost on them, was only a few feet from getting past the trees and between them, with luck before blood was spilled, because nothing attracted shifter attention quicker than the scent of fresh blood—and, of course, two drunk chicks fighting.

Yet before he could take those last steps, she was there, shoving the two females apart before they'd made contact. With her fangs out, a low and deadly growl rolling past her lips, she held her arms out from her body to keep them separated.

"A mixed breed," some lioness had sneered about her earlier in the evening when this feline had passed. The more politically correct term was, of course, hybrid. A ridiculously gorgeous hybrid, too, whom Lock had first caught sight of at the ceremony. At the time, he'd felt someone staring at him, but that wasn't unusual. People stared at him all the time. Yet when he'd finally glanced over his shoulder, out of mere bear-curiosity, to see who it was . . . well, he'd looked right at her. And, for the rest of the evening—through the synchronized wild dog dancing, the county-wolf line dancing, and the incessant conga lines led by some annoying male lion—Lock had watched her any time she'd come into his line of sight.

It was hard *not* to watch her when she was wearing that deliciously thin sleeveless black gown, equipped with only two little strings tied around her neck to hold the delicate material up, displaying the shoulders of an Olympic swimmer, while the thigh-high slit slightly off to the side revealed the legs of an Olympic gymnast. Or maybe he was fascinated by that striking face with those almond-shaped, bright gold eyes; the small nose that made him think of a house cat's muzzle; those full lips that made him think of nothing but hot, sweaty sex; and those almost razor-sharp cheekbones that made him think she might be nothing but trouble.

Was it really any surprise he'd been unable to look away—or that he'd spent most of the evening thinking about asking her if she wanted a drink? Yeah, he'd *thought* about it. He was a bear and bears were notorious thinkers. They'd study, they'd think, then they'd move. Unfortunately he'd never found the chance to move. Not with her flitting all over that reception. Not that she was being social, though. She wasn't. He watched her talk to a few people, but mostly she seemed to be on the hunt for something or someone, her gold eyes ever watchful, ever scoping out a target. He was surprised the Marines hadn't recruited her. They'd snagged Lock right out of college and placed him with the Shifter-only Unit. He could easily see her as one of his teammates. Then again, probably not a good idea. He wouldn't have gotten much done if he was busy staring at her all day.

"Cut this shit out right now," she snarled at the two females. Her voice was low, a little rough. He liked it.

"Back off!" one lioness said. "This whore's mine."

"*Whore?*"

"That's it!" The hybrid let out a breath, lowered her arms to her sides. "That is it. Whatever Roxy O'Neill told you, it's a load of crap."

"How do you know?"

"Because I do. And if you weren't on your fifth martini and you on your seventh Long Island iced tea, you dumb bitches would know that, too."

"Watch how you talk to me."

"I would, if I thought you had a brain in that fat lion head of yours." *Does she really think this is helping?* "But you don't. So cut this shit out right now or—"

"Or what?" the other lioness demanded. "What are you going to do about it, rescue kitty?"

The first lioness laughed and suddenly the two enemies had bonded over a new target.

The hybrid knew it, too. He could tell by the way her body stayed relaxed, but her gold eyes sharpened. This wasn't her first time in a fight and she wouldn't feel bound by shifter-etiquette to fight with only her claws and fangs. He'd bet cold cash that she was armed. Not with a gun—too noisy—but with something sharp that could be quickly used and tossed away before the cops came.

The two She-lions were up against something they simply couldn't handle. Something deadlier than a mere feline or hybrid. They were dealing with a Philly girl. Or, as Lock also liked to call them, a Pennsylvania Pain in the Ass.

As a Jersey boy who'd spent many a childhood summer at the Jersey Shore with his vacationing parents, and then as a bouncer during the summer months when he was big enough to pass as "legal," Lock had dealt with more than enough visiting Philly girls to last him a lifetime. He'd never known anyone—regardless of breed—who liked to argue as much as the Philly females. They could—and would—argue over *anything*. And God help you if you took it past arguing, if you took it into something physical.

How did he know this particular hybrid was a Philly girl? Because she had it spelled out in easy-to-read script on the gold necklace hanging around her throat.

Knowing he had seconds to end this before he was forced to call the cops or dispose of bodies—both of which he'd really like to avoid, if possible—Lock moved around the three females until he was upwind of them. A small, summer-night breeze passed and both She-lions raised their heads, their noses sniffing the air as their bodies tensed, and they seemed to sober up immediately. He watched as they slowly faced him, their dark gold eyes wide as they gazed at him in mute horror. He could have done a lot of things at that moment, but Lock didn't need to. He kept the hardcore bluffing for his own kind.

Instead, all he did was curl his lip the tiniest bit and give off the softest, faintest grunt. Almost a hiccup. It worked like a charm, too, the two cats tripping backward, slamming into each other before they skidded on the damp grass and took off running into the wedding.

That left him and the hybrid. She hadn't moved at all while the cats were scrambling around her, trying to get away. But now that they were gone, she faced him. Her bright gold gaze traveled from his head to his feet and back again. He knew she might run, knew she might take a wild leap for the trees. Not hard when she had those legs.

She did neither. Instead a slow smile spread over those lips and she said, "Jersey bear to the rescue." Her head dipped a bit and she looked up at him through pitch-black lashes. "Because we both know what I would have done if they'd made a move on me, don't we, Jersey bear?"

Uh . . . yeah, yeah. Sure. Whatever. The bear in him could care less about all that . . . he only knew he wanted the pretty kitty. He wanted to pick her up and carry her back to the closest river he could find and offer her fresh salmon, honeycombs with desperate bees still clinging to them, and never-ending sex. Yeah. Sex. Lots and lots of sex.

Grizzly-Lock was so focused on the feline standing in front of him, looking sexier than anything he'd ever seen—or even *dreamed* of—before, that he wasn't at all aware of anything else. At least not until that hand roughly landed on Lock's shoulder and a male lion snarled behind him, "Just what the hell do you think you're doing with my sister?"

Startled, Lock reacted the only way the bear in him knew how. With complete and utter violence.

Spinning around, Lock grabbed the cat by the neck, lifting him up. The male's eyes grew wide, his hands turning into claws, but Lock chucked the imbecile fifty feet into the surrounding woods before he could do anything.

Jaw popping, the rage and fear ripping through him, Lock started to go after the big-haired bastard to neutralize the threat until there was no more threat, but the feline female jumped in front of him. "No, no, no, no, no, *no!*"

She placed her hands on his chest and he felt that touch go straight through his clothes and skin and right into him. Lock immediately stopped, his fangs and claws retracting. He'd never met anyone, who wasn't family or a very close friend, brave enough to risk touching him when he was like this. Brave enough not to run off, leaving friends, lovers, and blood relatives to fend for themselves. And that alone startled him back to rational thinking.

"Please don't," she begged. "They'll blame me and then the O'Neills will be responsible for another wedding brawl."

Lock watched her closely, barely aware that another She-lion—*How many did Jess know and invite to her damn wedding anyway?*—had come out of the reception in time to see the male go flying.

"Brendon!" he heard the She-lion gasp as she ran after the cat. "Oh, my God! Are you okay?" Her voice was high and weak-sounding because of her fear for the male, making the predator in Lock want to follow and finish the job. To finish both cats and carry this feline off for that fresh salmon meal. But when his gaze followed the sound coming from the woods, the feline pressed harder against his chest to get his focus back.

"As it is," she went on, her cool but tough Philly exterior dis-appearing in a flurry of panic and fear, "because of other people's stupidity, we've been banned from three Catholic churches, two Protestant, and one of the Lutherans'. And there are several re-ception halls where we've been added to the 'Do not allow' list."

Lock closed his eyes, more angry at himself than anyone else. "He startled me." And he winced at the growl of his voice, sound-ing more pissed-off grizzly than rational human.

"Everybody knows you don't grab a bear from behind. Not if you like having your face attached to your head." She rubbed her hands against his chest and Lock's eyes nearly crossed. She had painted nails that, although not ridiculously long, were longer than any he'd seen on predator females, with each nail painted dark red and elaborately decorated with flowers and other de-signs in black. It must have taken her hours to get those done, and the feel of them through his clothes was making him crazy. He should hate those nails. He normally considered that sort of thing tacky or gaudy, but damn if that look didn't work on her. And because it worked on her—it was really working on him.

"This is all my fault," she went on, oblivious to the effect she was having on him. "It's a domino effect that only my mother can cause, and I'm sorry. I was trying to keep an eye on her, but she got away from me." Mother? What did her mother have to do with this? Neither She-lion who'd been about to fight looked old enough to be her mother.

Swallowing, trying to keep his desire to maul in control, Lock motioned toward the woods. "That's your brother."

"Him?" She laughed. "No. He just wants to be. He's the half-brother of my half-brother. And the female who went in after him is his twin, who I really hate, but that's another story. Which makes her the half-sister of my half-brother, but neither of them have a blood connection to me." Lock was busy trying to place all that in some semblance of a family tree in his head when she tossed in, "Life in the Pride. It's not for everybody."

"I have one set of parents and one sister," he admitted, "and I've never been more grateful."

"I'm sorry about all this." She pulled her hands away and he almost made a grab for them so he could put them back where she'd had them. "Why don't you go before someone comes out here wondering what the latest drama is? I'll take care of this."

One side of him yelled at him to stay, to spend more time with the Philly feline, but his more rational side told him to get the hell out while he still could.

Because really, what was he going to do with a woman like her? Like most bears, he liked things calm and quiet, and something told him that even a moment with this woman would never be that.

"Thanks," he said, taking that first step back from her.

"No problem."

He told himself he didn't see regret in her eyes as he turned to walk away. He told himself, as he waited for his SUV at the valet station, a hot but clearly high-maintenance feline like her would never be interested in an average grizzly like him. He told himself, as he got into his SUV and drove away, that she would have only tolerated his quirky nature for as long as he could give her things or buy her things or pay off her debt for her.

And by the time he'd made it to Long Island's Southern State Parkway, he'd nearly convinced himself that all that was the truth.

CHAPTER 1

Now this was living. A warm breakfast that eventually stopped moving, a lovely swim in a big, empty lake, and now a chance to relax in the tall grass under the last of the summer sun.

Yeah. Gwen O'Neill could so easily get used to this.

Like most Philly and Jersey shifters, this wasn't Gwen's first time at Macon River Falls Park, where the deer were plentiful and the land full-human free, but it was definitely her first time in the "rich part." The section of Macon River Falls owned by some of the richest Prides, Packs, and Clans in the Tri-State area. When she and her best friend, Blayne, had pulled up in Gwen's work truck two days before, the guards at the gate leading to the private properties wouldn't let them pass until they'd spoken to Brendon Shaw himself and he'd vouched for them. Then the guards had acted like Gwen and Blayne were hookers hired for the weekend. Whatever. Gwen didn't let a stranger's bullshit get in her way of a good time. Family, however, was a different story.

Some days she was convinced that her family made sure their bullshit got in the way of Gwen's good time. She believed that so much, she had almost turned down Brendon's offer. He was the half-brother of her big brother Mitch, but with Mitch in Japan until the Christmas holidays and her mother off to some expensive spa with Gwen's aunts and cousins for this Labor Day weekend, Gwen knew she'd be without any go-between to help her deal with Bren's constant need to prove they were all "family." Then last week sometime, it hit her—if she came to Macon River this weekend that would mean no Mitch, no Ma, and according to Brendon, no Brendon twin, Marissa "I'm a pissy slash" Shaw. And that meant, for Gwen at least, no bullshit to deal with—for once.

Gwen would actually be able to go somewhere and relax. Simply relax. She mentioned it to Blayne and got an extremely enthused, "*Oh, my God! We absolutely have to go! Free-range hunting! Yay!*" Of course, Blayne had that type of response when Gwen mentioned stopping by a diner for breakfast before work. "*Oh, my God! We absolutely have to go! Pancakes! Yay!*"

Grinning, her long feline tongue hanging out of her mouth, Gwen rolled onto her back and stared up at the blue sky.

Nope. This was "bullshit-free" living all right, and Brendon was at least tolerable. Of course, he was also wonderfully busy. He hadn't just invited Gwen and "a friend." He'd invited the New York Smith Pack wolves and the Kuznetsov wild dog Pack. Normally, that much canine in one place would turn Gwen into a hissing, slashing house cat. But she had a secret weapon. She had Blayne and everybody loved Blayne. She was cheery, sweet, funny and, more importantly, she managed to turn herself into a human shield for Gwen. She blocked anyone Gwen didn't want to be around, somehow knowing who that was without Gwen saying a word. Blayne had a gift and Gwen used it for all it was worth.

Uh . . . *what was that?*

Rolling onto her stomach, Gwen listened carefully, positive she'd heard something.

Her ears twitched and turned, trying to locate the source—and they did. It was Blayne, who'd wandered off her own way nearly two hours before. Gwen recognized her friend's yelps of pain, the sounds intermingling with that of unknown canine growls and snarls.

Gwen took off running, using Blayne's scent to guide her.

When she saw bushy tails above the tall grass, she lowered herself to the ground and low-crawled closer.

They had Blayne surrounded. At first growl she thought it was some of the Smiths who'd maybe decided they didn't like Blayne and her confusing wolfdog ways after all. But no, it wasn't the Smiths. Their scent didn't match and their coats were much lighter than those of any of the Smiths, and a hell of a lot more raggedy, too. *Remember, people, conditioner—it's your friend.*

Gwen's teeth snapped together as she watched them slapping Blayne around. Tragically, it wasn't the first time Blayne or Gwen had been on the receiving end of group attacks by Packs, Prides, and Clans. As hybrids, they were often alone, making them easy targets for those who didn't like the idea of mixed breeds dirtying up their precious gene pools.

Blayne was going head-to-head with a She-wolf, a really big one, with twelve other wolves attacking her from behind. With so many on her, she wasn't getting a chance to defend herself properly. Even worse, Blayne was neither Alpha nor Omega. She was Blayne. And she had a high tolerance for crap until she didn't anymore—and that's when sweet, pretty Blayne would snap and what started out as general bullying turned into something that would either get Blayne killed or mean that the rest of the weekend was spent trying to figure out where to hide the body parts. Neither of which Gwen was in the mood for.

Standing up on all fours, she sprinted forward, shooting through the tall grass and right into the middle of the Pack before any of them even realized she was there. She tackled the female who'd been fighting with Blayne, the two of them rolling away in a snarling, snapping mess of fur and claws. While Gwen dealt with the female, Blayne was able to turn on the other wolves.

Gwen knocked the She-wolf away from her and into a tree, momentarily stunning her, which gave Gwen time to check up on Blayne. As always, she was holding her own, even with her smaller wolf body and tiny dog feet, but Gwen could see the whites of her friend's eyes. A sure sign Blayne was about to lose it. Gwen had to break Blayne's concentration now or clean up the destruction later. She sprinted at Blayne and caught hold of the back of her neck as she kept going right by her. Blayne yelped, more from surprise than pain, but it got the reaction Gwen needed, forcing Blayne to focus on something else. She dropped her and the two friends kept running, the Pack right on their ass.

Gwen couldn't run for long, though. She was a natural sprinter, but she didn't do marathons. So she needed to get the wolves off their ass because the fact that they were following meant this was no longer a simple—but painful—"teasing" of the mixed breed.

Turning her head, looking for a way out of this, Gwen caught a scent she'd been taught to recognize before she could even shift. She'd also been taught to run away from that scent. Far away, as fast as she could go. But that wouldn't happen now. Now she was going to use it to her advantage.

Gwen turned, steering Blayne with her body, the Pack staying right on them. As they neared where she wanted to be, Gwen pulled out ahead. Blayne sped up to stay by her side, but when Gwen was about ten feet from her destination, Blayne hit the brakes, so to speak. Her too-small wolfdog paws digging into the soft dirt, trying to stop and ending up flipping backward, the Pack trampling right over her.

Perfect. Just what Gwen wanted.

Homing in on her target, Gwen leaped up as a wolf paw hit her on the hind leg at the same moment. Pain tore through her limb, but she ignored it, instead focusing on where she was landing.

And where she landed was right on his back, biting down on the thick lump of muscle between his shoulder blades while her body slid across and off him. Considering his size, he moved faster than anything she'd ever seen. In one fluid movement of violent, cranky, *startled* muscle, the grizzly boar rose, unleashing his full rage on all who were near. What was probably seven feet as human was now an easy ten feet on his hind legs. What was about three hundred and fifty or so pounds of human muscle was now fifteen hundred of grizzly muscle. And what had once been asleep was now awake.

And pissed off.

The wolves tried to stop in time but they couldn't, and they slammed right into those enormous claws that were slashing and ripping wildly. The bear-roar sent calm birds screeching from the trees and Gwen got to her feet behind the grizzly, watching as he tossed two-hundred-plus-pound wolves into trees or lobbed them thirty feet out into the grass with no effort at all. She was enjoying every second of it, too, until that damn She-wolf came at her from the side, her fangs tearing into Gwen's already wounded hind leg. Gwen roared and hissed at the same time, going at the female again. Before she could get to her, though, before she could slap the crap out of her, there was suddenly a big bear ass coming right for her.

The Pack of thirteen turned out to be a Pack of twenty-three. They came out of the trees, charging the bear, startling him again and forcing him back. And back he moved.

Normally not an issue, until Gwen realized she was at the top of what the brochures called one of Macon River's "scenic" cliffs. Across the chasm was one of the falls, beneath that was part of the raging river.

Gwen tried to dodge out of the bear's way, but he must have felt her behind him and turned, his paw already swinging out. Yet when he saw her his small brown eyes grew wide and although he managed to not use those four-inch claws to rip her face open, his forearm still caught her and the strength of it sent her flipping back. She landed flat on her stomach, her legs dangling over the cliff's edge, while she caught hold of the ledge with her front claws. But the ground was softer in this spot and her three-hundred-pound tigon form was simply too much. She slid over the side, her claws leaving gouges in the dirt, so she quickly shifted to human, hoping her lighter weight would help. She was able to grab hold of a branch with her hand, but it started to break away almost instantly.

"Shit," she blurted out. "Shitshitshitshit!"

Then the biggest human arm she'd ever seen was reaching down, big long fingers catching hold of her hand.

"Hold on! I've got you!" he called out. She looked up into that face and immediately recognized him. The bear from the Smith-Ward wedding who'd chucked Brendon Shaw into the woods like a five-pound sack of potatoes. She recognized those dark brown eyes, that handsome if almost painfully sweet face, and that great brown hair with silver tips she'd stared at all through the wedding ceremony. And he recognized her, too. The pair locking gazes in a shocked moment of clarity.

Feeling the strength of the hand that gripped her so tightly and relieved that she knew the bear, Gwen began to smile . . .

Until that first bit of wet dirt hit her face and after a heart-stopping moment of feeling the ground beneath them begin to buckle from his weight, the bear rapidly hauled her up. But it wasn't fast enough. The earth gave way beneath him, raining down on Gwen, forcing her to look away. Yet she still managed to see that big, human male body tumbling forward—right into her.

She screamed as they went freefalling, tumbling through the air. Instinctively she shifted back to her cat form, knowing it could handle more damage than her weaker human one. But still—for this level of fall, she didn't have much hope. And all she could think was *I can't believe I'm going to die in fucking New Jersey!*

But before her life could flash before her eyes or she saw any white tunnels with her dead relatives waiting at the other end, Gwen felt long, unbelievably strong, fur-covered arms wrap around her, pulling her in close to all that hard muscle.

She buried her head against the bear's furred body, held her breath, and together they slammed into the rushing river beneath them.

CHAPTER 2

The salmon were everywhere, leaping from the water and right into the open maws of bears. But he ruled this piece of territory and those salmon were for him and him alone. He opened his mouth and a ten-pound one leaped right into it. Closing his jaws, he sighed in pleasure. Honey covered. He loved honey-covered salmon!

This was his perfect world. A cold river, happy-to-die-for-his-survival salmon, and honey. Lots and lots of honey . . .

What could ever be better? What could ever live up to this? Nothing. Absolutely nothing.

A salmon swam up to him. He had no interest, he was still working on the honey-covered one. Yet the salmon insisted on staring at him intently . . . almost glaring.

"Hey!" it called out. "Hey! Can you hear me?"

Why was this salmon ruining his meal? He should kill it and save it for later. Or toss it to one of the females with cubs. Anything to get this obviously Philadelphia salmon to shut the hell up!

"Answer me!" the salmon ordered loudly. "Open your eyes and answer me! *Now!*"

His eyes were open, weren't they?

Apparently not, because someone pried his lids apart and stared into his face. And wow, wasn't she gorgeous?

"Can you hear me?" He didn't answer, he was too busy staring at her. So pretty!

"Come on, Paddington. Answer me."

He instinctively snarled at the nickname and she smiled in relief. "What's the matter?" she teased. "You don't like Paddington? Such a cute, cuddly, widdle bear."

"Nothing's wrong with cute pet names . . . Mr. Mittens."

She straightened, her hands on her hips and those long, expertly manicured nails drumming restlessly against those narrow hips.

"Mister?" she snapped.

"Paddington?" he shot back.

She gave a little snort. "Okay. Fair enough. But call me Gwen. I never did get a chance to tell you my name at the wedding."

Oh! He remembered her now. The feline he'd found himself daydreaming about on more than one occasion in the two months since Jess's wedding. And . . . wow. She was naked. She looked really good naked . . .

He blinked, knowing he was staring at that beautiful, strong body. *Focus on something else! Anything else! You're going to creep her out!*

"You have tattoos," he blurted. Bracelet tats surrounded both her biceps. A combination of black shamrocks and a dark-green Chinese symbol he didn't know the meaning of. And on her right hip she had a black Chinese dragon holding a Celtic cross in its mouth. It was beautiful work. Intricate. "Are they new?"

"Nah. I just covered up the ones on my arms with makeup, for the wedding. With my mother, I'd be noticed enough. Didn't want to add to that." She gestured at him with her hand. "Now we know I'm Gwen and I have tattoos . . . so do you have a name?"

"Yeah, sure. I'm . . ." He glanced off, racking his brain.

"You don't remember your name?" she asked, her eyes wide.

"I know it has something to do with security." He stared at her thoughtfully, then snapped his fingers. "Lock."

"Lock? Your name is Lock?"

"I think. Lock. Lock . . . Lachlan! MacRyrie!" He glanced off again. "I think."

"Christ."

"No need to get snippy. It's *my* name I can't remember." He nodded. "I'm pretty positive it's Lock . . . something."

"MacRyrie."

"Okay."

She gave a small, frustrated growl and placed the palms of her hands against her eyes. He stared at her painted nails. "Are those the team colors of the Philadelphia Flyers?"

"Don't start," she snapped.

"Again with the snippy? I was only asking."

Lock slowly pushed himself up a bit, noticing for the first time that they'd traveled to a much more shallow part of the river. The water barely came to his waist. She started to say something, but shook her head and looked away. He didn't mind. He didn't need conversation at the moment, he needed to figure out where he was.

A river, that's where he was. Unfortunately, not his dream river. The one with the honey-covered salmon that willingly leaped into his mouth. A disappointing realization—it always felt so real until he woke up—but he was still happy that he'd survived the fall.

Lock used his arms to push himself up all the way so he could sit.

"Be careful," she finally said. "We fell from up there."

He looked at where she pointed, ignoring how much pain the slight movement caused, and flinched when he saw how far down they were.

"Although we were farther upriver, I think."

"Damn," he muttered, rubbing the back of his neck.

"How bad is it?"

"It'll be fine." Closing his eyes, Lock bent his head to one side, then the other. The sound of cracking bones echoed and when he opened his eyes, he saw that pretty face cringing.

"See?" he said. "Better already."

"If you say so."

She took several awkward steps back so she could sit down on a large boulder.

"You're hurt," he informed her.

"Yeah. I am." She extended her leg, resting it on a smaller boulder in front of her and letting out a breath, her eyes shutting. "I know it's healing, but, fuck, it hurts."

"Let me see." Lock got to his feet, ignoring the aches and pains he felt throughout his body. By the time he made it over to her, she opened her eyes and blinked wide, leaning back.

"Hey, hey! Get that thing out of my face!"

His cock was right *there*, now wasn't it? He knelt down on one knee in front of her and said, "This is the best I can manage at the moment. I don't exactly have the time to run off and kill an animal for its hide."

"Fine," she muttered. "Just watch where you're swinging that thing. You're liable to break my nose."

Focusing on her leg to keep from appearing way too proud at that statement, he grasped her foot and lifted, keeping his movements slow and his fingers gentle. He didn't allow himself to wince when he saw the damage. It was bad, and she was losing blood. Probably more blood than she realized. "I didn't do this, did I?"

"No. I got this from that She-bitch." She leaned over, trying to get a better look. "Do I have any calf muscle left?"

He wasn't going to answer that. At least not honestly. Instead he gave her his best "reassuring" expression and calmly said, "Let's get you to a hospital."

Her body jerked straight and those pretty eyes blinked rapidly. "No."

That wasn't the response he expected. Panic, perhaps. Or, "My God. Is it that bad?" But instead she said "no." And she said it with some serious finality. In the same way he'd imagine she would respond to the suggestion of cutting off her leg with a steak knife.

"It's not a big deal. But you don't want an infection. I'll take you up the embankment, get us some clothes—" if she didn't pass out from blood loss first "—and then get you to the Macon River Health Center. It's equipped for us."

"No."

"I've had to go there a couple of times. It's really clean, the staff is great, and the doctors are always the best."

"No."

She wasn't being difficult to simply be difficult, was she?

Resting his forearm on his knee, Lock stared at her. "You're not kidding, are you?"

"No."

"Is there a reason you don't want to go to the hospital?" And he really hoped it wasn't something ridiculous like she used to date one of the doctors and didn't want to see him, or something equally as lame.

"Of course there is. People go there to die."

Oh, boy. Ridiculous but hardly lame. "Or . . . people go there to get better."

"No."

"Look, Mr. Mittens—"

"Don't call me that."

"—I'm trying to help you here. So you can do this the easy way, or you can do this the hard way. Your choice."

She shrugged and brought her good foot down right on his nuts.

Gwen took off, shifting in midhop, which amped up her wounded speed another twenty miles per hour or so. She could see the path leading out of the riverbed and planned to get there and then to the trees. Grizzlies couldn't climb trees, and Macon had some really high ones. Yet, she didn't realize how fast grizzlies could move until the big, shifted bastard grabbed her from behind. He wrapped those furry arms around her waist, the four-inch claws a little too close to her tender underbelly, and lifted her up. Intent, it seemed, on carrying her cat ass to some horrible hellhole where human beings went to die so their organs could be harvested!

Well, Gwen O'Neill wasn't going out like that.

She started twisting and swiping at him with her claws. She could feel fur-covered flesh being ripped off, and although he never once lashed back at her, he didn't let her go, either—until he got slammed into by the full force of a six-hundred-pound male lion.

Gwen went down with them, but the bear had to turn his attention to the lion trying to kill him and removed his arms from around her waist. Relieved, Gwen scrambled away as the two beasts fought. It was brutal, bloody, and ugly—she enjoyed every second of it, too, until that multicolored long-furred wolfdog came running up to her, barking and barking until she shifted into a black woman who had a tendency to blame Gwen for everything. So, in a way, she was *still* barking, when she said, "What the hell are you doing? Stop them!"

"I shouldn't interfere," Gwen said blandly, as two apex predators fought to the death behind her.

"Gwen," Blayne chastised, her caring dog side out there on display, "he saved your life. I saw it. Now stop them!"

Gwen and Blayne had met in what Gwen still referred to as prison but others called Catholic school. Ninth grade detention specifically. After a rocky introduction, they'd been best and inseparable friends ever since, with more in common than people realized and a bond that was stronger than anyone dare risk trying to come between—as quite a few males had learned throughout the years.

And yet, none of that stopped Gwen from torturing Blayne when the opportunity presented itself . . . like now.

Giving a helpless shrug, Gwen said, "It's really none of my business."

"*Gwendolyn O'Neill!*"

She blinked. "Ma? Is that you?"

Blayne pushed her shoulder, so Gwen pushed her back.

Blayne's mouth dropped open. "Don't push me."

"You pushed me first."

So Blayne pushed her again and Gwen pushed her back.

"Don't test me, Gwen," Blayne warned. So Gwen pushed her again, this time using both hands and putting a little more "shove" in her push than she had before.

"So what ya gonna do? Huh?" Gwen gleefully taunted, ignoring the brutal pain in her calf and the blood pooling at her feet. "What are ya gonna do?"

And like she did that first time they met in detention all those years ago, Blayne Thorpe grabbed Gwen's hair and yanked like she was yanking weeds out of her garden.

The lion had managed to get him on his back, his paw raised above Lock's head, while Lock was moments from throwing him off and then batting him around the river until he was nothing more than a gold furry ball of flesh.

Unfortunately, both males were distracted by the screaming, naked women fighting while a She-wolf quietly watched from a distance and scratched her ear with her back leg.

Normally Lock would be right there with that She-wolf, watching two really attractive naked women fighting while scratching parts of himself he couldn't reach as human, but he was still worried about Mr. Mittens's calf and yes, if he had his way, he'd call her Mr. Mittens until the end of time.

Shoving the lion off him, Lock stood and shifted. He stalked over as the feline brought up her hands, her claws unleashing and the other female—a canine from the scent of her—covered her face, screaming, "Not the house cat, Gwen! Not the house cat!"

Not even wanting to hazard a guess at what the hell the canine might be talking about, he grabbed both females around the waist and yanked them apart.

"Stop it! Both of you!"

"She started—"

"*You* started—"

"I don't want to hear it!" he roared, silencing them immediately. "Again with the fighting?" he said to Gwen. "What the hell are you thinking? Your leg is hurt, or did you conveniently forget that part?"

"You're hurt?" the other demanded, looking guilty when she really shouldn't. "Gwen, why didn't you tell me?

"It's not that bad."

Lock released the canine. "We need to get this one—" he jostled Gwen a bit, much to her annoyance "—to a hospital. She refuses to go, I'm taking her anyway."

The other female placed her hands on her hips, her much shorter, less well-treated nails tapping against her waist in the same way the feline's had. "Again with this, Gwenie? Again with this bullshit?"

"I'm not going," the feline said calmly and with much certainty.

"Yes, you are," Lock told her.

"Oh, no, I'm not."

The canine put her hand on Lock's arm. "It's all right," she said. "Let's just get her back to the house and clean up that wound ourselves."

Lock scowled, not liking that idea, because he knew how bad the wound was, but the canine gave him the tiniest wink. He almost missed it.

"Okay, Gwenie?" the canine asked, smiling.

"Yeah. That's fine."

"Great."

Lock began to release Gwen, but a quick shake of the canine's head had him stopping and, instead, he tightened his grip. The feline looked down at his arm and then her head snapped up to look at the wolfdog.

"Blayne Thorpe, don't even think—"

The canine, Blayne, took her friend out with a beautiful right cross to Gwen's jaw. The impact of the hit so strong, Lock was forced to take a step back in order to keep the woman in his arms. He hadn't seen a punch like that since he was a recruit in training.

Lock gaped down at Blayne. She had this innocent look to her with that beautiful brown skin and those full cheeks with deep dimples that flashed every time she smiled. And yet . . .

"You hit her."

"Of course I hit her," she said, shaking out her hand and wincing. "Although she's got a jaw like granite. But if we tried to take her to the hospital wide awake, she would have put up one hell of a fight. Now we can just lift her up and go."

Lock sighed. "I forgot."

"Forgot what?"

"Philly logic."

Blayne laughed and patted his forearm. "Let's get her to the hospital before she wakes up."

Lock lifted Gwen in his arms and turned, but found an alley cat in his way. "Don't I know you?" Lock asked, feeling like he'd met the man before.

"Give her to me."

Turning away with his prize, Lock shook his head. "No. Get your own cat."

"She's *my* sister."

Lock looked at the Asian feline in his arms and at the Anglo lion standing across from him, seething. "You don't look re-lated," he said flatly.

"It's complicated." When Lock merely stared at him, he added, "I'm the half-brother of her half—"

"Stop," Lock cut in, remembering that impossible family tree, and in no mood to hear it again. "Look, I've got her, I'm carry-ing her, and I'm taking her to the hospital. So you can back off and let me do what I'm going to do, or you can get your ass kicked and I'm still going to do what I'm going to do. Your choice."

Lock saw a flash of lion fang, but the She-wolf who'd been sit-ting off to the side and watching all this time leaped between them, going up on her hind legs, her front paws landing on the big cat's shoulders as she shifted from canine to human. "Now, darlin'," she said in an accent Lock found kind of irritating, "you gettin' all upset ain't gonna help our Gwenie one little bit. We'll let him carry her and we'll be right behind 'em the whole way."

The lion leaned down a bit and whispered, "But she's naked."

Oh, yes. She was. And Lock was enjoying every second of it. She had the softest skin, and with her being so much smaller than he was, he could rub her all over his body like a loofah sponge. He wouldn't . . . but he *could*.

"Darlin', we're all shifters here," the She-wolf stroked the cat's shoulders. "Now don't you worry, we won't let anything happen to our Gwenie." The She-wolf looked over her shoulder at Lock and smiled. "You won't let anything happen to our Gwenie, will you, Mr. . . . uh?"

"MacRyrie."

"Will you, Mr. MacRyrie?"

"Nope. I won't let anything happen to her."

"Good." She patted the lion's chest. "See? She'll be fine, Shaw. Let's just get this done—okay?"

The cat sighed, but nodded his head. "Okay. But I'm not happy about it."

Lock walked off with Gwen tight against his chest and Blayne beside him.

"You didn't back down from him at all," Blayne whispered, her eyes wide in awe.

"Why should I?"

"Because he's the always-dominant male lion."

"Yeah. And I can use his thighbone to pick my teeth."

Laughing, Blayne patted his arm as they all headed to the medical center.

She looked up from her mystery novel and watched as the younger members of her Pack limped and yelped their way back to the cars. She knew those two hybrids couldn't have done this much damage. Then again, maybe they weren't as alone as she'd first thought.

It was an O'Neill she'd sent the younger members of her Pack after. She knew it was an O'Neill as soon as she'd seen the pickup truck by the Macon River pier that morning with the family name stenciled on both doors, and when she'd seen that the female getting out of the driver's side was Asian, she'd known without a doubt it was Roxy O'Neill's half-breed spawn. Years of hatred had welled up nicely, and she didn't even bother trying to let it go. Sometimes things were simply too perfect to pass up.

Too bad she'd relied on others for what she could have easily done by herself.

Her daughter came forward, probably not wanting to shift back to human until she knew her mother's mood. As usual, she seemed to have the least amount of damage, which was typical since she took after her mother and knew, instinctively, how to hit fast and strong while avoiding any real injury to herself.

Behind her daughter was that useless boyfriend of hers. A plotting little fucker, always up to something. No use complaining, though. He brought in money and that was something that made it easier to overlook his major flaws. She knew, though, watching him, that he was up to something again. That he was plotting again. He stopped, staring back the way they'd come. Her eyes narrowed as she watched him, wondering what was going on in that dense head of his.

Closing her book, she said to her daughter now standing in front of her, "Let me guess . . . you got your asses kicked by two freaks."

And when her daughter's head quickly turned away, eyes gazing off—she knew she was right.

CHAPTER 3

"**M**ind telling me what happened?" The lion sounded gruff and angry when he spoke to Blayne, who Lock now knew was a wolfdog hybrid, but she didn't seem to notice the cat's tone or to mind it.

Blayne grinned. "Oh, no. I don't mind telling you!"

Lock finished pulling on the hospital scrubs given to him by one of the nurses. He was grateful the medical center employed bears, because they had his size in stock. Nothing was quite as embarrassing as putting on pants that ended up looking like he was wearing knickerbockers. But as he pulled the green-colored shirt down his torso and shook his hair out of his eyes, he noticed that Blayne had yet to answer.

She was still smiling at the lion, while the lion and She-wolf sitting across the small waiting room near the front doors of the center were staring back.

Lock watched, fascinated, as the mutual staring went on for nearly a minute before the lion barked, "*Well?*"

Blayne jumped, her smile fading. "Well what?"

Gold eyes turned to him and Lock shrugged. What did the cat expect *him* to do?

The She-wolf, Ronnie Lee Reed—said in an annoying, almost singsong way, as if it was one single name, "ronnieleereed"—

placed her hand on the cat's arm while asking the wolfdog, "What happened, darlin'?"

"We got jumped." Blayne paused, thought a moment. "Actually, *I* got jumped. Then Gwenie got in the middle of it and it turned into a street fight, which was kind of fun because we haven't been in the middle of one of those in a long time. We've been trying to be less McFighty the last few years," she said to Lock. "But it turned nasty fast, which really sucks, because I didn't actually do anything wrong to deserve getting slapped around. I mean a girl is minding her own business, trying to catch a squirrel, and then she's jumped for no good reason other than someone's political agenda—"

Blayne abruptly stopped talking when the cat snarled at her.

Lock understood the cat's frustration. It seemed he felt responsible for Gwen or Gwenie or whatever the hell the feline's name was, and took it personally that she'd been hurt. Still, there were better ways to handle a skittish wolfdog, and snarling at her wasn't it.

Dropping into the chair beside Blayne, Lock cringed when the plastic squealed in protest. Sure, the center may have scrubs and operating tables big enough for bears, but they hadn't planned far enough for their chairs. But his reaction got Blayne to laugh a little, and he knew that would help.

"See how they treat the grizzlies?" he asked, smiling with her.

"At least it didn't break."

"Thanks. That makes me feel much better." She giggled a little more. "Did you know the wolves that jumped you?" he asked casually, but directly. He could tell that being direct with Blayne was important if he wanted direct back.

She shook her head, her smile again fading as she thought carefully on her answer. "No, but . . ."

"But?"

Her brows pulled down and Lock could see that she was remembering the whole fight. Of course, he could remember the fight by simply looking at her face, arms, and feet. She had bruises and cuts, but none like Gwen's wound. Meaning Gwen had pissed someone off. Although, it wasn't really a stretch for him to see how she could do that.

"Earlier today we went down to the pier to hang out a bit—we used to go there every summer when we were younger—and there were lots of wolves. They may have locked on to us from there. The scents *may* have been the same, but I'm not sure." She gave a frustrated little pout. "Yeah. I'm not sure."

"That's okay," Lock assured her.

"But the She-wolf who jumped me," Blayne went on, "she came after me like I fucked her father or something."

Lock snorted, then laughed. "But you . . . uh . . . didn't?"

Her smile came and went and came back again so easily, even as she wiped blood out of her eye, that Lock found her interesting and very sweet. "No. I'm not into the older sugar daddy–younger girl thing. But I've always had a father figure in my life. I call him Dad. So maybe that has a lot to do with why I can resist the temptation. I often go for unemployed losers my own age instead."

"Would you know any of that Pack if you saw them again?"

"Maybe."

"Wouldn't *you* know them if you saw them again?" the cat asked Lock, although Lock sensed there was definite sneering behind that question.

"Not necessarily," Lock answered honestly. "I was asleep and they woke me up."

"That was Gwen," Blayne filled in, answering the question that had been bothering Lock since he'd recognized Gwen's face as she hung off that cliff. "She aimed right for you. I thought she'd lost her mind, especially when she bit your big grizzly hump." Blayne blinked and then, slowly—and in a pathetic attempt at nonchalance—leaned back, trying to see between Lock's shoulder blades.

Lock leaned back with her and said, "It's not nearly as prominent when I'm human, Blayne."

She quickly sat forward. "I wasn't . . . I mean . . . I was only . . . um . . ."

"When I get startled awake," Lock went on to the lion and She-wolf, trying not to chuckle at Blayne's embarrassment, "I wake up swinging and anything in my way gets slapped around."

"How nice for your friends and family." And there went that sneer again.

"My friends and family know how to ease me out of my slumber." He glanced at Blayne. "Coffee's always good. Croissants with honey on the side, even better."

"I'll have to keep that in mind," the cat practically snarled.

Lock studied the cat for a long moment before finally asking, "Do I *know* you?"

The She-wolf leaned forward a bit and whispered, "You kind of slapped him around at Jessie Ann Ward's wedding."

Lock snapped his fingers. "You!"

"He didn't slap me around," the lion barked. "He assaulted me."

"You came at me from behind."

"You were near my sister!" As if that alone was a crime.

"I was talking to her. That is allowed, ya know?"

"Not in my world, it's not!"

As the two predators glared at each other across the room, Blayne suddenly sat up straight and said, "Uh-oh."

He didn't know if it was her tone or the expression on her face, but Lock's entire body tensed.

"She's awake," Blayne said simply.

Lock knew then something was *very* wrong.

Gwen's nose twitched, the smell of antiseptic nearly causing her to gag. Then she heard those telltale sounds—a high-pitched beeping, steadily going up; the tear of plastic on hygienically maintained bandages and equipment; and the gruff orders of medical personnel.

Her eyes opened and an older coyote female smiled down at

her. "Hello, Miss O'Neill. Everything is okay. I'm Dr. Davis and
you're going to be just fi—*ack!*"

She heard the nurses and other doctors yelling, but all she
could focus on was how this murderer, this coyote savage was
about to kill her! About to cut her open and remove her organs!

Die, doctor! Die!

Strong hands tried to pry her off the coyote's throat but she'd
never let her go.

"No one's killing me and taking my organs!" she screamed.

"Gwenie! Look, Gwenie! Look what I have!"

Recognizing Blayne's voice and knowing the wolfdog loved
her and would save her from having her vital organs sold on the
black market, Gwen glanced over.

"Look at the sparkly, Gwenie! Don't you wanna touch the
sparkly?"

Of course she did! Gwen released whatever she had in her
hand and reached for the sparkly, shiny thing Blayne held. Gwen
loved sparkly, shiny things. They were sooooo pretttttyyyyyyyyy-
yyyyy . . .

Blayne came back into the waiting room and, letting out a
dramatic breath, sat down beside Lock again.

"Whew! That was close. I had to steal someone's car keys off
their desk to distract her."

"What happened?" Lock had to know. He hadn't been this
entertained in years.

Blayne shook her head. "I told them when we came in how
they should treat her dosage, but they never listen."

Ronnie frowned. "Treat her dosage?"

"We're hybrids," she needlessly reminded them. "What works
for you as wolf doesn't necessarily work for me as wolfdog. And
it's the same with Gwenie. Her metabolism is way higher than
any lion's or tiger's. Most doctors try and base it on her weight
as cat, which is about three hundred pounds unless she's a little
bloaty. Then it's like three-hundred-and-twenty-five, but either

way, basing it on her weight never works. I told them if they didn't give her enough, she'd wake back up. 'Don't worry. We're giving her something that will paralyze her muscles,' they tell me."

"Probably pancuronium." When they all stared at Lock, he asked, "What?"

"Yeah," Blayne said. "That stuff. Which I, personally, piss out. It doesn't do anything for me."

"At all?"

"Nope. And I warned them it wouldn't work on Gwen unless they gave her enough. And what happens? She woke up and everyone is all shocked. 'Why is she up?' She's up because you idiots didn't listen to me in the first place."

"Is that why she's afraid of hospitals?" Lock asked.

"No. She's afraid of hospitals because she saw this documentary on PBS once about organ theft. Ever since then, she's been convinced they—the elusive 'they,' the terrifying '*they*'—want to steal her organs.

"Seriously?"

"I'm *not* that creative. Couldn't make that up."

"But everything will be all right now?" the cat asked. "She has the right dosage now?"

"Doubt it."

Clearly not the answer the cat wanted. He snarled, "What do you mean you doubt it?"

The wolfdog leaned away from him, and Lock got tired of his attitude.

"Don't yell at her."

"I wasn't yelling, and no one's talking to you."

"Now ask me if I care you're not talking to me?"

"Why are you still here?" the cat demanded.

The She-wolf reached for him. "Brendon—"

"Stay out of this, Ronnie." He glared at Lock. "Look, Baloo—" and if there was one thing Lock hated, it was those damn bear nicknames, even the ones from classic literature "—I think it's time for you to go."

"I think I'd like to see you try and make me."

The lion actually stood, but the She-wolf grabbed the bottom of his hospital shirt, desperately trying to yank him back to his seat. At that moment, the doctor walked into the waiting room. The expression on her face was . . . odd. Although "confused," might be a better word. But Lock knew that as a patient, he never wanted his doctor to look odd *or* confused.

"What's wrong?" The lion stepped toward her, forgetting Lock. "What happened?"

"She's . . . uh . . . disappeared."

"She . . . she what?" The cat stormed past the doctor and into the medical suite, Ronnie Lee and the coyote behind him. But Lock noticed how Blayne didn't move. Nor did she look very concerned.

Lock sighed. "Where is she?"

Blayne shrugged. "Knowing my Gwenie? Halfway back to Philly."

"You sure? She wouldn't be hiding in a closet? Or in the bathroom or something?"

"Nope. Out the window is my guess. She'll stay in the trees. She's got those fierce tiger legs but, because of her weight, she can go like fifty feet, easy. Double what most tigers can do. Even if she is hopping."

"And you want me to go after her." He wasn't asking because he already knew that's what she wanted before she sweetly smiled up at him.

"Would you?" she asked, those brown eyes begging. "Please?"

"Fine. For you." Lock stood, walked out of the medical center and around the building until he caught the feline's scent. He followed.

Gwen lounged on that tree limb, panting softly and enjoying the fresh air.

She detested hospitals. The way they smelled, the off-white or green painted walls, and that lingering vibe of death. Okay, so she hadn't been in an actual hospital this time but close enough. If there were doctors and nurses, she was in a hospital.

It drove her mother crazy. Roxy had been a registered nurse for years before she opened her first salon, and two of Gwen's aunts and several of her cousins had been doctors' assistants or medical technicians. Roxy had tried to put Gwen on the same track, starting her off as a candy striper. But that after-school job lasted about a day before Gwen took off running and spent the rest of the night throwing up in the bathroom from her full-on panic attack. She hadn't willingly been back in a hospital since. "Willingly" being the keyword, because Gwen had *found* herself in hospitals more than once. She'd wake up and boom! There she was. But she was older now and crafty. They couldn't keep her if she didn't want to stay. No matter how much her leg hurt or how weak she felt from blood loss, she wasn't going back to that death motel.

Of course, no worries on that. Not with her so high up. And even if they found her, they'd never get her down from here. Even Brendon, cat that he was, couldn't climb a tree.

Gwen rested her head on her folded arms and began to drift off to sleep.

"Comfortable?"

"Hmm," she answered. She liked that voice. It was so low. She could imagine waking up to that voice every day, with it whispering that breakfast was ready or asking her if she wanted to share the shower. She could imagine all sorts of dirty things to be done with soap if that voice was involved. And yet . . . why was that dirty, sexy voice so close?

Gwen opened her eyes and blinked several times. His arms were folded on her tree limb the same way hers were and his head rested on them as he watched her with those beautiful brown eyes.

"Christ, how tall *are* you?"

He scowled. "It's not that I'm so tall, Mr. Mittens, it's that you're not that high up."

"Bullshit." She had to be like, forty feet up. Maybe even fifty! Right? She glanced down. *Wrong.*

Still, she wasn't exactly lying on the ground either. "You're like seven feet tall, aren't you?"

"I am *not* seven feet tall," he snapped at her as if she'd really insulted him. "I'm six-eleven." When she smirked in disbelief, he added, "And three-quarters."

"And that quarter inch makes such a difference, too."

"That's it. I'm taking you back to the medical center."

Like hell.

As the grizzly reached for her, Gwen unleashed her claws and quickly scrambled up higher. She knew for a fact that grizzlies couldn't climb trees, either. *So there!* She was totally safe. She'd simply stay here until she healed up and then she'd head on back to the safety of her Philly streets.

"You're being ridiculous," he called up to her.

"I'm not going back there to die. I can do that just as well out here, in the fresh air." With all her organs intact in her decaying body.

"If you go back to the medical center you're not going to die."

"Like I'll believe that lie for two seconds."

"And what about when the fever hits? You're going to fall out of that tree eventually."

Gwen couldn't help but get kind of smug. "The O'Neills don't get the fever."

"Don't even try it."

"We don't. My brother got shot three times two months ago, and he didn't get the fever."

"I bet your family gets shot at a lot, huh?"

"Hey, hey!" Gwen said excitedly. "Look at this! Look at this!" She extended her arm and gave him the finger.

"I should leave your Philly ass up there!" he snarled.

"Like I'd ever need help from some Jersey rich boy!"

"Look, Mr. Mittens—" and Gwen didn't think she could explain how much she hated when he called her that "—either you get your ass down here or I'm getting you out of that tree the hard way."

"You have an enormous head," Gwen taunted, enjoying the way his entire body tensed. "It's like a giant kumquat." Then she giggled hysterically, liking the word "kumquat" way more than she should.

"You want it that way," he said low, "you've got it." He stepped back and pulled off the hospital scrubs he'd been wearing. She only had a moment to wonder why he was getting naked—and enjoying *that* astounding view for all it was worth—before he shifted to bear. His height increased considerably once he did, going from his nearly not-quite seven feet to a full ten, but she was still too high for him to reach.

Leaning over, she taunted, "Nice try but no—"

Gwen squealed, gripping the branch she was on. He didn't try and climb up to her, he simply took firm hold of the old tree and began to shake it. Christ, how much did she guess he weighed as bear? Fifteen hundred pounds? Maybe more? And all of it pure muscle. With his claws gripping the trunk, he simply shoved the tree back and forth. It was an old tree—sturdy, strong, and disease free—but it still wasn't strong enough to stand up to the grizzly, the roots beginning to tear from the ground as he relentlessly kept up his actions.

"Stop it!" Gwen yelped, but he ignored her.

The tree, loose from its anchor in the ground, swung forward, Gwen's lower half flying free of the branch and dangling in midair. She yelped again, and the tree came swinging back. Her body already weak, her hands lost their grip on the tree and she went headfirst toward the ground.

She closed her eyes, not wanting to see that last second of her life. Yet the bear again showed how fast he was for his size, plucking her out of the air and pulling her in tight against his body. She wrapped her arms around his neck, her hands resting on the giant lump of muscle between his shoulder blades.

Gasping for breath, she clung to him, burying her face

against his neck. She felt his fur recede, his body straightening as it shrunk down to its only slightly less freakishly tall height, while the dramatic hump between his shoulder blades grew smaller and smaller until she could only feel it as several extra layers of muscle. He began walking, briefly stopping to pick up the scrubs.

"I can't go back," she whispered against his neck, horrified she couldn't stop the shaking of her body.

He stopped, the tree he'd taken her from crashing to the ground behind them, and gently asked, "What are you afraid of?"

"Dying."

He stroked her side with his fingertips and she was surprised at how gentle his hands were. How gentle *he* was, considering he'd torn an eighty-year-old tree out of the ground and she'd told him he had a kumquat head.

"You'll be fine."

"You can't promise that. They're going to get me on that table and they're going to start cutting me open and they're going to—"

"Hey, hey." He leaned back a bit, trying to catch a glimpse of her face. "Wait a minute. Where's my tough Philly girl?"

"Dead, if you take me back there."

"Do you really think I'd let anything happen to you? That I'd let anyone hurt you? After everything I've done today to keep you breathing?"

"I'll be alone with those sadists and you'll be in the waiting room."

"I'll stay with you."

"They won't let you."

His smile was so warm and soft, she found herself wanting to trust him when she barely trusted anyone.

"Do you really think anybody can force me to do anything?"

"Another bear?"

"You'd have to find one who cares," he whispered. "Most of us don't. But we do keep our word. It's the MacRyrie bear way."

"You promise you won't leave me?"

"I promise."

With her free hand, she clutched his shoulder with what was left of her strength. "Tell me something about yourself. So I know I can trust you."

"Um . . . I was a Marine."

"No. Not that. Something else. Something . . . just about you."

"I do a little woodworking."

"Like birdhouses? Whittling?"

"Okay."

"And what else? Tell me something private. Something no one else knows."

He thought a moment before he lifted her closer and Gwen couldn't believe how good his skin felt dragging against hers. Whispering against her ear, he confessed, "When I'm really stressed out . . . I play with my toes."

Gwen leaned back a bit and stared at him. "Seriously?"

"It's really relaxing and very bearlike."

And very weird. And yet . . . "I'm oddly comforted by this information."

"When this is all over, I'll show you how to do it."

She gave a little laugh, her eyelids trying to close. "There's a specific way to do it?"

"If you want maximum benefit."

"Oh. Well, then . . ."

"I'm going to take you back now, okay?"

She tensed up but she could no longer fight her desire to sleep. "But you won't leave me?"

"I promise."

"And you won't let them kill me or remove any of my vital, healthy organs to sell on the black market? Or exchange my vital, healthy organs with crappy, full-human ones?"

"Not a chance."

"Okay." She snuggled in closer, her nose against his neck, breathing in his scent. "I have your word?"

"You have my word."

" 'Cause where I come from, your word means something."

"And you've got it. I won't leave you, Gwen. I promise."

"And you'll stop calling me Mr. Mittens."

"Let's not ask for the world, okay?"

And even as she felt him taking her back to that death trap, she still managed to smile.

Chapter 4

The doctor wasn't remotely happy that Lock wouldn't leave, but once he started tossing his sister's name around, she backed off. As the top neurosurgeon at McMillian Presbyterian in Manhattan, Dr. Iona MacRyrie's name held definite clout, and Lock wasn't above using it when necessary.

The surgery went well, but the damage to Gwen's leg went beyond typical Pack harassment. There'd been real intent behind that wound and, although the unknown She-wolf may have made Blayne her first target, it had been Gwen who had really set her off. Maybe it was the cat-dog thing, Lock didn't know or care. He simply knew that no matter how much that idiot lion glared at him from behind the glass of the operating room doors, he wasn't leaving.

Maybe Gwen was being irrational—okay, she *was* being irrational—it didn't matter. He'd made a promise, given his word, and he hadn't been joking. MacRyries kept their word. That had been drummed into him by his uncles since he was a kid. They'd felt the need to help raise Lock because, to quote them, "Your father's kind of a pansy, know-it-all. You'll need us to give you the basics about life." At five, he didn't know what they'd meant, but by his early teens he understood that "pansy, know-it-all" translated into "college-educated." And his father's position as a highly respected university professor of literature and philosophy? Simply a fancy way of saying, "no real job."

Strange thing was, they didn't feel the same way about Lock's mother. "Your father's saving grace" was what they called Alla Baranova-MacRyrie, Ph.D. Although a third-generation Russian-American, Alla was a direct descendent of the Kamchatka grizzlies of the Russian Far East. Tougher shifters one would never meet. There was only a small group of them in the States, but their bloodline was well-known and they were more feared than the Kodiaks.

In the end, though, none of that mattered to either of his parents. They were intellectuals and raised their children to be as well. Iona turned out perfectly. Brilliant, pretty, and married with three cubs, she was in medical school before she was old enough to legally drink. And only recently turning thirty-five, she was head of her entire department.

Lock, however, was pretty much . . . average. He didn't need a lot to make him happy. Fresh salmon, imported honey, and doorways that he could clear without having to duck usually did it for him.

"I think she's starting to wake up," the nurse said.

Lock stood and walked over to Gwen's bed. She was covered from neck to legs by a blanket, but he discovered when he pushed her hair off her forehead that she was cool to the touch.

"No fever."

"Yeah. That's what her friend said would happen." The nurse talked while quickly and expertly cleaning up the operating room. "Her Pride doesn't get the fever. Weird, huh?"

Things could be weirder.

"Gwen?" he called out softly when he saw her eyelids flutter. "Gwenie?" Her head rolled to one side. "Mr. Mittens?"

Her lip curled up as she snarled and her head rolled back so she could open her eyes and glare at him. "Stop calling me that," she whispered.

"But you're as cute as a Mr. Mittens," he teased. "Like a little house cat."

"Bastard," she mumbled, her eyes closing again. Then she was out.

"Is she supposed to drop like that?"

The nurse glanced at her and went back to her work. "It's normal for her, according to her friend." And typical that only the nurses listened to the helpful friend while the doctor almost got choked to death because she thought she knew better. "They really need to do more research on hybrids. Less chance of the doctors getting their throats torn out if we knew what we were dealing with."

"Uh-huh," Lock muttered, his gaze stuck on Gwen's face. She was so pale. He was glad he'd decided to stay and—

"Excuse me?"

Lock glanced over at the double doors leading in and out of the recovery room. He scowled. "You must be kidding."

The polar grinned and motioned to the hallway with a twitch of his head before disappearing outside. Lock looked back at Gwen, brushed stray hairs off her cheek and out of her eyes before he sighed and followed.

Lock knew the polar. Everyone called him "Toots." He'd been born and raised in Macon River Falls, New Jersey, and like everyone else in his family, he'd stayed on to become one of the Macon River Falls Rangers. Part peace officer, part animal-park ranger.

Stopping in front of him, Lock crossed his arms over his chest. "That big-haired bastard called the cops?"

"You didn't expect him to take you on himself, did you?"

"Yeah, he might crack a claw."

Toots laughed. Like most polars, he had a healthy sense of humor and white-brown hair. He was also a good eight inches taller than Lock and quite a bit wider, since the polars had a tendency to stay closer to their bear size in human form than the grizzlies did, which was one of the reasons more polars were found in smaller, out-of-the-way towns like Macon River than in big cities like New York or Boston, where they would receive more attention than they wanted.

"Personally, I'm thinking that hot little She-wolf stepped in to prevent it."

Hot, huh? "Her feet are as big as yours."

"The bigger the feet, the bigger the tits."

Never a big fan of "guy talk," Lock shook his head and said, "I promised her I'd stay."

"The She-wolf?"

"No." He motioned to the recovery room. "The tigon."

"Wow. Got a tigon in there and a wolfdog out there. Two hybrids in one weekend—that's gotta be a record for us."

"I'm not leaving."

"Yeah, ya are. Or I can arrest your dumb ass and you can enjoy some time in our lovely jail."

"I haven't done anything wrong."

"Part of my job is preventing anything from happening as much as it is to fix things when they do happen. You don't leave, that cat goes postal, you slap him around, the She-wolf calls her itty-bitty friends and, like the dogs they are, they come running. You'll slap them around. At that point, I'm back out here because the doc's called me to get you off the property. Or, you can leave with me now and everybody's happy and breathing."

"Everybody's happy but me."

"Sacrifices have to be made, and we know that lion ain't makin' any if he can help it." Toots winked at him, motioned to the exit door. "Come on, shorty. Let's go. You can seethe all the way back to Van Holtz territory."

"Gee, thanks."

How did he let this happen? He'd promised Mitch he'd take care of Gwen. One weekend out, and she'd been assaulted by interloping wolves and mooned over by that imbecile bear.

Talk about dropping the ball.

Blayne stormed back into the waiting room. At five-eleven, she was a good three inches taller than Gwen, but both hybrids were still pretty small as human compared to most of the breeds they were mixed with.

"You called the cops?" Blayne accused and Brendon could only stare at her.

"What?"

"You called the cops on the bear! I was standing out front and I saw them driving away in the Ranger's SUV."

Not sure what she was talking about, but not in the mood to get into a fight with a woman who would happily have a verbal argument with lint, Bren could only shrug. "I don't know what you're talking about."

"It was me," Ronnie cut in and they both looked at her.

"I'm sorry, darlin'," Ronnie said simply, "but he needed to go."

"Why?" Blayne demanded, looking surprisingly angry over a bear she didn't even know.

"Because he didn't need to be here." Ronnie's voice was calm and very controlled, which Bren knew was not a good thing. Happy and sunny equaled good. Calm and controlled equaled wolfdog without her head.

"I don't think that was your decision to make," Blayne practically snarled.

"And I think you should suck my—"

"Why don't you check on Gwen," Bren quickly cut in, grabbing Ronnie's hand and intertwining their fingers before she could finish that particular sentence. "She'll be waking up soon."

With a loud and rather dramatic sigh, the wolfdog stormed off, and Bren kissed the back of Ronnie's knuckles. "Thanks."

Ronnie's bubbling anger slipped away and she smiled at Bren. "Gwen will be okay."

"Yeah, but—"

"And there's no need to call Mitch about this."

He winced. "Are you sure?"

"You wanna see that little mixed-breed feline really mad at you, Brendon Shaw? You just call her brother back here over something like this. Take it from a 'baby sister' who knows. You leave that boy right where he is and let us take care of Gwenie."

He nodded and pulled Ronnie over until she sat on his lap. "I'm so glad you're here."

She kissed his cheek and put her arms around his shoulders. "I'm glad, too. Did you see the claws on that bear? And he was aiming right for your pretty face, too!"

Gwen opened her eyes and snorted. *Figures.*

"What?" Blayne asked, staring down at her.

Blayne was staring down at her. Not a handsome bear. But Blayne. She loved Blayne . . . but Blayne wasn't the bear. The bear who'd made a promise. Gave his word!

See? She couldn't rely on anyone but herself, her family, and Blayne. Crazy, never-knew-when-she-would-snap, anger-management-classes-are-her-friend Blayne. Anyone else—*not* to be trusted.

"Nothing's wrong," Gwen lied.

"You sure?"

"Yeah. I'm sure. So can I leave?"

"Brendon's signing you out now. You can't walk on that leg for at least four hours, so he's going to have to carry you. Or Smitty." Blayne's lips pursed. "The Pack's here, too."

Gwen didn't ask why the Smith Pack was here because she already knew. Ronnie Lee called one of them and said in that annoying country twang, "No, no. I don't need nothin'. I'll be fine. Y'all don't worry 'bout me none." And the dogs ran over like Ronnie was being locked into an Animal Control van.

"Whatever," Gwen sighed. Because really . . . would it have killed the bear to have stuck around at least until she woke up? At least until he knew she wasn't about to become another victim of body-part theft? Apparently it would have, because he wasn't here. Like he'd promised!

As Gwen always suspected, male bears were no different from any of the other breeds. All males were born liars. Every last one of them. And why the hell did she care so much that he hadn't stayed and she felt moments from pouting?

It must be the medication. That was the only thing that made sense. All those stupid meds flowing through her body were making her an emotional wreck.

Brendon walked in. "All right. Let's get out of here."

Blayne slipped her arm under Gwen's shoulders to help her sit up.

"I've got her." Brendon waited until Blayne stepped aside and then easily scooped Gwen up in his arms.

"You don't need to carry me like I'm an infant."

And proving how much like Mitch Shaw he really was, Brendon cried out dramatically, *"Would it kill you to let me help you?"*

Blowing out a sigh, Gwen looked at Blayne and Blayne looked down at the floor, her shoulders shaking from laughter.

"No, Bren. That's fine."

He smiled, happy he'd gotten his way. "Thank you."

Ulrich Van Holtz continued to read the latest tome on world economics, pretending to be bored, but in truth absolutely fascinated!

He loved weekends like this. Weekends without his father, Alder, or brother in attendance because if there was one thing that pair knew how to do really well was ruin a relaxing weekend among family.

But instead of enduring the presence of those two, Ric was instead getting a few days of downtime with his favorite cousins, a few hours on his own to read a dry, detailed exploration on failing economics, and a chance to watch his best friend storm into the house, slam the door behind him, and make all Ric's lounging cousins disappear in the face of that grizzly boar-rage.

Awesome.

Lock MacRyrie stalked by the living room entryway wearing

hospital scrubs, a scowl, and a series of fresh bruises on his face and neck.

"Lock?"

The grizzly walked back and stood in the archway. "What?"

"Should I ask what happened to your face?"

"It doesn't matter," he growled before storming off again.

Placing his book on the table, Ric followed his friend. When the grizzly started to head out a back door, Ric caught his arm and led him toward the kitchen.

Adelle Van Holtz, his father's first cousin but mature enough that Ric always referred to her as Aunt Adelle, glanced up from whatever she was mixing for tonight's dessert. Her mouth dropped open in shock when she saw Lock.

"Lachlan!" She put down her mixing bowl and rushed to him. "My poor baby. What happened to you?"

"I really don't want to talk about it," he muttered and Adelle pulled him toward one of the stools by the breakfast bar that separated the kitchen from one of the smaller dining areas.

"You sit right down here," she said, amusing Ric, who sat next to him. It fascinated him the way the older She-wolves pampered Lock like a giant teddy bear, while all the older males hated and feared him.

"You going to tell me what happened?" Ric asked, reaching for one of the berries from the massive bowl Adelle placed in front of Lock, but quickly snatching his hand back when she slapped it.

"I said I don't want to talk about it."

"You'll feel better."

"No, I won't."

"Did you end up on the wrong side of a buck again?"

"No. Wolves." When Ric and Adelle passed glances, both wondering who in their Pack would be stupid enough to go up against any bear, much less Lock, he shook his head. "Not your Pack. Some other flea-bitten Pack."

"Excuse me, but we haven't had an outbreak of fleas in years. And what other Pack?"

"I don't know."

Adelle cleared her throat, her face concerned. "I know some of the Smiths are staying out at Shaw's place this weekend. But I can't imagine Bobby Ray would—"

"These weren't Smiths. I've dealt with Smiths before, and met a few of the New York Pack at Jess's wedding. It wasn't them."

"Okay. Then who do you think—"

"She's going to think I deserted her," Lock blurted out.

Her? Lock didn't have a "her" in his life. He'd had a few "you remember, what's-her-names" over the past couple of years, but they'd come and gone quickly with little thought. The only females in his life that Ric knew Lock thought about on a regular basis were his mother and sister. Otherwise, Lock kept primarily to himself.

"And who would this *she* be exactly?"

"I said I don't want to talk about it."

"But I'm sure we can go to wherever *she* is and—"

"Forget it. It doesn't matter." Lock picked up his bowl of berries and walked out of the kitchen.

After they heard his bedroom door slam shut, Adelle asked, "Do you think his 'she' is a wolf?"

"He smelled like he'd been around a feline, but what kind, I'm not sure."

"A feline? For my Lock?" Adelle scrunched up her nose. "I'm not sure some feline's going to be good enough for him."

If Lock really liked her, whoever she may be, Ric wouldn't care. His friend had not had an easy life, so a little feline canoodling couldn't hurt.

Ric slid off the stool. "Let me see what I can find out."

"Good."

"Did you say Brendon Shaw was in town?" he asked, always wanting to get information up front before he threw himself into things.

"Yes. Brought out a bunch of people, too, including Smitty's Pack and Jess's."

Ahh. Sweet Jess. Ric had always liked her, and was not happy he couldn't make her wedding. But he should have known that a sudden demand for an important business trip would rise up out of nowhere as soon as Ric's father had found out he hadn't been invited to the wedding but Ric had.

"I'll let you know what I find out," he promised, heading to the back door and pulling out his cell phone.

CHAPTER 5

O ne small kitchen fire later and Jess Ward-Smith was racing across territorial lines and right into Ulrich Van Holtz's open arms.

Oh, and it was a small, controlled burn. Nothing to worry about. Simply a way to distract one overprotective hillbilly wolf and his hillbilly wolf kin while she illicitly met up with one of the coolest-named guys *ever*.

"I'm so glad to see you!" she said, hugging the wolf tight.

He hugged her back and kissed her on the cheek. "Me, too." He placed her down and studied her carefully. "You look astoundingly beautiful," he said easily. He had to be the only man she knew who made those kinds of compliments sound as if he was stating the obvious rather than merely trying to flatter her. "And very happy."

Jess Ward-Smith knew she was blushing now, but she couldn't help it. "Yeah, okay," she admitted. "I am."

Ric laughed and gave her another hug.

Like all the Van Holtz males, Ric was tall, well-built with a slightly overdeveloped diver's body, and handsome. Yet handsome was only the first stop on the beauty train for Ric, who managed to head all the way into the station for The Land of Gorgeous. With his sculpted cheekbones, Grecian nose, square jaw, and that always freshly tousled dark blond hair, it still surprised her he'd never done any modeling.

"And pregnant, too," he teased. "My, those Smith males move quite fast."

"Don't start." Jess stepped away from him, but kept a grip on his hand.

Knowing she was short on time once Smitty realized she'd sneaked out—would she have to endure his Smith protective streak through *every* damn pregnancy?—Jess asked, "I got your text, handsome, what's up?"

"Lachlan MacRyrie went out for salmon and a nap, but came back covered in bruises and in full boar-rage. Any idea why?"

Jess briefly covered her mouth with her hand, a small gasp escaping before she said, "Oh, my God! That was Lock?" When Bren had muttered something to Smitty about an "annoying, fatass, stubby-tailed bear," she'd assumed it was one of the local bears. Not her Lock! And the last thing that man had was a fat ass, but that was a treacherous un-mate-like thought for another day. "Is he okay?"

"Physically he's fine. But he's rarely this pissed off. I'd love to know why, so I can avoid any maulings this evening."

"Well, the men aren't telling me anything, so I brought Blayne along to fill in the holes. She was there with Bren's sister, Gwen. Right, Blayne?" Jess looked around, wondering where the wolf-dog she'd dragged along with her had gone off to. "Blayne?"

Ric picked up a pair of shorts from off the ground. "She's disappeared."

No. She hadn't. But she had found a squirrel. Jess and Ric watched as a shifted Blayne chased the squirrel, caught the squirrel, toyed with the squirrel, let the squirrel go, only to go chasing after it again. Until she was distracted by the crow that she tried to catch in her mouth.

"So . . . when are you due?"

Jess winced at Ric's question as Blayne ran into a tree, backed up, and went after the bird again. "Mid-March."

"And you're having a—"

"Yes. Yes, I'm having a wolfdog."

"Huh."

Blayne was turning in circles now, trying to catch her tail.

"Blayne," Jess called out. "*Blayne!*"

The wolfdog immediately stopped and started to walk over to Jess and Ric. Too bad the dizziness got the best of her, though, because she stumbled sideways into another tree and slid down, panting.

Picking up Blayne's clothes, Jess walked over to her. Blayne had an interesting look to her as wolfdog. Built like a wolf, with a heavy coat and muscular body, she still had the giant ears and tiny paws of the wild dog along with the coloring that included big splotches of white, brown, blond, black, and red all over her shaggy coat. Not surprisingly, Blayne dyed her human hair one solid color, like most wild dogs. They were the only shifters forced to do so if they hoped to fit in among full-humans.

"I don't have all day," Jess said, wondering how hard it would be to raise the one wolfdog she was currently pregnant with, much less the seven girls Smitty believed they were going to eventually have because his "prem'nitions" told him so.

"Sorry," Blayne said after shifting. She stood and quickly pulled her clothes on. "Got distracted."

Jess didn't mention that Blayne seemed to get distracted often. "Blayne, this is Ric. Ric, Blayne."

They shook hands and then Ric asked, "So what happened?"

"Well—"

"Don't ramble," Jess said quickly, which got her a harsh glare. In answer, Jess tapped her wrist, where her favorite watch usually was, but it had been taken by Smitty and hidden for the weekend. "I'm on a tight schedule here, sweetie."

"More like a tight leash with a hillbilly at the other end of it."

Jess gasped in outrage and Ric quickly placed his hand on Jess's shoulder. "So what happened?" he asked Blayne again.

"It was a hate crime."

Jess looked at Ric and back at Blayne. "You mean they attacked you because you're bl—"

"A hybrid. Exactly!"

"Oh." Jess rubbed her forehead. "All right then."

"You and your friend are both hybrids?" Ric carefully asked.

"Yup. I'm wolfdog, Gwenie's tigon. They jumped me, Gwen jumped in, we took off running, Gwen woke up the bear, they went over the mountain. There. That quick enough for ya, Jess?"

Ric's back snapped straight. "I'm sorry. Um . . . they went over . . . wait . . . what?"

"Not at first. At first, Lock was slapping those wolves around. Then they were going over the mountain."

"*Over* the mountain?" Jess shook her head. "Do you mean they rolled down a hill?" She'd lived in Tennessee for two years, she was used to hills.

"Nope. Over the mountain, into the river, down the river."

"You mean they fell into Macon River from one of the falls?" Ric demanded.

"It was more of a cliff than a fall, but . . . yeah. I met up with Bren and Ronnie about a mile away. Together we ran down to the mouth of the riverbed, and that's where we caught up with Lock. He was trying to take Gwen to the medical center, but she was putting up a fight because of the organ thieves."

Ric stepped back. "The what?"

Jess held her hand up to halt Ric, wanting Blayne to finish before she killed her. "Then what?"

"Then Bren fought the bear, I fought Gwen—"

"Why were you fighting Gwen? Because of the organ thieves?" *Wait. Did I just say that out loud?*

"Because she wouldn't tell Bren that the bear helped her and Bren thought the bear was attacking her when he wasn't."

"Why wouldn't she tell Brendon that?"

"Because she was torturing me."

"All right then." Jess was done. "This was fun but—"

"No, no, no." Blayne clutched her hands together nervously or excitedly . . . to be honest, it was hard to tell. "There's something else."

"You know the Pack who did this?" Ric, so cute when he was trying to maneuver a wolfdog into a nice, logical, *straight* line. *Good luck with that one.*

"No," Blayne said simply. "I have no idea who it was."

"Then what?" Jess pushed.

"I don't know if I mentioned it, but I'm planning some life changes."

"Life changes?" What did this have to do with *anything?*

"Yes. Huge ones, actually. And so lately I've been mostly focused on me, you know, kind of obsessing, worried about how I was going to do this and everything and then it hit me!" She grinned, showing all those perfect teeth that had to be the product of excellent dental care and childhood braces. "What a really cute couple Gwen and Lock are!"

Ric laughed as Jess shook her head, turning to walk away. "Oh, my God! You must be joking!"

Blayne jumped in front of her. "I'm serious! You have to see them together. They're so freaking cute!"

"He's bear, she's feline. He lives in New York, she lives in Philly. The list is endless of why this is a bad idea." Plus this was her Lock! Jess loved Lock. He was the sweetest, kindest, nicest bear ever. And all Jess knew about Gwen was that she threatened Brendon Shaw's cranky sister with acid during the wedding. Not that Jess blamed her or anything, because Marissa Shaw could be a real bitch, but Lock deserved a lovely sow who loved him, pampered him, and understood his obsession with honey. Not some vicious-tongued cat who'd greeted Jess the last two mornings with, "Hey, Fido. How youse doin'?"

"I'm telling you—cute. Adorable!"

"Blayne, forget it."

Blayne sighed. "Okay. You're probably right."

"Do you really think that pouty-face move is going to work on *me?*" Jess asked. "I perfected it."

"What about two pouty faces?" Ric rested his chin on Blayne's shoulder and blinked big brown eyes at Jess. "Will that work?"

"What are you doing?"

"I have no idea." Ric grinned. "But I have to say that I'm completely in for the ride."

"But this is my Lock," Jess argued. "I mean . . . who is *she*?"

Now it was Blayne's turn to gasp in outrage. "Are you implying my Gwenie isn't good enough for your bear?"

"I'm not implying anything. I'm saying it. Out loud."

"Breedist!"

"I am not!"

"Breed-*ist*!"

While the two females snarled viciously at each other, Ric grabbed a stick from the ground and waved it between Jess and Blayne. "Look! Look! A stick! Who wants it? Who wants it? Go get it!" He threw the stick and Jess and Blayne watched it flip across the forest floor. Once it landed, they looked back at Ric.

"Dude," Jess told him, "that was just rude."

Niles Van Holtz, Alpha of the Van Holtz Pack, briefly glanced up from the pan he was scrubbing. "Hold on."

His assistant watched him for several long minutes until Van was satisfied the pan was perfectly clean. If there was one thing he couldn't stand, it was crud on his dishes and cookware.

"What is it?" he finally asked while carefully drying the pan with a clean cloth.

"There was a territorial breach on Van Holtz property. Another Pack."

"Which property?"

"East Coast. Macon River Falls."

"Uh-huh."

He certainly hoped there was more to it than a simple territorial breach for his assistant to come in on his day off. Especially if it involved his cousin Alder's New York–New Jersey territories. As it was, Van didn't involve himself in the day-to-day operations of his cousins' territories and sub-Packs. He made the assumption that those who'd fought their way to the top could manage. Besides, the only thing he liked to micromanage was his restaurants, his kitchen, and his delicious wife when they were in bed. Any other time, she wouldn't tolerate it, and he couldn't be bothered.

"There were injuries."

"How bad?"

"Bad enough we were given a heads-up by the medical staff. And there's something else."

He hoped so because right now it didn't sound like anything his idiot cousin couldn't handle.

Van hung the now-dry pan from the rack over his counter before he faced his assistant. "And what's that?"

"The ones that were attacked were hybrids."

Van sneered. No, his cousin couldn't handle this. Or maybe Van should say that Alder *wouldn't* handle this, his opinion on hybrids having been made quite clear over the years. Yet Van understood what his cousin didn't when it came to hybrids—an attack was rarely just an attack when mixed breeds were involved. "Get my cousin on the phone."

His assistant sighed. "Which cousin, sir? At last count, you had—"

"I know how many cousins I have." And why did he allow his wife to hire his assistants? They were all like her in tone but without the added benefit of a great ass and genius-level IQ. "Get me Ulrich out of New York on his cell and put him through to my office."

Cousin Alder wouldn't like it, but it was time to see what Alder's youngest boy, or as Alder liked to call him, the "useless, worthless, prissy boy" was truly made of.

CHAPTER 6

Gwen sat on the top stair of the porch, her elbows resting on her knees, her chin resting in the palm of her hands. She stared off into the woods.

She stared and she sulked. She hated when she sulked.

As it grew later, finally drawing to a close this hellish day, Blayne sat down beside her, resting her elbows on her knees, her chin in the palm of her hands. She stayed silent a good five minutes, which for Blayne was pretty much a record.

"What's wrong?" Blayne finally asked.

"Nothing," Gwen answered. "I'm just sitting here. Staring." Maybe hoping a bear would wander out of the woods to say "hi and I'm sorry I broke my promise."

"How's the leg?"

"Healing." Although it did feel like rats were inside her calf, tearing the flesh apart with their teeth and then sewing it back together with a giant needle and some thread.

"Hurts like a bitch, huh?"

"I haven't started screaming yet, have I?"

"You have a point." Blayne took a deep, satisfied breath. "It's really beautiful here, isn't it?"

"Yeah."

"Beautiful house," she sighed. "Great weather."

"Yep and yep."

"And that grizzly—"

"*Left me!*" Gwen screamed out, startling the birds from the trees.

Lock brushed the attacking bees off his face and dug into the hive again, pulling out the honeycomb. He shook off the clinging bees and broke off a piece. Ric sat down against a tree opposite from Lock that was close enough so they didn't have to scream at each other, but far enough away to help Ric avoid the rampaging bees.

Once he seemed comfortable, he observed, "You've stripped the trees of their bark quite nicely."

"Yeah," Lock mumbled around the honeycomb. "Sorry about that."

Ric shrugged. "My father had them imported from Japan for a tidy seven-figure sum, had them featured in that *Vanity Fair* article on him and the Van Holtz dynasty, and got an award from the Tree Rescue Foundation for his efforts to resurrect nearly extinct trees—but I'm sure he won't be too upset."

Lock winced. "Now I feel bad."

"Don't," Ric said good-naturedly. "Now—" Ric cringed when Lock bit into a honeycomb and spit out a bee he'd started to chew on "—Adelle is going to make her honey-glazed chicken. Unless you're all honeyed out."

Lock stared at his friend, and Ric nodded. "As I thought. So dinner is set. But before we go back, perhaps you can fill me in on why you're sitting out here, tearing the bark off trees and abusing bees."

Ric cringed again when Lock spit out another bee.

"What?" Lock demanded, tired of being judged for his eating habits. "Would you prefer I eat them?"

"No, no. You keep doing whatever it is you enjoy doing. No matter how vile."

Lock stared down at the remnants of the hive and admitted what was bothering him. Something that even honey wasn't curing. "I should never have left her."

"Did you have a choice?"

"If I wanted to fight a polar."

"Weren't you the one who told me that when it comes to bears—bigger wins?"

"Yeah." And Toots was definitely bigger. "But I promised her I wouldn't leave her. I guess I just feel like I let her down by not being there when she woke up fully."

"Okay, so maybe you did let her down a little. But I'm sure when she calls, you can explain—"

"Calls?"

"To thank you, of course. It's proper etiquette to send a thank-you note or call after someone saves you from a violent Pack, Pride, or Clan attack."

"I'm sensing she didn't get much shifter etiquette training in Philly. Or, now that I think about it, *any* etiquette training in Philly."

"But you did give her your number? Or you got hers?"

Lock stared at his friend. "My number?"

"You didn't give her your phone number?"

"She was wounded. It didn't occur to me." When Ric sighed, his disappointment clear, Lock threw in, "And I'm sure that cat wouldn't have let me leave anything for her anyway."

"What did the cat look like?"

"I don't know. He was a little thing. Tiny. Lion . . . I think. You know, the breed with all the hair."

"Tiny. Right. The world is filled with tiny lion males. And the only *tiny* lion I know of this close to my territory is Brendon Shaw. And, if I remember what you told me correctly, he's the one you beat up at Jess Ward's wedding. Something I'm sure he did not forget since last you two met."

"He didn't. But I didn't beat him up," Lock quickly added. "I . . . I simply threw him five . . . or maybe it was fifty feet into a tree."

The two friends gazed at each other for a long moment.

Finally, Lock shrugged. "That does make it all kind of awkward, doesn't it?"

And that's when Ric started laughing.

* * *

"You don't want to talk about the bear?" Blayne asked.

"No."

"But you just yelled about him. So maybe we need to discuss—"

"No."

"Okay." The sun began to slowly set and that's when Blayne abruptly turned to Gwen and spewed out in one, never-ending sentence, "My father wants to retire and he wants me to take over his business and I'm moving to New York and I want you to move with me so we can be partners and run the business together, preferably in Manhattan rather than Queens, because you're my best friend and I love you and it'll be great!"

Gwen continued to watch the sun go down behind some trees. "Only you, Blayne," she said calmly, "would spit out life-changing decisions like bullets from a tommy gun."

"Is that a yes?" Blayne asked, with that hopeful eagerness that never seemed to die a humane death.

"No. That's not a yes. And what makes you think you need a partner to run your dad's business? You're smart, Blayne, no matter what Sister Mary Rose told you. You'll be fine."

"In business terms, I'm a big-picture thinker. I have big plans for this business. But details, Gwenie, are not my friends. *You're* the one who handles details beautifully. To sort of quote my dad, I'm the fuck-up with big ideas and you're the stabilizer."

Gwen chuckled. "You're not a fuck-up."

"Maybe not. But I don't want to do this on my own."

And Gwen knew why. Because Gwen had all the confidence but none of the courage to see her dreams through, while Blayne had all the courage but none of the confidence. In many ways . . . they were a perfect team to run a business. If only Gwen could walk away from her family. Walk away from Philly. But she couldn't.

"Why make me a partner, Blayne? In a year you'll have everything running fine and you'll resent me taking part of your profits. And I will take part of the profits if I'm a partner."

Blayne stared down at her feet. They were too small for her size and definitely too small for the She-wolf in her. Some days she could do amazing things with those feet, other days she could barely manage to make it down flights of stairs, escalators, or simply walk from one room to another without falling on her face. "Other than my dad, I don't have anybody but you, Gwenie. You're my Pack."

"A Pack of two? That's awfully sad."

"It doesn't have to be. Not if we do something with it. By myself I can keep the business going. Maybe for the next forty years. But together . . . we can really do something with it, and enjoy ourselves."

Gwen was fighting really hard not to get caught up in Blayne's excitement. She'd done it before, gotten caught up. And that way laid madness . . . and jail time. Yet the thought of their own business . . . just the two of them. No Pride or Pack to answer to, no decisions made that were not theirs and theirs alone. "Yeah. Maybe that's true."

"I know you've got a lot invested in Cally's business—"

Gwen barely stopped herself from snorting at that one.

"—and that it will be hard to walk away from that—and from your mom. But if you just give me a chance—"

"Stop." Gwen wanted to rub her calf. Actually, she wanted to shift, rip off the bandage, and lick her calf until the pain went away.

Blayne winced a bit. "Your mom at it again?"

"She wants me running the business." Roxy's business. The one Gwen had absolutely no interest in.

"Well . . . if it's your business, I guess that's the same as the two of us . . ." Her words died off as Gwen let out a bitter laugh.

"I said she wants me *running* the business. Not that she'd *give* me the business. That business belongs to the Pride."

"You're part of the Pride."

"No, Blayne." Gwen looked her friend in the eyes and said what they'd both known for a very long time but neither had ever said out loud. "I'll always be an outsider."

"But they don't treat you like—"

"They treat me like family. But where they go, what they do as a Pride—I'm never part of that. I never will be part of that."

Blayne's jaw clenched in frustration. "That doesn't seem fair, Gwen."

"Sweetie, haven't I taught you there is no fair among predators?"

"Then nothing should be holding you back. You should come with me. Screw 'em all."

"She's still my mother, Blayne."

"And?"

"I can't leave Roxy on her own. I'm her only daughter."

"And she's got a whole Pride watching out for her. A Pride you're not even a part of."

"Yeah, but—"

"Yeah, but what? Instead of spending your whole life worrying about family who love you but not enough to give you as much power as the rest of them, maybe you should think about yourself for a change. About what *you* want."

"Because it's that easy?"

"No. It's not that easy. It wasn't easy for my dad to walk away from his Pack. But he did it anyway. For me. Because they wouldn't take us both and he wasn't giving me up. He made choices to benefit me and . . ."

"And now you need to be there when he needs you."

"Because of me he doesn't have anybody else. Your mom can't make the same claim."

Blayne put her arm around Gwen's shoulder and hugged her. She'd always been affectionate, even though Gwen wasn't. But she was Blayne and she would always do things her own way.

"Just think about it before you say no, okay?"

Lie to her. Tell her what she wants to hear so you both *can pretend you have a choice.* "Okay."

After another quick hug, Blayne left her and Gwen sat there. She didn't know for how long, but the entire time her mind kept jumping back and forth between what her life would be like if

she left Philly—from the best possibility to the absolute worst—
to what her life would be like if she stayed. And although she loved
her mother for never giving her up and making sure the family
never turned on her, forcing her out, Gwen couldn't shake the feeling that her future was not meant to be in Philly. It wasn't meant
to be with the O'Neill Pride. She'd always be an O'Neill, but
would her future cubs be raised by the Pride, her life dedicated to
the Pride? No. She didn't see that. She didn't see that at all.

Eventually, as if she'd somehow summoned her out of sheer
will alone, the phone rang, and it was Roxy, checking in with
Gwen as she liked to do when they were apart. As her mother
rambled about the wonderful spa experience she was having
with her sisters and wishing Gwen was there with her, Gwen
suddenly heard herself say something she never thought she'd
hear.

"Ma?"

"Yeah, baby-girl?"

Gwen closed her eyes, swallowed, and took that step off the
ledge, "I'm moving to New York with Blayne."

Lock tossed aside the empty beehive and scratched at a few of
the bee stings on his arms and neck. "Who am I kidding? What
am I going to do with a girl like her?"

"We had this talk when we were fourteen. I even brought my
brother's *Hustler* for visual assistance."

"I don't mean *that*, you dweeb. You didn't see this girl. Not so
much today, 'cause we were both naked, but at the wedding.
She's high maintenance."

"I thought you said she was an average Philly girl?"

"Average Philly girl does not automatically translate into easy
maintenance. She probably wants a lot of jewelry and a nice
car."

"All of which you can now afford."

"That's not the point. I don't want somebody I have to buy."

"You don't even know this woman and already you're accusing her of being available for purchase?"

"Because it makes me feel better that I'll never get her!" Lock dropped listlessly against the tree. "She uses that shampoo," he sighed.

"What shampoo?"

"The one with honey in it."

Ric's eyes crossed. "Oh, my God."

"She was sitting in that tree, her leg bleeding out, and all I could think about was how good her hair smelled."

"Why was she sitting in a tree?"

"She was hiding from the organ thieves."

Ric blinked. "Sorry?"

"Do you *really* want me to explain it?"

"Not particularly."

Lock stood, wiping his hands on his jeans. "I need to get her out of my head. That's the bottom line."

Ric got to his feet and gave a quick all-over shake to get the dust and dirt off. "Think you can?"

Lock shrugged and headed back toward the Van Holtz summerhouse. "Not really."

Gwen continued to rub her forehead and seriously considered mixing the heavy-duty pain meds with some tequila. Dangerous to her system? Yes. Able to temporarily wipe out the conversation she'd just had with her mother? Possibly.

She should have waited. She should have waited until she was back home, her mother was back from that spa, and everyone was relaxed and calm. That's what she should have done, but she also knew she couldn't wait. If Gwen waited, she'd talk herself out of it. And, for the first time in a very long time, this was something she wanted more than her next breath.

Hell. It was a future. *Her* future. And she was going to build it herself. How could she walk away from that?

She couldn't. Not now, not ever. But Gwen forgot how much damage her mother could do simply with words. The woman didn't need claws or fangs, she had her mouth and the ability to wield Irish-Catholic guilt like a ninja sword.

Sticking her cell phone in the back pocket of her denim shorts, Gwen thought again about getting those pain pills, but without the tequila. Debating on calling for assistance or actually getting off her ass, she was relieved when someone came out of the house—until Brendon stomped down the steps and faced her.

He held up his cell phone. "Why did your mother just spend ten minutes yelling at me?"

"Oh, my God." Gwen dropped her head into her hands.

"You're moving to New York?"

"Look, Brendon, I'm really sorry about—"

"You'll stay at my hotel."

Gwen stared up at him. Did he have to look so much like Mitch? And did he realize that looking like Mitch only made him a giant, big-maned target? Especially when he was giving her orders the way Mitch tried to do.

"I appreciate the offer—"

"It wasn't an offer," Brendon told her flatly. "If your mother is going to blame me for this—and my God, the yelling—then you're staying at my hotel until we find you an acceptable place to live, in a neighborhood I've researched and approved."

That he'd researched and . . . "Actually, I'm gonna stay with Blayne."

"After Blayne finished squealing in joy about you moving, because apparently she didn't know—and breaking her cell phone in half when your mother called *her*—she told me there was no way you two would ever room together after what happened on your senior class trip."

Gwen would kill that wolfdog if she weren't her new business partner.

"Brendon—"

"I won't have my little sister living in some rat-infested hell-hole that I wouldn't put my worst enemy in."

All right. That was it. "First off, I am *not* your little—"

The front door banged open again, cutting off Gwen's pointed but brutal words.

"Hey, darlin'?" Gwen rolled her eyes in frustration as Brendon's backwoods mate came out on the porch. "Where's that fire extinguisher?"

"Fire extinguisher?"

"Dogs. Oven. You do the math."

"Again? Goddamnit! I can't trust those dogs alone for two minutes." He jogged up the porch stairs, patting Gwen on the shoulder as he passed her. "I'll be right back."

As Brendon dashed inside, the screen door slamming shut behind him, Ronnie Lee sat down next to Gwen.

After a full minute of silent seething, Gwen looked over at Ronnie. The She-wolf gave her that warm smile that always set Gwen's teeth on edge. At some point in her life, Gwen would admit it wasn't fair to take out her personal rage and anger on some helpless She-wolf, but she was cat and the canine was in her space. What exactly did the hillbilly expect to happen?

"What the hell you lookin' at?" Gwen snapped.

Ronnie's smile didn't fade, although, it did become a tad brittle. "Now, I know it ain't been easy puttin' up with my Brendon. He can be a bossy so-and-so as only a male lion can be, but he's doing what he thinks is best and he does that because he likes you so much and sees you as his little sister."

"I'm not his little sister. I'm not related to him. We have no blood ties. And I think it's time he learned that. In fact, I think it's time I explained it to him—directly."

"Now, darlin', I'm gonna ask you not to do that. Don't think for a second I don't understand what you've been going through. I have three big brothers of my own. And Lord knows some days I just wanna kill 'em while they sleep. But it's about family, and family is all that matters. You've got a man here who will protect you and care for you like he does his own twin. Like he does Mitch. So I'm gonna ask you, real nice, to take his offer for, let's say, a month. You'll get free room service, anything you could ever need with one phone call to that concierge guy, and free room and board in a suite that important and very wealthy dignitaries pay thousands and thousands of dollars for each night they stay. Now how that be?"

Gwen remained silent a moment, let out a breath, and almost giddily replied, "No." She didn't say the word often unless medical personnel were involved, but holy shit was it liberating! Could she tattoo it on her forehead? Could she legally change her name to No O'Neill? This was great! This was wonderful!

The She-wolf blinked. "No?"

"Yeah. No. N. O. That spells no, in case you weren't clear. And you wanna know why? 'Cause I'm tired of this. I'm tired of you. I'm tired of your hillbilly, down-home bullshit. I'm tired of *your* Brendon trying to be like Mitch. I'm tired of Mitch. I'm tired of my mother, her sisters, my uncles, the cousins. I'm tired of all of it. And that's why this shit ends here. And you know what the first step in my new life's gonna be? It's gonna be me going inside and telling *your* Brendon to shove that hotel up his fuckin' ass. Because I don't need him or his rich-boy hotel or his country-ass girlfriend who doesn't seem to know the meaning of the word 'shoes.' So how that *be*, Deputy Dawg?"

It happened fast. That linebacker-sized human body slamming into Gwen's, the weight and force of it pinning her to the stair railing. Then Ronnie forced her left forearm against Gwen's neck and slapped her left hand over Gwen's mouth at the same time, stifling Gwen's screams as Ronnie's right hand reached down and gripped the back of Gwen's wounded and still-healing leg.

Gwen struggled to fight her off, but the She-wolf had pinned her in such a way she couldn't move her arms and she had no leverage.

"Stop squirming," Ronnie Lee warned, "or I'll—" the hand tightened on her calf again and Gwen screamed behind the hand covering her mouth. She also stopped moving.

"Much better," Ronnie said, cheery as ever. "Darlin', I know from personal experience that changing your life is never easy. Especially when your family cares so much it smothers you. Trust me, I understand. But you need to understand that I want to keep Brendon Shaw happy. Because when he's happy, I'm happy. And—" her smile never wavered, never lessened "—if you think for a New York second that I'm going to let some little half-breed, gutter cat get between me and *my* happiness, you are sadly mistaken. So when *my* Brendon comes back out here and offers you the room, you're gonna take it. You're gonna take it, you're gonna say thank you—*like a lady*—and you're gonna be damn happy about it. And if you don't . . . I will sneak in to your room, hack your leg off in the middle of the night, and use it as a putter for when I go drunk-golfing with Sissy. Now do we understand each other?"

Gwen's answer was to scream again because the hillbilly bitch tightened her grip on Gwen's leg.

"I didn't hear you, darlin'. What was that?"

Ronnie squeezed again, but this time Gwen screamed out "Yes!"

"Good." Ronnie released her and stood, quickly and easily moving out of the way as Bren came back outside.

"They're unbelievable," he grumbled, trotting back down the stairs. " 'What fire?' he says. 'I don't know what you're talking about,' she says. Canines." He blinked when he saw Gwen bent over at the waist, holding her leg and crying.

"Gwenie? Sweetie? What's the matter?"

"Her leg flared up," Ronnie offered, sounding all sorts of concerned. "But the doctor warned that would happen throughout the day. Didn't she, Gwenie?"

Gwen nodded, gritting her teeth against the brutal pain.

"I'll get the pain pills."

"I'll get 'em," Ronnie offered before Brendon could step away. "You two talk." She winked at Gwen and sauntered back into the house.

Brendon crouched in front of Gwen, his big hand reaching up and gently brushing the tears from her face. "You poor thing. Maybe I should take you back to the medical center?"

Christ! That was almost worse than the hillbilly! Almost. Gwen shook her head.

"All right, all right. Don't panic. We'll get you your pills and let you rest on the couch. You'll even have control of the TV remote." He winked. "And then we'll talk about you staying at the hotel when you move to New York. I promise it'll be temporary but I know I'll feel better if—"

"I'll take it," Gwen said quickly, too quickly.

"You will?"

"Yeah. I'll take it." She nodded, desperately. "It's fine. I'll take it."

Surprised, Brendon grinned. "Wow. Okay." He carefully reached under her legs and behind her back, easily lifting her off the porch stairs so he could carry her inside. "I have to say, though, Gwen," he teased, "I definitely thought you'd put up more of a fight."

The male wolfdog fell to his back, the jaws clamped tight around his neck, the heavier animal holding him down against the blood-encrusted dirt floor. He slammed his claws into the throat of his opponent, tearing at the flesh, hoping to hit the arteries, but it didn't seem to do any good. His opponent only squeezed harder until, with his windpipe crushed, he could no longer breathe. As he struggled, his body was swung back and forth, and from side to side until it was tossed across the floor and into the low wall surrounding the pit.

As his life drained out onto the floor beneath him, he heard the roar of the crowd . . .

CHAPTER 7

Gwen stumbled out of bed and headed straight into the living room. She poured herself a cup of coffee and walked over to the window. She pressed a button and the drapes silently drew back. She smiled at the sight of the Manhattan skyline.

After nearly six weeks, she'd thought she'd be bored by the same view every morning, but she wasn't. It kind of felt like the entire world was at her feet, waiting for her. Stupid, but she enjoyed the delusion anyway.

The sun was barely rising and she had a busy morning ahead in Jersey. She didn't look forward to the traffic, but a job was a job. She and Blayne were doing better than anyone but Blayne's dad expected. Plus leaving Philly had not been an easy task. Her Uncle Cally gave her a hard time for leaving the family and her mother acted like Gwen was moving out of the country and joining a cult.

"I blame Blayne!" her mother had shouted dramatically, Gwen's aunts shaking their heads in disgust and tsk-tsking all over the place.

"You love Blayne," Gwen had to remind her. "Any new friends I've brought home, you were quick to compare them to Blayne and they were always not good enough."

"She tricked me. Goddamn wolfdog!"

"Ma."

Shoving that long and torturous argument out of her mind and lured by the delicious scent of food, Gwen wandered over to the small dining table and sat down. She pulled off the silver cover to one of the plates and smiled. Crispy French toast, bacon, sausage, and scrambled eggs. Then it hit her—she hadn't ordered room service. She'd planned on grabbing a couple of donuts from the bakery next door to the office before she headed out.

Where did this come from?

The hotel room door slammed open, and suitcases were tossed inside, followed by her brother.

"Don't blame this on me!" he yelled at the empty doorway. "If you'd kept your trap shut, we wouldn't be in this situation!"

"Me?" a female voice yelled from the hallway. "Are you actually blaming me for this, Mitchell Shaw?"

"Yes! I'm *actually* blaming you for this!"

Mitchell O'Neill in Philly, Mitchell Shaw in New York, kicked the bags he'd just tossed down out of his way. He was uncharacteristically pissed as he tore off his leather bomber jacket and threw it on the couch.

"Is it really that hard for you to listen to me—for once?"

"I did listen to you!"

Mitch came across the room toward Gwen. She watched him closely, ready to flee if she deemed it necessary. But instead of demanding to know what the hell she was doing in his hotel suite, he snatched a piece of French toast off her plate and dunked it into the serving bowl of maple syrup. "Only when it looked like we were about to go to prison!" He leaned down and kissed Gwen on the forehead. "Yo, little sis."

Gwen brushed her forehead against his chin in a proper Pride greeting, while forcing herself to remain calm. "Yo, Mitchie." Christ, why was he here? He wasn't supposed to be back in the states for another month, maybe two. "Closer to Christmas," was what she'd last heard.

It was not Christmas! Why was he here and it was not Christmas?

Sissy Mae Smith, her big brother's mate and Alpha Female of the New York Smith Pack, stumbled into the room loaded down with even more bags. "You pack like a woman," she snarled when she finally dropped the luggage to the floor. "How can one man have so much conditioner?"

His mouth filled with French toast, Mitch pointed at his hair and snarled, "Tawny *mane*! Do you think this shit stays this beautiful on its own? It needs care and love! Which is more than I'm getting from you!"

Storming over and swiping her own piece of French toast off Gwen's plate and dunking it in the syrup, Sissy snapped, "Keep pissing me off, Mitchell Shaw, and you won't get *anything from me*!" She shoved that French toast in her mouth and headed back toward the door. "As it is, you better learn to suck your own dick, 'cause you won't be gettin' nothin' from this mouth!"

"Hey! Do you mind? My baby sister is sitting right here!"

"She's twenty-five!"

"I'm twenty-six."

"*Who cares?*" the canine bellowed before the door slammed closed after her.

Letting out a sigh, Mitch dropped into the chair across from his sister. He glanced down at her breakfast plates, now with a hundred percent less French toast. "I thought I ordered more." Mitch grabbed one of the suite phones and called down to room service.

Okay, so he was back. No reason to panic because he was back. And he looked good. Better than he had the morning he'd gotten shot after Jess Ward's wedding. Gwen still woke up in a cold sweat from time to time, the image of her brother lying on the floor of his hotel room in a lake of his own blood. She closed her eyes, not wanting to think about that. She didn't want to think how close she'd been to losing the big idiot. Yeah, he was a pain in the ass. And yeah, he didn't know when to cut it out—no matter what "it" may be. And yeah, he could sometimes be the most overbearing, overprotective, and overly delusional big brother on the planet.

But he was *her* big brother, and Gwen loved the asshole even when he didn't deserve it, so all that mattered to her was that Mitch was safe and very alive.

Still . . . *it wasn't Christmas yet!*

After name-dropping Brendon, Mitch ordered several platters of waffles, French toast, and bacon, along with a vat of orange juice.

When he hung up, Gwen asked point-blank, "Why are you back so soon?"

"We didn't get thrown out."

Gwen glanced around the room, searching for who might have asked the question that led to that answer. "Huh?"

"Sorry. I'm practicing for when we see Smitty and Mace." Mitch's bosses since he was no longer with Philly P.D. Although Gwen couldn't imagine how annoying it must be to work for a slow-talking wolf and an even *more* superior-acting lion than Mitch and Bren put together.

"So you were thrown out?" Gwen asked.

"Not exactly."

She felt that distinct throbbing in her temple that she always got whenever she had to deal with Mitch or their mother. "Mitchell."

"There might have been a *slight* racing incident, but we won't mention that. Kenshin, Smitty's partner in Japan, is taking care of it anyway, so it doesn't matter. Kenshin loves Sissy. She can do no wrong. Besides, we were coming back for the holidays anyway; we simply came back a few weeks earlier to avoid a possible arrest."

"Is that what you two were arguing about?"

"Nah. She was complaining, yet again, how I make her carry more stuff, which led to a fight at the airport that attracted the cops. But I got us out of it—barely. But as I told her, I make her carry more stuff because she has all that upper body She-wolf strength and I have to make sure I don't hurt myself before football season starts."

Gwen's stomach grumbled, but she ignored it. "Ma said you were playing with those hillbillies, but I thought she was kidding."

"Those hillbillies are family now."

"That's enough," Gwen said, appalled her brother would even say that sentence out loud, and stood. "I've gotta go."

Her brother caught her arm as she tried to pass him. He eyed her closely, taking in her too-long flannel pants that couldn't quite cover her bare feet and her Uncle Cally's old Eagle's football jersey that reached to her knees while the sleeves covered her hands.

"Why are you here?" he finally asked.

Should she lie to him?

Christ, why bother? It would only put off the inevitable, which would make it much worse in the long run. Best to face up to this now and get it over with. A philosophy she'd never employed with her family until very recently. "I moved here. About four weeks ago."

"Moved here? Ma didn't tell me you were moving here."

Of course Ma didn't. She wanted to make sure Mitch didn't have time to think about any of this rationally, time to get over his concerns and worries. Nope. Ma wanted this meeting as raw and uncomfortable as possible. Easy enough, since Gwen didn't have the guts to call him herself and tell him.

"Yeah, well. I'm here now." She tried to pull away, but Mitch tugged her back.

"So you're just going to live off Brendon?"

"Live off—" Gwen slammed her mouth shut. *Don't let him goad you. Don't let him goad you.* Calmer, she replied, "I'm not living off anybody. I've *never* lived off anybody. Brendon was nice enough to let me stay here for the time being, but now that you're back I can go stay with Blayne."

"Blaynie's here, too?"

She couldn't help but roll her eyes at the annoying nickname Mitch gave Blayne from the first day he'd met her. "Yes. Blay*nie* is here, too."

"So I guess this was one of her dumb ideas. You two move here and . . . what? Be fashion designers? Supermodels—although with your thighs . . ." Gwen's eyes locked on her brother's throat and thoughts of tearing it out with her teeth ran through her head. "Or are you just going to be party people who hang out with the stars?"

"No." *Calm, Gwen. Calm. You can do this.* "She . . . we . . . have taken over her dad's business and moved it from Queens to Manhattan."

Mitch stared at her for a long time until he snorted, and then his snort turned into a full-blown laugh, with his head thrown back and everything.

"You . . . *you* and *Blayne* took over Petty Officer Thorpe's business? The man with Navy commendations up his ass gave his business over to *you two*?" He still held her with one hand while he repeatedly slammed the table with the other. "*That's fabulous!*" he crowed. She was surprised he wasn't rolling all over the floor as well.

"You done?"

Mitch's laughter sputtered off when he saw her face. "Wait." He sobered immediately. "You *are* kidding, right?"

"No. It's all done and legal. Had lawyers and papers to sign and everything."

"You're serious?"

"When am I not?"

Incredulous, Mitch stood, his six-four frame towering over her, his hand still gripping her arm. Only now a little more tightly. "You're not even licensed in this state."

"Yes, I am."

"When did that happen?"

"A year ago."

"A . . . a *year* ago. A year ago and you never told me?"

"Why did I have to? It's none of your business where I'm licensed. Here, Philly, Jersey, what do you—"

"*Jersey?* And what do you mean it's none of my business? Is that what you just said to me?"

"Yeah. You want me to say it again? Louder?"

He released her by flinging her arm away. "Does Ma know about this?"

"Ma?" Gwen took a breath. "Mitch, I'm twenty-six. Ma knows or doesn't know about my life based on what I wanna tell her. Now, if you'll excuse me, I've gotta get ready for work."

"Hold up! Work? You think I'm letting my baby sister out there—*alone*?"

"You have no choice."

"Like hell I don't!"

Gwen threw up her hands and headed toward the bedroom. But Mitch caught hold of the back of her jersey.

"Wait, wait, wait." When she spun on him, he quickly released her. "Wait. I just want to talk. Let's start over and talk. Calmly. Okay?"

Deciding a little rational conversation with her brother couldn't hurt, "Yeah. Okay."

Lock reached for his cell phone and brought it to his ear. "Yeah?"

"Good morning, son."

"Hi, Mom."

"I need a favor."

"Uh-huh."

"Are you awake?"

"Of course I am."

"Is there salmon?"

"Covered with honey," he sighed.

"Lachlan MacRyrie! You wake up this instant!"

Lock's eyes snapped open and he realized he was yet again not in his dream river eating salmon and taking cell phone calls from his mother while in bear form. "Dammit."

His mother laughed. "You sleep like your father. It took me years to realize that he didn't have some sort of brain disorder, but simply was never awake when I began speaking to him in the mornings."

"Sorry, Mom." Lock sat up, yawning and scratching his head with his free hand. "What's up?"

"I need you to go over and check the house this afternoon."

Lock smirked. "Check the house or check Dad?"

"What do you think? New workmen mean new curiosity. And you know how your father is."

"I've got some work to do here, but I can be there about lunchtime."

"That'll be fine. And make it sound like you're simply visiting. I don't want him to think we're checking up on him."

"But we are checking up on him."

"Yes. But we don't need to say that out loud, now do we?"

"No, ma'am. We don't."

"Good. And I appreciate this."

"No problem. It'll get me out of the house for a few hours."

"Sounds like you've been working too hard again."

"Eh."

"If you went back to school and got your master's, you could be doing something you actually enjoy doing."

Lock frowned. "Which is . . . what exactly?"

"Teaching at university level."

Lock's eyes crossed. "Yeah. And I get along so well with kids, too."

"You'd make a great professor. I don't know why you insist on sticking with this ridiculous course."

"Because it pays well."

"First the Marines, now computers. All that intelligence going to waste."

He must still be half-asleep, because he could usually steer his mother off this deadly topic long before she ever got there. Besides, he didn't need any reminders of his parents' disappointment with where his life was headed. And he didn't look forward to the day they found out that creating software was only so he could earn money, retire, and finally do what he *really* wanted to do.

"Are you afraid to ask us for help? Is that it?"

"Mom."

"I don't know why you think we wouldn't help you if you needed it."

It was too early in the morning for this conversation. He hadn't had his coffee or his honey bun yet. "Mom, can we talk about this later? Or do you want me getting to the house closer to four?"

"No, no. Lunch would be better. Who knows what damage that man will do by four? We'll talk more later."

"Great." They both disconnected without saying good-bye—not because they were angry, but because his mother considered it a waste of words—and Lock got ready to face the day . . . and his dad.

Sissy and Ronnie headed down the hallway back to the suite Sissy shared with Mitch and, apparently now, his sister. Thankfully, there were four bedrooms in the suite, and like the cat she was, Gwen stayed mostly to herself, so Sissy doubted it would be too bad.

As they paused outside the suite door, Ronnie and Sissy stared at each other a long moment before Sissy unlocked the door with her keycard and pushed it open. She paused briefly in the doorway, shocked at what she was seeing, before she marched right across that room and got between Mitch and Gwen.

Not an easy task with Gwen standing up on the table so she could tower over her brother while she screamed in his face and Mitch screamed back. Plus there was finger-pointing going on, Gwen's looking much more lethal because they had those excessively long and painted nails. Sissy had never seen the siblings act like this toward each other before. She hadn't known it was possible.

"*Y'all stop this right now!*" she screamed over their yelling.

"Stay out of this, Sissy!"

"Yeah, ho-billy, stay out of it!"

"*Hey!*" Mitch bellowed. "Watch how you talk to her!"

"Fine! Then I'll tell *you* to kiss my motherfucking—"

"Hey!" Sissy tried to cut in, but it was too late. It had turned

into an embarrassing spectacle of a slap-fight. Horrified that one
of her Pack could see this display from Sissy's mate, Sissy again
got between the two, shoving Mitch back. *"Cut it out!"*

Panting rapidly, the siblings glared at each other over Sissy's
head.

"Is this any way for a brother and sister to act toward each
other?" she demanded.

Mitch's brow went up as he looked down at Sissy. "I can't believe that *you're* throwing that particular argument at my feet.
Or do I need to get out the football helmet you keep mounted on
our bedroom wall as a reminder?"

"Let me rephrase. Is this any way for a brother and sister who
like each other to act? Now I want y'all to stop this foolishness
right now before someone—" *most likely me* "—gets hurt."

"Fine." Gwen said first. "I've gotta get to work anyway."

For some reason that made Mitch snarl, but Sissy had no idea
why. "That's fine, Gwen," she said while glaring at her mate.
"Y'all can talk about this later. Right, Mitchell?"

"No! It's not—"

"Mitchell. Shaw."

The cat flinched. "Fine. It'll wait."

"Good. Thank you." Sissy stepped away from them and took
a breath. Lord, this mediator thing was a hell of a lot of work
and she was glad she didn't have to do it too often. As Alpha
Female it was all about keeping *her* calm and appeased. Much
easier.

"Hey, Sissy," Ronnie said as she walked closer. "Why don't I
leave y'all—"

It happened so fast that if Sissy still hadn't been looking in the
feline's direction she never would have seen it. But as soon as
Gwen heard Ronnie's voice, her entire body went airborne like a
suddenly uncoiled spring, her claws unleashing on both her
hands and bare feet, as she flipped off the table and away from
Ronnie. She caught hold of the drapes and, to Sissy's horror,
Gwen's head snapped around about 180 degrees so that her nose
aligned with her spine.

Then she hissed at Ronnie like a terrified house cat.

She kept hissing, too, until Mitch finally walked over, grabbed Gwen by the waist, and pulled her free of the drapes. It wasn't easy and she shredded up the drapes something awful, but he finally managed it and took her to one of the bedrooms. He tossed her inside and closed the door.

With her hand to her own throat, Sissy asked, "That thing she does with her neck—"

"She's a hybrid," Mitch snapped. "We don't ask those questions." He turned to Ronnie. "Did anything happen between you and my sister while we were gone?"

Ronnie glanced between Mitch and Sissy, her eyes wide. She shrugged. "Not that I know of."

The smile Blayne had on her face faded as Gwen stormed into their tiny, one-room office. And she cringed when Gwen's backpack hit the floor and then Gwen dropped into her office chair as if it had physically harmed her.

Blayne placed the printed job sheet back on her desk. "What's wrong?"

It took Gwen a minute to answer as she seethed, but Blayne could only cringe when she did. "Mitch is home."

"I thought he wasn't coming back until Christmas."

"That's what I thought," Gwen spat out between visibly clenched teeth. "But apparently, their plans changed. And now he's home."

"What did he say?"

Gwen's expression said it all, and Blayne could only shake her head. "We both knew he wouldn't take this well. We both knew he was going to be an asshole. That's what Mitch does when it comes to his *baby* sister. But this doesn't change anything, Gwenie. You're here, contracts are signed, there's nothing he can do."

But instead of Gwen agreeing with her, she only sat up and said, "I need that job information for today."

Blayne covered the job order with her hand. "Forget it. You can do it tomorrow or something."

"No. I'll do it today."

"It's in Jersey."

"I don't care."

"Sweetie, wait until tomorrow. When you're in a better mood and don't look so pissed off and you're maybe wearing a little bit of makeup—"

"Just give me the goddamn job!"

Blayne held the job order out and Gwen snatched it out of her hand. "I'll see you later," she said before she picked up her backpack and stormed out of the office.

Waiting until she knew Gwen was definitely gone, Blayne picked up the phone and dialed the in-building number. She waited until she got an answer. "Hey. It's me. We have a problem." A six-four, two-hundred-and-fifty-pound, big-haired *problem.*

"So what else haven't you told me?" Mitch snapped at his brother as they walked down a quiet side street about four blocks from the hotel.

"Huh?"

"Don't 'huh' me. You didn't tell me Gwenie had moved here. So what else have you been hiding from me?"

"Hiding?"

Mitch stopped and faced his brother. "All right, bruh. You better . . ."

The brothers blinked at each other and then, slowly, they turned their heads to look down the street. There were seven wild dogs standing on the corner, facing them. Mitch recognized them. He'd had enough karaoke nights with them. They were all from Jess's Pack.

The brothers looked back at each other and then down the opposite end of the street—where there were more wild dogs from Jess's Pack.

But before either brother could say anything about it, Jess Ward was there, circling around them and glaring.

"What are they doing?" Bren asked out of the corner of his mouth.

"Trying to scare us," Mitch replied.

The brothers looked at each other again, and this time they laughed. They laughed and laughed until . . .

"Long time no see, Mitch."

"Aaaaaah!" both brothers screamed before Mitch spun around and glared at the pretty little wolfdog smiling up at him. And to say he didn't trust that smile was an understatement. He and Blayne had always had a strange relationship. She was like his second baby sister. He'd protected her, bailed her out of jail, and loved to make her laugh just like with Gwenie. But he also knew that Blayne was the kind of woman who, if he were writing a horror novel, would always be the one shoving Mitch down the stairs, cutting the brake line to his car, making it look like he'd killed one of his girlfriends, while in the story none of the other characters would believe it was her because she looked so damn innocent, but Mitch would know. And although he knew Blayne would probably never do those things, he also knew, in that deep-in-his-bones way he had that he had to watch Blayne Thorpe closer than he watched those enemies who had actively tried to kill him.

"Blayne," he said, watching her close—like always.

She nodded at his brother. "Hi, Bren."

"Hi, Blayne. You startled us."

"What are you doing here?" Mitch asked her, the hair on the back of his neck rising up.

"Came to see what the fuck you're up to."

"What the hell does that mean?"

"It means my best friend was upset and *you* upset her."

"I wouldn't have upset her if she were home, in Philly. *Where she belongs.*"

"She belongs right where she is, and who are you to say different?"

"I'm her brother."

"Barely."

Mitch gasped. "Blaynie!"

"Oh, don't give me that Blaynie-shit, O'Neill! You're going to back off my Gwenie and you're going to do it right now!"

"Or what?" He stepped into her, his anger making him ignore what eleven years of being around a wolfdog had taught him. "What are you going to do?"

Blayne moved in closer until they were nose to neck. "Gwen is my best friend and I'm going to do what I can to ensure her happiness."

"And Gwen is my baby sister and I'm going to do what I can to ensure her *safety*. Guess who wins?"

"The one not afraid to set you *on fire*?"

"Okay, okay." Bren stepped between them. "Everybody just calm down."

Blayne looked around Bren. "Don't fuck with me on this, Mitch."

"Don't get between me and my sister, Blayne. She's going back to her Pride."

"Like hell she is."

"Both of you stop it," Bren said again. "You both want the best for Gwen, isn't that all that matters?"

"Oh, shut up!" Mitch and Blayne yelled together.

Bren stepped back. "Fuck you both then."

"Look, Unstable Girl," Mitch said while poking Blayne in the forehead, "you know how far I'll go to protect my baby sister. Don't push me."

"And," she replied calmly, "I'll tell you like I told Frankie Caramelli in the tenth grade after he inappropriately touched me in gym class, and while I was bricking him up in the church wall after I bound and gagged him . . . don't mess with me."

Then she punched him in the chest and walked off, the wild dogs disappearing with her.

Rubbing his chest where she'd hit him, Mitch glowered blindly across the street. "She's up to something. She's trying to keep Gwen here for some reason."

"Maybe because they're best friends and she'd rather Gwen be here than in Philly?"

"Oh, please. Blayne Thorpe has never been that linear. Trust me, it's not that simple."

"Uh . . ." Bren said, "maybe we should let this go anyway."

Shocked at his brother, Mitch demanded, "Why would we do that?"

"Lots of reasons, but mostly because I don't want to be bricked up in a wall like Frankie Caramelli."

Mitch rolled his eyes. "Don't be such a wuss! They found Caramelli after, like, eight hours. He was a little dehydrated, but he was alive."

CHAPTER 8

Lock parked his SUV in front of his parents' New Jersey home and got out. If this had been the weekend, when he spent most of his time in his workshop, he would have been more rushed to get in and get out. But on this lovely October morning, he found he was in no rush. Besides, he enjoyed spending time with his dad. The old man could be quite entertaining in his own wacky way—unless you were some poor guy trying to fix the plumbing and move on to your next job.

Using the same set of keys he'd had since he was nine, Lock entered his parents' home.

"Dad? You around?" When Lock didn't get an immediate answer, he closed the door and headed through the sunroom into the living room, through the dining room, and straight in to the kitchen. A big bowl of berries sat on the table and he grabbed a handful. He could hear sounds coming from the basement, so he entered the tiny hallway, which had a doorway to the right that led out into the backyard and to his parents' two-car garage, and a set of stairs to the left that led to the basement.

Lock barely had his foot on the first step when he heard a, "No, no, no, don't!" Followed by a "woosh!" and a definitely girlish squeal that he refused to believe came from the old man.

Lock charged down the stairs but stopped when he hit the last step. He simply wasn't in the mood to get his boots wet.

He watched his favorite childhood stuffed dog float by before looking in the corner to see his father standing there, looking typically guilty and holding a giant wrench. Beside him stood . . .

Lock blinked, not sure he was seeing correctly.

"You," he said, too shocked not to show it. Then he did something he rarely ever did—he laughed. Bent-over-at-the-waist laughing. He couldn't help it. Not a day had gone by when he hadn't thought about her. Part of him still ashamed he'd left her alone, part of him mad she'd made him care one way or the other. But he never thought he'd see her again. At the very least he never thought he'd see her again in his basement, with his dad, drenched from her knees to her boots from whatever fuck-up Brody MacRyrie had managed to get himself into.

"Lock?" his father asked, most likely shocked at the laughter coming from his only boy. "Are you all right?"

Lock couldn't answer. He was laughing too hard, which did absolutely nothing but piss off the little feline with the hospital phobia. And even though she clearly didn't appreciate being laughed at, she decided to take it out on Brody rather than Lock.

Yanking the wrench from Brody's hand, Gwen shook it at him—although Lock would be eternally grateful she didn't use it to bash the man's head in.

"What did I say? I said *don't touch!*"

"I was just curious." And that only made Lock laugh harder. He'd lost count of how many bad days with his parents began with the sentence, "But I was curious!" It was true, almost all bears were curious by nature, even Lock, but Brody took it to an extreme that made those who knew him love him and want to punch him all at the same time. "I merely wanted to see—"

"*Out!*" the little feline roared, the sound a bit more frightening as it seemed to combine the roar of a territorial lion with the warning growl of a pissed-off tiger.

"But why? I didn't do—"

"Dad." Lock stood up, wiping tears from his eyes. For a moment he thought that wrench would come right at his head. "Upstairs."

"I'm your father, boy. You can't tell me—"

"Up. Stairs. Or I'm calling Mom."

"Traitor," Brody mumbled, but he mumbled while moving, so Lock didn't bother arguing with him. "And you're both being unreasonable."

Lock waited until his father marched up the stairs and back into the kitchen, then he focused on Gwen.

"*You're* the plumber?"

Those gold eyes narrowed dangerously. "What does *that* mean?"

"It means I'm having a hard time believing you can fix my parents' plumbing."

"Why? Because I'm a woman?"

"No. Because you're you."

The wrench slapped into her left palm with a "swack!" "First my brother and now you. What a perfect fucking day."

He sloshed over to her, grateful he'd worn his work boots rather than his sneakers. "I don't know your brother. Just the half-brother of your half-brother, which I still find entertaining." He took hold of her left hand and lifted it. "But these are not the nails of a plumber."

"What's wrong with my nails?" She snatched her hand back and studied them. "The polish isn't even chipped."

"Exactly! What kind of plumber has pristine nails?"

"A smart one."

Lock took her hand again, studied her nails. "Are these the colors of the Philadelphia Eagles?"

Once more she snatched her hand back. "I support my teams. You got a problem with that, too?"

"If they're the Eagles."

"At least we have a team," she shot back. "And just because I have style and my nails look good, doesn't mean I'm not the best plumber you'll ever know."

"Is that right? Are you even licensed in Jersey, Mr. Mittens?"

"As a matter of fact, I am."

"How did you manage that? You have to live in Jersey to get a license."

"What are you? The plumber police?"

"Only for the Tri-State area. And how come you won't answer my question?"

"Because I don't have to! And—" she threw the wrench to the floor, water spraying the front of his jeans "—*you left me!*"

And there it was. He couldn't describe how satisfying it was to know that she had cared he'd left that day and that she *still* thought about him. He'd hate to think he was obsessing all on his own. "I had to leave. They called the Park Rangers."

"Who did?"

"I'm guessing the half-brother of your half-brother—and can I call him that for eternity?"

"No. His name's Brendon. And you let some cop force you to leave me when you promised you wouldn't allow the organ thieves to get me?"

"The organ thieves didn't get you, and yes, I just said that out loud. And it wasn't some cop or some ranger . . . it was Toots."

"Who the hell is Toots?"

Embarrassed, Lock didn't answer her right away, and Gwen put her hands on her hips. "Well?"

"He's a polar. Okay? Seven-seven, almost four hundred pounds, and he beat me up once."

"He beat you up?"

"We were only fifteen at the time, but it was lasting damage."

"Physical?"

Lock cleared his throat. "Emotional."

"*Emotional* damage?"

"It can be just as devastating, Mr. Mittens!"

"Yeah. I can see it. You look completely devastated."

"At least I can admit to my fears, She Who Is Stalked by the Organ Thieves of America."

"That's it, I'm leaving."

Lock started laughing again. "Why? Because I'm rudely suggesting you have issues?"

"I don't have issues." She bent down and picked up her wrench. "I'm fine."

"You snuck out the window when no one was looking so you could get away from your doctor."

"I'm not talking about this."

He grabbed the wrench from her. "You brought it up."

"I brought up the fact you left me in that mortuary to die."

"You call a medical center a mortuary and you don't think you have issues?"

Snarling, she reached for the wrench, but he kept it from her by lifting it over his head. "You have to fix whatever damage my father's done before my mother gets home."

"Find someone else."

"Please. I promise I'll keep him upstairs and out of your hair."

"Another promise? You sure do toss them around."

"This one I can keep as long as the half-brother of your half-brother doesn't show up and ruin everything."

"Stop calling him that."

"No need to hiss, Mr. Mittens."

"*And stop calling me that!*" She leaped up and snatched the wrench from him. "Get out of my sight!" she ordered after she'd landed.

Unable to keep his smile under control, Lock pointed at the stairs. "I'll be upstairs if you need me."

"Yeah. Sure you will."

Lock went back up the stairs and found his father in the kitchen—sulking.

"How about some coffee, Dad?"

"I don't see why I can't observe."

"Dad," Lock asked sincerely, "do you even know the meaning of that word?"

His father shrugged. "Sometimes."

After a solid fifteen minutes of uninterrupted time, Gwen discovered three things. One, the MacRyrie family needed a new water heater. Two, she'd need to get the pump out of her truck to deal with the water on the floor that wasn't going anywhere in that concrete basement. And three . . . that deserting idiot was even cuter than she remembered.

Marching back up the stairs, leaving a trail of water behind her, Gwen walked into the kitchen and stopped. Father and son sat at the table, their elbows on the wood, their hands gripping extremely large coffee mugs, the same expression on their faces. So much father and son, Gwen felt this weird tug at her heart.

"Well?" the grizzly son asked.

"Do you need some help, dear?" the grizzly dad eagerly offered.

"No, Dad."

"But—"

"*No.*"

And all that anger she'd been carrying around since her argument with Mitch that morning washed away. They were just so damn cute, she couldn't stay mad at either one of them.

Biting back her smile, Gwen said, "You need a new water heater."

"That sounds expensive," the older bear said, his brow furrowing. "Your mother isn't going to like it if it's expensive, Lock."

"Mom has no choice." He shrugged at Gwen. "I've been trying to get them to get a new one for years. I did what I could."

"It lasted longer than it should have, so you did really well. But it's time to put her out of her misery and to get you folks up to the here and now."

"Of course, of course." Brody MacRyrie put his coffee mug down. "I understand."

Eeesh. Twenty minutes ago, she was ready to charge this guy out the ass simply for being a pain. Now she didn't have the heart. "Don't worry, Mr. MacRyrie. I got ya covered." She winked at him and the older bear's face turned red.

"Well . . . uh . . . um . . . would you like some coffee, my dear?"

Gwen grinned. "I'd love some."

*   *   *

By the time they were finished installing the new water heater, hauling out the old one—helped along by Lock being able to simply pick it up and carry it out—and ensuring the basement was dry, it was late. Nearly seven o'clock.

Gwen sat on the curb behind the MacRyrie family home. She watched the company truck driven by one of her employees head off down the street while she checked in with Blayne.

"How did your job go?" Blayne asked after complaining for nearly ten minutes about her own.

"New waterless water heater installed and working fine."

"Water heater installation. Ka-ching!"

"You're not going to believe whose house this is, though."

"Whose?"

She smiled, thinking of Lock keeping his father busy and out of her hair anytime the man even *glanced* toward the basement. "The bear's."

"What bear?"

"The one from the infamous Labor Day weekend fiasco. The one who left me at the whim of organ thieves."

"Stop saying that! I told you what happened."

"Yeah. Whatever. He apologized, anyway."

"You made that man apologize?"

"Yes! As a matter of fact, I did."

"You're unbelievable."

"I was owed an apology."

"I'm not arguing with you on this. I've gotta go."

Gwen's eyes narrowed. "Oh? Where to?"

"To . . . uh . . ."

Gwen's eyes narrowed more until they were nothing but slits. The wolfdog was up to something, had been for weeks, and Gwen was determined to find out what. "To . . ." she prompted.

"To the hospital."

Gwen's back went straight. "What the—"

"As a volunteer."

"A volunteer?"

"Uh-huh."

Blayne was lying and they both knew it. "That's where you've been going after work the last few weeks?"

"Uh . . . huh."

"To a hospital?"

"Yuppers!"

"As what? A therapy dog?"

Blayne's gasp of outrage came through the phone. "Low blow, O'Neill!" Yeah. It was. But she hated when Blayne lied to her. Still, that was too low, even for Gwen.

"Blayne, wait. I'm sor—"

Not surprisingly, the phone call abruptly ended, leaving Gwen to stare at the "disconnected" message on her screen until she heard something breathing beside her.

"You're supposed to lumber," she accused softly, looking over at the grizzly quietly sitting next to her. Poor full-humans. Without the same hearing as Gwen, they'd never know the bear was next to them until he said something or until the mauling started. She shuddered at the thought. "Because I can hear lumbering."

"I do lumber. Since I was eight."

"You need to lumber louder. No one wants to look up and see a bear sitting next to them. Breathing."

"Gee, thanks." He jerked his thumb toward his house. "My mother's home. She wants to talk to you."

"You're not going to get a better deal from anyone else," Gwen tossed out.

"Would you stop doing that?"

"Doing what?"

"Arguing a point before anyone's given you a reason to. Don't preemptive argue. It's annoying." He stood up and so did Gwen. "The reason I'm talking to you now is that I need to warn you about my mother."

Gwen put her hands on her hips. "Let me guess. She doesn't like cats. She's going to say snide remarks about climbing trees and hacking up hairballs, and you're going to apologize now for whatever she says. Right?"

"You're doing it *again*," he accused.

Shit. She was.

"If you'd let me talk for myself, I was going to say that my mother is a dyed-in-the-wool feminist and she's *dying* to meet you because she's completely in love with the idea of a female plumber putting in her new water heater. She also may ask to interview you for her monthly newsletter, but you're not obliged to do that unless you want to."

Gwen could say with all honesty she hadn't been expecting any of that. "Oh. All right then."

He leaned down until their noses almost touched. "Did you know that you're very frustrating?"

"Maybe, once or twice, I've heard that before."

His mother was in love. Lock knew it as soon as she set eyes on Gwen that she'd fallen head over heels in love.

First off, Gwen was dressed "correctly." Sturdy work boots, no cute shoes. Curly hair held off her face with a headband, no cute hairstyle more concerned with glamour rather than functionality. Cargo pants with lots of pockets for easy access to often-used small tools or pen and paper, no cute jeans with a thong hanging out. Long-sleeved Philadelphia Eagles sweatshirt that had seen better days but still did the job, no "I'm your sexy plumber" cute T-shirt in pink.

But what made it perfection for Dr. Alla Baranova-MacRyrie was that Gwen had those nails, because in his mother's mind that meant she embraced her femininity even while rejecting society's standards for women. Give Lock a couple of hours, he could write the paper that his mother would present at the next female empowerment rally she would be hosting in the New Year.

"So you've been doing this for years," Alla said to Gwen, ignoring the burning smell coming from the stove.

"Mom, when was the last time you checked the meat in the oven?"

"Mmm?"

"You're supposed to be warming this up, ya know? Not grilling it all over again." Lock motioned her aside so he could pull the oven door open.

"I used to follow my Uncle Cally around when he'd come over to fix Ma's plumbing and by the time I was thirteen, I had a regular summer job with his company."

"Now this Uncle Cally, is he an actual uncle or simply one of the many males your mother had around for breeding purposes while you were growing up?"

Lock bolted up so fast, his head slammed into the stove. "*Mom!*"

Perplexed, his mother studied him while he rubbed the back of his head. "Whatever is the matter with you?"

"*Me?* You can't ask Gwen a question like that."

Alla sighed in exasperation. His mother had often told Lock that he was much too polite to ever be a true intellectual. "But this is a Pride we're discussing, Lachlan. They don't keep males around except for protection and breeding purposes."

"Mom!"

"Any Breeding Males we had around the house," Gwen calmly cut in, "were never called uncle. Ma always thought that was creepy."

"I have to agree with her," Alla muttered, again ignoring the glare from her son.

"My Uncle Cally is one of Ma's brothers."

"Half-brother?" Lock asked.

Gwen scowled but he knew it was to keep from laughing. "Shut up."

Brody walked into the kitchen, happily clapping his hands together. "Dinner ready?"

"Mom burned the meat. Again."

Alla glared at her husband rather than her son. "If you wanted a housesow, you should have married one!"

"I didn't say anything!" Brody argued, pointing a damning finger at Lock. "It was the boy!"

"But you were *thinking* it," she accused. "Now, I'm going to take Gwen into the living room and you two can work out dinner." She smiled at Gwen. "You'll stay for dinner, of course."

"Okay," Gwen said easily, surprising Lock.

Alla walked to the refrigerator and Gwen stepped out of her way. The kitchen had always been too small for a family of four bears, but Lock wondered if Gwen was feeling a little overwhelmed. She was only about five-eight. His mother was six-four and had the sturdy hips and shoulders of a true breeding sow. Lock could never think of a time as a child when his mother didn't make him feel safe. Because who'd be crazed enough to try and get near him when his mother was around?

"I have iced tea, dear. Or beer?"

"Maybe a saucer of milk?"

Gwen and Alla looked over at Lock and he immediately pointed at his father. "It was him," he lied.

His father, oblivious as always, held up a menu from the stack they kept on hand in one of the cupboards. "How about Chinese food? They deliver and have those wonderful family-style meals to feed four. So I'll order eight of those."

Gwen was kind of amazed. A mother with several degrees and a prestigious position at an Ivy League college did not ensure that she'd be any less embarrassing to her child than a mother who became a nurse through night school. Gwen knew this when Alla launched into her "unfortunate changes in my vagina after the birth of Lachlan" discussion.

Lock had to put his big glass of milk down for that one, his head buried in his hands. The parts of his face not covered by his long fingers turned a lovely shade of crimson. Gwen had nail polish that matched that color perfectly.

"Was it his giant kumquat head?" Gwen asked, thoroughly enjoying every second of Lock's misery.

"No. It was his shoulders. He's always had very large shoulders. I mean look at him. Even as a baby they were freakishly long."

"Freakishly?" Lock snapped.

"They stretched me right out."

"Mom!"

Brody shrugged and reached for more moo goo gai pork. "I didn't mind."

"Dad!"

"Well, darling, you were always quite large, so it made things a little easier for both of us when it came to sex."

"Mom!"

Alla shook her head. "I don't know what happened to you, Lachlan MacRyrie." She turned to Gwen. "I've always insisted on being quite open about human bodies when talking to my children. There's no shame in a woman's body. And like everything else in the world, it ages. So while you still have the exquisite body you've been blessed with, Gwen dear, and that prebirth vagina—enjoy it."

"Is there any way to get you to stop?" Lock begged.

"Eat your food and stop whining, Lachlan. It's not attractive."

Brody's head lifted and he leaned back in his chair, staring off through the living room and into the front room. Their house was like one long building, everything linear. It fit them so well.

After a few moments the front door opened and Brody grinned. "Well, look who's here."

Three young children ran in, screaming. Brody stood and held his arms open, allowing the children to crash into him. He didn't budge an inch.

"Mom?" She walked into the room and Gwen immediately saw the resemblance between brother and sister. She doubted Lock and his sister had many "You two are related?" moments like Gwen and Mitch did.

"Hello, dear. What are you doing here so late?"

"I came to pick up the . . ." Her words faded away when she saw Gwen sitting at the table. Her nostrils twitched and flared and her eyes immediately went to her children, her body tensing.

"Stop it, Iona," Alla warned while she put more honey chicken with cashews on her plate. The woman had an appetite like Mitch and Brendon put together.

"Iona, this is Gwen O'Neill," Lock said. "Gwen, this is my sister Iona MacRyrie-Phillips." There certainly was a lot of hyphenating in this family.

"Hi."

Her gaze examined Gwen carefully before she finally replied, "Hello."

"She's our plumber," Brody said with an interesting amount of cheer. He returned to his chair and sat, pulling one of the children, a girl, onto his lap.

"Inviting plumbers to dinner now?" the sow asked.

Relaxing back in her chair, Gwen replied, "I'm so good at what I do, I always get a meal afterward. And sometimes, flowers."

Lock choked on his milk while Brody agreed, "She did an excellent job, dear. We have a new water heater now. A *waterless* water heater. I plan to examine it tomorrow."

"No!" his entire family said, making him jump.

Even the granddaughter on his lap looked up into his face and said with the solemn wisdom of a four-year-old, "Don't, Grandpa."

"This is a really nice table," Gwen said after Iona and Alla went into the kitchen to retrieve old family flatware for one of Iona's exclusive doctor-only parties. And yeah, Lock specifically did not mention to Gwen that his sister was one of those evil "organ thieves." Not with the evening going so well and all.

Gwen tapped the table. "Where did you get it?" She leaned down to examine the underside. "Was it expensive?"

Lock glanced at his father who quickly shrugged and muttered, "I didn't say anything."

"Didn't say anything about what?" Gwen asked.

"Why are you asking about the table?" Lock demanded, wondering what she was up to.

"Because it's nice and one day I'll need furniture."

Brody sat up. "Well, then—"

"Dad."

Gwen glanced back and forth between them. "What?"

"Nothing," Lock said. "The table was made for my parents," which wasn't a lie.

"Oh." She pouted a little. "This would probably be out of my price range then."

Brody threw his napkin down. "Yes, but—"

"Dad," Lock cut in again, scowling in warning at his father.

Gwen watched them closely. "What is wrong with you two?"

The MacRyrie men gave identical shrugs and answered together, "Nothing."

Gwen said good-bye to the MacRyries, giving them her personal cell phone number in case they had any problems with their new heater. As she walked back to her truck, Lock walked beside her.

"I'm sorry we kept you out so late," he said.

"No problem. I had a really good time."

"Sure you don't want me to follow you back to the city?"

She laughed. "Yeah. Right. I don't know how I survived this long without you shadowing me."

Gwen unlocked her truck door and pulled it open.

"So, Gwen . . . you want to go out sometime?"

And there it was.

She faced him, the open truck cab to her back. He had his hands in his pockets and his eyes focused on the bushes behind her head. He was shy and adorable and wouldn't last ten seconds with her or her family. Sure, in a physical fight and if they snuck up on him, startling him into a violent reaction, he could take Gwen's uncles and Mitch. But in the verbal duels that represented O'Neill get-togethers? Not two seconds. He got weird when she asked questions about his parents' dining table and couldn't even look her in the eye when he asked her out.

"Thanks, Lock, but no." See? Much better to let him down now, then crush him later when he got attached to the unattachable. "It's nothing personal, though," she added.

He laughed, now looking her in the eyes. "Yeah, being turned down for a date is always *not* personal."

"You know what I mean."

"Not really." But he was smiling and there didn't seem to be any bitterness or anger. She appreciated that and, to her way of thinking, it said a lot about him as a man.

"I had a great time tonight. Let's leave it at that, okay?"

"Okay."

Hmm. Maybe he was taking it *too* well. Couldn't he even put up a little fight for her? Jeez. She was glad she hadn't wasted her time.

She got into her truck, and Lock closed the door for her. He leaned into the open window, looking around at everything, as curious as his father, if not as grabby about it.

Gwen started the truck and put on her seat belt.

"You've got the check, right?"

"Yup. Thanks." She adored prompt payers.

"Okay. See ya."

"Yeah." She turned her head to say good-bye and then his mouth was there, on hers.

It was . . . strange. His lips . . . they . . . uh . . . she didn't know. But as strange as his lips felt on hers, they also felt wonderful. Amazing wonderful. And instead of pulling back, horrified by the awkward moment or freaked out by his strange lips, she ended up kissing him back. She leaned into that kiss, her mouth opening under his, tongue pressing inside until she felt inundated with the taste of Chinese honey chicken.

She released the steering wheel, her hands reaching out for him, and that's when he stepped back. His eyes were closed and his tongue swiped his lips, as if he were still savoring the taste of her.

When he looked at her again, he said, "Night."

And walked off!

Gwen watched him, moving from a slow burn to a nice, frothy rage as he left her sitting there in her running truck.

Again! He'd left her again! This time was worse than the last, too, because she was awake and fully aware he was leaving her!

You turned him down for the date, her rational cat side reminded her. And her human side told her cat side to shut the fuck up!

"Bears," she growled. "Tricky, eating-out-of-trashcan Jersey bears! I hate all of them!"

She slammed the truck into reverse and tore out of the MacRyries' driveway, promising herself never to return no matter how much she liked his parents or what a great kisser Lock MacRyrie was.

Never. Again!

Lock walked up to his parents' house, the sweet taste of Gwen still on his lips.

It had been a long time since he'd felt like this about a woman. A long time since something had caught his interest other than food or survival. And he liked it. He liked feeling something other than hunger or dread, panic or calm, anger or absolutely nothing. For the first time in years he felt warm from the inside out and he loved it. Wanted more of it.

He wanted more of Gwen O'Neill.

She wouldn't be easy to get, though. Like a cat staring at him from a hundred-foot tree, Gwen kept herself safe from outsiders, only the chosen allowed in to her world.

But Lock was nothing if not persistent. He had pulled ancient trees out by the roots to get to a beehive, and battled full-blood grizzlies to get the best spot in a salmon-filled Alaskan river. So if Gwen thought she could motion him out of her life with a wave of her hand and an "It's not you, it's me," she was dead wrong.

"Nicely handled, son," his father praised as Lock stepped into the house, the old man patting him on the shoulder as he passed.

Lock smiled in return, feeling surprisingly pleased with himself. "Thanks, Dad."

Niles, exhausted to his bones, rubbed his forehead and glared across the boardroom table. They'd all been arguing for the last three hours and he'd just hit his wall.

As he slammed his hand on the table, every predator eye locked on him. It was a disturbing sight, but one he'd gotten used to over the years since he'd joined the Board. "We can't keep having this same argument. Nor can we ignore how things are changing."

The ancient matriarch of the Llewellyn Pride, Matilda, tapped her claws against the table. She was so old, she couldn't retract them anymore. "What are you suggesting, Van Holtz?"

"You know what I'm suggesting, and I'm tired of talking. Do we do this . . . or not?"

"Do we have much of a choice?"

"Not anymore."

The representatives of every major Pack, Pride, and Clan, as well as reps for nonsocial breeds, glanced at each other. After a much-too-long stretch of time, each nodded, silently giving their agreement.

Matilda was the last. She nodded, white-gold mane briefly covering her face.

"Good," Niles said, signaling to his assistant. "Then we're done."

They rose to leave, one of Matilda's nieces helping the old lioness out of the chair. But before she left, and after everyone else had, she focused still-sharp gold eyes on Niles. "I hope you know what you're doing."

"Matilda, you just agreed—"

She waved one white claw. "I'm not talking about the decision that was made here, young Niles. I'm talking about your new hire."

Oh. That. Well, he'd known there would be some uncomfortable with his choice, but that was too damn bad. "I was empowered by the Board to make those decisions. Without getting prior approval by you . . . or anyone."

"You were. But be careful, poodle." She made her slow way toward the door, her niece gripping her elbow. "That one's predecessor . . . that didn't end too well, now did it?"

"Perhaps," Niles murmured, hiding his smile. Because as Niles's father used to tell the story, it actually only ended badly for the Llewellyn Breeding Male who'd gotten in that one's way.

"She's going to be difficult," his assistant reminded him once Matilda was gone.

"True. But there's something to keep in mind ..." Niles picked up his papers and shoved them into his briefcase "... the old bitch can't live forever."

His assistant looked at him with what Niles could only interpret as amusement mixed with pity. "Perhaps not, sir. But she's clearly going to make her best effort."

CHAPTER 9

With extreme care, Gwen pulled the sheet back until nothing blocked her from all six feet, four inches and 280 pounds of naked Mitch O'Neill Shaw. Raising her hands, she unleashed her claws. While her fingernails still sported Eagle colors, her claws sported the Steelers.

And her brother *hated* the Steelers.

Grinning, Gwen leaped straight into the air at the same time that Sissy Mae's eyes opened, instantly growing round and huge as Gwen landed on her brother's back with all her weight and slammed her front claws right into his ass.

"*Owwwwwwwwwwwwwwwwwwwwwwwwwwwwwwwww!*"

Ignoring his howl of pain, Gwen quickly and efficiently dug her claws in and out of her brother's ass cheeks until she was satisfied she'd left a proper—and memorable—pattern. Because if nothing else, he needed to learn that she wouldn't tolerate him treating her like a child and talking down to her as he'd done the day before. Even more important—it was fun!

Impressed with her work, Gwen nimbly leaped off her brother's back and strolled toward the hallway. She waited until she heard Mitch's snarling rage only a few feet behind her before she grabbed the door and yanked it shut. The satisfying sound of Mitch running face-first into it would sit with her all day, and she couldn't be happier.

* * *

The doorbell went off again and Lock glared at the clock next to his bed. Not even seven and someone dared to wake him up? Especially when he'd only gotten to bed a few short hours ago. Unacceptable.

Marching through his apartment, he snatched his front door open and ended up glaring at Ric, who grinned at him from behind five-hundred-dollar shades.

"Morning, Mr. Sunshine." Ric held up a bakery bag. "I've brought treats to gently ease you into wakefulness."

"Fuck off." Lock slammed the door shut, engaged the industrial-strength security system he'd recently had installed, and went back to bed.

Thirty minutes later he smelled fresh coffee under his nose and bacon throughout his house. He opened his eyes and glared at the smiling face of Ulrich Van Holtz. "How did you get past my security system?"

"Security system?" The canine's grin turned into a smirk, making Lock's eye twitch. "Is that what they call it?"

"You're annoying me."

The smug canine eased the coffee under his nose again. "But doesn't that smell delicious?" he crooned. "And I'm also going to make you my perfect French toast. All you have to do is ease your way out of bed. That's it. Good boy."

"Shut up." Lock placed his feet on the floor and buried his face in his hands. After all these years, only Ric had discovered the perfect method to get Lock out of bed and reduce any early-morning maulings.

Lock reached out for the coffee, but Ric pulled it back. "Why don't you come to the kitchen first?"

In response, Lock roared, the windows rattling behind Ric.

"Or I could just hand this over now." Ric gave him the mug as Lock's upstairs neighbor slammed a broomstick against the floor. So Lock roared again and the sound immediately stopped.

"As always . . . the perfect neighbor you are."

Gripping the mug and baring a fang, Lock let out a small snarl. What his sister called the MacRyrie family's "Early Warning System."

Knowing that warning system as well as anyone, Ric headed toward the bedroom door. "I'll just go and get that French toast started. And you'll just *ease* your way out."

By the time Lock had finished his coffee, taken a shower, and put on a pair of jeans, Ric had a full breakfast waiting for him.

Sitting down at the table, Lock looked over the platters of freshly made French toast, scrambled eggs, bacon, sausage, and rolls, as well as bear claws from the nearby bakery. There was also butter, honey—European, from the scent of it—and warm maple syrup. Lock reached for the French toast first, but Ric slapped his hand away and placed a carefully prepared plate in front of him. As Lock waited, Ric went to the counter and returned with a small strainer. He tapped the side, covering the French toast with powdered sugar. Somehow the wolf managed not to get any on Lock's bacon or sausage.

"There. Isn't that nice?"

"I have to say our relationship is getting stranger and stranger as we get older."

"Why? Because I enjoy taking care of you?"

"Now you're freaking me out." But that didn't stop Lock from digging into his food. As always, it was perfectly cooked, but he expected no less from any of the Van Holtzes. Many of them, including Ric, were known for their superior chef skills among the most elite food snobs. Each Van Holtz pup was taught from very early childhood to cook, with the plan that one day they would work in or manage one of the family restaurants spread across the States and Europe.

"I thought you were working today," Lock said when he got to his third helping, and the coffee had finally done its work of making him a tolerable human being and bear.

"I was, but Adelle is covering for me. I wanted to do something before practice tonight and I'm hoping you'll come with me."

"Where are we going?"

"Staten Island."

"What are we going over there for?"

"To talk to Sharyn McNelly of the McNelly Pack."

"Why?"

"Because they were the ones who attacked your little feline and her canine friend."

Lock looked up from his food. "You sure?"

"Of course I'm sure. And I've gotten the approval of the imperious Board to handle it." Ric had gotten the Board involved? Yikes.

"And that's why we're going over there?"

"Yes."

Pushing a piece of bacon around his plate with his fork, Lock asked, "Why do you need me to go?"

"To kill them all."

Lock's gaze snapped to Ric's and then they both burst out laughing.

"You're such an idiot."

Smiling, Ric filled up his own plate with food. "I know. I know."

"Why do you really need me to go?"

"To watch my back, of course." Ric shrugged and bit into a piece of bacon. "And, you know, just to be your usual wonderful and interesting self."

Sharyn McNelly, Alpha of the McNelly Pack, cringed again as she heard bending metal snap like a toothpick.

"Oh. Wow." The bear lumbered out from her laundry room, holding a piece of broken pipe in his hand. "This kind of snapped off." She'd lost track of how many things had "kind of snapped off" in the ten minutes the grizzly had been on her territory. From the second he'd walked into her house, he'd been "exploring" and the level of damage was killing her. "I was just trying to see how sturdy it was . . . not very, I'd have to say."

"I'm sure it was an accident, Lock," the Van Holtz wolf said casually while watching Sharyn. That bastard had unleashed that beast on her home, proving what she'd always known—the Van Holtzes were assholes.

"It was. Definitely." The bear gave a small shrug. "I'm really sorry about that. I'll be happy to replace it."

Shaking her head, Sharyn focused back on the wolf. "So we were on your territory? So what? Who gives a fuck?"

The bear stood in front of Sharyn's prized curio cabinet. She'd spent years getting that together. Hitting yard sales all over Staten Island, Long Island, and Jersey. She swallowed as the bear leaned around to examine the back of the case.

"The Van Holtzes give a fuck, Miss McNelly. Even more troublesome, your Pack attacked guests on my territory."

She didn't bother to hide her sneer. "Mixed breeds? That's what you're protecting?"

The wolf smiled. "Mixed breeds . . . and guests. That's the important part, don't you think?"

Fed up, Sharyn pointed a finger at the wolf. "You show up at my fucking house in your fancy limo and you think I'm just going to roll over and give you what you want? Over some crossbreeds? Is that what you think?"

"No. I think you'll do what I want because it's the right thing to do and because . . ."

He let the sentence dangle out there as the bear tugged on her cabinet and her hands turned into fists, her eyes cutting back to the wolf. He smiled at her.

"Don't mind him. He's naturally curious." His head dipped down a bit. "You know how bears are."

Yeah, she knew. That's why she wasn't surprised when she heard something tear and turned back to see the bear easily holding her six-foot-tall cabinet in one hand and feeling around the now-tattered wall it had once been attached to with the other.

"I didn't know this was attached to the wall until it came out." The bear winced. "Sorry."

He pushed the cabinet back into place, but with such force the curios inside were slammed together. "I'm sure I can fix it."

"No!" She stood up and the wolf rose with her. "Just leave it." The bear stepped away from the cabinet, but his attention was quickly snagged by her television. Since that television was worth nearly seven grand and she'd only paid one grand for it in a back alley, she wasn't about to lose it to a frickin' bear. "Spit it out already, Van Holtz. What do you want?"

"What the Board says anyone with a first-offense territory breach is owed. Twenty-five hundred for me and twenty-five for Brendon Shaw."

"You want me to pay that cat?"

"The Board represents all of us. It protects all of us."

"Fine. Whatever. Just get out."

"Of course. And thank you for your assistance. You can send the money directly to the Board secretary. He'll be expecting it and it will be split up appropriately."

He headed toward the door. "Lock? You—"

A snap of thick plastic cut off the wolf's words and they both looked over. The bear held the sixty-five-inch flat screen in one hand like it weighed nothing and half of the TV's base in the other. "Um . . . do you have another stand for this TV?"

"*Just put it down,*" Sharyn growled out between clenched teeth.

"I can get you a new stand or—"

"*Down.*"

The bear did as she asked and she walked the two interlopers to her front porch.

As the limo pulled off, Sharyn's daughter and her idiot boy-friend walked up to her.

"Everything okay?"

Staring after the limo as it drove off her Pack's Staten Island territory, Sharyn calmly asked, "You went off neutral territory to nail that mixed cat on Labor Day weekend?"

Donna Noreen Maire McNelly blinked a few times, which meant she was debating whether to lie or not.

"Well . . . you said to get her. So we got her."

"Got her where?"

Donna licked her lips. "We tracked them to lion territory. Found the mutt first, went after her, and O'Neill showed up."

"Then you chased them into Van Holtz territory?" And brought that rich asshole wolf right to her door.

"Well . . . yeah."

Sharyn backhanded her daughter, sending her flying across the porch.

"*What the fuck was that for?*" Donna screamed, blood dripping from her cut lip, while her useless boyfriend, Jay Ross, leaned against the porch railings and kept busy by texting his "clients."

"First you didn't even kill the bitch like I told you to. Then you opened that fat yap of yours and led a goddamn Van Holtz to my fuckin' door!"

"It wasn't me!"

"Then who?"

Sharyn looked over at the boyfriend and without even looking away from his phone, he said, "Don't even."

"I look at you," Sharyn sneered at her daughter, "and I think again why didn't I make him wear a goddamn condom? Too bad I never have an answer that doesn't make me throw up a little." That said, Sharyn went back in to her house and slammed the door shut.

Donna McNelly glared at the hand held out to her, then slapped it away. "Fuck you!"

"Whatever." Jay went back to his cell phone and her eyes narrowed. Useless. He was absolutely useless!

Pushing herself off the ground, she wiped the blood from her lip. "I can't believe you didn't do anything."

"I'm not getting between you and your mother."

Angry and needing to take it out on somebody, Donna slapped the phone from her boyfriend's hand. He stepped toward her but stopped when she didn't back down, their eyes level as they were the same height, the same build.

"Why do I bother having you around?" she sneered. "You're fuckin' useless."

"You have me around because I give you what you *need*."

She blinked, briefly studied him. There were only two things she ever really needed from the man. Money, to keep her mother off her back, and a good fuck.

Oh, wait. There was something else her boyfriend provided—information. "You know where they are."

"'Course I do." He smiled, showing his fangs. "And those bitches are closer than you ever knew."

Chapter 10

Gwen was inputting the information from recent receipts and was taking her sweet time about it, too, when Blayne received yet another text message. She responded quickly and shut her phone. Placing the phone in her backpack and her backpack over her shoulder, Blayne got up and headed toward the office door.

Gwen kept typing, waiting until Blayne's hand was on the door handle before she said, "Where you going?"

Blayne stopped, her body tensing. "Huh?"

She continued to work. "I said, where are you going?"

"Out."

"For drinks? I haven't had a Guinness in forever."

Blayne stared at her. She'd been a nervous mess all day, jumping when the phone rang, tearing papers she had on her desk into shreds, and twisting and untwisting poor, defenseless paperclips. When it came to emotions, Blayne was always an open book.

"No," she finally answered. "Not drinks. I'm ... uh ..." Gwen could see her out of the corner of her eye, struggling with what she wanted to say. Struggling between lying and telling Gwen the truth. After a minute, she went with the lying. "I'm going to the hospital. Again."

"The volunteering. Right. Okay."

Blayne nodded, stared at Gwen for another moment—her frustration evident in the way she was twisting and untwisting her fingers—and went out the door.

Gwen went back to work . . . for about thirty more seconds. Then she shut off her monitor, pulled her backpack onto her shoulders, and ran to the office door. She stopped long enough to lock the doors and took off running. It still amazed Gwen that Blayne had finagled office space in the Kuznetsov Building. It was a small space, barely big enough for their two desks, small fridge, and coffeemaker, but the rent was too good to pass up and there was basement space to accommodate their company trucks and supplies. Really, Gwen couldn't ask for better, especially in this city.

Stopping at the main doors of the building, Gwen stuck her head out and looked both ways. She could see Blayne running west and she took off after her. She didn't get too close, though, not wanting Blayne to catch sight of her.

Thankfully Blayne didn't grab a bus or take the subway, which was good because Gwen was still learning her way around this nightmare town. Still . . . the door Blayne disappeared into nearly fifteen minutes later did nothing but convince Gwen that she'd have to rescue Blayne from herself yet again.

Gwen walked to that door, stopping immediately when she stepped inside. Nope. Not a hospital—a place Blayne knew Gwen would never willingly go into—but an ice-skating rink. The entire floor teeming with full-humans watching their children skate, all of them hoping to be the breeder of the next gold Olympian.

Yet Gwen's powerful sense of smell told her that full-humans weren't the only ones using this building.

Sniffing like a bloodhound on the trail of a murderer, Gwen followed her nose to a discreet door behind a set of stairs. That discreet door led to another discreet door. She pulled it open and came face-to-face with several bathrooms and closets filled with cleaning and maintenance supplies. She almost got sidetracked by some copper pipes in the maintenance closet but made herself focus.

She sniffed the air and went to another set of stairs and a locked door. She sniffed at the door and pawed at it a couple of times. It opened, a wolf standing on the other side.

"Hi."

"Hi." Gwen walked in, ignoring the way the male automatically sized her up, and quickly examined everything around her. This area of the building was huge, with its own set of elevators, a food court, several sports-related stores, and a Starbucks. This was a shifter-only space, huge and all-inclusive. A safe zone for every breed. That meant no fighting of any kind, including Pack, Pride, or Clan wars, and no hunting or bloodletting. Shifters got bitchy when they had to clean up any messes that required cops or disposing of carcasses.

"Can I help you?" the wolf asked.

"Uh . . . yeah. I'm looking for my friend. She's a little taller than me, black with brown hair . . . she was probably talking to herself."

He grinned. "The wolfdog? Yeah, she went down those stairs over there."

"Thanks."

"Want me to help you look for her?"

Gwen chuckled at that, sure of the kind of help the wolf wanted to give her. "No, thanks."

"If you change your mind, let me know."

"Yeah, yeah, sure." Because she obviously had nothing better to do than hook up with some horny wolf for ten minutes. How She-wolves tolerated any of them, Gwen would never know.

As directed, she went down the stairs and stopped in the hallway. The really big, multidoor-filled hallway. Because finding Blayne shouldn't be easy, now should it?

Sighing, Gwen went from door to door. Some were locked, and some opened to a practice or training session. She wished she could have stayed and watched the gymnasts. Nothing like

watching all those eight-year-old cubs and pups vaulting themselves twenty to thirty feet in the air and then screaming on the
way back down because they had no real idea yet how to land
properly.

She didn't have time for that, though. She was snooping, and
she wouldn't let anything get in her way. Because who knew
what Blayne was up to? Gwen was betting it had something to
do with a man. She'd already seen the basketball players working out and Gwen was surprised she didn't find Blayne there in
the stands, watching and waiting on some freakishly tall loser to
come over and smooth talk her. The woman had the worst taste
in males. She picked what seemed to be the nicest, sweetest guys,
and they always turned out to be full-fledged sociopaths. And if
she was sneaking some guy in behind Gwen's back that meant
one thing—another nutbag Gwen was going to have to deal with
down the road.

Why did she have to work so hard to protect her friends and
family? Why couldn't Blayne find normal, cranky shifters with
dominance issues like the rest of them?

Gwen heard male voices coming from a door close to her and
she reached for the handle, figuring she'd find Blayne. But before
Gwen could get a grip, the door flew open and she barely moved
out of the way in time. She caught sight of ice skates and knew it
was the hockey players. Her uncle Cally had played hockey on a
shifter team for years when he was younger.

She was trying to move around the player, when he snarled,
"Do you not answer your phone?"

Gwen tensed and looked up—and kept looking up until she
burst out laughing. "*You* play hockey?"

"What do you mean by that?"

"It can't be fair. You battin' the other players around the ice
with your giant arms."

"I don't have giant arms."

She kept laughing and shook her head. "Forget it. Is Blayne in
there?"

"No. And why didn't you answer your phone?"

"I shut it off because my brother was driving me crazy after I lacerated his ass this morning. Why?"

"I found out who jumped you and Blayne at Macon River."

Gwen stared up at the grizzly. To be honest, she'd forgotten about that Pack. Forgotten they'd existed or had attacked her and Blayne. Not that she didn't care, but the past few weeks had been so crazy busy, it had gone to the bottom of the heap of concerns she already had.

"Who was it?"

"I was calling to tell you that, but when I thought about it, I realized I couldn't tell you."

"Why not?"

He took several gulps of water from the bottle he held in his hand. His hair and skin were drenched in sweat and he was panting. He must have had a hell of a workout. "Because it's been handled, and I don't want you going over there to start it up all over again."

"I won't."

"You say that now, but then you'll be sitting around . . . thinking. And you'll remember what went down—and the next thing I know, I'll be hearing about you in the news."

Disgusted he was probably right, Gwen ignored him with a flip of her hand. "Whatever."

" 'Whateva,' " he mimicked back at her and then smiled.

Goofball.

And Gwen was about to tell him that, too, when she noticed seven females dressed in black latex minidresses and carrying black-and-gray pom-poms walk by in latex boots with six-inch heels. She peered at Lock, figuring she'd have to get his attention back to ask him a question, but he was still gazing down at her. Or maybe he had a really quick response time like Mitch.

"Who are they?"

"Who are who?"

Did he really not see seven big-breasted females in black latex walk by? Or was he the biggest liar this side of the Atlantic?

"The chicks in latex." She pointed and he glanced over, but focused back on her in less than a second.

"Oh, yeah. They're the derby pep squad."

Oh, no. No. No. No. No. No. No!

"*Derby* pep squad?" *Please, Christ! Let it be something other than what I'm thinking!*

"Yeah. Some leagues use cheerleaders and some use pep squads. The New York Roller Derby League uses a pep squad."

Goddamnit! Gwen took a breath, trying her best to stay calm. "Is there a bout tonight?"

"Yep. In the stadium, one floor beneath us."

Without saying another word, Gwen walked off.

"You'll never get in."

She looked at him over her shoulder. "Why not?"

"The bout's already sold out."

She faced him and quickly realized he was wearing a practice jersey for one of the professional shifter league teams. "But you play for the New York Carnivores."

"I do."

"So I'm sure with your connections you can get me in."

"I can."

Letting out an annoyed breath, she walked back over to him. "What do ya want?"

"I don't want anything, Mr. Mittens." He leaned down until their noses nearly touched. "In fact, all you have to do is ask me."

"That's it?"

"Yeah, that's it. I try to avoid blackmail. It always works out badly in the end."

"Can you get me into the bout?"

"Sure. Wait here." He walked off and the door he'd come through opened up again, more hockey players streaming out. She barely noticed any of them, too busy stressing out over what she'd see in a few minutes, until one walked over to her and sniffed her hair. Normally she'd be pissed off at some strange wolf sniffing her hair without permission, but he was gorgeous and . . . friendly

"Honey shampoo," he said with a smile. "You must be Gwen."

"Do I know you?"

"We have a mutual friend. Lock. I'm Ric." He pulled off his glove and held his hand out. Gwen shook it. "Nice to meet you."

"You, too."

"I recognized your scent from when Lock came back to the house after his run-in with that invading Pack. Sorry about all that, by the way."

"It wasn't your fault."

"Perhaps. But it was brought to the attention of the Board, and you and your friends should see some recompense for the attack." She would? But before she could ask for more details— because ya-ha! Free cash!—Lock returned. He'd changed into sweatpants, sneakers, and a light gray T-shirt that looked like it had been molded to his body. And . . . uh . . . *yowza.*

"Hey," Lock said to Ric.

"Hey," Ric said back. Then he walked away.

Nope. Gwen would never really *get* guys.

Lock smiled at her. "You ready?"

Lock had never been so grateful for being on the hockey team before today. It was an excellent way to work off nervous energy and earn a few extra bucks. He'd joined the team about six months after his return from the Marines. Nearly a year after that, Ric had become the team captain and Lock his backup. Which meant he had access to all the cool little benefits that all the team captains and managers had . . . like primo seats at derby bouts.

What he didn't expect was to find half the Kuznetsov wild dog Pack taking up most of those primo seats.

"Hey."

Jess Ward-Smith glanced up from her program and broke out in a huge grin . . . until she saw Gwen standing next to him. Then her eyes grew wide and . . . yeah. He definitely saw panic.

"Hi!" she said, way too brightly. "What are you guys doing here?" She elbowed the wild dog next to her without giving Lock or Gwen a chance to answer her. "Hey, Phil. Look who's here."

Phil glanced over and then barked, "Oh, shit."

He then elbowed Sabina, who elbowed Danny, who elbowed Maylin, who yelped at the sight of them. Considering the wild dogs had actually allowed Lock to be around their pups on a regular basis, he somehow doubted they suddenly feared him.

"Where is she?" Gwen demanded, confusing Lock more by her aggressive tone.

"Whoever could you mean, Gwen?" Jess replied, again, way-too-brightly and with a higher pitch to her voice than Lock could ever remember her having.

Gwen pointed her finger at Jess. "Don't lie to me, Benji. Where is she?"

"What's going on?" Lock had to ask. And, as if in answer, the lights shut completely off and a rough female voice came over the speakers.

"Ladies and gentlemen, I hope you're ready for a night of raw brutality and unrepentant violence. You've been waiting for it . . . you've been wanting it! And now you're going to get it! The new girls on the block against the most vicious broads known to derby. Welcome, one and all . . . to Boroughs Brawlers Banked Track Derby!"

The crowd roared, especially the wild dogs—except for the "top five," as Lock called Jess and her best friends. They were all whispering and generally panicking.

"So let's get this party started," the announcer yelled. "And let's all put our hands together for . . . the Assault and Battery Park Babes!"

The response was not exactly enthusiastic, the Babes being pretty new and mostly hybrids. Lock had been hearing a lot about them this past year, though, as they steadily moved up the ranks in the league, taking everyone by surprise.

The spotlights hit the track as the Babes came tearing out to John Lee Hooker's "Boom Boom." They moved fast and looked really cute in tiny red shorts, black fishnets, bright sparkly red derby skates, and three layers of too-small tank tops in red, black, and white. As each player zipped around the track, the announcer called them out by number and derby name.

"Number thirty-eight, and team captain, Pop-A-Cherry! Number sixty-two, Marlon Brandher. Number twenty-four, Our Lady of Pain and Suffering." Lock laughed, kind of wishing they had cool names like that on the professional teams, when he heard Gwen gasp as the announcer called out, "Number seventy-six, Evie Viserate!"

Lock heard the wild dogs barking and was about to ask who she was when Jess yelled, "Lock, get her!"

Get her? Get who? Following where Jess pointed, Lock watched as Gwen marched down the stadium stairs toward the track.

"What the . . ." Glad he'd changed out of his skates, Lock went after Gwen and grabbed her around the waist, hauling her back up the stairs.

"*Put me down! She's not doing this!*"

"Who?" he demanded.

Jess motioned to the track again and Lock looked at Evie Viserate. Really looked at her. She had her hair in two ponytails and a bright white helmet over that. But when she smiled Lock could only cringe. Because he'd recognize that smile anywhere.

"Uh-oh."

Gwen was still putting up a fight. "Put me down! *Right now!*"

"I'll be back," he said to Jess. "Hold our seats." And then he hauled the crazed feline back up the stairs and out into the stadium hallway.

"*How could she lie to me like that?*" Gwen demanded as soon as Lock put her down on the ground in the hallway.

"Maybe because she knew you'd get a tad hysterical."

"I'm not hysterical. I'm *pissed off*! She's going to get herself killed out there." She tried to go around him again, but Lock took one small step and immediately blocked her way with that insanely beautiful body of his.

"How do you know that?"

Arms folded under her chest, Gwen demanded, "Have you ever watched derby? *Real* derby? Not that full-human one," which was pretty tough for a bunch of full-humans but, compared to shifter derby, totally lightweight.

"No."

"Then you have no idea how bad this could get."

"But you do?"

He really thought she was being a little drama queen for no reason, didn't he? That her whole life was built around stopping Blayne from having any fun because she was Gwen the Fun-inator.

"Yeah. I do. I'm the daughter of The Rocker."

Lock frowned. "The baseball player?"

Taking a deep breath, "No. Not the baseball player." *You pinhead!* "The derby queen."

His frown faded and she watched him try not to smile. "Your mother was a—"

"Yes. But not 'a,' she is *the* derby queen. Even now. She and my aunts ran the Philly league for years. Just *surviving* bouts against the Philly Phangs was considered an accomplishment by most teams. For shifters, derby hasn't changed that much. The uniforms are hotter, the girls cuter, but the rest of it is exactly the same."

"And you don't think Blayne can handle it."

"I know she can't."

"Because you tried and failed."

Gwen paced away from him. "Yeah. I did try." She leaned against the wall. "I did fail."

Lock stood next to her, still towering over her even as he leaned back. "That doesn't mean Blayne will fail."

"I'm not worried about that, her failing like me. I mean, I was eighteen and daughter of The Rocker. I didn't stand a chance, and everybody knew it. Even my mother. The whistle blew on my first game and I froze. Just froze. I've never experienced fear like that before." She shook her head. "That won't happen to Blayne."

"Then what are you—"

"Her name was Marla the Merciless with the Pittsburgh Steal-ers—that's 'Stealers' as in thievery. She slammed into me like a two-ton truck. I hit the ground and then she came down on me, breaking my leg in five places."

"Ow."

"My pelvis."

"Uh . . ."

"My right hip."

"God, Gwen—"

"My tailbone."

"Okay, okay." Lock shuddered. "I get it."

"I woke up in the hospital."

"Because you'd never go there on your own."

"Exactly. It took weeks for me to fully recover."

"Did you play again?"

"No. But not only because I was terrified, which I was," she freely admitted. "But because when Marla was crawling off me and before I blacked out, she called me a 'mixed-breed whore.' And the way she said it, I knew whether I'd been the worst or best player out there, whether Roxy was my mother or not, she would have made sure she hurt me."

"That was a long time ago, Gwen."

"So? Nothing's changed. Am I the only one who remembers Labor Day weekend? That Pack went after Blayne for one rea-son and one reason only."

"Maybe. But Blayne's entire team is mostly made up of hy-brids. She's not alone out there."

"She's the new girl, Jersey. Fresh meat." She shrugged in frus-tration, knowing there was nothing she could do. "They'll want her broken in right."

"So when does the ball come into play?" Jess asked, earning a scowl from Gwen.

"There's no ball in Roller Derby," Gwen snapped. "That's a movie—and I only acknowledge the James Caan version, not that other one."

"If there's no ball, then what are they doing?"

"Going around in circles," Phil explained incorrectly. "Until someone dies."

Lock could feel the feline bristling next to him, which only got worse when he started laughing. He hadn't thought he'd be able to convince Gwen to come back in to watch Blayne—watch, not rescue—but he had. Now they sat with the wild dogs, and there was something quite entertaining about watching Gwen deal with them.

"All right," Gwen said. "*Very* short lesson in derby before the whistles blow. Four girls from each team that includes three blockers and one pivot make up the pack. The whistle blows, they take off. Two other girls, one from each team, are jammers. When a second whistle blows, the jammers' whole goal is to get through the pack as quickly as possible. Whoever passes the other team's Pivot first becomes the lead jammer and she'll earn points for every player she passes from the other team. This all happens within two-minute intervals called jams, although the lead jammer can call off the jam before then. The whole thing wraps up in about two hours, including time-outs and a thirty-minute halftime break. There. That's derby."

The wild dogs stared blankly at Gwen, the disappointment evident on their faces.

"That's it?" Jess finally asked. "That's the entire game?"

"It's called a bout, not a game. And yes. That's it."

"That sounds kind of . . ."

"Boring," Phil finished for her.

Gwen shrugged. "To each their own," she said, focusing back on the track.

As Gwen said, five females from each team rolled onto the track. Blayne was among them. She looked terrified as she rolled to a stop, lifting her gaze to the crowd, her eyes searching. She saw Jess and the wild dogs first, her smile painfully forced as she waved at them. Then Blayne's gaze moved over to Lock and Gwen.

She blinked, her head tilting like a confused German shepherd's. Then she smiled—and the power of it nearly blew out the stadium lights.

She lifted her arm high and waved. "Hi, Gwenie!"

Laughing, Gwen waved back, but both women jumped when a large hand slammed down on the rail in front of Blayne.

"Who is that?" Gwen asked, her eyes targeting the good-sized player leering down at Blayne.

"She's one of the Staten Island Furriers." Jess smiled around her chocolate-dipped banana on a stick, like most canines ignoring the potential risks of eating chocolate. Even her wedding was a veritable chocolate fiesta that every dog attending indulged in. They were fine the next day, but Lock didn't understand taking the risk. Then again, if someone told him he couldn't have honey . . . "Her name is D.F.A."

"D.F.A.?"

"Death From Above."

Gwen and Lock looked at the wild dog. "That's her *name?*" Lock asked.

"It's her derby name. And considering her size . . . kind of fitting."

"Muzzles on," one of the refs ordered and Lock could only stare.

"Uh . . . Blayne's wearing a muzzle."

"Yeah," Gwen clenched her hands together. "I heard some leagues insist on it if wolfdogs, coyote-dogs, or wolf-coyotes play. They have to wear muzzles."

"Tell me you're kidding."

"Nope. It's the only way the leagues would allow them to play against nonhybrids."

Well, at least the muzzles they wore were fitted, snapping on to their helmets, the crisscrossed strips of white leather stretching over their noses and mouths and under their chins. Not only did they protect the other players from bites, they also looked pretty cool. Lock's dweeby side was impressed.

The first whistle blew and the pack of females shot off. Lock and Gwen leaned forward and he wondered if they saw the same thing when it came to Blayne as a player. She had solid strength, holding her own against the other players in the pack, but she was a little timid and she needed more confidence on her skates. A few times it looked as if a strong wind would knock her on her ass.

The second whistle blew and the two jammers sped off after the pack, working their way through when they reached them. The Furriers' jammer tried to get past Blayne, and Blayne was nicely holding her off so the rest of her team could get their jammer through. But as the pack tightened up, Lock suddenly heard Blayne snarl, and Gwen sat up straight as they watched her best friend lifted into the air by D.F.A.

It was strange how he knew, how he sensed it without actually knowing, what Gwen would do. Automatically his hands reached out and caught hold of her waist as she tried to shoot past him. He yanked her onto his lap only seconds before she could launch herself over the seats and probably onto the track.

Holding Gwen tight, Lock watched as D.F.A. shot out from the pack with a struggling Blayne still in her arms, rolled toward where Gwen and Lock were sitting, and, when she was about ten feet away, shot-putted Blayne right at them.

The entire section instinctively ducked as Blayne's body flew over the railing and into the protective glass between the audience and the track. He'd never been so grateful for protective glass as he was right now.

Slowly lifting his head, his mouth open, Lock stared at the spot where poor Blayne's body had hit.

Had he really just seen that? Had he really just witnessed one player throwing another *at the crowd*? And, more importantly, why wasn't that player thrown out of the game?

"Do you know her, Gwen?" he had to ask, because D.F.A. had been staring right at Gwen when she'd lobbed Blayne at her.

"No. I've never seen her before."

"Why is she still playing?"

Gwen was sitting up, straining to see Blayne, who'd hit the floor between the banked track and the stadium seats. "You're kidding, right?"

"No, I'm not kidding."

"You've gotta do a hell of a lot more than toss around a player before they'll throw you out. Marla the Merciless didn't even get a thrown out after she took me down."

Lock didn't know what to say, but then Blayne managed to get to her feet. She had to grip the railing for several seconds and then she realized she was blind, but that was quickly remedied when she readjusted her helmet and muzzle.

Giving her body a once-over shake, she waved at Gwen again, a happy smile on her face, and rolled off to get back in the game. Admiring the will it took for her to get back in there, the crowd cheered, but none so loud as the wild dogs.

Gwen applauded, but again, Lock knew from her body language how stressed she was. And he didn't blame her one bit.

CHAPTER 11

By the tenth time Blayne was flung at the crowd like a Frisbee, Gwen didn't even cringe anymore. And Lock simply sat there, no longer jumping or snarling when Blayne came flying at them.

Yet what amazed Gwen was that no matter how many times Blayne got tossed around by that giant bitch, she not only got back to her feet seemingly undamaged, but she was always smiling. Gwen knew Blayne was tougher than most people gave her credit for, but even she had no idea how resilient her friend was. Like heavy-duty Tupperware, Blayne kept bouncing back.

"Kill her!" Jess screamed at Blayne, Gwen and Lock looking over at the cute wild dog with the unnatural bloodlust. "Wipe her from the face of the earth, Evie!"

"They're pulling her out," Phil announced and Gwen saw that it was true. Blayne was being benched, confirmed by the announcer. The crowd booed, but Gwen understood the decision. Although it might be entertaining for these people to watch Blayne Thorpe get tossed around by a blond missing link, it didn't exactly advance the bout.

The last quarter went fast and hard, neither team willing to back off. But when the final whistle blew, the Furriers had beaten the Babes by a good twelve points.

"That was great!" Jess cheered. "I'm so coming back."

Gwen smiled. Another derby convert. She knew the signs.

"We're going out to see Blayne," Jess told her. "You want to come with?"

"Yeah. Okay."

Gwen stretched, yawned, and that's when it hit her—she was still on Lock MacRyrie's lap! Had been for the entire bout, including halftime—and he hadn't said a word about it. Sneaky Jersey bear!

"Why don't I meet you guys there?" she suggested.

Nodding, Jess got up with her Pack following. They filed out and Gwen waited until they were gone. Then she scrambled off Lock's lap, turned, and began slapping at him with her hands.

He held his arm up to block his face and laughed at her.

"What did I do?"

"You let me sit on your lap that whole time!"

"I was comfortable!" He caught hold of her arms and pulled her forward. "And so were you," he taunted. At least it sounded like taunting.

"That's not the point!"

"Besides, I figured you'd temporarily deemed me your feline throne."

"Very funny." She pulled her arms away. "I'm going to see Blayne."

Frustrated and embarrassed and a tiny bit confused—because she really had been comfortable on his lap—Gwen marched up the stairs and out the door, Lock right behind her.

"This way," he said, catching hold of her hand and leading her around a corner, through a small hallway and into a much larger one filled with girls on skates and their adoring fans.

The wild dogs were already hugging Blayne, but as soon as she saw Gwen, she pulled away and skated over.

"Gwenie! I'm so glad you're here."

Gwen hugged Blayne tight. "I am, too."

When Blayne pulled back, Gwen couldn't help but wince. "Blayne . . . your face."

"It'll heal," she dismissed with a wave. She caught sight of Lock behind Gwen. "Hi, Lock!"

"Hi, Blayne. You were—"

"I know, I know," she said before he could finish. "I need work. I know."

"I didn't say—"

"I was pathetic, hopeless! You don't have to tell me."

"But I wasn't—"

"Just a mess! I know!"

Gwen patted Lock's chest. "Let it go."

As Blayne continued to rhapsodize on how bad she was, a group of Furriers came down the hallway, heading toward the locker rooms. They had a large group of fans and friends around them as they made their way, but that didn't stop Gwen from coldly eyeing the one who kept going after Blayne.

And the female eyed Gwen right back as she rolled by, an annoying smirk on her face.

Deciding to let it go, for now, Gwen turned back to find Blayne still listing her flaws. She was about to tell her to stuff it already, when Gwen's nose twitched and her desire to hiss nearly strangled her.

"You all right?" Lock asked.

Surprised he'd noticed since she hadn't made a move, Gwen said, "Yeah. I'm fine . . . I'll be back." Then she calmly walked off down the hall.

Jess tugged on Lock's arm, pulling him away from staring after Gwen, wondering what she was up to. "So . . . ?"

Lock shrugged at Jess's vague question. "So . . . what?"

"You, hanging out with Gwen." She grinned and danced on her toes. "A good thing?"

"We ran in to each other before the bout. I just tagged along."

"She sat on your lap for almost two hours, Lachlan MacRyrie of the Clan MacRyrie." A name she insisted on calling him any time she saw him.

"I know what you're thinking and forget it. I already asked her out, and she turned me down."

"Are you that naive?"

"Possibly."

"Lock, she's a cat. She wouldn't deign to sit on your lap for two whole hours if she wasn't interested."

"Don't start, Jess."

"I'm serious." He knew she was and he didn't want to discuss it, because he didn't know what was going on between him and Gwen. He only knew that it was a fragile thing, easily destroyed. He didn't want that to happen.

Deciding to torture his favorite little wild dog in the hope of distracting her from this topic, Lock gripped her nose between his thumb and forefinger.

She scowled. "Let me go."

He didn't.

"Now."

Nope.

"Dammit!" Lock laughed as Jess tried to pull away from him, her hands slapping at his. When Jess got like this she always reminded him of a dog trying to wiggle out of her collar.

"Where did Gwen go?" Blayne asked, seemingly oblivious to the wild dog trying to fight him off.

"Down the hall—"

Lock's body jerked, his fingers immediately releasing Jess as he heard the unmistakable roar-hiss of Gwen. Yet before he could move to find out what the hell was going on, she came slamming out of the locker room, her body wrapped around the behemoth derby girl who'd tortured Blayne. Pounding her fist into the female's face, Gwen roared again, oblivious to the Furriers streaming from the locker room to help their teammate. Derby girls were notoriously protective of their own, and Lock quickly saw how bad this could get.

Even worse, D.F.A. wasn't the type of female to quietly take a beating. She swung Gwen off her and slammed her into the opposite wall.

"Holy shit!" Jess burst out as Blayne charged past them, intent on getting to Gwen. She did, too, tackling the She-wolf and shoving her to the ground. The timidity Blayne showed on the track disappeared in an instant now that Gwen was involved.

Now D.F.A. had two Philly hybrids on her, both of them slamming their fists into her face, screaming profanities that Lock hadn't heard since one of his teammates had been "accidentally" shot in the ass by his resentful girlfriend.

Lock moved forward but the Babes' captain caught his arm, gold cat eyes watching Gwen and Blayne take on the vicious She-wolf. Based more on her size than her scent, Lock guessed she was a liger, a normally sweet-natured hybrid. He found it odd that she'd play on a derby team.

The Furriers jumped in to help their teammate, one of the wolves grabbing Blayne around the waist and throwing her off D.F.A. and at the rest of them.

Lock caught Blayne before she could crash into them, but before he could pass her off to the wild dogs, she screamed out, "House cat her, Gwenie! *House cat the bitch!*" Still not wanting to know what the hell that was, Lock tossed Blayne at a couple of the male wild dogs as Gwen got slammed onto her back and her face pounded by the She-wolf. That's when the two teams merged, the fight getting ugly fast since no points were at risk and no refs were there to stop them.

That was also around the time that Lock had had enough.

He slammed one foot down, the sound ricocheting around the hallway, and followed it with one of his roars. The two teams separated, each breed reacting instinctively, which meant the cats took off, the wolves snarled and backed up, looking to each other for someone to lead them in to that particular fight, while the hyenas laughed and ran but didn't go too far because they wanted to see someone hurt. Some of the hybrids reacted in similar fashion, but at least two broke down into tears, a wolf-coyote tried to dig through a concrete wall, and their liger team captain smiled at him.

"Thanks," she said. "I wasn't sure I could break that one up on my own."

Lock nodded at her and reached down to tear the two still-battling women apart, both of whom appeared completely unaffected by his roar.

Once he separated them, they both scrambled to their feet, but Lock stepped between them before they could go at each other again.

"She's the one!" Gwen yelled, trying to go around him but he kept pushing her back. "She's the one who jumped Blayne and me at Macon River!"

"That little half-breed whore started it, you fuckin' bitch!"

In answer to that, Gwen leaned around Lock and spit blood into D.F.A.'s face, and the She-wolf—who he now realized *must be* a McNelly—came at Gwen again by trying to climb over Lock. That's when Gwen slipped her hand into one of the pockets of her cargo pants. He saw the flash of silver and knew what she was about to do. Refusing to let this go that far, Lock shoved McNelly back, sending the She-wolf flying down the hallway. He grabbed hold of Gwen, pinning her right arm against her body so she couldn't pull out the blade she had on her, and carried her in the opposite direction.

"Bring it, bitch!" Gwen yelled, those scary nails of her left hand pointing at McNelly over Lock's shoulder. "I will kill you, you fucking whore! You touch my friend again, *I will kill you!*"

Lock slammed into the men's locker room halfway down the hall and shoved the door closed. He released Gwen and pushed her farther inside, but once loose, Gwen tried to go round him. He shoved her back again and, again, she went for the door. When he shoved her back a third time, Gwen went up and over him, using those powerhouse legs to leap from a standing position. She was at the door when he grabbed her from behind and spun her around.

Angrier than he'd ever been with anyone not trying to kill him, Lock lifted her up and held her there. She was fully out of control, the two felines inside her roaring for blood. Her claws were out now, tearing at his favorite T-shirt, and Lock couldn't imagine either a full lion male or a full tiger male being able to handle her when she was like this. He wasn't even sure she knew what she was doing.

Out of ideas, he did the only thing he could think of. He carried her to the showers, turned her so she faced away from him, and flipped the water on full blast and cold.

Gwen screamed, but she finally sounded human. He held her under the water even as she kicked to get away. He wasn't taking any chances.

"You son of a bitch! Put me down!"

He spun her in his hands until she faced him again. "You have control of yourself?" he demanded.

She answered him by slapping his face. So hard he actually felt his teeth rattle, then she was kissing him and he . . . uh . . . kind of stopped caring about the whole teeth rattling thing.

Attacking someone without warning for something they did weeks before? Check. Ready to turn a simple breed dispute into something far uglier with the razor blade she kept on her at all times? Check. Using blood as a weapon of rudeness? Check. Threatening death? Check. Attacking a helpful stranger or friend? Check. Kissing a helpful stranger or friend without warning or permission? Check.

Yeah, it only took Gwen six weeks to become her mother.

The horror of that was staggering and perhaps that was why she was making out with Lock MacRyrie in a men's locker room. She knew it belonged to the men because of the testosterone funk permeating every corner. Normally she'd gag, her delicate feline senses unwilling to accept the lingering aftereffects of too many male breeds mulling around the same area after a game. But for some reason kissing this man focused her attention on him and only him. Not only distracting her from the "man funk," as Blayne called it, but from her rage. A rage that, once unleashed, could rarely be contained or controlled by anyone, which was why she fought so hard to hold it in—but when she realized who that bitch was . . .

Yet none of that mattered right now as all that anger and

hatred slipped back into its safe place and she allowed herself to enjoy this kiss. She still didn't know how he did that . . . that . . . *thing* with his lips, but it did make her wonder what effect those lips would have on other locations of her body.

And God, he tastes so sweet. It must be all the honey he eats.

Was there a way to make this kiss last forever? With the freezing cold water pouring down on them from the showerhead, she could almost imagine they were standing under one of the Macon River falls, fresh from a swim in the river, and making out like two teenagers.

She briefly wondered how far she could take this little fantasy when Gwen heard Blayne come into the bathroom. "Gwenie? Hon, are you ooooooooooo—wow. Okay. Yeah. Uh . . ."

Blayne wasn't alone, either. She had Jess with her and the two canines, in their pathetic attempt to leave quickly without being noticed, slammed into each other and then tripped over the other as they tried to make it to the door.

By now Lock had stopped kissing her so he could watch the two boneheads over his shoulder. Although Gwen didn't blame him. Some things simply couldn't be ignored.

Jess yanked open the door, slamming it right into Blayne's face.

"Ow!"

"Oh, shit. Sorry!" Jess pushed her out the door and smiled back at Gwen and Lock. "Sorry," she mouthed before she spun away and right into Blayne, who hadn't moved.

"Ow!"

"Oh, Blayne! Honey, are you okay?"

The door swung closed and there was a moment, maybe two, before she heard that first snort from the bear. After that, it took forever for them to stop laughing.

CHAPTER 12

He drove her back to her hotel, everyone having cleared out of the hallway by the time Gwen and Lock came out of the bathroom. He'd assumed he'd drop her off and go, but when he stopped amid all the limos and cabs to let her out, she'd asked, "You're coming in, right?"

That had been forty minutes ago. Forty minutes for Gwen to shower, change in to sweats, clean up all those facial lacerations, and somehow—some*way*—end up in Lock's lap.

How he got her in his lap, he still didn't know. They'd barely glazed over the fight with McNelly when she'd blurted out, "You need a damn haircut!"

When he'd disagreed, she'd suddenly crawled onto his lap. Not that he minded. Not at all. Especially with her facing him, her knees resting on either side of his hips and her amazing little ass resting right over his cock. So nope, he didn't mind at all.

Gwen put her hands in his hair and pushed it off his face. She studied him for a moment and then pulled her hands out. "I'm not talking a major haircut here."

"I don't want a haircut. I'm enjoying my wild side."

"There's wild and there's unruly. You don't want unruly, do you?"

"There's a difference?"

"You're the guy with all the degrees. Shouldn't you know that already?"

"Much to my parents' disappointment, I only have one degree."

"Pieces of paper," she muttered, still playing with his hair. She seemed fascinated with the silver-tipped ends, studying them closely. "Seems to me you got more of an education in the military. Especially if you saw combat." She leaned in closer, her studious gaze moving up the strands of hair. She smelled wonderful, especially with that damn honey shampoo she was using. "Did you see combat?" she asked.

"I wasn't in a combat unit." She turned her head to look at him and her mouth was so close. It took everything in him to not kiss her again, to not slip his tongue in her mouth and lick his way to heaven. "We're stalkers. We hunt the ones who hunt us."

"You were in the Unit?"

He nodded and she released the strands she held and picked up another handful. "You really do have amazing hair," she said, not asking him anything further about his military past. "I know women who would pay a fortune for this kind of coloring."

He didn't think she was changing the subject because she was uncomfortable with it. Almost all shifters knew about the Unit and what their role in the full-human military was. Instead he got the feeling she was changing the subject because what he once did didn't bother her one way or the other. At least not the way it bothered his parents. Then again, Gwen was a take-no-prisoners kind of female. That's how she'd been raised, that was how she lived. He knew that from the way she'd brutally fought McNelly. No bluffing, no warning growls or cat scratches to get her point across. He could easily imagine the two females fighting until one or both were dead.

"What shampoo do you use?" she asked.

"Whatever's on sale at the grocery store when I go shopping."

Her mouth dropped open and she laughed. "My brother's head would explode if he heard that. The first job he ever got when he was sixteen was so he could pay for his conditioner. And before you ask, yeah, it was *that* expensive."

"I'm too lazy for all that."

"You don't have a *mighty* mane. A sign of a lion's sexual maturity and power."

Having had more than his fair share of male lions to deal with while in the military, Lock could do nothing but roll his eyes in disgust.

She lifted another handful of his hair. "It wouldn't hurt to shape it a bit. I've got my clippers, I could do it here."

"No."

"If you're worried, I've got my license."

"As a plumber."

"And stylist. When I work in Ma's shop, I get a lot of guys coming in for me to cut their hair." He *bet* they did. The bastards probably stampeded the door.

"You can do hair?"

She counted off on her fingers as she answered, "Hair, makeup, pedicures, manicures, and I can wax whatever part of the body you want me to."

"You're not waxing anything of mine."

She leaned in, her thumb rubbing across his brow. "Maybe pluck a few stray hairs?"

"No."

"Okay, but you'll have to deal with it later."

"Deal with what?"

"Your father is getting a unibrow. And since you two look so much alike . . ."

He brushed her hand away. "The world will have to deal with the horror of my old-man unibrow."

"Fine. Be that way."

"I will." Lock studied her for a moment as she continued to exam his hair. "I don't get it."

"Get what?"

"You don't like doing hair, but you're determined to cut mine?"

"I don't like doing hair for money, every day. But I do my friends' hair all the time. That's fun. Besides, if we don't clean this up a bit—" she combed his hair down until it covered his face and laughed "—you're never going to get yourself a nice housesow to breed your cubs and make your dinner."

He pushed her hands away and shook his hair out of his face. "Because that sounds *hot.*"

With her fingers resting against his chest, and those intense gold eyes watching closely, she asked, "If a nice housesow's not to your taste . . . then what do you want?"

You. I want you.

Yet something told him this was not the right moment to say that, to admit how she was driving him and his poor cock crazy. So the answer was the much more mundane but safe, "Dinner. I want dinner."

And to prove it, he reached to the side table and picked up the room service menu.

"Hope they have moose," he muttered as she watched him closely but said nothing.

Gwen didn't know who she was more pissed at. The bear, for resisting her charms, or herself, for trying to be charming in the first place.

She'd admit that she never bothered working hard to get a guy interested, mostly because there were none who made her feel as if they were worth it. For those she did feel were worthy, she'd put out signals that suggested she was interested in sex and most would respond in kind. Eventually they'd end up in bed together. If it was good, Gwen would usually go back for a little more. If it wasn't, she wouldn't bother.

Her life was usually so simple. Now it was complicated because she didn't feel like she was going after this guy simply for sex.

Okay, she wouldn't lie and say she wasn't interested in having sex with him. Because, Christ! Was she interested. But there was more to it than that for both of them.

They ate their dinner at the dining table, but when it was time for dessert, Lock moved the table and coffee table out of the way and opened up the blinds. Removing their ice cream sundaes from the freezer, they sat on the floor, their backs against the couch, and stared out over the New York City skyline.

"Do you ever miss Jersey?" Gwen asked.

"How can I?" He gestured with a tilt of his head. "It's right over there."

She laughed. "Good point."

"Besides, I was going to schools in Manhattan from the time I was ten."

"From where you live in Jersey?" He nodded. "That must have been a hell of a daily haul for your mother."

"Not when there's a bus and subway system available."

"When you were ten?" He nodded again and Gwen moved around until she could look at him without turning her head. "Your mother sent you into the city on your own at ten?"

"My mother is a big believer in self-sufficient children."

"So is my mother, but she never put me on a bus alone at the age of ten."

"But then how else would I have accidentally discovered the Bowery—and learned at such an early age exactly how fast bears can run?"

Gwen shrugged helplessly. "I have no response for that."

"Yeah," he said after swallowing another spoonful of his sundae. "Most people don't."

"I have to go," Lock said.

Of course, he should have said it forty minutes ago, but they were having such a nice conversation about the ins and outs of copper plumbing, he hadn't wanted to leave. But they'd run out of things to say and she was staring at him, waiting for him to make that move. That move to put him in her bed.

He knew his uncles would cuff him in the back of the head and ask him what the hell was wrong with him and "didn't you learn anything from us? Or have you been listening to that idiot father of yours again?"

The truth was, Lock had learned a lot from his uncles, but there was one big difference between the MacRyrie bears of Jersey and Professor Brody MacRyrie—Brody had the woman he wanted. Had her and had managed for over thirty-seven years to hold on to a sow that everyone said would never be caught, much less kept. Lock didn't know if that's where things were going with Gwen, but if he hoped to have a chance in hell with her, something told him he needed to follow his father's path down this road. *Not* his uncles'.

"Already?" She glanced at her watch and gave a small wince. "I didn't know it was so late."

"Yeah. And I've got work . . . or something." *Or something? Is that the best you can do, you idiot!* "I mean, I'm working on a job and I'm running behind."

"Okay." They were sitting on the couch again, Gwen facing him, her legs tucked up under her. Those gold eyes watching him with that heavy-lidded, barely blinking, feline stare. Yet she wasn't tense. She simply waited. For him.

An enticing move, but he wasn't falling for it. At the same time, though, a little good-night kiss couldn't hurt, right?

Leaning forward, he slipped his hand behind her neck, his fingers massaging the muscles there. Gwen groaned and closed her eyes, her lips parting in what he could only see as a personal invitation.

Gripping the back of her neck to hold her in place, Lock kissed her. He'd meant to keep it short and controlled, but Gwen's small hands gripped his shoulders, those damn nails grazing against his throat, behind his ear. It drove him nuts! He tilted his head to the side, allowing himself to be pulled in to that kiss as his tongue stroked hers, as his lips played with hers. She abruptly pulled as far back as the hand holding her in place would allow.

"Your lips," she whispered, her eyes still closed. "What is that thing you do with your lips?"

"What thing?" he asked and then pulled her in again. She groaned deep and long, the sound coming from the back of her throat as she rose up on her knees, her hands releasing his shoulders so she could wrap her arms around his neck.

He knew he had to stop, he had to pull away. God knew he didn't want to but . . .

Lock pulled back, untangling her arms from around his neck. "I have to go."

Gwen's eyes blinked open. She stared at him with unabashed surprise but also passion. Deep, raw passion that he'd never seen from another female before.

"You're . . . ?"

The word "going" hung out there between them.

He kissed her forehead and released her, pulling away as a card was swiped in the front door and it swung open. A male stepped in. Lion. He looked like Brendon Shaw. *Must be the infamous half-brother of the half-brother.*

The lion strode into the room yawning, glanced at them, and waved.

"Where's Sissy?" Gwen asked, moving farther away from Lock.

"Off with her She-wolves. I don't know how she does it, because the jet lag is kicking my ass." He grabbed a bottle of water from the minifridge underneath the end table closest to Lock, waved again, and headed down a hallway. "Night," he called out seconds before a distant doorway slammed shut.

"Huh," Gwen said. "That went well."

Lock wasn't sure what she meant until they heard a roared "*Who the fuck was that?*" and that distant doorway crashed back open.

Jet lag! She forgot about jet lag! Of course, since Gwen had never traveled off the East Coast, this wasn't exactly surprising. Plus, an early night in for her brother and his mate was usually around six in the morning. But Gwen had forgotten that Mitch wasn't used to traveling the way Sissy—a hardcore traveler since she'd turned eighteen—was. And because of that miscalculation,

her brother was here—exhausted, pissed off, and ready to kill a
bear. *Her* bear!

Mitch Shaw went right for Lock, too, his claws unleashing as
he moved in for the killing blow, the power behind those claws
capable of snapping a human spine with one well-placed slap.

Even worse, Lock wasn't startled. A startled Lock meant he
could put up a healthy fight. A sedate Lock simply meant he
could get his ass . . .

Oh. Oh.

Well she hadn't expected that.

Not only was Lock not startled, but he wasn't frightened either. Nor was he mad. And as Mitch lunged at him, Lock casually
reached out and batted the lion down. Gwen couldn't even call it
a vicious mauling. More like a simple sow-swat from a momma
bear to her cubs when they were doing something stupid. She
doubted Lock put any real strength behind that sow-swat either.
But Mitch went down, grunting as he hit the floor hard.

Raging now, and roaring, Mitch got back up and came at
Lock again. Again, Lock slapped the big cat down. Even worse,
Lock still wasn't upset. He was laughing. Not mocking laughter,
either, which she knew well from when Mitch and her uncles had
done it to others. More like entertained chuckles as if he'd found
a really great toy.

Again Mitch got up and, again, Lock batted him to the floor,
Gwen's brother going down with a bam!

Lock grinned at Gwen. "He's fun," he said, reaching out and
cuffing Mitch without even looking at him. "He just keeps trying
to get back up." Bam! "It's great." Bam! "Like 'The Little Lion
Who Could.'" Bam!

Mitch, bruised and perhaps permanently brain damaged, tried
to struggle up again, but Lock held him down on the floor by
using the same hand he'd slapped Gwen's brother around with.

"I've got to go," he said to Gwen again, oblivious to the
curses and promises of violent retribution being tossed at him
from the floor. "But I want you to know I had an amazing time
tonight."

The words were said with such sincerity that Gwen completely forgot about her poor—now special-needs—brother struggling on the floor. She gazed into those big brown eyes that were almost too big for Lock's human face and too small for his bear one and said, "I had a great time, too."

"Then I'll talk to you later?"

"Okay."

He kissed her again, keeping it short this time, but then he pressed his forehead against hers, his silver-tipped brown hair feeling soft and silky against her skin, tickling her cheeks and chin.

"I've got to go," he whispered.

"You said that. At least three times."

"I know. I'm saying it again." He took a deep breath and then moved away from her, but not before brushing his skin against hers. It was an almost feline move, and she barely stopped herself from climbing onto his back and steering him like a horse to her bedroom.

He made it to the front door before he looked back at her. Then his eyes grew wide. "Oh! I almost forgot." He came back over to her and handed her a card. "These are my numbers, e-mail addresses, business URL, physical address, and mailing address. You know . . . if you need to get in touch with me."

Get in touch with him? But he left out his social security number, his date of birth, and his high school GPA. "Thanks."

"If you need *anything* you let me know. Okay?"

Melting. She was so melting. "I will. I promise."

"Okay." He walked back to the door, looked at her over his shoulder. "Bye, Gwen."

"Night." He opened the front door and Gwen said, "Lock?"

He stopped immediately. "Yeah?" Did he have to sound so eager when *he* was the one making the decision to go? Damn him! "Uh . . . could you leave him here? He kind of comes with the place."

Frowning, Lock glanced down. "Oh, jeez!"

Oh, jeez?

"Sorry about that." He immediately dropped the lion he'd dragged from the couch to the door, back to the couch, and back to the door. "Habit. Usually I bat my prey around until they stop fighting and drag them off to the brush to . . . well . . . you know." He looked down at Mitch. "Sorry about that . . . uh . . ."

"Mitch," she told him.

"Mitch. Right. Sorry about that, Mitch. And nice to meet you."

Lock lifted his gaze toward hers, but shook his head and walked out, closing the door behind him.

Letting out a breath, Gwen buried her face in the couch cushions. She didn't know how long she stayed there, pressing her face into the fabric, but she didn't have any intention of moving. That is, until she couldn't stand the constant moaning anymore.

"I'm dying. Help me," her brother whined.

"What?" she demanded, glaring at him over the back of the couch. "What are you whining about now?"

"Hospital. Need hospital."

Gwen snorted. "You're not even bleeding."

"Internal. Bleeding inside. Slowly *dying*."

She got up and headed to her bedroom. "Such a drama king!" she yelled over her shoulder. "How does Sissy put up with you?"

CHAPTER 13

With her work gloves on, protective eyewear in place, and a small white mask over her face, Gwen began pulling out the wall she and Blayne had just demolished to get to the pipes behind it. What started out as a simple sewer-line job for the do-it-yourself couple rebuilding their recently purchased fixer-upper had quickly turned into a much larger project that would bring in some nice cash. Gwen loved when that happened.

Of course, they were only tearing down the walls to replace the plumbing. Putting the walls back up would be down to the homeowners, which was fine with Gwen, since she loved tearing down walls but detested the tedium of putting them back up again. Besides, she wasn't very good at that part.

"So why didn't you tell me about the Babes?" Gwen asked as Blayne dumped the pieces Gwen tossed to the floor into the large industrial trash. "Or about your first bout?"

"You know why."

"Because I'd ruin it for you?"

Blayne looked up from the trash, her eyes wide. "Of course not! I didn't want you to be embarrassed by me. I know I'm a mess," she finished sadly.

"Stop saying that. You weren't a mess. And can I just say you must be made out of rubber, because you kept bouncing back up, completely unharmed."

Blayne grinned. "The beauty of the mutt. You can do that weird thing with your head and I'm indestructible."

"What weird thing with my head?" Gwen asked, unclear what Blayne was talking about.

Blayne blinked up at her. "Nothing."

Before Gwen could push her on that, the full-human couple stepped into the doorway. "How's everything going here?" the male asked. They were very cute in that earthy, save-the-world, "I'm always green" way, and probably not much older than Gwen and Blayne.

"Fine," Gwen said. She stepped closer to the wall. "Blayne, we're going to have to move the toilet out."

"Okay."

"Move it out?"

"Yup. And you know you have a severe mold issue, right?"

"We do?"

"Yep."

Gwen looked into the dark recesses of the walls and quickly stepped back. "Plus, you've got a snake."

The couple stared at her. "What?" the wife asked, looking moments from bolting.

"In the wall. A really large, living, breathing, uh, snake."

Blayne smiled and leaped forward. "They do?"

"We've never had a snake," the wife said desperately. "It must have been the people we bought the house from. They were hoarders. Had cats, dogs," she swallowed, "and mice. Frozen ones in their freezer. We just figured they kept the bodies of their pets!"

Then her husband added, "I guess our little Cotton Ball didn't run away."

The wife gasped, tears welling, and Gwen reached for her cell phone. "We need to get Animal Control over here and—"

Before she could dial, Blayne reached into the wall.

"Blayne Thorpe! Don't even think—"

Then Blayne dragged the hissing snake out of the wall by the head. Not only was it hissing but Gwen could now hear rattling as well.

Panicked, Gwen jumped back. "Holy shit!"

The husband got in front of his wife but Gwen never understood the whole waiting-for-a-guy-to-protect-you thing. She was a runner and hopefully the guy could keep up.

Moving wickedly fast, Blayne got a grip along the snake's body and slammed its head into the ground three times. As the snake lay there, stunned, Blayne pulled out the small hacksaw from their tool bag and sawed its head off. She tossed the body into the trash with the remains of the moldy plaster walls and tossed the head in after it.

While the couple and Gwen watched her in mute horror, Blayne grabbed a flashlight and took another look inside the wall. "Hey!" she called out cheerfully. "A nest!"

That's when the couple and Gwen took off running.

Sissy stood in the doorway of the office she shared with Mitch at Llewellyn and Smith Security. They rarely used this office with both of them out of the country for the last few months, but it was theirs whenever they came home.

She watched Mitch stare out the window. He was rarely pensive. Not her Mitch, but she couldn't shake the feeling he was up to something.

As she stepped into the office, Mindy walked by and said, "Mitch, I finally got your mom on the line. Line two."

"Thanks." He turned and reached for the now-buzzing phone, but Sissy slapped her hand over his. "Why is your mother calling?"

"Because she loves her only son?"

"Try again." His mother rarely called unless there was something wrong or she wanted to see him.

"She's returning my call. Now do you mind moving your paw?"

"*Why* did you call your mother?"

"I can't talk to my own mother just to talk?"

"No." Sissy's eyes narrowed. "This better not be about that bear."

"What bear?"

"The one that Gwen said dragged you around the room like a little boy dragging around his favorite toy."

Now Mitch's eyes narrowed and they stared at each other while his phone continued to buzz away.

"Whatever you're planning, Mitch Shaw—"

Mitch gave a little snarl before tossing Sissy's hand off his and lifting the receiver. "Hi, Ma," he said while staring at Sissy. "How's it going?"

With their job on hold until Animal Control could clear out the rattlesnakes living all over one poor couple's property, Gwen and Blayne had the rest of the day to themselves unless another job came in. They went to their office to get paperwork done, but it was Friday and, to be honest, the desire to do anything *but* work got the better of them.

Around lunchtime they ended up in the basement of the Kuznetsov building. Most of their trucks were out on jobs and that gave them a huge space to utilize.

Gwen had Blayne put on her skates, and then she ran her through the drills her mother used to put her through back in the day. Because it was Blayne, Gwen had way more fun than she thought she would. No matter what she told her to do, no matter how many times she told her to do it, and no matter how often Blayne fell on her ass, the wolfdog never got upset, never complained, and always kept that smile.

After a couple of hours, while Blayne raced around the basement and Gwen threw things at her head, trying to catch her off guard, one of the wild dogs wandered by. He watched them for a few minutes before wandering away again. About twenty minutes later, they had all the wild dogs down in the basement with them. They brought food, and since Gwen and Blayne had never gotten around to getting lunch, they ended up eating with the

Pack. Gwen usually hated being around crowds of canines, but maybe it was the wolves she didn't favor as much because the wild dogs weren't that bad. They were extremely friendly as only dogs could be, and they were also funny and, unlike the wolves and cats, very welcoming of mixed breeds.

Around four o'clock, two pups showed up. Both teenagers. One was Kristan, the daughter of Maylin, and the other Johnny, wolf and adopted son of Jess. Much bigger than any of the dogs who currently ruled Johnny's life, Gwen wondered if the pup appreciated that Jess had married another wolf. Maybe he felt a little less alone? Gwen could relate after having spent her whole life surrounded by lions who were much taller and never understood Gwen's desire to not constantly hang out with her cousins.

Not surprisingly, Kristan eventually wandered over to Gwen and started chatting with her. Like fellow wolfdog Blayne, Kristan was a happy girl with a big smile, but Gwen also felt a kinship to the sixteen-year-old canine because they were both half Asian. Although Gwen knew more about her Irish side and her ancient druid relatives who may have liberated the people of their small village from the Romans or . . . uh . . . enslaved them. It wasn't really clear, and it depended on who you talked to.

None of that mattered to Gwen and Kristan because, just as it was between Gwen and Blayne, they were outsiders among outsiders, making them instant allies. So before Gwen knew it, she'd grabbed what Blayne called her "magic case," which held all of Gwen's favorite hair and beauty products, wet the teen's multicolored wild dog hair and, with the reluctant blessing of her mother, Gwen began to remove a lot of the length to give Kristan's hair more body and shape and make her look more like she was sixteen rather than twelve.

While Gwen worked with a blow-dryer and curling iron, Kristan sitting at her feet, one of the wild dogs pulled out his MP3 player and attached it to speakers. Great eighties music pumped while Blayne had fun on her skates with a few of the other wild dogs on their skateboards.

"She's good, isn't she?" Kristan asked, not even bothering

with the mirror Gwen had given her to watch the progress of her hair. Her immediate trust in Gwen was humbling, if not daunting.

"She's very good. She'll get even better."

"Are you on the team, too?"

"Me? Nah."

"How come? I bet you two would make an awesome team. And you guys could have your own nicknames like the Terrible Twosome or the Battling Bitches."

Laughing, Gwen finished with the curling iron, unplugging it before setting it aside to cool. "Oh, yeah. That sounds like us."

"I'm serious!" Of course, she was serious. Wolfdogs were always serious, even when they had no idea what they were talking about.

Gwen worked her hands through Kristan's hair, playing with the curls until they fell the way she wanted them to. She stood and walked around, crouching in front of her. She fussed with the multicolored locks for a bit longer, wondering how long before Kristan would start dyeing her hair so she didn't stick out as much.

Leaning back and looking Kristan over, Gwen had to admit she'd done a pretty good job.

Gwen picked up the mirror and held it up for her. "What do you think?"

Kristan glanced at herself, began to smile pleasantly and look away, but her gaze shot back and she snatched the mirror from Gwen. "Oh, my God. Oh, my God! *I look amazing!*" She jumped to her feet, forcing Gwen to scramble out of her way.

"Mom! Oh, my God, look!"

May's hands covered her mouth as she stared at her oldest daughter. "You look—"

"Older," Blayne muttered in Gwen's ear after she'd rolled up behind her.

"It had to happen sometime," Gwen muttered back.

"Yeah, but that young pup over there is a lot more fascinated with her than he was when he walked in." The friends peered over at Johnny, and Gwen had to bite back her smile. Blayne was right. He was *really* interested. Kristan threw her arms around Gwen's neck. "Thank you so much! I love it! You're a miracle worker!"

"I always thought so," a voice said from the doorway and both Gwen and Blayne went tense.

Looking over her shoulder, Gwen stared at her mother and— *betraying bastard, son of a bitch, hope he burns in hell*—Mitch.

With a walk that made men stop whatever they were doing to watch, Roxy O'Neill sauntered over, her purse swinging from her hand, her hips moving from side to side. To anyone who didn't know her, she looked too busy being sexy to be worried about anything else.

But Gwen knew her.

Drawing her hands through Kristan's hair, Roxy nodded in approval. "Nice. Very nice. It fits her face and lets her look her age rather than too young or too old. You've always had an eye, baby-girl."

Looking around, Roxy smiled. "I see the plumbing biz is keeping you busy."

Gwen's jaw clenched at the direct hit, and Blayne immediately put her arm around Gwen's shoulders.

"Early afternoon," the wolfdog explained. "It's been a long week."

"Uh-huh." After turning in a complete circle, Roxy focused again on her daughter. "I'd love to see your office, baby-girl."

"Absolutely!" Blayne said and stepping forward, she took Roxy's arm and steered her back to the double doors that led to the building elevator. "Let's go see it. Gwen will be along in a bit."

As Blayne walked with Roxy, she managed to slam her skate-wearing foot on Mitch's instep as she passed him.

"Ow!" As he lifted his foot to rub it, Blayne turned into him, knocking the lion to the ground. "*Ow!*"

"Oh, Mitch! I'm so sorry!" No, she wasn't. Nor did she stop propelling Roxy toward that elevator.

Once they were gone, Gwen realized she was clutching her

hands together. Jess approached her, reaching out to touch her shoulder. Immediately Gwen stepped away. "Don't . . ."

Jess pulled back and the dogs gave Gwen her distance.

Determined to face her mother, Gwen let out a breath and headed toward the elevator. Although she did stop long enough to kick her brother in the balls before moving on.

Roxy watched her daughter walk into the office. She didn't look like any of her cousins, yet she was naturally more beautiful than all of them. A face like her father's, she had. With those bright gold eyes and that sweet grin, when she bothered to use it. Which, to be honest, was also like her father.

"Can you leave us alone for a minute, Blayne?"

"But I haven't finished showing you how our billing system—"

"Out."

Unlike the good old days, when her daughter and canine friend used to jump at Roxy's orders, Blayne didn't move until Gwen motioned toward the door. "Give us a minute, would ya?"

"Sure." Blayne got up and rolled out the door.

Roxy couldn't help but study the quads on those tiny dog feet. The four-wheeled skates derby girls played in, unlike those ridiculous inline skates for the masses.

Roxy remembered when her daughter wore the black and gold skates of the Philly Phangs. And she'd worn them for all of one bout. She never thought Gwenie would quit so easily, even with all the injuries she'd suffered that day. Never had she quit anything before or since, but something else must have happened, because her daughter never went back and she would never discuss it. Not with her, Roxy's sisters, not even Cally, whom she held in highest esteem among the O'Neills.

"How is she?"

Gwen frowned. "How is who?"

"Blayne." When Gwen frowned, she added, "I saw what you two were doing in the basement. That's derby training, baby-girl."

Gwen shrugged. "She's good. But that's not why you're here."

She moved around her daughter. "Can't a mother come visit her only daughter?"

"Not my mother, no."

And this was why she adored her baby-girl. Gwen was all about the direct approach.

Roxy lifted her arms, sweeping the room. "You give up everything I have to offer you for this? A cruddy little office and no real work? What did I do? Why do you hate me?"

Gwen dragged her hands through her hair. "I don't hate—"

"You must if this is what you've resigned yourself to. And if it's not me, what is it? Your cousins? One of your aunts? Did they say something to you?"

"Ma, stop. They didn't do anything. *You* didn't do anything. I love what I do."

"Did you see what you did with that little girl downstairs? How beautiful you made her look with a set of shears, a blow-dryer, and an iron?"

"Yeah, but—"

"You could be doing that every day and running the business. Making real money. Have a high-end clientele. And you'd have family around you, baby-girl. Family to protect you."

She brushed her hand against the still-lingering bruises on Gwen's face. They must be recent, since bruises for their kind didn't last much longer than a day or two. Was no one watching her baby's back? Other than that wolfdog who was too sweet for her own good? And Blayne's face hadn't looked much better.

"Who did this to you?"

"It doesn't matter, Ma."

"Tell me."

"Why? So you can make it worse?" Gwen smirked. "And we both know you'll make it worse. Besides, it was just a fight."

"And no one watching out for you. No one covering your back."

"Blayne watches my back. Blayne always watches my back."

"But for how long, baby-girl? She's a canine who's making new canine friends. Canine friends with money. Where does that leave you? I know you're not comfortable with meeting new people, and that's okay. You always have your family. The ones who love you and will always be there for you."

Roxy put her arm around Gwen, kissed her forehead. "Let's get your brother and go grab some dinner. We can talk then."

"No."

"Don't be mad at Mitch. He was only trying to—"

"No. I mean I can't. I'm . . . uh . . . meeting someone."

"Oh?"

"Yeah. A bear I've been seeing."

Roxy smirked at her daughter. "Really?" A bear? And her Gwenie? Well, *that* was interesting.

"Yeah. In fact—" Gwen glanced at a wrist with no watch on it "—I'm going to be late if I don't get a move on."

She kissed Roxy on the cheek and grabbed the straps of her backpack. "I'm really sorry, Ma, but you should have called first before coming all this way."

Gwen walked to the door and saw her brother standing on the other side of it. She *saw* him. And yet she flung that door open like she hadn't. Thankfully, Mitch had always been quick and he managed to keep the door from hitting him in the face.

"Off for a date. See ya."

Mitch scowled. "With that bear?" he yelled after her.

"Damn right, bitch!" she yelled back, and Roxy had to rub her nose to hide the smile.

Mitch walked into the office, looking around in distaste, but Roxy didn't know if it was distaste for the room or the bear.

"So you're going to let her go out with that bear?" he demanded.

Okay. Distaste for the bear it was.

Mitch walked his mother to the overpriced parking lot across the street from the Kuznetsov office building. "I can't believe you're letting her get away with this."

Roxy remotely unlocked her gold Lexus SUV and tossed her bag into the car. "I don't know what you want me to do."

"Tell her she has to come home. You've done it before with the cousins."

"Yes, but they were . . ."

Mitch, not sure how there could be a "but" there, motioned to his mother to continue when she stopped talking. "They were what?"

Roxy gave him that soft smile that fooled a lot of nonrelated male lions but not Mitch. She patted his chest. "You need to come to Philly for a family dinner, baby-boy. Make sure to bring your girl with you."

Mitch grinned. "And I'll bring Gwenie."

"Mitch—"

"Invite the whole family. We'll be there. Tomorrow night."

Roxy shook her head and got into her vehicle. "I swear, baby-boy, sometimes . . . just like your father."

"I'll try not to take that as an insult, Ma."

He closed her door and waved at her until she turned out of the lot and onto the street. Already working on how he would get Gwen home for a family dinner—also known among the O'Neills as a Family Pile-On—Mitch never saw that fist coming until it grabbed a hold of his hair and yanked.

"*Not the hair! Not the hair!*"

"You rat!" Blayne accused, while using her other hand to slap Mitch in the face and head. "You big rat!"

Desperate as he felt precious hairs pulled from his head, Mitch grabbed hold of Blayne's arms and twisted them back until she let him go.

"Off!" he ordered, pushing her away. "Did you think I was really going to let this go? *Especially* after last night?"

She put her hands on her hips, reminding him of Gwen. "Because he batted you around that hotel room like a Tonka toy?"

"No. Because he had my precious baby sister on his lap for your entire derby bout."

Blayne's eyes grew wide. "How . . . how did you find out about that?"

"Don't think you can hide anything from me, little girl. When it comes to my baby sister, I know all." He walked up to her and leaned down until their noses touched. "And this isn't over." And it wouldn't be until he got Gwen away from that circus freak bear and got her back to her Pride where she belonged and would be safe.

Smirking, and feeling pretty damn smug, Mitch headed toward the corner and a cab, but he froze when Blayne tossed after him, "You know everything, huh? Did you know that when your hair started falling out in clumps back in your senior year it was because me and Gwen put Nair in your leave-in conditioner?"

When he spun around, roaring in outrage, Blayne yelped and skated off in the opposite direction.

Jay Ross stared at the cash in his hand. "This is it? I usually get twice this."

Bobby B., who owned the Staten Island bar Jay was in, shrugged and carried another case of beer behind his bar. "What do ya want me to tell ya? You're not the only dealer out there. And the product you've been givin' us ain't been that great."

"I need more money." Donna's bitch mother had been on a rampage since she'd found out that her kid once again nearly got her ass kicked by an O'Neill, but who'd counted on that goddamn bear being there *again*? And the only way to calm the evil bitch down was with cold, hard cash.

"Then bring in better product. The last two died pretty easy and that don't make for much of a show," Bobby B. complained, dismissing him.

Jay started to head to the door but stopped, an idea hitting him. "What about females?"

Bobby's head came up, the older full-human looking at him with definite interest. "Females? A name will get you three times what you used to get. Bring one in yourself . . . and it's six times."

"Six?"

"They're popular and hard to grab." Bobby smiled. "Deadlier than the male."

The man had no idea.

Jay walked out of the bar and headed to his car. No way could he move that product on his own, but if he could get the Pack involved . . . He shook his head, resting his arms on the roof of his car. Sharyn McNelly happily took his money, but she didn't want any involvement in what he did. Still, there had to be a way, and Donna pretty much ran the younger Packmates. But her mother ran Donna . . .

Then again hate like that didn't just go away. And that bear couldn't be there every time to protect O'Neill. No way.

Yeah . . . Jay just needed to bide his time. And he was good at that.

Knowing what he needed to do to make some quick money now and a lot more money later, he unlocked his car and pulled the door open. He was about to get in, but he stopped, quickly scanning the street. It was weird. He felt like someone was watching him. He could feel eyes on him.

He shook his head. It was probably the cops. They were always watching him, trying to find something on him, but never could. And they never would.

CHAPTER 14

Lock parked his SUV in his allotted space under his building and climbed out. He took the stairs to the first floor, checked his mail, and then was heading to the elevator when his nose lifted, catching the air . . . and that scent.

Honey. Honey shampoo.

Making a quick turn, he walked out the front door and stopped at the top step. She was sitting at the bottom of the building stairs, staring across the street at the twenty-four-hour deli. She didn't make a move, even as he sat down next to her. His narrow hips had no problem fitting in beside her on that stoop, but his shoulders nearly shoved her off.

Startled, she viciously hissed, but cut it short when she saw his face.

"Do you need to take lumbering classes or something?" she demanded. "Where is the lumbering?"

"I thought I was lumbering. I was definitely not walking on my tippy-toes."

She didn't say anything, her attention returning to the deli across the street. After five minutes of silence, Lock asked, "How was work?"

"Found snakes."

He blinked. "Actual snakes?"

"Yup. The kind that rattle."

"Are you . . . are you okay?" He felt like checking her for bite marks.

"I'm fine. Blayne had a nice little hack and slash party and I got to see a couple of cute guys from Animal Control." She looked at him. "Do you wanna have sex with me?"

"Uh . . ."

"Good enough," she said, getting to her feet. She grabbed his hand and pulled. "Come on. Let's get a hotel room and have sex. Or we can go up to your place to have sex. Let's go have sex."

"Or you can tell me what's really bothering you."

"Nothing. Nothing's bothering me. Are you saying you don't want to have sex with me?"

"Well . . ."

"If it takes you that long to think about it, I'll find someone else to have sex with."

And with that, she headed off down the street.

Lock watched her go. He still felt where her fingers had held his, could still smell her shampoo all around him, and he'd woken up that morning thinking about how he'd kissed her from the night before.

And after all that did she really think that he'd let her walk off?

Gwen was moving down the street, heading toward a corner where she could see cabs. She needed to get out of her head. She felt trapped by doubt, by insecurity. Even worse, she didn't think she'd ever escape it. Would she still be like this in another ten years, another thirty? Would her family still be able to walk in her life and simply fuck it up by their mere presence?

And what the hell did the grizzly mean by "Well . . ."? What did "Well" mean? She couldn't figure him out. He kissed her like he could eat her alive, but then he turned down an offer of sex. Why? It drove her insane that she couldn't figure him out, couldn't label and box him away appropriately.

"Hey, legs," some little prick standing on the corner with his friends called out to her. "Where you goin'? Want some company?"

In the definite mood for a fight, Gwen stopped and turned to them. "What do you want? What have you got to say? What do you think you'll do, little man?"

The full-human sneered, looking ready to give her that fight she needed, but then he backed up, his friends stumbling away from him. By the time they were charging down the street and Gwen was wondering what the hell happened, big hands caught hold of her and spun her around.

Lock gripped her denim jacket in both hands and leaned over, forcing her to bend back until she was practically U-shaped.

"I want you to listen to me very carefully, because I've never liked repeating myself. First off, don't come here, dump your shit at my door, and then walk away before you've even given me a chance to figure out what you're trying to tell me. Second, don't ever assume, for even a second, that my pauses imply anything. I'm a thinker, O'Neill. Thinkers pause. And third, you're absolutely right that I want to have sex with you, but I'll be damned if I let you fuck me because you're in a pissed-off mood and you want to get even with whoever the hell you're pissed with. When I have you, it's because we'll both want the same thing, at the same time. Not because you think you can walk all over me. Do you understand what I'm telling you?"

"Hello, Lachlan," an elderly man said as he leisurely walked by with a female on his arm. The couple appeared to be about the same age, and Gwen could only guess they were married.

"Hello, Mr. Guzman. Mrs. Guzman. Nice night, isn't it?"

"Very nice night. Very nice."

They continued on their way, apparently oblivious to Lock intimidating some poor feline with his overwhelming boar-rage.

"I'm still waiting for my answer, Mr. Mittens."

Gwen's eyes narrowed, but she checked her desire to punch his face and chose to nod instead.

"Good."

He stood tall, but kept his hands on Gwen's jacket so that he pulled her up in the process. Tugging her jacket into place, he said, "Let's get something to eat. I'm starving, and we can talk at the restaurant. Does that work for you?"

"Well—"

"Good." Keeping hold of her jacket with one hand, he pulled her along behind him as he stepped off the sidewalk and into traffic.

Lock moved in front of a taxi and the driver hit his brakes, the vehicle's grille stopping no more than an inch from him. Walking around to the passenger side, Lock opened the door and pushed Gwen inside.

"Fifty-first and Fifth," he said.

Shaking, the terrified driver pulled back into traffic and Gwen wondered if going out to dinner with her mother and brother would have been that bad an idea after all.

"Okay, okay. Can I have everyone's attention?" Blayne Thorpe smiled at the room full of people and Bobby Ray Smith, Smitty to nearly everyone who hadn't grown up in Smithtown, Tennessee, or were related to him by blood or Pack, wondered yet again what he was doing here. "Great. I wanted to thank all of you for coming tonight on such short notice. As you know, we're all involved in Project: Code Name Bear-Cat. And things seem to be moving along very nicely."

The audience applauded and Smitty let out a bored breath, which got him a kick from a tiny little wild dog foot under the table.

Blayne pointed at an older bear couple and said, "The MacRyries said the reunion went better than expected *and* they got a new water heater at cost!" More applause and Smitty debated slamming his head into the table until he blacked out. "And although yesterday's bout was a bit of a surprise for all involved, it worked out well! So thanks to everyone for all their help and involve-

ment. That being said, we do seem to have two unexpected ob-
stacles to our intended goal. Uh . . . the first is . . . uh . . . Danny,
could you?"

Danny tapped on his laptop and an image of a long-haired,
air-guitar-playing, eighteen-year-old Mitch Shaw came up on the
big TV screen beside Blayne. "Sorry about the oldness of the pic.
I don't have anything more recent of Problem Number One. We're
working on what to do about him, but he's not an easy one. Especially when he's a big, fat tattletale who calls his mother at the
slightest provocation!" She let out a breath. "However, I think
we may have some assistance there. Right, Jess?"

"Right!" Smitty's beautiful, if annoying, mate cheerily replied.
Why she was involved in this weirdness, he had no idea. "The
Insider. And the Insider is working on our behalf as we speak."

"Excellent! Now on to our second problem. No pic for that
one because, well, he's sitting right over there."

Smitty looked around, wondering who Blayne was talking
about, and then quickly realized that she was talking about him.

"Me? How am I in the way of something I didn't even know
was going on?"

Jessie Ann slammed her hand down on the table. "You told
Mitch what happened at the bout last night!"

"I didn't know that was a secret."

"Of course it was!"

"Then you should have made that clear when you told me."

Jessie's mouth dropped open and Smitty knew he was in for it,
but then that *other* wolf spoke up. Just 'cause he liked the man's
Aunt Adelle, didn't mean he liked him none. Of course, Smitty
didn't know him either, but he still didn't like him.

"Out of curiosity," the wolf asked, "what did you say to
Mitch Shaw?"

"What Jessie Ann told me. That his baby sister spent the
whole night on the bear's lap. Cuddlin'."

The wolf laughed, but the wild dogs, the one wolfdog, and the
pair of older bears gasped as if he'd called up Satan himself.

Even worse, Jessie slapped at his arm. He hated when she did that. Those hands may be little, but they could still cause pain.

"What did I do now?"

"You are such a . . . why do I . . . Oh! Never mind!"

"Fine. Does that mean we can go?"

"You sit your ass back down, Bobby Ray Smith!"

Grumbling, he did just that.

Blayne walked over to him and smiled again, but he wasn't fooled by that smile. Like a weak, two-dollar poodle collar worn by a pitbull that smile did nothing but lull a man into a false sense of security.

"Hi, Smitty."

"Blayne."

Still smiling, "You know it would really help us if you kept things about Gwen and Lock that you may hear from Jess to yourself. At least until Project: Code Name Bear-Cat is finalized."

He had to say it. "That is the *dumbest* name I've ever heard."

And "snap" went that collar.

Blayne slammed her hands against the table and leaned in. "Now listen up, you Navy-loving son of a bitch! If my friend wants that bear, she's gonna get that bear. And neither hell nor you nor some big-haired, twenty-hour-sleeping king of the idiots is gonna stop me from *making sure she gets that bear!*"

Van Holtz took careful hold of Blayne's shoulders and pulled her back. "Excellent, Blayne. Very effective."

He gently pushed her back toward the front of the room and faced Smitty. He wasn't an Alpha, was he? But he was no one's Omega, either. Smitty could dismiss him as a Beta, but that didn't fit this one either. Naw, this wolf was . . . something else. And as laid-back, nonconfrontational, and fancy-talkin' as he was, Smitty didn't trust him for a damn second.

"Smitty . . . is it okay if I call you Smitty?"

"As you like."

"Excellent. Smitty, we're trying to achieve something here

with two incredibly difficult yet loving people, and the assistance of our friends would be greatly appreciated."

"I ain't your friend."

Blayne stormed back over to the table and the wolf held up one finger, stopping her in her unhappy and ranting-ready tracks.

"Understood. But Lock is friend and family to almost everyone in this room—especially your wife. They've been so close for years. I'm sure she told you about that." And they both knew she hadn't. MacRyrie had been at their wedding, but so had three hundred other people. If the grizzly had a special connection with Jessie Ann, neither had mentioned it. "She was there for him during his hardest time. Fresh out of the military, really not adapting to civilian life after all those years in the Unit." The back of Smitty's neck tightened with tension. The bear they were talking about had been in the Unit? The same Unit his cousin Dee-Ann had been in? Even Smitty's shifter-only SEALs team stayed away from Unit members. The job requirements for the Unit made them more . . . *troublesome* than others.

More than once, Smitty's team had been called in to "put down" a Unit member who had "snapped his bolt." It was always one of their worst assignments. Not only because it was one of their own but because the Unit team members were the hardest to track and kill. And God forbid they ever came up behind you. God forbid they ever caught you unaware.

And leave it to Jessie Ann Ward to go waltzing up to one of 'em and say, "How do ya do? Come on over to my wedding, which is chock-full of defenseless people!"

Damn, but that woman was going to drive him into an early grave!

"I'll admit, I'd hoped that something would develop between Lock and Jess, but . . . well . . . it didn't work out that way, now did it? Although I think Lock was open to it. Of course, she's with you now, and I'm sure her heart is forever yours, but wouldn't it make us all feel a little better if we could get Lock settled with a girl of his own?"

Smitty sized the wolf up. Typical Van Holtz. Not much brawn but wily.

"You smooth-talkin' mother—"

"Problem!" Adelle yelped as she ran into the room. "Mary was throwing out the trash and she said she saw Lock and a female who sounds like Gwen heading this way!"

The dogs scattered in seconds. Like the cats, they were good at that. But one wild dog wasn't going until she got Smitty to move . . . and he wasn't in the mood to move.

"Smitty, please!" she begged, holding on to his leather jacket and trying to pull him out of the chair.

"Not sure I'm in the mood to go. You promised me steak and I'm still waitin'."

"He has to get out of here," Van Holtz practically snarled.

"I'm trying," Jessie said. "But he's in a mood."

"Y'all do know I'm still in the room?"

The older bears cleared their throats. "Uh . . . and we're a little too old and big-boned to scatter," the She-bear kindly explained.

"Okay, okay." Van Holtz took a moment. "Let's do this. Adelle, please take Doctors MacRyrie through the side exit." Adelle nodded and showed the older couple the way out while Van Holtz focused on him. "And what do you want, Smith?"

"World peace?"

"*Bobby Ray!*"

He didn't even look at Jessie, too focused on the conniving wolf in front of him.

"How about information?" Van Holtz offered.

"What information can you give me?"

The wolf leaned in and what he whispered in his ear had Smitty's body tensing as he scowled at him. "You're lyin'."

"I don't have to."

Smitty stood and stormed out of the dining room, Jessie behind him, desperately trying to keep up.

* * *

Gwen stared around the restaurant and again looked down at her clothes.

"We are so out of here," she whispered.

"Why?"

"One . . . I'm still in my work clothes. And two, there's no reason for you to pay so much for a lousy steak dinner."

"There are no lousy steak dinners at the Van Holtz." Gwen blinked in surprise as the wolf she met from the night before appeared beside her and leaned down to kiss her cheek. "Hello again, Gwen."

"Uh . . . hi."

Gwen couldn't help but eye him. He was wearing a chef's coat and a dark-green bandana around his forehead. Last she heard, only Van Holtzs cooked in Van Holtz restaurants.

"Dinner?" he asked Lock.

"Is that a problem?"

"Not at all."

Grabbing two menus from the hostess, he motioned them past the extremely long line of those waiting to be seated, through the packed dining room, and into the back. She knew she was dressed badly, but were they going to have to eat in the alley?

It seemed, however, that the Van Holtz flagship restaurant was more than a dining room and a kitchen. It also had a huge reception hall, and several private dining rooms in the back.

As they passed one of the bigger dining rooms, Lock abruptly stopped, his head lifting, his nose casting for a scent. "Were my parents here?"

Ric stared at him for a long moment before finally answering, "Yes. Earlier. For dinner."

"My parents came *here* for dinner? Why?"

"Why?"

"Yeah. Why? There's an IHOP down the road from their house. That's usually all they need."

"Um . . . your father was feeling . . . romantic."

"What?"

"Frisky, might be a better word."

"Okay, that's enough. I don't need to know any more."

"If you're sure."

"I'm sure. I do not need to hear about my 'frisky' father."

With a shrug, Ric led them to a smaller private dining room with a small table and two chairs. Everything was draped in dark reds and browns, the furniture made of dark wood.

"Does this work?" Ric asked.

"Perfect."

Lock held her seat out and Gwen stared at it. "What are you doing?"

"Would you get in the seat?" She did, since he snarled at her, and then he took his own seat.

Ric handed them both menus. "Whatever you want. Your waiter will be with you shortly." He started to walk out and then said, "Oh. Wine?"

Lock and Gwen looked at each other and both shook their heads at the same time.

"Okay. Let me guess." Ric studied Gwen before offering, "Sprite?"

She grinned. Shrugged.

And without looking at Lock said, "Big glass of milk?"

"Several."

Shaking his head, Ric walked out. "An award-winning wine cellar at your disposal and you want milk. Philistine!"

The door closed and Gwen said, "What's Ric's full name?"

"Ulrich."

Cute. "And last name?"

"Van Holtz."

That's what she'd thought! One of the richest and most powerful Packs in the world and Lock was best friends with one of the direct bloodline. "It never occurred to you to tell me that?"

Lock gazed at her. "Tell you what?"

And she got the feeling . . . he really didn't have a clue what she meant.

* * *

Although Lock couldn't shake the feeling Ric was hiding something from him, he would still remember this night as the best one he'd ever had at *any* Van Holtz restaurant. Perhaps the addition of Gwen had in fact made it his best night *anywhere*. Ever.

It didn't take long for him to get out of her what had her so upset and even less time to get her to smile and stop thinking about it. He understood her frustration with her family, though. Understood it more than she realized. He also knew she was braver than him because she'd taken the leap while he was still working up the nerves and the cash.

But soon, instead of ruminating about their frustrations, they focused more on talking about their childhoods, swapping stories about growing up in Jersey and Philly. About his time working as a bouncer at one of the many bars on the Jersey Shore and her early days taking her school's plumbing apart to see how it worked.

They had no idea how late it was until Ric finally stuck his head in. "Sorry to do this, guys, but we're shutting down for the night." That's when Lock knew they were the last there; Ric wouldn't toss him out unless they were.

So he took Gwen back to her hotel and they stood outside in the chilly night, the hotel still alive with activity, even at the late hour.

"Do you want to come inside for a drink?" she softly offered.

"No. No. No, no, no, no. No."

Gwen stared at him. "One 'no' would have been clear."

"Those 'no's' weren't for you. They were for me. I was simply saying them out loud."

Smiling, her hands stuffed into the front pocket of her cargo pants, she said, "It seems like you're fighting with yourself there, Jersey."

"I am. Because I want to come up with you, but . . ."

"But . . ." she pushed when he didn't go on.

"Something tells me not now."

She blew out a breath and it was cold enough to see it. "Why not?"

"I have no idea where this is going, Gwen. But I'm not going to wake up tomorrow and find myself dismissed. And I think if I go upstairs with you now . . . that's exactly what's going to happen."

"You're that sure?"

"Yeah. I'm that sure."

She nodded. "Okay. Then how about a date?"

Lock smiled. He couldn't help it. "You're asking me out?"

"I'm asking you out."

"I'd love to."

"Tomorrow? It's Saturday."

He winced. "I can't tomorrow. Family thing at my parents' house. Unless you want to—"

"For our first date?"

He shook his head. "Good point."

"What about Sunday?"

"Sunday's great." And if it wasn't, he'd *make* it great. "How about I pick you up here? Around one o'clock? We can get lunch, maybe catch a movie or something, and then dinner."

"Perfect."

"Okay. Sunday. One o'clock."

"Sunday, one o'clock."

Lock had no idea how long they stood there, grinning at each other like a couple of idiots, but when she turned to walk away, he snapped out of it.

Catching her arm, he pulled her back. "I said I wouldn't go up with you tonight. I didn't say anything about not getting another kiss."

"Good. I was afraid you were going to leave me hanging."

He leaned down and took her mouth gently, wanting to show her how much he liked her beyond the mere physical. But there was something about this woman that short-circuited every synapse he possessed. Because right there, in the middle of Manhattan, he pulled her close, his arms tight around her, his kiss moving from gentle to territorial in seconds.

And she gave it right back to him. Her arms so tight around his neck, an average shifter might be strangled, her mouth hot on his as their tongues met.

She was driving him crazy! How was this fair? And how was he supposed to make it until Sunday without seeing her again?

Pulling away and standing up straight, Lock let out a shuddering breath. "You're trying to kill me."

"Not yet," she teased, stepping away from him. "But give me time."

Her gold gaze moved over him, the tip of her tongue swiping across her top lip. Then she smiled and said, "Night."

Without another word, she walked off, leaving him—and his hard-on—devastated.

Lock headed back to the sidewalk. He wouldn't bother with a cab. He'd walk. The cold air would do him good and as late as it was, he never worried about anyone bothering him. Because no one ever did.

Well, except for . . .

"Hey, you bear son of a—"

Lost in thoughts of Gwen, the growling voice startled him and Lock spun around. Immediately the two lions stumbled back and Mitch shoved Brendon ahead of him.

"Take him!" Mitch ordered Lock.

Brendon glared at his brother. "What do you mean 'take him'?"

"Well, bruh," the lion explained, grinning, "I *am* the pretty one."

"You betraying son of a bitch!"

"There's no need to get nasty, you big baby! Take your bear-mauling like a man!"

Once again glad he'd never had brothers, Lock headed down the street, leaving the Shaws to beat the crap out of each other in front of their five-star hotel like ten-year-olds.

He'd only gone a couple of blocks, debating about getting a taxi, when he saw the dark-blue van behind him. He stopped and studied it closely. The van rolled to a stop, those inside not even trying to pretend they weren't following him. So Lock didn't pretend that it didn't bother him. Instead, he charged the van, flat out, slamming his body into the side and putting most of the power in his shoulder. He heard roars and yelping from inside as he shoved the van over.

It landed with a loud crash and Lock stepped back, grinning. *They must be new.* And apparently no one had warned them about how to handle the "difficult and highly emotional" bears as per the Unit's breed breakdown.

Hands in his pockets, still thinking about Gwen and humming to himself, Lock headed on home.

Chapter 15

"Gwennnnnnnie! Gwennnnnnnie! Gwennnnnnnnnnnie!" Gwen tried to cover her ears, but something had her hands trapped. She started kicking and fighting but something was on her, holding her down.

"Gwen! Wake up!"

Gwen's eyes opened and she stared into a face she knew all too well.

"You idiot!"

"And an excellent afternoon to you, too, lazy head!" Mitch, still holding her hands, leaned down and breathed in her face.

"Jesus Christ!" she screamed.

"That's right! Just got up myself and haven't brushed my teeth yet!"

"You asshole! Get off me!"

He started slapping her in the face with her own hands, something she'd hated when she was six and, twenty years later, she *still* hated.

"Why are you hitting yourself, Gwen? Why are you hitting yourself?" he demanded while laughing maniacally.

"Get off!"

"I'm taking Sissy to Philly with me today," he said, still slapping her with her own hands. "You'll come, too. Mom says you haven't been home in weeks. Not okay."

"Can't. I have plans!" she yelled, trying to kick him off her.

"With who exactly? It's not Blayne, because I already checked in with her and she's spending the day with her dad, or as I like to call him, Petty Officer Thorpe, Master of the Sea." He took her hands and pulled them down her face. "Now look at you, Gwen! You're trying to scratch your own eyes out! This is a cry for help!"

"Stop it!"

"A cry for help that only Ma and someone else's apple pie—" *because Christ knows Ma can't bake* "—can fix." He released her, but when she went to slap the living hell out of him, he leaped neatly away. "And pack a bag. We're staying a couple of days."

Quickly sitting up so he couldn't pin her to the bed again, Gwen scowled at her brother. "I said I can't. I have plans."

"If it's not Blayne, then who? It's not like you have any other friends."

Gwen's hands balled into fists. "You are *such* an asshole."

"But an honest asshole, baby sister. Painfully honest. Now let's get going."

He was determined to get her back to Philly and she knew why. The O'Neill Family Pile-On. It was a horrifying event where every O'Neill aunt, uncle, and cousin in a hundred mile radius would be at her mother's house for dinner so they could spend the entire time telling Gwen what a fuck-up she was.

They'd had their chance to do this before she left, but none of them had taken her very seriously, figuring she'd be home after a week or two.

But Gwen didn't want to go home . . . wait. She briefly closed her eyes. She didn't want to go back to *Philly*. She was already home. True, she didn't have an apartment of her own yet, but she would. The business was doing well, their client list was healthy, and the wild dogs had cut her and Blayne an unbelievable deal on their office space.

And the family is testing you.

Yeah. She knew that. Although not as purely evil as a cult,

Prides had their pull on a lioness. There was no denying that, and Gwen would be no different. But she wasn't ready yet, and her mother knew it.

"I accepted another invitation for tonight. Sorry."

Mitch crossed his arm over his chest. "Uh-huh. An invitation with . . . ?"

"What do you care?"

He chuckled. "Look, the rest of the Philly cops may believe your line of bullshit, but I'm your brother. I know better. So stop fooling around, get your shit, and let's go."

He turned to walk out, completely dismissing her and pissing her off so badly that she lied like she hadn't lied since Philly P.D. found her ex-boyfriend's gun on her in the tenth grade.

"I've been invited to Jersey to spend time with Lock MacRyrie's family. They're expecting me for dinner and no way I'm not going."

Mitch slowly faced her. "The bear? You've made dinner plans with a family of *bears*? You sure you're not just dinner, Goldilocks?"

"That's very funny," she replied flatly. "Hilarious. But yeah. Plans to spend time with the family. They like me." She hoped. She liked them and they seemed to like her, but who the hell knew and she was having such a bad day already. "Tell Ma I'll see her at Thanksgiving, when I *plan* to be back in Philly. Not before."

She was expecting her brother to throw one of his lion-male hissy fits, but it seemed Mitch was in as much of a game-playing mood as Gwen. Smiling, he said, "Even better . . . why don't we drop you off in Jersey on our way home?"

"That's not necessary. It's out of your way."

"Not by much, I'm sure," he said easily. "And it's no big deal. We'll drop you off, I can meet the family, and even apologize to your bear. I think Bren and I might have startled him last night . . . after seeing you two *making out* in front of the hotel."

Don't you dare cringe, Gwendolyn O'Neill!

And drop her off? Meet the family? Oh, he was good. Gotten

better in fact. She'd bet money he'd picked up tips from that damn ho-billy girlfriend of his! Manipulative canines!

Yet the one thing Gwen knew, she couldn't back down now. "Sounds good."

"Excellent."

He turned away from her and Gwen reached for her phone to call Lock, but Mitch spun back around so fast, she immediately moved her hand away, trying to appear as if she hadn't moved at all.

"And, to make it really interesting—" he walked over to her bedside table and picked up her cell phone "—why don't *I* keep your phone, so you're not tempted to let your bear know I'm coming? It'll be a surprise! Doesn't that sound like fun?"

Bastard! "Surprising a bear? That sounds like fun to you?"

"Oh, come on. He knows me now. I'm sure it'll be great. I can't wait!" He grabbed the in-room phone and yanked it off the table, ripping the cord from the wall.

This had quickly gotten out of hand. And Gwen knew why. Because Mitch expected Gwen to do what she always did when it came to her family. Take the path of least resistance. If it kept them quiet, Gwen usually did it simply to keep the peace and to avoid the whining, complaining, and roaring.

But not this time. This time she was going to play this out. Even if it blew up in her face—and she kind of knew it would— she had no intention of backing down. None!

"You better get ready," Mitch said cheerily. "We'll be leaving soon."

"Fine," she said, also with a cheeriness that could kill a twenty-foot boa constrictor. "Sounds good."

She kept smiling until he walked out of the room, then she went to her closet and grabbed the high school football jersey Mitch had kept at their mother's house. Gwen had taken it, because she liked to wear it even though she knew her brother would lose his mind if he found out. She dropped it to the floor, unleashed her front and back claws, and proceeded to rip the living shit out of it!

When she was done, she put the shreds in a paper bag and stuck it in the back of her closet. When the time was right, she'd hand it right back to him. Maybe with a bow on it.

Lock had his nephew on his lap and one of his nieces hanging from around his neck. His mother was in the kitchen arguing with his sister, and his oldest niece, the seven-year-old, was learning how to flirt on Ric.

Ric had an open invitation to the monthly MacRyrie meal, even attending when Lock was in the Marines and didn't come home for over a year. And Lock didn't begrudge Ric a moment of that time, either. Because he knew it was one of the few times Ric truly felt like he was part of a *family* as opposed to just part of a Pack.

Tragically, however, Iona had also brought a friend. For the first time in ages, she'd dragged that unhealthy looking carcass over, Judy Bennington. A one-time supermodel and now an agent, Judy was a sun bear who needed to eat more. No bear, boar or sow, should be that thin. Even worse . . . she apparently still had a thing for Lock, and she'd had that thing since he was a senior in high school. Yet unlike most predator males, Lock's libido was actually attached to his brain and nothing about this woman had ever gotten him hard or even made him smile. She was a shifter who'd walked into his parents' house wearing real mink, for Christ sakes!

Lock was also smart enough to know that Judy's current interest in him was more about the fact that, at least in modeling terms, she'd passed her prime. She wanted a man to take care of her as she grew older. Not that he'd begrudge her that, but he wasn't that man. She was so busy being "fabulous" that she was never very interesting. Lock liked interesting.

I like Gwen, he thought with a smile. And if there was nothing else he could say about that woman, he could sure say she was interesting.

"So how have things been going with you, Lock?"

His real smile faded and he forced on a fake one. "Fine, Judy. And you?"

And that, as he knew it would, sent Judy off on a good ten minutes of talking about herself. At the seven-minute mark, he looked across the dining table at Ric, who crossed his eyes and tried not to fall out of his chair with boredom. If Lock were more of a predator and less of a bear, he'd toss Ric to Judy and hope for the best. But Judy detested wolves and Lock couldn't do that to any man.

Iona placed two large bowls of berries on the table, swiped up the empty cheese and crackers tray, slapped her son's hand away from the berries, and said to Lock, "Did Judy tell you about her newest client?"

"She's in Paris," Judy said, gripping her glass of chardonnay. "For a photo shoot. She's gorgeous and I snagged her young. Thirteen."

Lock glanced over at his young niece and could only think of one response. "Eew."

Ric snorted and looked away, but his sister cuffed him in the back of the head. A skill she'd picked up from their mother.

"Lachlan!"

"Sorry, but she's thirteen! She should be dealing with zits and telling boys 'no.' Not whoring herself out to European designers so Judy can make her twenty percent." And before his sister could yell at him, Lock snarled to Ric, "And are you going to answer that phone or am I going to break it?" The wolf had it on vibrate and the sound of it was driving Lock insane.

"I know it's my father. We had one of our . . . disagreements earlier today."

"Then either turn that phone off—" Lock said, standing when he heard the front door bell "—or throw it out the window. But do something."

Lock walked through the house and had his hand on the doorknob when he heard his parent's home phone ringing and Ric urgently whispering at him, "Don't look surprised!"

Jumping a little, Lock glared back at him. The wolf had his phone to his ear and was watching him. "What?"

"Don't look surprised." He was still whispering. "Whatever you do."

"Okay." Shaking his head, wondering when everyone around him had lost their minds, Lock pulled the front door open—and stared.

Gwen gazed up at Lock, her eyes wide. What a nightmare this had all been! First, her brother had to drag her into the car. Not because she'd been fighting him on going—oh no, she was more than ready to take this stupid, ridiculous sibling fight all the way to its stupid, ridiculous conclusion if it killed them both!—but because Ronnie Lee felt the need to come along and Gwen had refused to get in to the car with her. In the end, Gwen had sat up front while Bren, Sissy, and Ronnie Lee got the back. Although any time Gwen had heard any strange noises from the backseat, she'd look at them—and while Sissy was busy texting someone from her cell, Ronnie and Bren just looked horrified. Gwen didn't know why, though. She was just looking at them over her shoulder . . . or maybe more her spine. But so what?

Tragically, that wasn't the end of the evening . . . it was only the beginning. Now she was trapped on the MacRyrie porch with Mitch behind her, his hand gripping her shoulder. He'd insisted on walking up to the house with her, and Bren had insisted on coming with Mitch because, "They're bears, dumb ass . . . they kill." And that had meant Ronnie insisted on coming with Bren because, "The Lord knows I gotta protect that pretty face from those bear claws," and of course that meant Sissy had tagged along, " 'Cause I don't wanna be left out, y'all!"

Really? Has my life come to this? Really?

Now here they all stood, the grizzly gazing down at her, then at Mitch, Bren, Ronnie, Sissy, and finally back at her. Gwen was seconds from giving up and saying, "Fine. Take me back to Philly," when Lock said, "You're late."

She almost collapsed right there, at his feet. She fought the urge.

"Traffic," she managed to get out.

"Lucky for you that when it comes to dinner parties, my mother is always running late." He stepped back and held the door open for her. "You have time for a drink before dinner."

"Great!" Mitch said, pushing past his sister and walking inside, the rest of the psychopaths following.

Panicked, Gwen turned to Lock, and he shrugged.

Acting like the King of the Jungle Idiots that he and Bren were, the brothers walked right through the MacRyrie house like they owned it until reaching the dining room.

Gwen rushed in behind them, skirting around Ronnie to get to her brother. "I thought you were just dropping me off."

"We'll leave in a minute. What's the rush?"

"Hi, Gwen."

Gwen forced a smile at Ric Van Holtz—because why should she keep her embarrassment between her family and the bear? She shouldn't. Everyone should know!—"Hi, Ric."

Grinning, Ric smiled at Bren. "Brendon Shaw. Nice to see you again."

"Ulrich."

"Did you get the payout from the Board for the territory encroachment and the attack on your sister?"

Uh-oh.

Bren's eyes grew wide in panic and Mitch asked, "Someone attacked Marissa?"

"Uh . . ."

"No," Ric answered, probably trying to be helpful. Maybe. "Gwen. And Blayne. By the McNelly Pack out of Staten Island." It was a toss-up of who Mitch would go after first—but he went with Brendon.

"My sister was attacked on your territory, and you didn't tell me?"

"I can explain—"

"*My baby sister!*" Mitch threw his arm around Gwen's shoulders and pulled her into his side. So tight, she was positive bones were breaking. "The most important woman in my life—"

"Hey!" Sissy snapped.

"—and you don't tell me this?"

"Ronnie said not to."

Outraged, Ronnie snapped, "No you didn't just toss me under the bus!"

"I was going to call him from the medical center, but you said not to."

"Medical center?" Mitch glared at Gwen. "Why the hell didn't you tell me you'd been attacked?"

"I was too weak . . . you know, with dying and all."

"*What?*"

"I'm kidding, Mitch. It wasn't a big deal."

"Like hell it wasn't! And what exactly did you or Blayne do to start this fight?"

Gwen pushed away from her brother. "Blayne and I didn't do a goddamn thing! It was an assault!"

"Yeah. Right. You and Blayne—the innocents. When did that happen? Did hell freeze over, too?"

"You are an asshole. And you know what else?" she hissed "You're getting *split ends!*"

Mitch gasped and stepped back while Sissy shook her head and said, "Low blow, Gwenie. Low blow."

Lock leaned in, studying Mitch's hair. "Kind of accurate, though."

Eyes narrowed to slits, Mitch scowled at the bear. Lock leaned back, shaking his silver-tipped hair out of his face. "I've never had that problem. It must be genetic." He glanced at Brendon. "On your father's side."

Gwen snorted before quickly covering her mouth, which was around the same time Lock's sister, Iona, came out of the kitchen, three children behind her. She stopped and stared at Gwen. "Why are you here?"

But before Gwen could reply with an adequate lie, Alla burst from the kitchen, her arms wide.

"Gwendolyn!"

Shocked, Gwen stumbled back, but Lock stood behind her, keeping her from panicking and running. Alla smothered her in a warm hug, the embrace only lasting a few seconds, but Gwen could feel the strength running through Alla and she had to admit—it humbled her.

"Hello, Alla."

"You're late," she said with a wink, "but that's okay." Gwen smiled at the She-bear, adoring her for eternity in that instant. "And who do we have here, dear?"

"This is Mitch, Brendon, Sissy, and Ronnie."

"Nice to meet you. I'm Dr. Baranova-MacRyrie."

"Doctor?" Mitch asked, raising his brows to his sister.

"A Ph.D.," Gwen happily tossed back, as if she'd spend more than two seconds with an actual butcher.

"And this is my daughter, Iona, my husband, Brody. You all know my wonderful son Lock, his friend, Ric, and the always-emaciated Judy."

That's when they all noticed the weak-looking sow sitting at the table.

Glaring at Alla, her mouth briefly twisting in hatred, the too-thin She-bear said, "Nice to meet you all. I'm Lock's date."

Alla's mouth dropped open and Iona's blinked wide in confusion while the silence in the room grew oppressive as everyone waited for Lock's response. But he was too busy staring out the window. Then, as if he'd suddenly heard her, Lock glanced down at Judy. "Since when?"

"Oh, Lock," she giggled and Gwen thought about strangling the bitch. "I'm sure Iona told you I was here to be your date."

"Not that I remember."

What kind of answer was that? And if she was lying, why wasn't he livid? Gwen was used to men who got livid over not having enough maple syrup for their pancakes, much less some heifer lying about being their date while standing in front of their date for the following day.

Lock shook his head, "I'm pretty sure I'd remember that conversation with my sister."

"Oh, my God!" Gwen suddenly burst out, startling the bears in the room, which made the rest of the predators nervous. She grabbed Lock's arm in order to drag him outside so she could slap some sense into his big bear head, but he didn't actually move when she tugged, pulled, and yanked. He simply kept looking at her with those big, innocent bear eyes.

His mother tapped Lock's shoulder. "Son, remember when I taught you how to give the smaller, weaker ones the *illusion* they're dragging you places? This is one of those times."

"Oh. Right." He smiled and let Gwen drag him out to the backyard.

"She's your *date?*"

Lock stared at Gwen, wondering what she was going on about. Why was she here? Why were her brothers here? Why did his mother and Ric seem to know what was going on? When had Judy Bennington lost her mind and started thinking they were dating? And how could Gwen be even prettier than the last time he saw her? Not a spot of makeup, wearing only jeans, a T-shirt, jacket, and sneakers—and she easily outshined all the overpaid Judys of the world.

"Not that I'm aware," he answered.

"Not that you're—" She gritted her teeth together, her hands curling into fists. "You're not getting this, are you?"

"Not really."

Pacing in a circle, Gwen snarled, "Are you fucking her?"

Shocked and hurt, Lock said, "I'm not fucking her. Or anybody," he rushed to add. But especially Judy—skin and bones does not a good time in bed make.

"Is that why you walked away last night? Is that why you couldn't see me today? Because of *her?* Because you were planning to be busy fucking her while you're busy turning me down? Is that what's going on here, Jersey?"

It suddenly occurred to Lock that Gwen's scent had changed, but it wasn't a new scent. No. It was the same one she had when she'd slammed her fist into that She-wolf's face and spit blood in her eye.

So Gwen having that scent now . . . probably not a good thing.

While Sissy unknowingly kept the bears busy by rambling—and Christ knew, the woman could ramble—Mitch slipped into the bears' kitchen. No matter what his baby sister thought, he wasn't stupid. Someone had tipped off that grizzly, but he had no idea who. Who among his friends would betray him? Who among his friends would risk the wrath of the mighty lion in order to help out a frickin' bear?

He didn't know, but he was determined to find out. Determined to know who was getting between him and his ultimate goal of getting Gwen back to her Pride and her family. New York was no place for someone so sweet and delicate and vulnerable as his Gwenie. And he definitely wouldn't leave her in the hands of some . . . some . . . *bear.*

Oversized, larvae-eating, easily startled, toe-playing, carcass-stealing bears! His sister deserved a nice, solid lion . . . well, maybe not a lion. A tiger? No. He detested tigers. A mountain lion? Eh. Perhaps a full-human? He rolled his eyes at the thought, but at least a full-human was easily controlled. Unlike those bears.

Moving over to the landline phone attached to the wall, Mitch eased the receiver out of the cradle and hit star six nine. Less than a full ring later, the other end was picked up and he heard a female voice ask, "Alla? Did it go okay?"

His eyes narrowed. He knew that voice. Where did he know that voice from? He was waiting for the voice to speak again so he could narrow it down, when a very large arm reached around him and disconnected the call. Swallowing, the scent of She-bear nearly choking him, Mitch turned and looked directly into large brown eyes.

The She-bear took the phone from Mitch's hand and placed it back in the cradle. He watched her closely, refusing to cower in the face of an old bear. Sure, she was his height—and wider—but she was older and the intellectual type. Nothing to be worried about.

"You and your sister have the same cheekbones . . . and eye color. But you look more much more like your brother." She gently placed big hands on Mitch's shoulders. "She had so many funny stories about growing up in Philly with you and her mother's Pride."

"*Her* Pride," Mitch was quick to correct. "Gwen's Pride."

The sow's head tilted to the side. "Really?" She blinked, then said, "Anyway, while we were exchanging stories, I did tell her about a family vacation we had in Alaska one year. A bison bull, about seventeen hundred pounds or so, came out of nowhere and I guess I just panicked, but . . ." she shrugged, her gaze drifting up to the ceiling ". . . it did provide a lot of meat for the rest of the camping trip."

That's when Mitch tried to walk away, but she gripped his shoulders tight, and it took all of his strength not to drop to his knees from the pressure of it. "I guess I just felt my cubs were being threatened by that bison. Silly, huh? They do say that the most dangerous place anyone could be caught is between a bear sow and her cubs, but both Lock and Iona were adults when this happened, so I thought I'd be over all that by then." Her hands briefly tightened again and Mitch was sure he heard something "pop" in his shoulders. "But I discovered that one is never too old to feel protective of their cubs and to destroy whatever may be threatening the life and *happiness* of their offspring. Isn't that fascinating?"

Not waiting for an answer, she put her arm around Mitch and steered him back out to the dining room.

"Well," the sow said sweetly to everyone in the room, "it

looks as if it's time for us to get our dinner under way." She smiled over at Van Holtz. "I think it's time to get that steak in the oven, Ric."

"Yes, ma'am."

As the wolf passed, she added, "And remember, *very* rare."

"As if I'd cook it any other way."

She focused back on Mitch and the rest of the interlopers. "I'm so glad I had a chance to meet and chat with Gwen's friends, and I'm sure we'll all be seeing each other again soon." Her arm still around Mitch, she ushered them out of the dining room, briefly pausing by the way-too-thin She-bear. "You, too, Judy. Time to go."

"Yes, but I was invited—"

"Not by me, and I don't like you." Her daughter started to disagree, but when her mother jerked her hand up, the younger sow quickly moved behind her father. And Mitch didn't blame that female one bit.

"But it's been great having all of you over!" the older sow said cheerily. "It's so rare for us to have so many wonderful breeds in our house at one time. For some reason, only bears ever come here."

CHAPTER 16

Gwen walked around Lock, heading back to the house. "I'm going to Philly with Mitch, get some dinner, and let my family harass me into moving back."

She was only a few feet from the door when she went airborne. She gave a short squeal, her body preparing to be flung across the small backyard, but luckily, he didn't fling her anywhere, simply lifted her up until she could look him right in the eye . . . which was still a hell of a drop if he decided to let her go.

"Listen to me, Mr. Mittens. I have not, nor will I ever, fuck Judy 'I desperately need a sandwich' Bennington. I wasn't mean to her because she's friends with my sister and poor Iona never had many friends. It's really hard to make them when you're twelve and smarter than most multidegreed scientists. So I put up with Judy being around, but I have no interest in her. None. And never will. Understand?"

Not wanting to be dropped on her head, Gwen nodded.

"Good." He lowered her to the ground. Gently. "And before we go back inside, I want you to understand something." He released her arms and rubbed his hands against his thighs. "I am really not complex. I eat, I sleep, I work. That's it."

"Don't forget the woodworking and playing with your toes."

He chuckled. "Right. But that's it. When I'm with someone, I don't screw around on them, whether we've started having sex or not. I'm not one of those guys who can manage more than one woman at a time. And to be really honest, Gwen, emotionally you're like three women. There's a lot going on around you and I have to keep my focus at all times."

"Gee, thanks."

"It's true. Besides, you've come to mean way too much to me to screw it all up now."

She wanted to believe him and, to her surprise, she did. She wasn't using her head here, either, but her gut. Her gut was never wrong. "Fine, but if there's anything else you need to tell me, now is the time. I don't want to find out later."

Lock let out a breath. "Uh . . . there is something I haven't told you that I've been avoiding telling you."

Gwen nodded. "Let's hear it."

"You're not going to like it."

"Tell me anyway."

Lock licked his lips and admitted, "My sister's a neurosurgeon."

Gwen didn't say anything, but the blank expression on her face said it all.

"She's *not* an organ thief," he argued.

"Uh-huh."

"This is why I didn't tell you before."

"Because we both know she'll try and kill me if she thinks I know too much?" she asked flatly.

"You're insane."

"Have you paid attention to the last twenty minutes with my family?"

She did have a point. But instead of arguing with her about any of that, he did what he'd wanted to do since he saw her standing on his parents' porch.

Lock leaned in and kissed her. Instantly, her arms wrapped around his shoulders, and she groaned into his mouth, the sound making his knees feel weak and his stomach clench. From only a kiss. Damn.

"Lachlan, my dearest," Alla called from the back door. "Sorry to interrupt, but dinner's almost ready."

Lock pulled back and gazed into Gwen's face while he answered. "Okay, Mom. We'll be right in." He brushed stray curls off her cheeks. "What is it about you that makes me so crazy?"

"My incandescent charm?"

"Heh."

"You're not supposed to laugh."

"Oh."

"You're supposed to agree."

"Painting your nails with the team colors and logo of the Philadelphia Flyers does not mean you have incandescent charm. It just means you're kind of weird."

She held her nails up, making his skin itch to feel her hands on him. "But tonight they're playing against the Islanders. It's all about team loyalty."

With a wink, she slipped her hand into his, and together they walked into the wonderful-smelling kitchen.

The first day Abby Vega could shift, she knew two things: She wasn't crazy—no matter what her foster mother said—and she needed to get out on her own. That was three years ago, and she'd been living on the streets ever since. Of course, she'd lived on the streets as a canine. Much easier than as a girl. This was one of her favorite spots, too. An alley that had a restaurant on one side—amazing the kind of stuff they threw out—and a bar on the other. That gave her a good sideshow while she was eating.

Tonight would be no different. The guy opening the doors of the white van owned this Staten Island bar. Other than the liquor, she still wasn't sure what else he sold, all those deals happening in this alley, but she knew it wasn't anything legal. She'd seen him do all sorts of stuff in this alley, too, and not once, in all the time she'd come here, had she ever seen him picked up by the cops. She had, however, seen him giving money to cops.

And that's who Abby thought she was at first. The woman crouched on top of the van, watching the deal go down. But she wasn't, was she? Too many scars, and her eyes . . .

Abby's own eyes narrowed, trying to get a closer look.

There were three men now, haggling over whatever they had in that van, completely oblivious to the woman watching them. Was one of them setting up the others? Were there a bunch of cops around here? It didn't matter to Abby. If and when she bolted out, tail wagging, the cops would let her go. They always had before. Always patting her on the head, giving her a few treats. They never bothered calling Animal Control. Although they all asked the same question: "What the hell kind of dog is that?"

Abby chewed the steak bone, trying to get the marrow, and watched the men and the woman above them. The woman was silent until she pulled out a gun complete with silencer. Not a tacky homemade one, either, but a real one that was made for her gun. The woman sized up all three men, but shot only two. They dropped, and Abby's bone fell from her mouth. The other man, the bar owner, turned to run. The woman didn't shoot him. She did, however, take a large hunting knife from the back of her jeans and throw it.

The blade slammed into the guy's lower back and he flipped forward, landing flat on his face. The woman dropped easily to the ground. She lifted up the two men she'd shot, one in each hand, and tossed them into the back of the van. Then she went to the other male.

Unlike the first two, he wasn't dead, but he was unable to do more than crawl, his legs dragging uselessly behind him. And he was crying. The woman followed behind him, watching him. When she got tired of that, she stepped on his ass, pressing her foot down to hold him in place. She reached down and yanked the blade out of his spine, silencing his screams with a simple

"Shush." She slid the blade into the holster attached to the back of her jeans and crouched beside him, rolling him over.

"Names," she said.

She didn't even have to say it twice. He began rattling off names between his sobs. The woman nodded, but didn't write anything down because she probably never forgot anything.

Once he'd finished giving her those names, the woman lifted him up by the neck and carried him to the back of the van, where she tossed him inside. Those strong arms reached in after him, and Abby cringed when she heard something snap.

The woman stepped back and slammed the doors shut. She held a set of keys in her hand. She started to walk around the van but stopped and turned, her nose lifted, nostrils flaring. A few sniffs and she homed right in on Abby, walking over to her. Abby backed up as far as she could, but she had the alley wall behind her. She bared her fangs, but the woman only smiled, the light from the open back door reflecting her eyes.

"Pup." She looked down at Abby, cold, reflective eyes looking her over. "Hungry, pup?"

She was, but . . . ?

"Come on then." She motioned to the van and walked away. Did she think Abby would follow? Why?

"Ain't got all day, pup," she said.

Abby wasn't crazy but . . .

She crept out from behind the trash can, her body low, her legs tense and ready to run at the slightest provocation. But the woman opened the passenger door and casually walked around to the driver's side. She got inside and waited. She waited for Abby. Creeping closer, Abby stared up at the woman in the driver's seat. She was on her cell phone. "I got the names," she told someone. "Nope. I'll handle it."

The woman closed the phone and stare down at Abby. "Move your ass. I'm starvin'."

Glancing around, Abby carefully climbed into the van, and the woman reached across the seat to pull the door closed. She relaxed back and said, "Guess no one ever told you not to get into vans with strangers, huh?" She started the engine and added, "If anyone asks, you didn't see those bodies back there." Then she winked at her and backed out of the alley.

Something told Abby she wouldn't be back to this alley anymore for those free scraps.

CHAPTER 17

L ock was starting to see a pattern here. Adding a little Gwen to his life seemed to improve his meals exponentially. In addition, his parents seemed to adore her, and his sister tolerated her, which was more than Iona did with most people. So, using basic science, if he were to add Gwen to more of his life in general, she'd improve it all around.

At least that was his conclusion. And who was he to argue with basic science?

Lock held Gwen's jacket open for her. She reached for it, and he stepped back, continuing to hold it open.

"Are you going to give me my jacket or what?"

"I'm holding it open for you."

She studied the jacket and then him. "Why?"

"Just put your arms in the damn jacket!"

"Okay, okay!"

He helped her put her jacket on and once he had her in it, leaned down and wrapped his arms around her from behind, kissing her neck. "That wasn't so hard, now was it?"

"The MacRyries are so polite—except when you eat."

"We were hungry. And you still have all your fingers and toes."

"Barely."

Lock lifted her in the air, making her legs swing out, and Gwen squealed.

"Lachlan, put her down," his mother ordered, although she was smiling. She handed Gwen a take-home bag filled with leftovers from their meal. "Here you go. Lunch for tomorrow."

"Thanks so much."

She hugged Gwen. "I'm so glad you came tonight."

"And thank you for covering for me."

"Anytime." Alla went up on her toes and kissed Lock's cheek. "Talk to you soon?"

"Yes, ma'am." He opened the door and they walked out onto the porch, his mother behind them.

"What about Ric?" Gwen asked.

"His car is here to pick him up, but he's staying to do the dishes."

Gwen stopped and said to Alla, "Ulrich Van Holtz is doing your dishes?"

"Of course. He always does the dishes when he eats here. Always a very polite boy. And unlike that idiot father of his, he has a brain."

"Mom." Lock chastised, although he knew his mother meant every word.

"I'm merely pointing out that the gene that controls intelligence skipped a generation in the Van Holtz household. Like red hair or blue eyes."

Lock stood on the porch and watched as his father gazed down the street at a dark-blue van with dark windows. It was easy to spot on a small street that hadn't had new neighbors in more than ten years. Everyone knew everyone else and strange vehicles on the block caught one's attention. Especially the attention of curious bears. But that van wasn't strange to him. Hell, it still had the dent on the side from his shoulder.

"Stay here," he said to Gwen and his mother before going over to his father. "Dad?"

"That van. I think someone's inside, but the windows are so dark I can't tell."

The father and son looked at each other and then back at the van.

* * *

"What are they doing?" Gwen asked.

"Being curious," Alla replied. "My husband and son are very curious."

Brody leaned against the van and sniffed at the window. When that didn't seem to work, he grabbed hold of the door handle and pulled, ripping the handle from the door.

Gwen's body jerked. "Oh."

Lock walked to the back of the van and tugged on the door handles there . . . before ripping them off. Like his father, he dropped them to the ground and focused on the doors. He pressed on the two darkened windows in the back of the van with his fingertips. Nodding, he stepped back, balled his hands into fists, and slammed them forward, breaking through the glass.

The motor on the van roared to life as Lock reached into the broken windows and grasped the doors from the inside. Brody broke through the driver's side window with his elbow and grabbed hold of that door. Tires spun as the vehicle shifted into Drive, but it sat in position for several long seconds, tires churning up gravel and dirt, until there was a hard squeal of metal and the van shot off—leaving its three doors behind.

Gwen charged down the stairs and across the street.

"*Have you two lost your minds?*" she yelled.

Holding the thick, steel-enforced doors in both hands while blood dripped down his arm from where he'd been cut by the glass, Lock watched her curiously. "Why would you say that?"

Lock took her back to his apartment, parking his SUV in the garage under his building. When he turned off the motor, they sat inside his vehicle until Gwen said, "How the hell did you find an apartment with parking in this city?"

Not what he expected her to say, but Gwen always seemed to surprise him. "My uncles helped me get this place."

He got out of his SUV, and by the time he walked around to the passenger side, she was out and heading toward the elevator.

Neither spoke in the elevator nor while walking down the hall to his apartment.

Once inside, he took off his jacket, hung it up in his closet, and headed off to the bathroom so he could take off the gauze bandages his mother had wrapped around his arms. His mother handled it, because Gwen wouldn't let a very pissed-off Iona near him. "You just keep your Hands of Evil away from him, butcher girl," she'd said plainly with a completely straight face.

Tossing the bandages into the trash, he quickly examined his forearms. The wounds had already healed up, appearing more like scratches one might get from their pet rather than the gouges they were a couple of hours ago.

Lock rinsed off any residual blood, washed his hands, and tracked Gwen down in his kitchen. Coffee was percolating in his twelve-cup coffeemaker, and she was invading his cabinets for sugar and mugs.

"I can't believe how much ice cream you have in your freezer," she said.

"I like ice cream."

She shut the cabinet door and placed the small container of sugar on the table, along with a generic bottle of honey he kept for emergencies and two large mugs. Glancing at his arms, she held her hands out. "Let me see."

Lock dutifully held his arms out and she grasped his wrists, examining his forearms closely. "They're healing up nicely. See? I knew your mother could handle it."

He didn't respond, too busy noticing how close his hand was to her chest, the curious bear in him desperate to discover how her breasts would feel. Always one to explore when he had the chance, Lock simply lifted his right hand until her breast filled his palm.

Gwen froze, but she didn't push him off.

Lock closed his hand around her breast, gently squeezing, amazed how such a simple action could feel so good.

Gwen gasped and, to Lock's great appreciation, stepped in closer.

He used his left hand and gripped her other breast, squeezing until Gwen reached for him. Her hands dug into his sweatshirt and she tugged at it, trying to lift it. He released her long enough for him to bend at the waist, allowing her to yank the shirt off over his head and toss it somewhere.

Moments later she had those small, soft hands of hers gliding over his shoulders and down his chest. She moved in closer, pressing her head into him and brushing her hair against him in a way that was totally feline. He trembled and slipped his hands into her hair, lifting her head and tilting it back so he could take her mouth fully, his tongue and lips exploring hers as he'd been wanting to do since he met her at Jess's wedding.

Gwen gripped his hair, her fingers holding the strands tight as her tongue met his and she moaned into him. Lock let himself get lost in that kiss, let his body take him where it would without thinking much on where it was going.

Abruptly pulling back, her eyes wide, Gwen gaped at him. "The way you kiss," she gasped. "You do something . . . weird."

He scowled. "It's not weird."

"Not bad weird but," one finger slid across his bottom lip and his entire body shuddered, "amazing weird."

Weird was still weird to Lock, but she didn't seem freaked out or anything. Besides, he might as well tell her and get it out of the way. "It's nothing, really. We, bears I mean, have, uh . . . well, the technical term is prehensile-type lips."

Gwen's eyes focused on his mouth, her brow furrowed as she studied it for a long moment. "You have what?"

Gosh, this was awkward. "I mean . . ." Damn, what did he mean? "They can move independently. When I'm bear, they're completely unattached from my jaw, and as human—I can kind of play with that."

She leaned back a little more, her furrowed brow turning to an outright frown and well on its way to a healthy scowl. "Are you telling me that your lips are like . . ." She had this look on her face that could be a look of disgust or a look of confusion, he had no idea which one. Confusion he could handle . . . disgust, however . . .

"Your lips are like fingers?"

He swallowed, terrified he was about to lose everything with this answer, but Lock had never been one to lie about much, especially himself.

"Yeah," he admitted, reluctantly. "I guess that's one way of—"

She shoved and Lock moved back from her, watching in stunned silence as she ran out of the kitchen.

Gee, is that my broken heart lying on the floor? Yes. Yes, it is.

Wait. He wasn't going to let her go *that* easily, was he? Simply because she didn't understand? No way.

Determined, Lock stalked out of the kitchen, through his dining room, and into the hallway. He looked toward the front door, expecting to see Gwen struggling with the security system. She wasn't.

More curious than panicked now, Lock sniffed the air and followed Gwen's scent . . . to his bedroom.

As he walked in a sneaker hit him in the forehead.

"Why are you still dressed?" she demanded, standing in the middle of his bed. "Get naked!" Another sneaker hit him in the head.

"Uh . . . Gwen?"

"What? You're asking me questions *now*? Why are you asking me questions now?"

Because she was freaking him out?

Gwen tore off her socks and then went for her jeans.

"What are you doing?" he asked, completely confused.

"I know, I know." She was panting. Heavily. "You want something more organic or romantic or some other bullshit, but I don't have time for that."

"Why? Do you have to be—"

"I mean, seriously . . . how many times in a girl's life can she hope . . . even dream?"

"Gwen, I don't under—"

"I swear," she begged while wiggling out of her jeans before she sent them flying, "you take care of me, I swear, swear, *swear* I'll take care of you. I just need you to do this for me."

And there went her panties.

"That sounds great, but I guess I'm unclear—"

"Unclear?" she snapped. "You tell me your lips function like fingers and you're unclear? On what exactly?"

Lock took a moment to luxuriate in the wonder that was Mr. Mittens. Because, holy hell, he adored this woman!

"I see."

"I hope so." Completely naked from the waist down, Gwen stretched out across Lock's bed, her feet pointing at him, and spread her legs. She fisted her hands at her side and said, "Okay, do it. Wait!" She reached over and grabbed one of his pillows, covering her face. "Okay," she said behind the pillow, "*now* do it."

Unable to help himself, Lock teased, "If you're sure."

The pillow slammed against the bed, and that desperate feline glared at him from beneath a mass of unruly curls. "Oh, my God! *I will kill you!*"

"Okay, okay." Laughing, Lock kneeled on his bed. "No need to get crazy. I've got it covered."

She made a little whimpering sound and covered her face up with the pillow again. He wasn't sure why, but who cared? Because at this moment, in his perfect universe, he had Gwen O'Neill right where he wanted her.

Gwen caught her lip between her teeth and peeked around that pillow like a nervous virgin. She watched, barely able to breathe, as Lock hooked his arms under her knees and lifted her legs up and back, giving him complete access to her pussy. He gazed down, giving her a brief second of concern, before he licked his lips and lowered his head between her thighs.

To Gwen, there was absolutely nothing sexier than that first moment a man went down on a woman. In this case, however, she knew she'd never find anything sexier than Lock MacRyrie doing it. He'd given her that explanation about his mouth earlier as if he'd had no idea the power of what he was telling her. Did he not know that some women searched their entire lives looking for a man who'd developed the kind of talents Lock had gotten naturally from his DNA? Of course, this explained why She-bears never talked about their men. Why would they? Why would they give up the secret of their happy marriages? Only a fool would do that, and bears were never fools.

Lock kissed the inside of her thighs, gently licking and nipping the sensitive flesh. He took his time, and Gwen refused to say a word. She wouldn't say anything that would ruin this. Not with her big mouth. Not a word. Not a syllable. Nothing.

His tongue slid inside her and Gwen's eyes closed, her back arching a bit. Well, if nothing else, the man had the basics down, using his tongue to make her wet and crazy while he held her firmly. As he licked her, Gwen quickly forgot about anything but what he was doing to her. He teased her, taking his time, playing with her body. She enjoyed every second of it and, as she felt that first orgasm coming her way, his mouth moved and she felt his lips wrap around her clit. She groaned, the first orgasm easing through her. Until Lock did . . . something. Something so as-tounding, her entire body quaked, his lips tightening around her clit and twisting one way, then another, then tugging. Or some-thing. Whatever he was doing, the original, slow-moving orgasm was brutally shoved away for the promise of something stronger and more powerful than she could have ever dreamed of. Gwen's entire body bowed, her hands holding the pillow against her face out of courtesy to his neighbors. His lips twisted again, tugged, pulled, and Gwen almost shot off the bed. Her legs started to close of their own volition, but big, powerful hands pinned them down, making her eyes cross from the simple action.

Shaking, sweating, the orgasm bearing down on her yet still somehow out of her reach, Gwen allowed her body and desires to rule this moment with this man. She trusted him to take care of her, and knowing that made her groans deeper, her gasps louder.

His hands began to move, and the touch of his fingers against her skin was more intense than anything she'd ever known. Ever felt. One hand wrapped around her breast, his fingers squeezing and tugging the same as what his mouth was doing to her clit. Two thick fingers from his other hand pushed inside her, fucking her hard. He was relentless, almost brutal. But he didn't hurt her. Far from it.

It was that mix of restrained strength with unending determination that took her over the edge. She came so hard that only his strong arms pinning her thighs down kept her on the bed, and his wonderful-smelling pillow muffled her screams.

Gwen's body shuddered and writhed until she relaxed back, her breath coming out in hard pants. But her panting quickened, her body tightening again, and she realized as her brain cleared that he hadn't stopped. His lips were still tugging and pulling, his fingers still playing. As the first wave left her body, the second slammed into her. The pillow went flying and Gwen gasped out his name, gripping the back of his head. She had no idea if she was trying to shove him away or hold him in place. She couldn't think straight. Hell, she couldn't think at all.

Every muscle of her body was taut and straining as the second wave roared through her. The pillow was no longer needed because she could barely breathe, much less scream. She held him to her as she rode out the second climax, immediately trying to push him away as it finished with her. But the bear didn't pull back. He took her up again, his lips twisting and turning her clit until Gwen's body snapped taut once more. Her fingers yanking at his hair, she begged him to stop, knowing she couldn't handle more, but he told her, "Not yet, Gwen. One more." And it crossed her feverish mind that he was speaking clearly while his lips were still working her over.

A third finger was inside her now, stroking and pushing, making her pussy feel too full. But it was the bite of pain that cut through everything and took her one more time. She came screaming with no pillow to block the sound, her body twisting and fighting as Lock held her down.

He finally pulled away, and Gwen crashed onto the bed, not

realizing until that moment that only her shoulders had been resting on the mattress.

Once Lock moved away, Gwen managed to drag herself into a ball, shuddering and sweating, her teeth chattering, her body shaking, and she wondered if she'd ever recover from this.

Lock stared down at Gwen and wondered if he'd gone a bit too far. But he couldn't help himself. The more she came, the more he'd wanted to see her do it again.

He leaned in a bit. "Gwen?" He touched her shoulder. "Gwen? Are you okay?"

Hospital. He had to get her to a hospital. Whether she wanted to go or not. Lock went to stand up, but Gwen's hand reached out, gripping his throat. *Uh-oh.* She raised her head, her sweat-drenched hair nearly covering her eyes, and said, "Marry me."

Hiding his immense relief, Lock replied, "Shouldn't we get to know each other better?"

"What else is there to know?" she asked, her eyes gazing hungrily on his mouth, the fingers of her free hand reaching up and brushing against them gently. Lock's eyes closed from the contact, the pleasure of it making him shudder. "I have all the information I need."

"You do know there's more to me than these lips, don't you?"

"I don't care." And Lock laughed as she went on. "Until you I've only found men perfect from the neck down—and that's only if they work out regularly and watch their carbs. But you? You're perfect from the neck up *and* the neck down. You're a god."

"And once the euphoria wears off, you're going to be kicking yourself."

"Then—" she said, slapping her free hand against his face.

"Ow!"

"—the euphoria better not wear off."

He frowned in concern. "Are you sure? Maybe we should wait a little while before we—" Lock's eyes crossed as her hand reached down and gripped his cock through his jeans.

"I want you inside me. Now, Jersey."

Panting, his brain unable to think past *Fuck. Girl. Now,* Lock quickly gripped the hand trying to get his jeans unzipped. "Wait."

"For what?"

He had no idea. Oh! He remembered! Condoms. He needed condoms.

Lock pushed her hands away and rose up on his knees. Shaking his head in an attempt to clear it, he reached over to his side drawer and pulled out the unopened box of condoms. He managed to tear the box open and had a condom in his hand when his zipper slid down and Gwen sunk her hand into his jeans.

He dropped the condom and choked as she gripped and stroked. Frowning, she pulled her hands out and proceeded to push his jeans and boxer briefs down to his knees.

"Oh, my God," she gasped.

"What?"

"It *is* bigger."

Lock peered down at his cock. "Well," he offered as explanation, "it's in a good mood."

"You're a grower *and* a show-er."

"Gwen? Are you crying?"

"Just a little." She wiped the tears. "Nothing to worry about."

"Yeah, but—"

Her hand slapped over his mouth. "Silence is your friend right now."

When he didn't try to speak, she removed her hand and placed both on her hips. "Do you know I'm actually concerned I won't be able to handle this thing?" A few more tears fell. "Do you know how many women actually get to say that sentence in a lifetime . . . and *mean it?*"

He kept his mouth shut, not wanting her distracted or upset. Not when he wanted her this badly.

"Give me a moment," she said, and he was afraid she was going to leave the room to sob in private. She didn't. She simply spread her knees wide, which lowered her down a bit, allowing her easier access to his cock.

And when her mouth wrapped around the head, he really thought he saw God and, not surprisingly . . . God was a bear.

Lock tasted so good. Better than she'd hoped. Especially when all she could think about was putting his mammoth cock in her mouth. If for no other reason than she wanted to see if she could swallow the whole thing.

Over the years, Gwen had found there were two kinds of men. Men who made eating a woman an art form because they were average—or barely—in size so they had to compensate. And men who were hung like horses but felt that nine-incher somehow exempted them from one of her favorite forms of entertainment.

Yet somehow that Irish luck that had kept Gwen alive all these years deigned to reward on her the highest blessing a woman could hope for. A well-hung man who loved to give his woman head.

Nirvana. She had it.

Gwen took him in her mouth, swallowing him whole. She felt the tip hit the back of her throat and she almost cried a little more when she realized *she wasn't done!*

Relaxing her throat, she kept going until she'd managed to get all of him in. Lock gripped her head and it took her a moment to understand what he was fervently whispering.

"Thank you, God. Thank you." Over and over again he kept saying it. A more complimentary mantra a woman was not likely to hear. She sucked and used her tongue, shocked when he actually got *thicker* inside her mouth. She growled in the back of her throat, making sure he felt the sensation of it vibrating against the tip.

That's when she felt claws against her head and Lock pulled her off.

"I wasn't done," she said.

"You are for now." Taking deep breaths, he pushed her back

on the bed and grabbed the condom. She relaxed back, her elbows keeping her chest up as she raised her knees and spread her legs wide. She wanted to make sure he could see how wet she was for him.

Lock moved so fast, she only had a chance to blink before that condom was on and he was over her. He kissed her first, and the kiss was wonderfully passionate . . . and desperate. So desperate, she didn't bother to try and hide the desperation building in her. Why bother when she wanted him so badly?

Gwen kissed him back, her arms wrapping around his neck. His thick arms gripped her under the knees and lifted her legs until they rested over his thighs. He pushed her farther back against the bed and pressed home, his cock sliding into her, filling her, making her ache and come at the same moment. He hadn't even done anything yet, nothing but pushed inside her, but she came hard on that way-too-big cock, her mouth pressing against his chest to stifle her screams.

What was this woman doing to him? First that blow job that almost had him coming down her throat long before he was ready to and now . . . God, now, she was coming again. Her muscles tightened around his cock and he felt it down his back and to his toes. He gritted his teeth, ordering himself not to come yet. How unfair would that be? He was not a sixty-second man, and he wouldn't start now, no matter how amazing Gwen's pussy felt.

After a few minutes she stopped, her breath coming in hard pants against his nipple—which was definitely not helping—and her hands dug deep into his sides. Then Lock waited a few moments longer. He didn't want to catch the tail end of anything, so he waited, even while it was killing him, he waited.

Finally, she let out a sigh and relaxed back. The sign he needed, Lock started slow, doing what he could to maintain control, keeping his movements even and . . . and . . .

"Oh . . . oh, God!" she cried out, arching into him.

Wait, wait! He hadn't even—

But it was too late. Gwen was coming and those damn muscles of hers contracting around him were just too much. He lost it. Pressing his hands against her shoulders, Lock pinned Gwen to the bed and fucked her hard. So hard he knew he couldn't be doing much for her, except maybe hurting her, but he couldn't stop. He *couldn't* stop. Not when it felt this good. God, so good. Nothing. Nothing had ever felt this good be—

He barely bit back a roar as he came, his entire body jerking in time to each ejaculation. When there was nothing left to give, his body collapsed, too weak for anything more. He did, however, manage to fall to the side and not on top of her, but barely.

One of his arms lay listlessly across her chest and he cringed when she pushed it off.

"Gwen—" He had the apology on his lips, all the right words to explain how bad he felt, but she turned toward him, burrowing deep against him.

"Put your arms around me," she demanded and he did, pulling her tight into his chest and wrapping one of his legs around both of hers. "Perfect," she sighed seconds before she fell asleep.

Knowing she was the type of woman to tell him if she were disappointed or not, he let his worries go and fell into his own deep sleep a few seconds later.

CHAPTER 18

Lock woke up when he felt claws kneading his chest. Not actual claws, thankfully she had those sheathed, but those girly claws she insisted on keeping.

She wasn't awake, either, but seemed to enjoy using him as a scratching post while she slept. And it didn't help that she was purring and rubbing her body against his.

Unable to go back to sleep and unwilling to wake her up, Lock stared up at the ceiling and thought about how relaxed he felt. He hadn't felt this relaxed in . . . years. Definitely not since he'd joined the Marines and perhaps even before then.

Whatever. He only knew he liked feeling this way. Liked waking up with Gwen on top of him, and he was willing to do whatever it took to keep her purring like that.

He was so engaged in his thoughts, Lock didn't immediately realize he'd started petting her, brushing the tips of his fingers against her sides, down her back, across her ass. And when he did realize, he didn't stop. She had such smooth skin and he loved the feel of it, and thankfully she didn't seem to mind his rough hands brushing against her.

Soon after, her kneading hands became more insistent, earning a few winces from Lock, but then the kneading stopped and the licking took over. With long strokes of her tongue, she moved up his chest until she reached his neck. Lock groaned when she began to nip at his throat while her fingers dug into his hair and massaged his scalp. He knew she was awake now, turning his head to get a kiss. Her eyes still closed, Gwen instinctively raised her mouth to his.

Their kiss was long, yet moving from sweet to desperate in seconds. Lock's hands stroked down her back to grip her ass and hold her in place while Gwen pushed her hips into him, the feel of her pussy getting hotter and wetter against Lock's chest driving him crazy.

He slipped his hand over her ass and between her thighs, pressing his finger deep inside. Gwen pulled from their kiss and threw her head back, the movement of her hips matching that of his hand. "You . . . you're the best kisser," she stuttered, biting her lip as he added a second finger to the first. "I could kiss you for hours . . . days."

That sounded perfect to him.

"I . . . I think I'm gonna come again."

And that sounded even better. "Then come."

She still had her eyes closed as she placed her palms on his shoulders, raising herself up as she rocked her hips against his fingers and his chest.

"I could watch you come for hours," he said, paraphrasing her, "days."

Her breath caught, her back arched, and her body stiffened. Then, as the orgasm shot through her, her breath left her lungs in a hard rush, thighs shaking as they clung to him, and hands gripping his shoulders in a brutal hold, her nails digging past flesh.

He didn't care.

She gave a small sob and crashed hard on top of him, her hair covering his chin and neck. He pulled his fingers from her, loving how drenched they were, and carefully rolled to his side while he placed Gwen on her back. She didn't say anything as she lay there, her eyes still closed. She might have slept again, but Lock didn't know. And, again, he didn't care.

He wiped his wet fingers across her right breast and lowered his head, his lips wrapping around her nipple, the taste of Gwen flowing through his mouth. Using only his lips, he twisted and plucked her nipple. Gwen's body jerked, her hands immediately reaching for him, clinging to him as Lock took his time playing with her.

He'd never enjoyed a woman so much. And even though his cock was so hard it hurt, he had no problem holding back his own release in the entertaining pursuit of hers.

Besides, he had bigger issues to handle than merely coming.

Christ almighty! Were they all like this? How did their females keep this secret for so long? And no wonder there was that exclusive group of cat and canine males who seemed to only date She-bears. She'd never understood it, considering how much bigger and stronger those females sometimes were, but now Gwen got it. She could only imagine what those lips could do to a cock.

The grizzly also had an unbelievable amount of willpower. She could feel his cock pressing against her leg, hard and hot, leaking from the tip, but still he seemed more interested in playing with her nipples and watching her writhe than taking care of himself.

Time meant little as he managed to bring her to the brink of coming again and again—using just his mouth and her nipples— only to pull her back time after time. When she finally thought she might actually lose control and tear his face off with her claws, his hands gripped her ass cheeks and he said, "Gwen."

She opened her eyes and glared at him. She didn't want to talk. In fact, she wasn't sure she *could* talk.

"I really like you."

Huh? What? What the hell was he rambling about? Shit on a stick! Couldn't this wait?

"A lot."

Yeah. Sure. Whatever. Just finish!

"So I want to make this exclusive."

Wait. What?

"We'll see how that goes."

She sensed she should be debating with him for some reason, but his mouth was on her again, and Gwen's eyes rolled back in her head, her legs shifting restlessly against his sheets, and she started making this mewling sound that on any other day she'd be too embarrassed to make.

"Okay?" he asked after another few minutes.

Huh? What?

"Okay?" he asked again while his fingers tugged at her nipples and although that kept her on the edge it wasn't his mouth. It wasn't those lips. "Tell me that's what you want, too."

Fine! Whatever! "Yes. God, yes!" She gripped his head between her hands. "We'll make it exclusive. I'll be your girlfriend. Go with you to weddings, help you pick out underwear—whatever you want. Anything you want. *Anything.*"

She saw that adorable little-boy smile of his right before he said, "Okay" and lowered his head, taking her nipple back into his mouth. He twisted and tugged until she cried out, her hands clinging to him as she came hard.

She crashed to the bed, spent, but she saw his arm reach out to snag a condom before he was inside her, fucking her. She laid there, willing to let him do whatever he needed to after getting her off so perfectly, but to her shock, her body began to respond.

No, she tried to tell him, I can't do this again. Not again. But she couldn't manage to speak the words, because she was too busy panting and mewling, and instead of trying to push him off, her arms were wrapping around his shoulders, holding him tight, and instead of trying to get out from under him, her legs were going up and around his waist.

It briefly crossed her mind that this might be how addiction started, but she couldn't focus on the thought for more than a second or two as the big bastard managed to throw her over that edge again. She screamed against his chest as she clung to him, felt him come with her, his hips jerking against her, burying his cock deeper inside her.

Even after coming like that, he was thoughtful, pulling out of her and moving off to the side before he crashed onto the bed. Thoughtful, but she still didn't like the loss of his heat and strength when he moved away.

Still panting, she rolled to her side and closer to him. He immediately reached for her, pulling her against his body. She could feel him trembling and knew he had no shame over it. She might have liked that more than anything else.

When she knew she had her voice back, she asked, "So I'm your girlfriend now?"

"Yup. We're going to attempt what's known in the nonintellectual world as a rel-a-tion-ship." He sounded the word out and Gwen struggled not to laugh.

"That was a little tricky," she accused. "Asking me at that particular moment."

"I know." Yet he didn't apologize, and that made her smile. Bears could be fascinatingly tricky, and she liked that she could no longer pigeonhole them as mere teddy bears with a honey fetish or psychotically unstable killers when frightened.

"Are we still going to be friends?" Because she liked him, too. No, really. She did.

"During my research I've discovered that friendship is a large part of it."

"Your research?"

"Yes. Knowledge is a powerful thing and can lead to many new discoveries."

Geek. "All right, but don't whine to me later when I piss you off." And she would piss him off. She always pissed them off.

"I won't. Besides, you make me goofy-happy."

Gwen leaned her head back so she could see his face. "Goofy-happy?"

"Yeah. When you can't stop smiling? That's what you do to me, Mr. Mittens. I figure feeling goofy-happy is completely worth the pissing-off risk."

Gwen nodded, realizing that at this moment, she completely understood what he meant by goofy-happy.

"Yeah," she said, smiling and loving the smile she got in return. "I guess you have a point."

Chapter 19

Gwen woke up starving and annoyed someone woke her up. But it was Lock, and she stopped feeling so annoyed. "What's up?"

He held out his cell phone. "It's for you."

"Me?" She'd forgotten Mitch still had her cell phone. It was probably him, too. Good. Let him find out she'd spent the night with a bear.

Sitting up, Gwen ran her hands through her hair and glanced at the clock on the side table. It was almost noon. She took the phone and said, "What?"

There was an incredibly long pause and when she didn't hear her brother say anything, Gwen squeaked out, "Blayne?"

"You're with the bear?"

"Blayne Thorpe—"

"Ha-ha-ha!"

Then her best friend disconnected the call. "*Goddamnit!*"

Laughing, Blayne closed her cell phone. When it rang again two seconds later, she yanked out the battery and threw it out of the wild dog's dining room.

"He's in!" she cheered, arms in the air, and the wild dogs who'd invited her over for Sunday brunch cheered and badly howled right along with her.

*   *   *

Lock watched as Gwen kept redialing Blayne. She must have tried six times before she threw the phone across the room, flipped over, and buried her head in the pillows.

"Is something amiss, my love?"

"Shut up!" she screamed with her head still buried in the pillows.

"Okay." Lock stretched out beside her and began kissing along her back, down her spine.

Gwen instantly scrambled away. "Oh, no, you don't! I need food before we can start all that again."

"Can't we eat after—"

"No!"

"We'll order in then."

"No, because we'll have to wait and you'll look at me with those big bear eyes and before I know it, I'll be flat on my back again, and afterward I'll be too weak to eat."

"You know I'll feed you."

She slipped off the bed, stumbling as her legs almost went out from under her. He reached for her but she backed away, holding her hand up to ward him off. "I'm taking a shower and then we're going out to eat."

"Like boyfriend and girlfriend?" he asked, making sure to look particularly eager.

"What are you? Twelve?"

"Perhaps in an alternate universe where bears rule."

She rolled her eyes. "Geek," she muttered, turning away from him.

Lock stood up. "I need a shower, too."

"Back off, Jersey. I go alone."

He let his shoulders slump. "Okay. Of course . . . it'll take us longer to get to the food."

"Don't even." She headed to his bathroom.

Should he mention he had a second bathroom? Nah. "I thought you were hungry."

"Fine. But don't touch me!"

Should he mention that the shower was almost too small for him alone? Nah. "Okay. I'll try not to."

Mitch watched his mother file her nails at the kitchen table. "You know, Ma, you don't seem real upset that Gwenie didn't come with me."

"I'm disappointed. I miss my Gwenie."

Funny, she didn't *look* disappointed. "If you miss her so much, tell her she has to come back home. Tell her she can't just walk away from her Pride."

"Oh, baby-boy, you know how your sister is when she makes up her mind." She studied her nails for a moment, then went back to filing. "She's an adult and can do what she likes."

"You didn't have that attitude when Patty Anne took off."

"Because Patty Anne can't handle living on her own. She can barely handle *not* setting herself on fire when she makes soda bread. *My* Gwenie doesn't have that problem."

"Because she hates soda bread?"

Roxy glanced at her son over her reading glasses. It was still early—for them—barely noon, so she'd yet to put in her contacts. She looked more . . . *motherly* with her glasses on and less Rockin' Roxy as the neighborhood kids called her.

"You don't consider Gwen part of the Pride, do you?" He'd had that thought since his mother had come to New York and then left again without Gwen. Before that moment, he'd never considered it—even when Gwen had told him as much over the years.

"My daughter," Roxy answered, her gaze still focused on her nails, "has no constraints on her. She can do whatever she wants as long as she has the guts to follow through."

"But she doesn't belong here. Just like I don't." Although he didn't belong because the males born to a Pride never stayed with that Pride. Some were bartered off, although that mostly happened in the richer Prides, but most left when they hit eighteen and found a Pride of their own or, like Mitch, a life. Yet it had never occurred to Mitch that Gwen wasn't considered part of the Pride, if for no other reason than she was Roxy O'Neill's daughter. Yet even without that, Gwen had lived her life for the Pride, she'd taken care of them, helped them, and at least eighty percent of the gang fights she found herself in the middle of was because of her cousins. How could they not make her part of the Pride? Hell . . . how could they not put her in charge of it? Just because she wasn't full lion?

Roxy looked up from her nails and leveled gold eyes on her son. "The O'Neills will always be your blood, always your *family*. For you and Gwen. And we always protect our own, whether you're in the Pride or not." Roxy smiled at him. "Now how about waffles for breakfast? Or is too late for breakfast?"

Mitch rested back in his chair. "Maybe too late for breakfast, but it's never too late for waffles."

"Good."

A newspaper landed in the middle of the kitchen table and his Aunt Marie sat down across from him, taking the seat his mother had just vacated, with a glass of orange juice in her hand. "Morning, handsome."

"Hey, Aunt Marie."

"Where's your girl?"

"Sleeping."

She smiled and began to read the business section.

Mitch watched his mother with her sudden urge to be domestic and his Aunt Marie not gossiping or yelling at him about leaving the toilet seat up again, and it hit him that they were relieved he hadn't brought Gwen home with him. That they wouldn't have to explain to her that she was family but would never be Pride. He felt anger for his baby sister and, more importantly, worry. Who'd take care of her now, if not her Pride? Who'd protect her? Did they understand that she'd be nothing more than another hybrid wandering the streets with no Pack, Pride, Clan of her own? Did they care?

Well, if nothing else, Gwenie had him. She had Bren. The Shaw brothers would protect Gwen O'Neill. It was perfect actually. She'd stay in New York, where they could keep an eye on her, but that bear . . . that bear was going to have to go. Between the grizzly's clearly unstable mother—Mitch was never one to trust those "intellectual types"—and Gwen's tendency to be squirrelly, the whole thing was a recipe for disaster. Mitch couldn't take the risk his baby sister's beautiful face would be mauled should that bear misplace his vat of honey or she startled him by hissing or something.

But first he needed to figure out who was helping Blayne in her evil plan to destroy Mitch's happiness . . .

Tamping down his growing rage that things weren't working out exactly as he wanted them to, Mitch brought up to his mother the one thing he'd sworn to Sissy he wouldn't. "So Gwen and Blayne got jumped while away at Brendon's on Labor Day weekend."

Not remotely surprised by this information—*am I the only who didn't know?*—Roxy nodded and pulled eggs and milk from the refrigerator. "I know. She told me. Couldn't hide that limp from me."

"Her leg healed up nice, though, huh, Rox?" Marie asked.

"Better than I would have thought from one of those Jersey doc-in-a-box centers."

"Yeah." Mitch scratched his chin, watched his mother walk back over to the counter. "But did Gwenie mention she was jumped by the McNelly Pack?"

When the eggs and milk hit the floor and his aunt's juice sprayed across the room, Mitch leaned back in his chair and reminded his mother, "Uncle Cally warned you McNelly would *never* let that go."

It wasn't until the waitress slammed the food down in front of her that Gwen opened her eyes.

"Don't worry," Lock told her while he reached for the ketchup. "You weren't snoring."

She sneered but kept her fangs in, since it was a full-human restaurant. "It would be your fault if I was snoring."

Lock grinned around the burger in his mouth. He seemed to

be a regular in this place. The waitress didn't blink an eye when he ordered four of their "Big Enuf 2 Kill a Man" Burgers. But the way the same waitress eyed her, Gwen got the feeling he'd always come in alone before, and the waitress was hoping she'd one day be the one sitting on the other side of the table with him.

Too bad. He's with me, and apparently I'm his girlfriend.

For the moment, anyway.

Gwen gave a big yawn before she dug into her pancakes. It was almost two o'clock, but she'd been all geared up about getting some breakfast. Thankfully, this diner sold breakfast twenty-four hours a day.

"You knew them, didn't you?" she asked.

"Knew who?"

"The guys in that blue van from last night. You knew them."

"Probably."

She didn't mention the Unit, because she didn't have to. Mitch had told her once what they did. Portraying prey to lure out the full-human hunters who focused on shifters—and then killing them. "It's been three years. They're still following you?"

"Maybe. There's been a few problems lately with former members, so they may be checking up on me."

He wiped his hands on a napkin now that he'd finished devouring those four burgers in record time and dug into his basket of fries, leaving it in the middle of the table to share with Gwen.

He pulled out his cell phone and Gwen tensed, thinking it was Blayne again. Lock let out a sigh after reading a text message, glanced at Gwen, and asked, "Would you mind if we hit a bar after we're done here?"

"A few hours with me and already you need a stiff drink?"

He grinned. "No. But I figure you could use a little more rest before we head back to my place."

And damn him . . . he was right.

Lock walked into the Jersey bar with Gwen behind him. He'd given her what Ric called "The Speech" when they'd driven over. "They're mostly full-humans there. Don't talk to anybody. Don't

look at anybody. If someone moves toward you, let me know
and I'll deal with them."

He'd practically grown up in this bar and he'd seen enough
over the years to know what the lowlifes at the bar went for and
what they didn't. Lock had learned early that full-humans were
worse than any predators he'd ever encountered in the wild, and
being in the military had only driven that belief home. Yet it wasn't
what was in the main bar that he wanted. It was in the back
room.

As soon as they entered, every full-human eye turned their
way. They immediately turned away from Lock's direct gaze as
they always did, but they all latched on to Gwen the second after
that. He popped his jaw and those who'd watched him grow
from five-foot nothing to what he was now instantly refocused
on their drinks or racing forms. A few of the newer, younger
ones were unaware of past incidents and their gazes stayed right
on Gwen. Lock could see them debating whether she'd be worth
the fight—and she was. For him.

Gwen, being a true feline, seemed not to notice anyone or
anything. She moved casually through the bar, her gaze examining the framed pictures tacked to the wall and the ancient juke-
box shoved into the corner. But as they neared the hallway
leading to the backroom, a new full-human Lock had never seen
before spun his bar stool around and made a move to stand. It
wasn't that Gwen turned to look at him. It was that only Gwen's
head turned to look at him. A good 180 degrees if Lock were to
guess. She didn't say a word, she didn't hiss, she didn't do anything because that one move was all it took.

Freaked out, the full-human spun his stool right back around
and faced the bar again. Smirking, Gwen moved into the hallway,
and together they walked to the last door. Gwen reached for the
doorknob, but Lock pushed her hand away and shook his head.
He raised his fist and knocked. Two times. Pause. Two times.
Pause. Three times.

A minute passed and the door slowly opened. The seven-two

glaring Scotsman stared down at Gwen, and Lock felt her press her body closer to his. Not that he blamed her. He could see her nostrils flare as she caught the scent of a bear-filled room. The grizzly raised his gaze and the scowl turned into an enormous grin.

"Lachlan, my boy!"

Lock grinned back. "Hi, Uncle Nevin."

Gwen discreetly let out the breath she'd been holding. They were related. Thank Christ, they were related! For a minute there, she'd thought Lock had lost his ever-loving mind bringing her to a bear den. But the way his uncles descended on him, she realized Lock was greatly loved here.

"You're looking fine, boy. Fine."

"Thanks." He grabbed Gwen's hand and pulled her forward. Although she felt like running, she plastered on a fake smile instead. If she could handle his parents, she could handle his uncles.

"This is Gwen. Gwen, this is my Uncle Nevin, my Uncle Duff, my Uncle Hamish, and my Uncle Calum."

"His *Scottish* uncles," Calum said, bowing low from the waist. "The MacRyrie bears. The loving, caring side of his family. Not those rough brutish Russian bears, the Baranovas."

"Don't let Mom hear you talking crap about her family . . . again."

Calum took Gwen's hand and kissed the back of it. "And such a beauty you are, dear Gwen."

Lock pushed his uncle aside. "Lay off."

"I was greeting her properly."

"Yeah. Right."

Lock's Uncle Duff moved behind Gwen and sniffed her neck. "Mmm. She smells like the sweetest honey."

"That's shampoo," Lock said, moving on Duff. "And don't crowd her."

"Who's crowding her?" Hamish, who seemed to be the youngest, asked. They all seemed to have held up well for men in their late fifties and early sixties. He sat on the round table in the middle of the room and added, "We're trying to get a better look at her, is all."

"Where do you come from, sweet Gwyneth?"

"It's Gwendolyn," Lock corrected Calum. "And she's from Philly."

"Well we can't hold that against her."

Gwen laughed while Nevin rested his butt on the table, his arms crossed. "And who are your kin in Philly, dearest Gwendolyn?"

"The O'Neills."

"A lioness? You seem too pretty to be a mere lioness."

"I'm half lioness, half tiger. A tigon, if you want to be technical."

Calum raised a brow. "Ahhh. The delicious fruit of forbidden love."

Gwen laughed harder and Lock pulled her against him. "All right, that's enough. Leave her alone."

"What's wrong with you, boy?" Calum asked. "You're not attached to this one, are you?"

"Attached enough to keep her away from you."

"That's because you have the sense of your dear mother," Hamish laughed.

"And we're not staying long. You said you wanted to see me, so I'm here. What's up?"

The uncles exchanged glances and then Calum said, "Your father's birthday is coming up in December."

"Yes."

"We thought we'd throw him a party this year."

"No."

Duff crossed his arms over his chest. "Why not?"

"After what happened last time?"

"That was twenty years ago!"

"And Mom has not forgotten."

*   *   *

Apparently, it wasn't just Lock that Gwen had this effect on. His uncles were falling over themselves to be accommodating. Wiping off a chair so she could sit down, getting her a clean glass for her beer, and offering her some of their honey-wheat pretzels to munch on.

What Lock found really interesting was the way she giggled and fluttered those eyelashes like some average female. He'd thought she must have banged her head at some point and lost her mind until she said, "So what are you gentlemen doing with these cards?"

Nevin gathered the cards together and showed off his Vegas-learned shuffling skills. "Just a little five-card stud."

"Oooh. Can I play? I've always wanted to play."

"Gwen—"

She turned pleading, wide cat eyes at him. "Please, Lock? Can I?"

He was so stunned she was asking his permission to do *anything*, he could only manage to say, "Uh . . ."

"Thanks."

She dropped a wad of cash big enough to choke a goat on the table. "Is this enough?"

Before Lock could blink, three of his uncles had grabbed chairs and quickly sat down.

Lock crouched next to her and whispered in her ear, "Where the hell did you get that cash from?"

"I don't know. Some guy outside." He'd be shocked if it was anybody but Gwen. "I didn't like the way he glared at you."

"So you took his cash?"

"It's a skill."

"Out of the way, boy." Calum pushed him back. "We need to teach sweet little Gwen here how to play poker."

"I'm not sure you want to—"

"Don't argue with me, boy."

Hamish shoved a racing form in Lock's hand, then grabbed his arm. "While they do that, I need to talk to you outside for a minute." He smiled and winked at Gwen. "We'll be right back, gorgeous."

She giggled—*giggled!*—and focused back on the rest of his uncles. "So . . . um . . . how does this game work?" she asked sweetly.

While the rest of his uncles practically fell over each other in an attempt to "assist" Gwen, Hamish pulled Lock out the back door that led to the alley behind their bar. More than once, his uncles had used this door to get out during police raids. The fact that none of his father's brothers were in prison still amazed the entire MacRyrie family. Lock loved each and every one, but the only difference between his uncles and the average felon was that the MacRyrie brothers had never done any hard time.

"What'cha bring the girl for?" Hamish asked once he'd closed the thick metal door.

"Why wouldn't I bring Gwen?"

"Why do you always answer a question with a question?"

"Why are you always upset when I do?"

Hamish gritted his teeth and briefly closed his eyes. "I swear, some days you are just like your old man."

"I no longer find that an insult." Lock shrugged. "So what's going on?" He knew something must be up, because his uncles had never cared before when he brought a girl over . . . of course it had been more than ten or twelve years since he had. And then he'd only brought the girls to impress them with his bad-boy side—important since he didn't really have a bad-boy side—but he'd brought Gwen because he hadn't been ready to let her go. And he wasn't sure when he would be.

His uncle motioned him farther into the alley. It was one of the few in New York that didn't have a few people living in it— even before they'd "cleaned up" the city—but that was because who'd be crazy enough to set up house near bears? Even full-humans who didn't know the MacRyries were bears knew better.

Hamish crouched down and pulled back a large piece of cardboard. Heart sinking, Lock crouched beside him.

"How long?"

"We found it this morning."

"Is this the first?"

"No. The third one in the last five months. Always male . . . always a mixed breed."

This one was a wolf-coyote mix. Lock leaned in closer. "He hasn't been shot."

"No. I'm thinking he died from the bites." Hamish let out a breath. "This isn't hunters, is it?"

"No. They sometimes use dogs for tracking, but these bites are too deep for dog bites. And they wouldn't go for such lethal spots. Hunting dogs only track the prey, corner them, but these wounds are to kill." Lock sat back on his heels. "These are fight marks."

"The first two, we got rid of the bodies ourselves. But third time's the charm, ya know?"

"I'm glad you told me."

"You gonna take care of it?"

"No. I don't have any connections any more. No authorization to do anything. And lately the Unit has been watching me, I'm still not sure why."

" 'Cause of this?"

"Doubt it. We were never sent out on assignment over a hybrid." Mostly because the other breeds didn't care about the hybrids.

"So we should just get rid of the body, then?"

"No. Don't touch anything." Lock pulled out his cell phone and hit his speed dial. "There's someone who does have connections." By the second ring, Lock heard that familiar voice through the phone. "Ric . . . we've got a problem."

Gwen set up her cash into little piles based on denomination. The MacRyrie bears glowered as she did, since all that money she was organizing had been theirs.

"You certainly did pick up the game real quick," Nevin observed.

She smiled and kept piling and counting.

"You said you're an O'Neill?" Calum asked.

"Yes."

"And exactly who is your mother, sweetheart? Maria? Mary Patrice?"

"Roxy."

And, as she expected, the four males turned and now glowered at their nephew.

"You idiot!" Hamish yelled.

Lock looked up from the racing form he'd been studying and marking for the last two hours. Whatever he and his Uncle Hamish had discussed while they were gone, it had bothered the bear, but he was doing a good job of hiding it. She didn't think it had anything to do with her, because his uncles seemed to like her . . . and Ric was outside that back door. She'd scented him and a few others nearly ninety minutes ago. Since the wolf didn't come inside and Lock didn't mention him or go out to greet him, she knew they were hiding something. Did they really think she wouldn't notice? Or did they think that their metal door and thick concrete walls blocked her senses? Well, whatever. She'd just get it out of the grizzly later.

"What did I do?" Lock demanded.

"Roxy O'Neill is her *mother*? You could have warned us!"

"Warn you?" Lock frowned. "Why?"

"You bring a baby shark into our den and it doesn't occur to you to mention the baby shark's mother?"

"That analogy makes no sense to me."

"Anybody have something I can carry all this money in?" The bears returned their glares to Gwen. "What did I say?" she asked, attempting to keep it innocent.

"Here." Calum slammed a bank-deposit bag on the table. "Take your winnings and go, feline."

"Where did the love go?" Gwen pouted.

"It went with our money," Nevin muttered.

Duff snatched the racing form out of Lock's hand, scowled, and turned accusing brown bear eyes on his nephew. "What is this?"

"Uh . . ."

"You were supposed to mark winners and times and everything else we need on the races."

"What did he write?" Hamish looked over his brother's shoulder, easy for him since Duff was only about seven-one. "A door? You drew a door?"

"For Dad's birthday."

Gwen stopped putting her money in the bag. "You're giving your father a picture of a door for his birthday?" And she'd thought Mitch marking up pages in her copy of *Vogue* and telling her, "This is what I'd get you for your birthday if I had money" had been cheap.

"I'm not giving him a *drawing* of a door."

"Then what are you giving him?" Gwen liked Brody and she wouldn't have Lock give him some half-ass birthday gift.

"Don't worry about it."

"But I do worry about it. Because you're male and instinctively lame."

"There are those claws she's been hiding," Duff chuckled.

"Well?" Gwen pushed, ignoring Lock's uncles.

"I've got it covered."

Hamish folded his arms over his chest. Or, perhaps it was more like his massive arms over that massive chest. Huge didn't even begin to describe the size of these men. She knew she should feel uncomfortable around them, but she didn't. Not anymore. And honestly? She'd never felt safer in her life. "You haven't told her?"

"Quiet."

"Told me what?"

Calum grinned. "What Mr. Sensitive Bear does in his spare time."

"Shut up."

"Which is what exactly?" Gwen pushed.

"It's nothing." Lock motioned toward the door. "Let's go."

Gwen rested her hands on the table and began to tap her fingers. She tapped and she stared.

"You can stop that right now," Lock said. "Because there's nothing to tell."

Gwen kept tapping. Gwen kept staring.

"It's not going to work."

Tap. Stare. Tap. Stare.

"I don't have to tell you anything. I don't owe you an explanation. So let it go."

Gwen never changed her expression, she never said a word, and she never stopped tapping her nails.

With a short roar, Lock snatched the racing form back from Duff. "Fine! This will allow me to take care of something tonight anyway. Now move your skinny butt!"

Gwen shoved the rest of the money in the pouch and headed toward the door. Lock stopped her.

"Where is it?"

"Where's what?"

He raised a brow—and she now knew where he'd gotten *that* particular expression from—and Gwen gave a short snort of disgust before handing him the small wad of money. Small compared to what she now had.

"This better be all of it."

"Like that guy would know one way or the other." He probably didn't even know Gwen had taken his money, and she wouldn't have thought about giving it back to him if it wasn't for Lock. To her way of thinking, the guy owed Lock big for being so gracious.

Lock opened the door and motioned her out.

"We'll see you soon, Lovely Gwen."

She turned to wave at the MacRyrie bears, but the door had already slammed closed and Lock stood in front of her, glaring.

"What?" she demanded. "I like them."

"Figures." He spun her around and pushed her. "Come on. If we're going to do this, let's do this."

CHAPTER 20

It was bad enough he let his uncles goad him into things he didn't want to do, but now he was letting Gwen do it, too. And all she did was stare at him with those gold eyes.

Yet he couldn't shake the feeling that maybe, just maybe, he wanted to show Gwen. That he wanted to let her in to the part of his life that only a chosen few had access to.

Lock pulled into one of two parking spaces at the warehouse and shut off the motor. They sat in silence for several minutes until Gwen asked, "So what exactly was going on behind your uncles' bar?"

Surprised by her question, Lock could only stare at her.

"What?" she demanded. "You think I'm stupid? You disappear with your uncle, then Ric shows up, but he never comes inside. No one discusses what's going on out there, and even though everyone is trying to be quiet, I can still hear 'em all out there. And I know I smelled something dead in that alley."

Realizing that trying to get anything over on Gwen would be futile, Lock shrugged and said, "They found a shifter corpse behind the bar. And before you ask," he said when she opened her mouth, "no, my uncles didn't have anything to do with it."

"Someone sending them a message?"

"Doubtful. It's no one they know and it's happened randomly

over the last five or six months. Chances are it's just a good dumping ground."

"For what?"

"So far it's been hybrids. Male wolf mixes."

"Hunted?"

"I don't think so."

"You worried?"

"Don't know yet."

"Why bring in Ric?"

"It's the kind of thing that gets him all up in arms. He's a big believer in protecting all shifters, full-blood or mixed." He took her hand. "That being said, I want you to be careful. At least until we know what's going on. You *and* Blayne."

"No worries there. We're always careful. We have no choice. I'm an O'Neill and she's the best friend of an O'Neill. Now are we going inside to see what your uncles were talking about or are you hoping I'll completely forget and you can totally puss out?"

Dropping her hand, Lock snarled, "Fine. Get out."

Lock stepped from the SUV and slammed his door. He walked to the warehouse and unlocked the door, shutting off his alarm system and heading inside, assuming Gwen would follow.

Gwen stood in the doorway and gazed up at the high ceiling. The place was an old warehouse, but even in New Jersey it couldn't be cheap to own or rent a place like this, even for storage. Which she was sure it was with all the furniture lying around.

And nice furniture, too. *Really* nice.

Captivated by the first thing that caught her eye, Gwen wandered over to a sweet little side table. It was made entirely of wood, and she was amazed at the craftsmanship. Gwen crouched down in front of it and ran her hand over the smooth wood.

"Well?"

She heard tone from the bear behind her, but she chose to ignore it. Besides, the more she touched the end table, the more she wanted it. "Where did you get this from?" When he didn't answer right away, Gwen glanced over her shoulder and was surprised by how uptight he looked. "What's wrong?" She stood, gently placing her hand on his forearm. "What's the problem?"

"Nothing." He shrugged and admitted, "I made it."

Gwen looked down at the table and back at the bear. "No, seriously."

"I am serious. I made it. And I was drawing a front door for the house. Dad's been wanting a new one."

Gwen reached into Lock's back pocket and pulled out the racing form. She'd grown up looking at these and helping her own uncles with their winnings and losses. It surprised her that she and Lock had that much in common. It surprised her even more what was drawn on that racing form.

It wasn't simply a door, as the MacRyrie bears had put it. The design was intricate, beautiful. As someone who worked with carpenters and construction people most of her life, Gwen knew when she was looking at something amazing. But could he actually create this?

Gwen stepped closer to the end table and examined it again. Straightening, she walked down to the next piece. A rolltop desk that looked like something out of the nineteenth century but had been kept in impeccable shape. She pushed the rolltop up and then down. She studied every inch carefully.

"*You* did this?" she pushed, really not sure she believed him, but he looked so nervous and embarrassed, she was beginning to realize he wasn't lying. And if he could do this, then she doubted the door would be much of a challenge for him.

"Yeah. I did."

"*This* is your hobby? The woodworking you like to do?"

"Yeah."

Momentarily speechless, she stepped to another piece. This one a long dining table that she knew her mother would kill for.

"Hobby?"

"Why do you keep saying that?"

She whirled on him. "Because hobby means whittling. Or bird-houses. Remember the birdhouses?

"*You* said birdhouses. I never said birdhouses."

"It means," she went on, ignoring him, "a badly put-together table that your friends only pull out of the garage when they know you're coming over. This—" she gestured around the room at all the amazing pieces surrounding her "—this isn't that."

Without waiting for him to say anything else, she ran her hand over the dining table. It looked similar to the table in his parents' house. No wonder he'd gotten so weird when she'd asked about it. He'd made it! And although this table had a similar style, she could see a marked difference in skill level between the two. He was growing, getting better, becoming a true artisan at his craft.

"Okay, so how much for the table?"

Lock's head tilted to the side. "How much?"

"Yeah. Ma would love this and Christmas is coming up."

"Uh . . ."

"And don't try and out-haggle me. I've learned from the best."

"I don't haggle."

"All right. How much then?" She gestured to herself with her hands. "Hit me with it. I can handle it."

"Gwen . . ." he seemed so confused ". . . you can have it."

"Have it?" Gwen looked at the table that was slowly going from Christmas gift to her mother to Christmas gift to Gwenie.

"Lock, I can't take this. I mean you'll lose what? Four, five grand for it? Okay, it's true, the sex is great and all but four or five grand? That's a lot of money for the sex to live up to."

"I don't mean . . ." He dropped his head but she saw the smile. He wasn't laughing at her, it was a surprised smile. A smile of pure pleasure. "What I mean is I don't sell my work. At least not yet."

It took her a moment to understand him. "You don't sell your work? At all?"

"No."

"Why? What are you waiting for?"

He shrugged. "I'm waiting for it to be . . . better."

"Better?" Wow. The man had higher standards than she realized. "Lock, I mean this in the nicest way possible, but . . . you're an idiot."

"How do you mean that in the nicest way possible?" Lock demanded, *never* knowing which direction Gwen would come from.

"I mean, you're an idiot if you're not selling this stuff. And I don't mean at yard sales. I'm talking about selling it to a furniture specialist shop. Where rich people go. You want rich people to buy your shit because they tell their rich friends and they tell their rich friends and on and on."

"None of these are ready for sale," he argued. "These are all just . . . drafts."

"Drafts?"

"Right. Because I'm still learning."

"Okay. So you're saying everything isn't perfect yet."

"It doesn't need to be perfect." Just as close as humanly possible. "But I have to be comfortable getting money for it."

"Fair enough." She pointed at the dining table. "So what needs work on this?"

Lock walked over and refreshed his memory on the dining table he'd made a year ago. "Um . . . this." He crouched down and pointed. "See those crossrails? They're slightly . . . off."

"Off?"

"Uh-huh." He stood up. "I'll make another one and try and fix that."

"Right. Okay. And you said you had to take care of something here, right? What was that?"

"Since my uncles goaded me into coming here, I figured I could grab a chair I made for Jess, and we could drop it off at her place. If I give her the chair now, she can't guilt me into going to her baby shower later . . . and she'll try." Oh, she would try.

"Can I see the chair?"

"Sure." He walked her over to the chair and took off the drop cloth he kept over it to protect the wood.

Gwen studied it for several long moments before she dropped her head into her hands and groaned.

"Was it the Viking runes?" he asked, wincing. "Too much? I wouldn't put it on anyone else's chair, but this is Jess and she's—"

"You're not charging for this?" Gwen cut in.

"No." He looked at the rocking chair, admiring the lines but easily spotting all the flaws. "I made it as a gift."

"Let's say you didn't make it for a gift, but you simply made it. Would you sell it then?"

Lock frowned. "Probably not."

"Another crossrail problem?"

Lock laughed. "No. Not this time. It's just . . . I'm not real happy with this joint. Right here."

She nodded. "Is that a problem that would have Jess falling on her ass when the chair broke?"

Insulted, Lock said, "Of course not. I'd never give her anything that wasn't absolutely sturdy and reliable."

"So it'll last, let's say, a hundred years or so?"

"More than that, I hope. And it can handle at least fifteen hundred pounds." He knew this because he'd sat in it as bear. If it could handle his weight, it could handle a pregnant little wild dog.

Abruptly, Gwen paced away from him.

"What?" he asked, already planning to start a new chair for Jess tomorrow. "Is it that bad?"

"No, Lock. It's perfect." She whirled on him again, but he was glad she didn't do that 180-degree thing with her head instead. "But, hon, I was right . . . you're an idiot."

"Why am I an idiot?"

"You're an idiot because you're not selling this."

"It's a gift."

"Not the chair, you mongrel. I'm talking about all of it. You have a fortune sitting here."

"No," he said, even as his pulse raced. "It's not—"

"What? Perfect? Art is supposed to have imperfections. That's what makes great art." She stopped, blinking in surprise. "I can't believe I remembered that from Sister Ann's stupid art history class. And let me tell ya . . . not exactly an 'A' student with her."

"Not a big art history fan?"

"Not a big fan of Sister Ann. She was the one who started all the nuns and Father Francis calling me the devil's whore and Blayne the devil's whore's lackey, which did nothing but hurt Blayne's feelings."

As always, amused by Gwen's random comments, Lock smiled as he reached down to lift up the chair he would be giving Jess, but Gwen placed her hand on the seat, halting him.

"Wait."

He looked up at her.

"Are you telling Jess you made this?"

Immediately, Lock shook his head at the uncomfortable thought. "No."

"Why not?"

"I don't want to."

"Don't be silly. She'll appreciate it more if you tell her."

"I don't want to tell her."

"So you'll lie to her."

"I won't have to lie to her. She never asks, so there's nothing to admit to."

Gwen's eyes narrowed the tiniest bit, and he knew he was in trouble. "How much stuff have you given her?"

"A few things," he hedged.

"And you haven't charged her for any of it?"

Her voice was even and controlled, but he could still hear the outrage in it. "No. I haven't charged her. And I don't plan to start now."

As always when annoyed, Gwen placed her hands on her hips, those Philly girl nails of hers tapping against her cargo pants. "What is your deal with her?" Before he could answer, she held up her hand and went on. "What if she asks? Then will you tell her?"

"She won't ask."

"But if she does?"

"She won't.

Her eyes flashed wide in warning. "But. If. She. Does?"

"Breaking one simple sentence into several sentences won't change the fact that she won't ask. She never asks and, like most dogs, Jess is a creature of habit."

Gwen suddenly relaxed, which made Lock tense up instead.

"How about a bet then?" she asked.

"I don't gamble."

"Because once you start you can never stop or because you have moral issues with it?"

"Because I hate to lose."

She smiled. "That's valid."

"Your other two options weren't valid?"

"Valid but a little more depressing."

Not sure where she was going with this, Lock rested his arms against the back of the chair. "Okay. So what bet?"

"We take your chair over to Jess's and if she asks where you got it from—you tell her."

"No."

"Again with the 'no'?"

"Gwen, I saw you clean out my uncles. You're what we in the high-stakes military game refer to as tricky." She laughed and Lock smiled but was honest. "I know you, Gwen. You're going to slip her a note or spell out my name in semaphore."

She frowned. "I don't even know what semaphore is. And I swear not to say a word about you making the chair."

"Yeah, right."

"Seriously. No looks, notes, sema-whatevers, or smoke signals to imply you had anything to do with its creation. I won't say, write, or mouth one word about who made this chair or any of the other furniture you've stupidly given rich dogs for no pay."

He couldn't believe she wasn't letting that go. "I like giving Jess stuff. She's a good friend."

"Yeah," she said, turning away. "A good friend with big perky tits and a round, wild dog ass, but I'm sure that has nothing to do with it."

"Wait . . . what?"

"Nothing." She headed toward the door. "Let's go."

"Wait." She stopped and faced him. "The bet?"

"What about it?"

"Aren't you supposed to have stakes for a bet?"

"According to the bookie I had in tenth grade . . . yeah."

No wonder she'd beaten his uncles at cards. "You had a bookie in the tenth—"

"We'll keep it simple. If she asks about the chair, I win and you give me that dining table free of charge."

"I was going to—"

"If they say nothing and you win . . ." She shrugged. "I'll fix your plumbing for free."

Lock frowned. "What makes you think I have plumbing problems?"

Gwen silently walked across the large room to the one and only bathroom, far off in the corner. She disappeared inside and flushed the toilet. Lock cringed when the pipes shook and shuddered throughout the entire building.

She walked back to him and stared.

"All right!" he yelled over the shuddering pipes, flinching when the noise abruptly stopped and his voice ended up echoing around the room. "It's a bet."

The front door opened and Gwen could see through the metal-and-glass security door the eyes of wild dog pups. They didn't notice her, however—too busy staring up at Lock.

"Hi," he said, keeping his voice low and even. "Your moms home?"

The cutest little girl with big blond curls turned and yelled, "*Mommmmmmm! Bearrrrrrrrrrrrrrrrrrrrrrrrrrrrrrrrrrrrrrrr!*"

"There's a welcome," Gwen teased Lock.

"And it only gets better."

Sabina, the Russian wild dog that even Blayne called "prickly," came to the door and unlocked it, pushing it open with one hand. "Why are you here?"

"To see Jess."

"Will you be long? We are going to eat soon and I don't want us all starving like peasants while we wait for you."

The woman, with her thick Russian accent, did simply reek of warmth and hospitality, didn't she? Gwen knew gang members who were nicer to crackheads who owed them money.

"No. We won't be long. I just want to give something to Jess."

"Then come." Sabina started to turn away than turned back, her left forefinger raised. "We will not feed you, bear. We don't have enough food. You and the cat must starve."

Gwen hissed and Lock urged Gwen forward with his hand against her back. "That's fine."

Sabina went back into the house and Gwen asked, "Is it only fear that keeps you from tearing her head off that puny dog body?"

"Pretty much. Because even missing her head, I'm not sure she'd actually die."

They stepped into the long hallway and found more children than had originally been there. They stood around Lock, staring up at him with wide eyes. They were waiting for something.

Jess walked up to them and raised her brows at Lock.

"I'm not a dancing bear," he complained.

"Please?" Jess pushed lightly, giving him a smile that made Gwen want to deck her.

Appearing more embarrassed than Gwen had seen him, Lock looked down at the children—and roared.

The children screamed and took off running, scattering in all directions while Jess clapped and laughed.

"And today's Lack of Dignity award goes to . . ." Gwen muttered.

"Shut up."

"They love the roar!" Jess enthused, before her attention was quickly snagged to what was resting on the stairs. "What's that out there?"

"It's for you," Lock explained. "A little something in honor of—"

"Getting knocked up," Gwen cut in.

Instead of being insulted, Jess clapped her hands together again. "Gifts for me! Gifts for me!" she cheered, making Gwen and Lock laugh.

"Show me," Jess insisted.

Lock went back outside and grabbed the drop cloth–covered chair; together they followed Jess into the living room. Setting the chair down, Lock pulled off the cover and stepped back. Gwen could tell from the look on his face that he was nervous as hell about his gift. She didn't know why. It was exquisite.

Jess gazed at the chair, May and Sabina coming up behind her. Then they all gazed at the chair. Gazed and said nothing.

It was a rocking chair, large and roomy. Definitely too big for Jess alone, but once her baby had gotten much bigger, the chair would be a perfect fit for mother and child to sit in together. Maybe while Jess read to him or her. Gwen could picture it perfectly in her head and it made her smile.

"Do you like it?" Lock asked. "If you don't, I can—"

Jess held her hand up. "It's . . . perfect." She swallowed and walked around the chair. "Really. Perfect."

Gwen almost rubbed her hands together in villain-style glee. *Excellent.*

Lock watched Gwen closely as she leaned forward, studied the arms of the chair, said, "Huh," and leaned back.

While all three women peered at her, Sabina spoke first. "What was that?"

Gwen blinked, giving that same innocent expression she'd given Lock's uncles. "What was what?"

"That 'huh.'"

"Nothing."

"You lie, feline. Tell me what you know!"

"Y'all," May cut in. "No reason for everybody to get crazy." She ran her hand across the back of the chair. "Maybe this chair is simply not to Gwen's tastes. If she's tasteless."

Sabina didn't seem to be buying that as she walked around the chair.

"What are these?" Sabina demanded, pointing at the wide arms of the chair. "Cut into the wood."

"Those are Nordic runes," Lock explained.

"Nordic?" Gwen asked. "Oh! You mean like Nazis?"

Turning on her, Lock exploded. "*Nazis?*"

"Hey, hey," she said, holding up her hands. "It was just a question."

"You give us chair owned by Nazis?" Sabina demanded.

Lock couldn't believe this. "Of course I didn't!"

"You are Nazi lover!" Sabina accused.

"I am not!"

"Everybody calm down!" May let out a huff. "This is ridiculous. We all know Lock. Been knowin' him for years. He's not a Nazi lover. Are you, Lock?"

"Of course I'm—"

"So you say," Sabina cut in. "But you tell us nothing of this chair. Perhaps it was made by Nazi lover."

Lock glared at Gwen. "This is ridiculous."

Gwen gave the smallest of shrugs, a tiny smile on her lips.

"Ridiculous or not," Sabina said, "our Jess will not sit in your Nazi chair until we know where you got it from."

Jess, who'd been about to put her butt in the chair, stood back up. "Oh, come on!"

"Do you want to promote Nazism?" Sabina demanded of her Alpha.

"Jesus Christ!"

"Blasphemy," May muttered under her breath.

"Shut up." Jess folded her arms over her chest. "Lock, just tell us where you got the goddamn chair from so we can stop all this foolishness."

Lock's jaw popped as he kept his focus on Gwen. How the hell did she manage it? For the last three years he'd been giving his stuff to Jess and her Packmates and not once had they asked where he got it from. They'd never cared, usually too busy amusing themselves with the gift instead. But without breaking her word, Gwen had gotten them to do what they'd never done before!

Understanding his body language more than she should this far in to their relationship, Gwen explained to him, "I've been best friends with Blayne Thorpe since ninth grade and she's more dog than wolf. So do the math, Jersey boy."

"Well?" Sabina pushed. "Tell us where you got this or get your Nazi chair out of here."

"It's not—" Lock stopped, took a deep breath in an attempt to remain calm and keep the embarrassment at bay. "It's a combination rocking chair and Viking throne," he explained. "I looked at some of the old *Conan the Barbarian* art and stole some ideas for the chair from that and combined it with a standard rocking chair design. Hence the *Viking* runes—not Nazi."

Sabina looked at the chair and back at Lock. "I do not understand."

But Jessica did. "You made this, Lock?"

He shrugged, livid with Gwen. Could he wring her neck and get away with it—legally? "Yeah. I made this." He cleared his throat. "But if you don't like it, I can definitely—"

Lock's words abruptly halted as Jess burst into tears, his gaze quickly swinging to Gwen's in panic, but all she could do was shrug helplessly.

"Jess," he began, desperate, "if you really don't like it, I can make you something else."

Jess took a step toward him, still sobbing, and raised her arms.

Lock briefly closed his eyes. "Jess, come on."

She slammed her foot down, her arms still raised. Lock glanced at Gwen again before he reached down and picked Jess up.

Gwen's eyes narrowed as Jess buried her face in his shoulder, her arms around his neck, and continued to sob.

Chewing her lip, May slowly moved around the chair and was about to sit down in it, when Jess's head snapped up.

"Your ass hits that chair and it's the last thing it'll ever do!"

"Oh, come on, Jess!" May begged. "Just let me sit in it."

"No! It's mine!" Jess rested her head against Lock's shoulder. "All mine. My throne of power. By this chair I rule."

"I can't believe you're being so selfish!"

"*Mine!*" Jess screamed.

Sabina slapped Lock's arm and pointed at the chair. "Make me one but with Russian words I will give you."

"Hey!" May snarled. "That's not fair."

"What is not fair?"

"Why should you get a chair first? *I'm* the one pregnant again. So if he's making another chair, it's gonna be for me!"

"You spawn like the salmon this bear eats," Sabina accused. "Why should you get something special for something you seem to do constantly?"

"Why? Because I'm creating the future leaders of the United States of America. You, however, are breeding thugs!" May smiled at Lock. "I'm sure Lock wouldn't mind making my chair first."

"He make your chair first in hell."

"Back off, Putin!"

"I pay," Sabina offered Lock, gripping his arm. "Three thousand for chair."

"I'll give him five thousand."

"Ten, hillbilly."

"Fifteen, Chekhov."

With Jess still in his arms, Lock stepped between them. "Stop it. Both of you. I can make you both chairs for—*owwww!*" He glared down at Gwen while a spot on his thigh throbbed from where the little psychopath had pinched him. "*What the hell was that for?*"

"I'll handle this," she said, grabbing hold of an arm from each wild dog and pulling them out of the living room. "You show Jess her new . . . uh . . . throne."

Lock glanced at the woman in his arms. She was no longer sobbing, but was now smiling and giving her best Queen Elizabeth wave to her nonexistent "people."

"I," she somberly intoned, not to Lock but her invisible "people," "as your ruler and sovereign, do thank you for this lovely throne."

She motioned to the chair. "You may now place me in my throne."

"You have got to be kidding me, Jessica."

"*Place me!*"

"All right. All right." Lock placed her in the chair and Jess leaned back, sighing and smiling. "I love it, Lock," she said. After she rocked back and forth a few times, she stopped and looked up at him again. "The other stuff you've given me. The desk, the dining table—where did you get those from?"

Lock let out a breath and wondered how Gwen could manage to cause so much trouble without really trying.

CHAPTER 21

"A ren't you a little interested in finding out how much—"
"No."
Lock got out of the SUV and slammed the door shut behind him. Gwen followed after him, trying to keep up as his long legs quickly took him across the parking garage interior.

"I didn't break my promise, ya know?"

"I know."

He slammed his hand against the elevator button and Gwen flinched, certain he was going to shove the entire wall back.

"Then I don't see why you're so ticked off."

"I don't like being embarrassed. Okay?"

"Then you shouldn't be hanging around me." Gwen blinked. "Wait. That came out wrong."

"I'm bettin' it didn't."

Gwen's mouth dropped open, shocked at the insult. And a little hurt.

"Fine," she finally said as the elevator doors creaked open. "I'll go back to the hotel then. I don't need this shit." She turned away from him, figuring she could take the stairs back to the street. But Lock caught hold of her denim jacket and hauled her into the elevator. It wasn't even a struggle for him. He simply caught hold of her and yanked her in like she was a bag of dirty laundry.

Christ! What was she thinking getting involved with a guy this strong? He seemed nice enough, but what if he wasn't? What if the whole shy, sweet bear thing was a sham and he was a dangerously unstable man-eater? Then what would she do?

The doors opened on the first floor and Gwen tried to walk out, but he put that Thor's Hammer he called an arm in front of her and pushed her back.

"If you're so mad at me, I don't know why you'd want me around."

He didn't answer her but pushed her out of the elevator when they got to the second floor. He walked behind her until they reached his apartment, his arm reaching around her to unlock the door, and he didn't move until she went inside. She walked away from him and into his living room.

Lock came in behind her and she gaped at the way he filled that large entryway.

"Look, I'm not mad at you," he said.

He wasn't? Holy shit! What about when he was? He would be eventually and then what? He'd snap her neck like a deer's? Crush her tiny, insignificant head with his bare hands?

"You're not mad?"

"No. I'm—" Snarling a little, he tore off his jacket and threw it at the couch. "I'm not used to people talking about my work. Looking at it. Knowing it's mine."

"Because you never told them."

"Because they'd talk about it!"

Oh, boy.

"They love your work."

"They were probably being nice. But now that I'm gone and they can really analyze it—"

Clearly he needed to face the harsh reality of his current situation, and Gwen was the kind of woman who'd give it to him. Besides, she was pretty sure she could make it to the window and out it before he ever got close to her.

"I got you five for the chairs. One chair for May and another for the Russian nutbag."

He blinked in surprise. "Five? Really?" He gave a small smile. "Wow. That's . . . that's really nice. That's a thousand bucks. That's—"

"No."

"No?"

"It's ten thousand."

Lock's entire body went rigid. "It's . . ."

"Ten thousand. Five grand apiece. And they've recently purchased the last building on their block, so the entire block is pretty much their territory. Anyway, they've already gutted part of it. Most will be more bedrooms, but they've started on a library for all their books. They had a guy who was going to design it for them, but they're firing him and hiring you. We're talking thousands of books that they have. I told them for that many shelves we're looking at at least six figures for the design and the building. They said that was fine and they want cherrywood or something equally dark and smooth."

Lock shook his head, took a step back, quickly gripping the archway with his hand to keep from falling back. Gwen was at his side in seconds, her arm around his waist and her free hand gripping his forearm.

"Can't breathe," he said. "Not breathing."

"It's okay. It's a panic attack. Blayne gets 'em all the time." She tugged him toward the couch and sat him down. She pressed his back down so his head was between his knees. "Don't worry. You're going to be fine."

He raised his head. "You don't understand."

"I do." She pressed him back down. Pulling off her jacket, she got on the couch behind him and pressed her chest against his back. She kneaded his neck with her fingers and kept him down with her weight. "This is what you've wanted all along, isn't it?" Because no one could do all that he had merely for a hobby. No way. "To create stuff with your hands, to make money from it. And now it's going to happen."

"It's not that easy."

"Why? What's holding you back?" *Other than himself.*

"This wasn't supposed to happen now. I was supposed to do the software thing for the next few years until I saved up enough money to retire. Like when I was forty-five or fifty. And then I was going to move out of New York and maybe up to New Hampshire or Massachusetts, where I'd work on my stuff full-time and at my discretion. No demands, no risks."

"Well, life has decided to speed up that little vision. And everything is a risk."

"But I had it all planned out." He looked at her over his shoulder, an out-of-control fear in those big brown eyes. "It's on paper."

No wonder people were fooled into thinking bears were these adorable, cuddly toys they could give food to and risk getting close to—because they were so damn cute!

"Yeah. I get it. I was there." She moved off his back and rested on her knees by his side, her arm around his shoulders. "I figured I'd be working for other guys and my Uncle Cally until I was about forty and then, if all went well and I'd built up a good enough name, I'd be able to open my own business. It was my goal, and it was miles off. And then here comes Blayne, tossing the opportunity of a lifetime into my lap. And I almost walked away from it. Because it meant leaving Philly and Ma and my family. Then it hit me . . . I couldn't walk away. This was the right time for me, even if I didn't want it to be. I'm not mated, no cubs, no mortgage. Nothing holding me back except my need to protect my mother from herself. I knew I had to take the chance. I'd never forgive myself if I didn't."

"Is that why your brother is riding you so hard? About this?"

Gwen blew out a breath. "Mitch has never taken me seriously. Not ever. So in his mind this is something cute and sweet between me and Blayne, but I need to get serious and go back to Philly and Ma. Until I do, he won't be happy."

"Well, you're not going back now." Lock sat up and she was glad to see some color had returned to his face, and that it wasn't the beet red it sometimes got when he was thoroughly embarrassed.

"I'm not?"

"If you go back, who's going to haggle for me?" He relaxed back into the couch and gazed up at the ceiling. "And we're not charging them five grand each for two rocking chairs."

"Rocking chairs created entirely by hand by the eminent local artist Lachlan MacRyrie." His gaze shot over to hers and Gwen didn't even flinch. "In three years' time those chairs will be worth four times as much. They're getting in early and should be damn glad they're getting the chairs that cheap."

"Not five."

"Fine then. Four."

"Gwen—"

"I'll go as low as three, but that's it. And if that Russian gives you a ton of crap she wants you to do, it goes back to five."

"Yeah, but—"

"I'm not arguing this with you. And you're going to let me handle the library estimates or that little wild dog will walk all over you."

Lock snorted. "Sabina?"

"I'm talking about Jess and her weepy eyes."

"What are you talking about?"

"You carried her around their house."

"It's not like I *wanted* to, but I'm the only one who can get her up high enough so she can do her queenly wave."

Gwen gave Lock a sidelong glance, amazed she was becoming jealous over a pregnant, happily married wild dog. "That's pathetic."

Lock's heart began to slow down and he felt the panic pass. He hadn't felt panic like that since he'd walked into the middle of his first firefight. And even then, he didn't really have the luxury of panic since he'd been way too busy trying not to die.

Yet all this would throw off his carefully timed plans. Should he take the risk and possibly lose all he'd built up so far, thereby setting his ultimate goal back several years? Or not take the risk and end up still doing work he barely tolerated well into his sixties because one excuse after another got in his way?

One thing he did know, he didn't need the answer tonight. He'd think about it tomorrow.

Gwen checked her watch and winced. "I should get back to the hotel. I've got work tomorrow."

"You're not staying?"

"I better not."

Lock grabbed her hand even though she hadn't moved away. "Don't go. Stay."

"I don't have a change of clothes or even fresh panties, and I can't go to work without them. I just can't."

Tugging her closer, Lock admitted, "I don't want you to go. I want you to stay with me tonight. I want to wake up with you next to me. If I remember correctly, that's what boyfriends and girlfriends do."

"Not all the time."

"We're still in the honeymoon stage. Indulge me."

"Yeah, but—"

"I promise we won't stay up late." He could tell she was weakening, barely putting up a fight. "And I'll get you up early tomorrow so you can get changed before work."

He pulled her onto his lap, close to his chest with her knees on either side of his hips. He wrapped his arms around her waist and pressed his face against her chest. "Stay with me, Gwenie." He moved his lips across her collarbone. "Stay with me tonight."

Her arms slid around his neck, her hands buried deep into his hair. "I've got you so figured out," she said, her voice soft.

"Me?"

"Yeah. You." She pulled back a bit and peered into his face. "You call me Gwenie when you want something and Mr. Mittens when you're trying to tick me off."

Slipping his hands under her sweatshirt, he lifted it up and off. He nuzzled her bra and then used his mouth to undo the clasp holding the pieces of gray cotton together. "What can I say? I'm busted."

Gwen shuddered, smiled. "I knew it."

Lock used his nose to brush the bra cup off her breast and used his lips to tease her nipple. Her hands moved back into his hair and she pulled him closer against her. He suckled her and Gwen's hips moved against him, soft whimpering sounds turning harsh as he toyed with her. Taking hold of her hands, he pulled them from his hair and to her sides. He then took hold of her bra straps and pushed them off her shoulders, down her arms. She moved her hands behind her and that's where, instead of removing Gwen's bra, Lock used it to bind her wrists behind her.

She made a faint choking sound in her throat and arched her back, giving him complete access to her body. He took it, using his hands to roam every part of her chest, back, sides, and face while he let his mouth give her as much pleasure as she could handle. Gwen continued to rock into him, her moans and whimpers slowly turning into cries. He could do this all day if she let him, for days at a time. There was something about giving her pleasure that he couldn't get enough of. He craved it like he craved honey and salmon.

As he slid his hands behind her back, his fingers trailing up and down her spine, Gwen's body began to shake, her thighs gripping him tighter and her head thrown back.

"God . . . Lock . . . Christ . . ."

With one hand braced against her back and the other gently pulling and twisting one nipple while he did the same to the other with his lips, he felt Gwen's orgasm as her body desperately moved against him, heard it as she cried out his name.

As the last of it slammed through her system, she sat up abruptly, both her hands free. He had a bad feeling about what happened to her bra. She gripped his jaw and kissed him with so much passion he knew he was only falling faster now. So fast he wouldn't be able to stop if she changed her mind.

Then, with her forehead braced against his and her sweet breath pelting against his mouth, she was tearing at his jeans.

"I need to fuck you so bad."

He wouldn't deny her even if he could. He raised his hips and she slid back enough to pull his jeans down far enough to release his cock. It was brutally hard and ready. So was he. While she struggled with her cargo pants, he pulled the condom out of his back pocket. He'd only just slipped it on when Gwen straddled his waist and dropped down on him.

Lock's eyes briefly closed as the heat of her pussy nearly seared him, the wetness only making him want her more. He'd gotten her like this, nothing else meant more to him than that.

Her arms went around his neck and she growled with absolutely no pity, "My God, Jersey, I'm gonna fuck you so hard."

Good thing he'd had that condom in his pocket, because she might have taken him without it. Shocking, since there were some things Gwen didn't fuck around about, and protection was at the top of that list.

But Christ, there was something about him. She couldn't explain it. He wasn't like the kind of guys she'd ever been with before. You know . . . assholes. Guys who kept unlicensed guns under their pillows, always walked off the other way whenever they saw a cop coming, and thought grabbing her by the back of the head and trying to force her head into their lap was sexy.

Lock wasn't anyone's bad boy, and there was a time Gwen thought that was the only kind of guy who could get her off. She was wrong. Really wrong. Because not only did the grizzly get her off, he kept her going. Kept her wanting more. And, even more important, he made her want to make sure he got as much pleasure as he gave to her. Even she'd admit she wasn't a very "giving lover" and had been told so more than once. But why should she give when she didn't think they deserved it?

For the first time ever, though . . . she'd met someone who deserved it. Who might deserve everything.

She moved her hips slowly at first, her gaze staying right on his because she couldn't seem to get enough of that, either. The way he looked at her. Not like he thought she was just pretty, but like he . . . well, respected her or something. It was weird, she couldn't explain it, but it turned her on more than if he treated her like the hottest European supermodel. Maybe because in this world looks only got you so far for so long, then they went on their merry way and all you were left with was what you had inside.

And that was it, wasn't it? Lock looked at her as if he could see exactly what she had inside—and he liked it.

Realizing that, knowing it was true, Gwen got turned on more and she tightened her muscles until Lock's eyes crossed.

His hands gripped her waist and he said her name. A few times.

She rode him harder, faster. She wanted to see his face when he came, see the pleasure she brought him. She was thinking so much about him, watching him so close that it wasn't until she came—the strength of it tearing up her back and causing her to scream out—that she realized she'd been that close to coming.

As he watched her go over, he gripped her hips tight and brought her down hard once, twice. He exploded inside her, his entire body one rigid line of muscle. Gwen instinctively gripped his cock again, squeezing him dry until he fell back against the couch, gasping for breath. She dropped on top of him, working hard to get her own breath back when those big arms wrapped around her and held her close.

"So . . . you'll stay the night?" he asked after a few minutes.

And if Gwen weren't completely wiped out, she would have laughed. "Yeah," she sighed against his neck. "I'll stay the night."

She'd never found watching other people have sex very interesting, but tonight it was part of the job. Part of what she had to do to get what she needed.

Truth be told, she had the equipment to drill a precision hole in the back of this idiot's head and was tempted to do it. Right here, right now. But she was older now and she'd like to think she was smarter, too. She'd discovered that getting information was more important than instant gratification. Unfortunately, getting information required waiting, which she could tolerate, and watching, which was beginning to make her ill.

She'd do it, though, because it was her job now. Maybe. She was still making up her mind. And it was a nice night anyway. A beautiful night.

CHAPTER 22

Lock was still arguing with Gwen at his front door. "Let me take you home."

"I'll catch a cab."

Leaning against the door frame, Lock gripped her denim jacket by the lapels and tugged her closer until she was flush against him. "It's polite to see a woman to her door—and then make out with her."

"Yeah, exactly. I have a job today, so I can't afford to let you get me confused and horny when I'm dealing with a sewer line."

"Eew."

"Wuss," she teased. "Besides, not all of us are artists."

"Stop calling me that."

"You're so friggin' cute when you blush."

She went up on her toes and Lock came down so she could kiss him. "I'll call you later today. Okay?"

"Yeah. But remember what we talked about . . . be careful."

"I always am."

Lock watched her walk down the hallway and disappear into the elevator. He wished he could have taken her home, but she was right. He would have been forced to try out that Kingston Arms bed, and she'd have lost a whole day of work. The last thing he ever wanted to do was get in Gwen's way, but he also wanted to make sure she built time in for him.

He closed the front door and walked into his living room, retrieving the jacket he'd thrown at his couch the night before so he could hang it up. His phone went off and he pulled it out of his pocket and glanced at the text message from Sabina.

WHEN WILL I GET MY CHAIR, JERSEY BEAR?
DON'T MAKE ME WAIT.

How long exactly before she got on his nerves? She was always pushy, always demanding the software jobs sooner than they were contracted for. But this wasn't some software job and he sure as hell wouldn't let her bully him when it came to his . . . Oh, God.

He'd been about to say "his art." What had the feline done to him?

Flipping his phone so he had access to the extended keyboard, Lock focused on typing and retyping his reply. He hated these keyboards. The were simply too small for his thumbs. He ended up hitting three to four keys instead of the one.

Lock was seriously starting to get frustrated when he glanced up and saw the She-wolf standing in the middle of his living room.

The phone went flying, he roared, and before he even realized it, his claws were swinging for her face.

She caught his arm with her left hand and pressed her gun to his throat with the right.

"Easy, boy," she said. "Easy."

It took Lock a minute, but then he let out a breath and his claws retracted. As soon as he was calm again, she lowered her weapon—and smiled. "Miss me, hoss?"

"You crazy little—" Lock grabbed her around the waist and hugged her right off her feet.

"Dee-Ann Smith," he snarled against her neck. "Where the hell have you been?"

Gwen eased the hotel door open and stuck her head in. The room was dark, the drawn curtains keeping the seven A.M. sun out. But she didn't need light to see. She was nocturnal, after all. Searching carefully, her brother nowhere in sight, she quickly but silently eased inside. Closing the door, Gwen tiptoed to her room to get fresh clothes.

She closed the door behind her and tossed her bag onto the bed. Moving to her closet to grab a pair of her work boots, Gwen opened the door as her mind debated on a headband or stubby ponytail for her hair. Perhaps the ponytail in case baby rattlesnakes fell into her hair. *Ick! Snakes!* How she would manage going back into that snake farm—which is what she and Blayne kept calling the home of that poor couple with the snake infestation—Gwen didn't know. But if she could just keep—

"*Ahhhhhhhhhh haaaaaaaaa!*"

Gwen yowled and spun up, her claws digging into the ceiling and holding her there as her brother stormed out of the closet.

"*Where the hell have you been?*" he screamed up at her.

And Gwen screamed down, "*What the hell do you think you're doing?*"

"Don't try and change the subject on me, missy! You've been gone all goddamn weekend and didn't even let me know if you were alive or dead!"

Gwen retracted her claws and dropped from the ceiling, landing on her hands and feet.

"I want you to learn a new phrase," she said as she stood up and shoved him with both hands. "None of your business!"

Mitch waved his hand in front of his nose. "Christ almighty! What is that *funk* on you?"

Gwen smirked. "Eau de Grizzly."

"I knew it!" Mitch threw his hands up. "And you're crazy if you think I'm lettin' this go. I'm not letting my little sister hook up with some idiot bear!"

"You can't stop me!" she yelled at him as he stormed out of the room. "But maybe you can call Ma and rat me out again, *you overgrown tattletale!*"

Gwen slammed her door shut, but she could still hear the

window-rattling yell of a pissed-off She-wolf, "*Would you two shut the fuck up? Some of us are trying to sleep off a hangover!*"

Lock was still laughing when he opened his front door. "Hey!" he slapped Ric on the back and ushered him in.

"Should I assume the weekend went well with the lovely Gwen?"

"It went great. But remember when I told you about the van that had been following me?"

"Yeah."

"Well, now I know why. It wasn't me they were interested in."

"Aw, little bear. I'm sure someone, somewhere is interested in you."

"Very funny. Come on." He motioned to the living room. "I want you to meet somebody."

Ric stopped walking, head lifting, nostrils flaring. "You have another woman here."

"Yeah. That's who I want you to—"

"Why do you have another woman in your house?" Ric demanded, turning on him. "What if Gwen came back over? You know women do that all the time. What if she wanted to surprise you and you, imbecile, have another woman in your house? Did you not see how she reacted to Peggy?"

"You mean Judy?"

"*Does it matter?* Don't be an idiot!"

Before Lock could ask Ric when he'd gone completely off the rails, Dee-Ann sauntered out of his living room. "I could eat. You hungry?"

"Yeah, uh . . ." Ric suddenly gripped Lock's bicep, cutting off Lock's words and the flow of blood. "Ow! Do you mind, Van Holtz? I'm rather attached to that arm!"

Dee-Ann smiled, sauntered a little closer. "Who's your friend, MacRyrie?"

Lock pried Ric's fingers off his arm. "This is Ulrich Van Holtz. Ric."

"Oh, yeah. Lock talked about you all the time."

"And, Ric, this is Dee-Ann Smith. My old Marine buddy. We were in the Unit together."

"Nice to meetcha," Dee said, grasping Ric's hand and shaking it.

Lock didn't even realize he was waiting for Ric's return greeting until it never came.

He watched his friend continue to shake Dee's hand while he gawked at her, his mouth open a little.

"Ric?"

"Huh?" Ric mumbled, his eyes still on Dee, his hand still holding hers.

"You're embarrassing me."

Dee laughed and pulled her hand back. "Leave him alone, MacRyrie. Now you boys want to go out and get some breakfast or not?"

"No!" Ric snapped and Lock, startled, growled.

Dee's smile faded. "No one's twistin' your arm, hoss."

"What I mean is," Ric said quickly, staring directly into her eyes because they were both the same six-two height—in fact they could probably share each other's clothes—"*I'll* make you breakfast."

Dee's smile returned, bigger this time. "Now, darlin', you don't have to make me breakfast. A breakfast that don't come out of a packet is like a dream to me."

"But a fresh, hot breakfast is what you deserve."

Dee shrugged. "Well, if you really want—"

"I want. Oh, God do I want."

She laughed. "Have it your way. Lock, you don't mind if I use your bathroom, do ya? Figure I'll get showered and changed before I see the cousins and since I'm gettin' my very own Van Holtz–made breakfast."

"Sure. Down the hall and to the left."

"Thanks, hoss." She picked up the duffel bag she'd left by the door and ambled off to use Lock's bathroom.

Once gone, Ric turned on him, gripping his shirt and yanking. But instead of yanking Lock toward him, he only managed to pull himself closer to Lock.

"Who. Is. *She?*"

"That's Dee. Remember? I've told you about her."

"No one told me she was a goddess."

"A . . ." Ignoring the strange way Ric phrased that, Lock studied the hardwood hallway floor where Dee had stood, leaving scuff marks from those damn boots of hers. "Dee? A goddess? Really?"

It wasn't that Lock didn't find Dee attractive but . . . well . . . hmm.

"Yes. Really." He pushed Lock away—or tried—and began to pace. "You'll need to run down to the store for a few ingredients."

"What for? I'm sure I've got everything you—"

"*Don't argue with me!*" Ric dug cash out of his front pocket and shoved it into Lock's hand. He stared at the amount for a moment, which had to be several hundred dollars, and then grabbed his wallet from his back pocket, pulling out a credit card and placing that on top. "I'll give you a list. And everything *must* be of the freshest quality. I insist on that."

The freshest quality for Dee-Ann Smith? Who'd been living the last ten years on whatever rations the Marines gave her and whatever she could take down on her own?

Lock watched as his best friend jotted a list in the small notepad Ric always kept in his back pocket.

The bear debated. Tell his friend now he didn't stand a chance with Dee-Ann or let Ric learn it for himself? Lock flinched, remembering the ways Dee-Ann had of letting a guy down when she was done with him. Nope. Bad idea. Very bad idea.

"Hey, Ric . . . look, uh . . ."

Dee-Ann came back in the hallway and both men stopped and stared at her.

"Just came back to get some water out of the fridge." When neither man said anything to her, she asked, "Somethin' wrong?"

Ric stepped forward. "How many children do you want?"

Lock grabbed Ric by his hair and yanked him back, slamming him into the front door. "Ow!"

Dee-Ann smirked. "What's going on, MacRyrie?"

"Nothing."

Arms crossed over her chest, her foot tapping, Gwen asked Blayne, "And you said we'd do this . . . why?"

She shrugged. "Because it's a nice thing to do."

"And because you have no concept of shame?"

"Come on, Gwenie. It's not a big deal. They *like* you."

"I'm not sure what that's supposed to mean to me."

"It means they don't trust just anybody with this task."

Gwen stared down at the panting, slobbering animals at her feet.

"I don't buy it, Blayne. Not even from you. There has to be a reason we're doing this. And not 'cause today's job was postponed."

Hands on her hips, sweet Blayne left the room and direct, father's-a-Navy-man Blayne stepped in. "What? You think we got such a great rate on this place due to my big grin and your implacable charm? We had to make concessions."

"So we're walking their dogs? We're a plumbing-and-dog-walking service now?"

"We walk 'em when we can."

"Couldn't you have offered them sex, blow jobs . . . *something?*"

"*That's* less humiliating than dog walking?"

"In my world."

"Gwen!"

"All right, all right. But if we're going to do this, we might as well get something out of it . . ."

"So what are you doing here?"

Dee reached for the bowl of warm maple syrup. "Thinking about joining my cousin's Pack. If the mood grips me."

"You'll work in his company, too?"

"Don't know about all that." She shrugged. "Don't like feeling hemmed in."

"Yeah. I remember that."

Lock smiled easily, like he used to when she'd first met him and he was just another raw recruit from the wilds of New Jersey. To be honest, Dee didn't know how she'd find her old friend faring. Staying in the Unit wasn't an easy thing and those in charge had to cycle the Unit's team members out to protect not only the other team members but the Corps itself. The Unit's assignments took their toll and sometimes, when it got too much, shifters "broke"—the unofficial term for going rabid without actually having the disease. So, ten years was the max unless you were an officer, although some didn't even last that long. Lock hadn't. He'd made it through seven years before he looked at Dee one day, his eyes dead, his soul deader and said, "I missed my mother's birthday."

That was all he said in a thirty-hour stretch and Dee knew, knew it was time for her best friend to go. Go before he did something they'd be forced to put him down for. And now that she'd seen him again, spent time with him, she knew she'd made the right decision that day three years ago . . . when she told Lock MacRyrie that he had to leave not only the Unit but the Corps. It had been the right call for both her team and for Lock. She was sure of that now.

"So if you don't work for him, what will you do?"

"I've got some lines on things."

"If you need anything, just let me know."

"Thanks, darlin'. Much appreciate it. Do have a question, though."

"Sure."

She leaned in a bit and asked, "He gonna keep starin' at me?"

The Van Holtz wolf smiled at her when she glanced his way. Funny, she'd been raised that Van Holtzes were nothing but stuck-up rich boys. Although her daddy always added that they weren't as easy to kill as they looked.

"We're going to ignore Ric, because he's lost his mind. Temporarily, I'm sure."

"We all need to do that from time to time." She winked at the wolf, and he let out a breath.

"Marry—"

"You know—" Lock said loudly, cutting the wolf a hard glare "—um, you know lots of Pack gossip, right?"

"Not of my own doing to find out, but I hear things. Why?"

"You know anything about the McNelly Pack?"

Chewing her bacon nice and slow, Dee asked, "Now why would you bring them up?"

"My girlfriend has been having problems with them, but from what I can tell she hasn't had any past problems with that Pack. So I'm thinking it's some old problem come up, ya know?"

Dee knew well enough because the Smiths were all about holding grudges. It was one of the reasons they were so feared, they didn't forget anything. Of course, she was far more interested in something else. "That feline you were talking to earlier is your girlfriend?"

Lock's grin grew, revealing pure male satisfaction. "Damn right she is."

"All right then. Who's your girlfriend connected to?" When Lock gave a small frown, she added, "You mentioned her first name but not her kin connections."

"Oh. She's an O'Neill."

"An O'Neill?" *Oh, Lord.*

"Yeah. From Philly."

"And she's been having problems with a McNelly?"

"Yeah."

Dee put down her fork and focused on her friend. "She an O'Neill through her momma or daddy?"

"Her mother. Roxy O'Neill."

The laughter poured out of her before she could stop it and then she couldn't stop at all.

"What? What's so funny?"

But Dee was laughing too hard to even answer.

*   *   *

"What I can't believe is how he acted, Blayne!" Gwen yelled, her hold on the leashes tightening as the three dogs tore down the Manhattan sidewalk. "Like he had the right to be jumping out at me from closets, demanding to know where I'd been!"

"You know how your brother is!" Blayne yelled back. "He's always been superprotective! He doesn't know any better!" She had four dogs pulling her and was doing much better than Gwen would have hoped.

Actually . . . they both were.

"And then I was lying to him on Saturday! Like a child! What's wrong with me?"

"Nothing! He took you by surprise and he did it for that reason! I'm glad you lied!"

So was Gwen. It had led to the best weekend of her entire life.

"What I want to know is—" Gwen let out a brief squeal when she hit a rough patch of sidewalk and almost fell on her ass, but she caught herself and kept going "—how the hell did Lock know?"

"Know what?"

"That I was coming over. He wasn't surprised at all. Nobody was! They all can't be such good liars."

"Uh . . . it was Jess."

"What do you mean it was Jess?"

"She told me Sissy called to complain to Smitty that Mitch had lost his mind. Smitty told Jess, and she called Ric."

"Why?"

"Why?"

"Yeah. Why?"

"Uh . . . she knew Ric was going over there?"

"Are you asking me or telling me?"

"Look, woman! All I know is that Ric, Jess, and Lock are good friends."

"Yeah," Gwen muttered. "I know."

"Truck!" Blayne called out cheerfully before she easily maneuvered herself and the dogs around an eighteen-wheeler that had backed into a loading dock. The loading dock's entrance cut through the sidewalk and Gwen tried to halt the dogs by pulling on their leashes the way she saw people in movies pull on a horse's rein. Sadly it didn't work; the dogs kept going. But, thankfully, they went off the sidewalk and into the street—causing Gwen to screech like a full-human—went around the truck, and then back on the sidewalk. Gwen jumped the curb, all her pre-teen training coming back to her during that forty-five-second nightmare. The dogs she held followed behind Blayne and the others, making a right onto a main avenue. And wasn't that wonderful? *More* people yelling at them to "slow the fuck down!" or "get off the fuckin' sidewalk!" or a myriad of other sugges-tions, some of which involved Gwen's mother.

Her phone rang and Gwen called out, "Phone! Need to get phone!"

"Okay!" Blayne happily yelled back. She easily stopped her dogs and Gwen's dogs automatically followed suit. Gwen rolled to a stop until she was standing right in front of Blayne.

Panting, Gwen asked her friend, "How much do we rock?"

"Like gods."

Laughing, Gwen answered her phone. "It's Gwen."

"It's Lock."

She bit her lip and rolled away from Blayne. "Hey. What's up?"

"Hey. Um, an old Marine buddy of mine showed up this morning. She's in the Smith Pack—"

"She?"

"Yeah. And I mentioned McNelly to see if there was any Pack gossip that she may know that we don't."

"Yeah?"

"And . . . uh . . ."

"What, Lock? Spit it out."

"You're going to be mad."

Gwen shrugged. "Tell me anyway."

"Okay, but . . ."

"But what, Lock?"

"It involves your mother."

*   *   *

Blayne held the leashes for all seven dogs while Gwen took her call. She crouched down and petted them, adoring each one. They were all so cute. Every one of them mutts, rescues that the Kuznetsov Pack had picked up over the years, and every one happy and healthy and adorable.

As was Gwen at this moment. Sure, she was pissed at Mitch, but few days went by where she wasn't. But this . . . this was amazing. Gwen exuberant, Gwen happy . . . Gwen satisfied. Blayne felt like buffing her nails against her T-shirt because she was *that* damn good. She'd known Gwen and Lock were perfect for each other the second she saw them together.

Even better was how amazing everyone was at helping out! She didn't think they'd come through like they had, but wow. Everyday she learned to love the Kuznetsov Pack more and more. And Ric? What a great guy!

Mitch, however, was still a problem, but Blayne had her surprise ace in the hole. A sneaky She-wolf who knew how to text message. No, no. She hadn't *lied* to Gwen . . . officially. It was more about massaging the truth to help her friend. And that was okay, wasn't it? Of course it was! Because it was all coming together and Blayne couldn't be happier!

Really, could the day get any better?

"*Goddamnit!*" Gwen yelled out, making the dogs bark and Blayne realize the day apparently would *not* be getting any better. "*That woman will be the death of me!*"

Blayne knew "that woman" could only be one woman and she wasn't even sure she wanted to hear the rest of it.

CHAPTER 23

Lock waited until he heard the shower shut off and then he made her a mug of hot tea. When he walked into the room with it, he found her sitting naked in the middle of his bed, her knees up and her arms tight around them. He sat down next to her and offered her the tea, but she shook her head.

Sitting next to her, he quietly said, "Gwen—"

"She fucked McNelly's husband!" she screeched, causing his upstairs neighbor to bang on the ceiling with a broom. But Gwen unleashed that combo hiss-roar and, not surprisingly, the banging stopped.

Lock grimaced, and offered, "Wolves don't really get married." Gold eyes filled with rage fastened on him and he quickly amended, "What I mean is, I don't think they were mated or anything. Wolves are big on that. They take it very seriously. I think this fight was more of a 'You took my man' kind of thing. Rather than 'You took my mate.' And it sounded like it happened years ago. Like before you were born."

"And everyone knows?"

"Not everyone. Ric had no idea. And Dee-Ann—"

"Right. The—" she made air quotes with her fingers "—'Marine buddy.' "

"She is. And one of my trainers. When I started, we were—"

"*Does it look like I care?*"

"O . . . kay." He held up the mug. "Tea?"

"I hate hot tea."

"All right." He put it down on the side table.

"I thought New York meant a new start," she said. "But not when you're the idiot daughter of Roxy O'Neill. A woman determined to haunt me!"

"Gwen, you're not an idiot."

"Whatever. It doesn't matter. Right? Because I'm an O'Neill and that's what O'Neills do. Fuck other people's husbands, get shot at, fix boxing matches, and set things on fire for money."

Lock blinked. "What?"

"And we do that because we're O'Neills and that's what O'Neills do. I might as well accept it. And *you* need to accept it, too. Because according to you I'm your girlfriend and I'm also an O'Neill—*so prepare yourself for the humiliation!*"

Letting out a breath, Lock lifted Gwen into his arms and moved her around until she was sideways on his lap, her head against his chest, her legs resting over one of his thighs. He held her and his hands smoothed up and down her back.

"What are you doing?" she asked, sounding pissier than he'd ever heard her.

"Being nice to you. Whether you want me to or not."

Gwen didn't struggle; there didn't seem to be a point. Instead she sat there while he held her. He didn't try and make a sexual move, he didn't do anything but hold her. She had no idea what he was waiting for, what he wanted from her.

Gwen was too busy seething to notice the tears until they fell on her chest. Mortified, she tried then to pull away, but Lock wouldn't let her go.

Would he understand these weren't tears of sadness, but of frustration? Her frustration for having a mother she adored but who somehow managed to torture her without trying?

And all this violence and fighting, poor Blayne turned into a human shotput, over an old grudge that involved Roxy, Sharyn McNelly and, tragically, Donna McNelly's *father*.

And here was this thing, this precious, delicate, *amazing* thing between her and Lock. An amazing thing she could see growing into more. But how could she hope to keep a man used to intellectual discourse over grilled salmon and wineglasses of cranberry juice, when her own mother was busy nailing the wolves of her derby rivals? An event so well-known it had once been the hot topic of conversation as far away as frickin' Tennessee. A place O'Neills never ventured willingly until Mitch and Sissy hooked up.

Yet Lock wasn't running away from her. He'd picked her up at work, taken her back to his apartment, and made her vile tea. Even now he was holding her, stroking her naked body while managing to not make it sexual, but comforting. And as much as she tried to hold back from him, as much as Gwen tried to keep this part of her life separate from Lock, she couldn't. He wouldn't let her.

Gwen gripped his T-shirt, knowing she should push him away, knowing she shouldn't drag him into any of this, but she ended up burying her face against his chest and crying. She cried until she couldn't cry anymore.

She had no idea how long they stayed like that; even after she stopped crying, they stayed like that. But when Gwen was done, she was done. She sat up straight, but Lock's arms stayed loose around her.

"I'm done now."

"Okay." She adored that he didn't want to talk things out or psychoanalyze the situation. She hated that.

"And we can't let my mother find out what happened Labor Day weekend, or she'll do something stupid."

"You don't think Mitch—"

She waved her hand, cutting him off. "He's so freakin' occupied with trying to get in the middle of my business, it won't even cross his mind."

"Okay." He brushed her hair off her cheek. "You're staying tonight, right?" he asked.

"If you want—"

"Good." Lock kissed her forehead. "Now, do you want to feel better?

Oddly phrased question, but okay. "Sure."

"Do you really want to feel better or would you rather sit around wallowing?"

She chuckled. "No. I'm done wallowing." And she really wanted to feel better. Of course just having Lock here was making her feel better.

"I can help you feel better." He lifted her off his lap and placed her carefully on the bed, before he scrambled off.

Gwen wasn't exactly surprised when he took his clothes off, nor did she mind.

Naked, Lock got back on the bed and stretched out next to her. "Lay down." She reached for him but he shook his head. "No, no. Stretch out. Next to me."

That seemed weird but whatever.

"Now . . . you lift your legs up straight." Not sure what the hell he was doing, Gwen lifted her legs up. It was kind of humorous to see the two pairs of legs raised up considering how much longer his were. "And using your hands . . . grab your toes."

Gwen dropped her legs and sat up. "You want me to do what?"

"Trust me. You'll feel so much better."

She quickly scrutinized the room. "You don't have a hidden camera around here or something?"

"Of course not."

"This isn't going to end up on the Internet or something, right? I'll be really pissed if this ends up on the Net."

"Trust me," he said again. And when Gwen looked at him he was playing with his toes.

With a shrug, Gwen stretched out beside Lock, lifted her legs up, and grabbed her toes.

"You can roll back and forth, too."

All right then.

"What do you think?"

"This is . . . uh . . . kind of . . . nice actually."

"I know. I do it anytime I'm really pissed or depressed or bored or . . . playing."

"You do it every day, don't you?"

"Sometimes. There's no shame in the toe grab. And look! You can cross arms and grab opposite toes."

"Rebellious."

"I live on the edge, Gwen."

Laughing, Gwen dropped her legs and curled into Lock's side. "What? What's so funny?"

Sharyn McNelly pulled her truck into the strip mall and parked in front of the hair salon.

Walking inside, she didn't bother to look around. For the last two years, she'd been coming to this salon every other week just before closing. The owners were cats, but they were cheaper than the other places and worked fast. She dropped into the chair and opened her bag to toss in her phone. "The usual, Ling," she told her stylist. "And make it quick, I'm meeting someone tonight at the bar down the street."

There was a rare moment of silence from the chatty stylist and then, "Man, you got fat."

Sharyn's head came up, her fangs instantly extending as anger roared through her system. "*You.*"

Roxy O'Neill grinned back at her in the mirror, seconds before she gripped the back of Sharyn's head and slammed it into the table that held the stylist's tools.

Stunned, Sharyn fell back in the chair as Roxy moved around her. "You went after my daughter? What made you think that was okay?"

"I don't know what you're talking about, bitch."

Sharyn's head hit the small table in front of her again. "*Goddamnit!*"

"*My* baby girl. Did you really think I'd let you get away with that?"

Gripping her head and panting, Sharyn watched the cat. "She was there. It was convenient. And I still *owe* you."

"Are you kidding? You did it over that idiot?" Roxy leaned down and stared Sharyn in the eye. "He fucked everybody in the league, sweetie. And actually, it was Marie who fucked him. I just gave him a blow job."

Sharyn wrapped her hands around Roxy's throat and they crashed to the floor, but the cat wasn't alone, her sisters grabbing Sharyn's arms and pulling her off, dragging her across the floor.

Roxy stood, shook out her gold mane of hair. "There's a thing about the O'Neills you need to know, pooch. Mixed-blood or full. Dark hair or gold, we always protect our own."

Even though she struggled, the cats easily yanked Sharyn into the chair and held her there.

Roxy smiled down at her. "The other thing. Never start shit with a lion when it's lions that are doing your hair."

"And FYI," Marie tossed in. "Just because she and her sisters are Asiatic lions, doesn't mean her name is Ling."

"It's actually Tracey. And look!" Roxy held up clippers. "She's letting me use her equipment. Now let's see if we can fix that mess you call hair."

Marie patted Sharyn's shoulder. "You know, hon, conditioner? It's your friend."

Gwen pulled on one of Lock's T-shirts and laughed when it went past her knees. He grinned at her from his bed. The lone white sheet was pulled up to his waist, but he had one leg out and raised. She'd always enjoyed the male body but . . .

She sighed softly. All that hard muscle and so damn much of it. And she'd spent the last three hours enjoying every inch of him. It simply dazzled her how he went from goofy bear, rolling on his back and playing with his toes, and right into sexy-beyond-belief Jersey grizzly who'd worked her body like a love god.

"It looks like you're wearing a muumuu," he joked.

"And if I were wearing a muu-muu?" Gwen asked, her hands on her hips. "Then what?"

"Gwen, I don't care how big you get, you're never wearing a

muumuu around me. But . . . feel free to wear any of my shirts, anytime you want."

The way he looked at her sometimes . . . it wasn't cute and cuddly, that was for sure. And it made her feel sexier than she ever had before. "I'm going to call Blayne before she calls me, panicking. I ended our training session a little abruptly this afternoon."

"Okay. I'll scrounge up something for us to eat."

"Sounds good. I won't be long." She started for the door, but she heard the grizzly grumble and then what she could only describe as tongue clicks. She faced him. "Yes?"

"I want a kiss."

Gwen shook her head. "Uh-uh."

"Why not?"

"Don't give me that innocent bear look. I start kissing you and we'll never eat and I'll never call Blayne and then we'll starve while crazy Blayne tries to track us down in all the wrong places." She pointed at the door. "So I'm going out there and you're going to get us food."

"Not even a little kiss?"

"Stop it." She again moved toward the door, but paused before she went through it. "And stop humming."

"I didn't know I was."

She looked at him over her shoulder. "You do it while you sleep, too."

"And you purr in your sleep."

She didn't normally. Of course, the last few nights in Lock's bed she'd been purring a lot.

Leaving the bedroom, Gwen grabbed her phone and speed dialed Blayne. She dropped facedown on Lock's couch as Blayne answered.

"Chello?"

Gwen smiled. "You sound in a good mood."

"I am! Cherry says I'm doing so much better since I've been training with you. Everybody's really happy. Thanks so much, Gwenie."

"Anytime, Blayne. You know that."

"Well . . . since you mention it—"

"I'm not joining the team, Blayne," Gwen cut in, knowing exactly where this conversation was headed.

"But they like you *so much*."

Lock sat down in the big king chair across from the couch. He wore boxers and was eating honey from a jar with a spoon.

"That's really sweet, but—"

"Won't you even consider it?"

"No."

Gwen glanced over at Lock, watched him trying to shake the spoon off his right hand. When that didn't work, he used his left to pull it off and then tried to shake it off that one. Since he seemed more entertained than frustrated she didn't bother saying anything.

"Why not?" Blayne asked.

"I'm not trying to be a bitch."

"I know."

"I just . . . I can't."

"Okay. I understand. But that doesn't mean you can't be a teammate in spirit!"

Only Blayne. "Okay, fine. I'll be a teammate in spirit."

"Yay!"

Lock used his mouth to pull the spoon off his hand, then realized that both hands were too sticky from honey to have anywhere to put it. He stared at his hands for several seconds, shrugged, and then flicked the spoon in the air, catching it with his mouth when it came back down.

"Christ," Gwen murmured, "he's a goofball."

"Huh?"

Focusing on the couch cushion, Gwen said to Blayne, "Nothing."

"Okay." Blayne paused for a moment and then asked, "So . . . are you at the hotel?"

Blayne Thorpe. Obvious Girl. "No, Blayne."

"Where are ya then?"

"I'm hanging up, Blayne."

"Gwen—"

"Blayne, we're not going down this road."

"Just tell me this . . . are you happy?"

"You mean at this second?"

"Yeah, Miss Specific. At this second."

Lock was now staring at his toes while using the sticky spoon to eat more honey. In another two minutes he'd be playing with those toes using his sticky fingers.

"Yeah," she replied honestly to Blayne. "I am."

Gwen disconnected the call and demanded, "I thought you were going to get food?"

Licking the spoon, Lock admitted, "My mind wandered."

And laughing, Gwen buried her face in the couch.

Blayne put down her phone, stared intently across the table and said, "My nefarious plan is almost complete. And soon, everything I could imagine will come to fruition."

Her father glanced at her over the top of his reading glasses. "Must you always be as odd as your mother?"

"You adored my mother. You told me so. And I'm your little princess." Blayne grinned and her father snorted out a laugh but cut it short like he always did.

"And what is next in my little princess's plan to get her feline friend a bear? Although why anyone would want a bear . . ." he ended on a grumble.

"We're almost there, Daddy, but . . . we're . . . we're not there yet."

"That made no sense. What have I told you before about not making sense to me? You know I hate that."

"I also know you should be used to it by now." Her father's lip curled and Blayne quickly threatened, "If you snarl, I start crying."

"Please don't." He leaned back in the chair and said, "Okay. Remember what I taught you."

"About knife fighting and skinning animals?"

"No. Although that's good information. I'm talking about seeing the final outcome of what you want and seeing where you are right now. From there, you figure out that final step. And keep in mind that you're dealing with predators."

Blayne thought for a moment before she said, "She needs to claim him."

"I thought she had."

"That was to her brother. She'd claim Genghis Khan if she thought it would piss off Mitch. She needs to claim Lock as her own, in front of the world. Or, at the very least, me. That's the final hurdle."

Her father picked up his copy of the *Navy Times*. "And for a feline, Blayne, that will be the hardest hurdle of all."

"I know, Daddy." She picked up her cell phone. "And that's why you need friends."

Chapter 24

An envelope appeared in front of Lock's face, his name embossed in silver on the front and his response was immediate, "Not in this lifetime."

"You have to go," Ric said, leaning against Lock's desk, ignoring all the papers, CDs, DVDs, hard drives, and small tools he had littering it. "If you don't, I assure you there will be tears. You know you can't handle that."

"I'm not putting on some stupid costume and parading around—"

"Already discussed and you're off the hook."

"I am?"

"Yes."

"You have that in writing?"

"For a costume party?"

"Not just a costume party. A *wild dog* costume party. That means a costume, a copious amount of chocolate, and an inhuman amount of knowledge on the *Lord of the Ring* movies."

"Why are you arguing this with me?" Ric demanded with a laugh. "She already said if you say no, she's coming over here to sob until you agree."

"Why? She didn't care I didn't come to last year's party."

"That was last year. Not this year. This year she wants you.

And I have yet to see you turn down a sobbing, *wailing* wild dog."

Because he couldn't! His weakness sickened him.

"I'll think about it."

Ric smiled. "Of course you will. And then you'll say yes anyway." Ric glanced around. "So . . . are you here alone?"

Lock dropped back in his industrial-strength office chair. "I wish I could believe you were asking to be nosy about Gwen and me. But you're not. You're asking about Dee-Ann."

"Well, is she here or not?"

"Not. And if I were you, I wouldn't try and track her down."

"Why not?"

"Because when it comes to Dee, you're better off not knowing where she's going or what she's up to. You'll only have to lie to the authorities later."

"Oh. All right then."

Smitty looked away from his computer monitor and over at the big feet resting on his desk. Relaxing back, he interlaced his fingers and rested them on his belly.

"Look who's put her big, fat hooves on my desk."

"And a good day to you, too, Bobby Ray."

"Where the hell have you been, Dee-Ann?"

"I didn't know I was on some sort of schedule that I might be late for."

"I thought you would have been here a couple months back."

"I told you I'd think about it."

"And why didn't you tell me you were in town as early as last week?"

Dee smiled. She had her momma's warm, pretty smile, but her daddy's eyes. Eyes like the wolf she shared her body with. And although when Smitty shifted to wolf he had the same eyes, Dee's and Eggie's never seemed to change, whether they were human or wolf. They remained as watchful. As cold.

He loved his cousin, but Smitty would never cross her. Because the older she got, the more like her daddy she became. Just as dangerous, just as lethal.

"How did you hear I was in town?" She asked, watching him closely.

"A Van Holtz said one of my cousins was in town. He didn't give me any names, but I figured it was you."

She studied him for a moment. "You want me to leave?"

"No, darlin'. I want you as part of the Pack."

"I don't like feeling hemmed in."

Smitty had to smile. "And the one thing my daddy always taught me was to never hem in Eggie Smith—or Eggie Smith's daughter. You join the Pack on simple terms. We're always here for you and, when I need you, you're there for us."

Dee-Ann nodded. "Give me a few days."

"If you like."

Dee-Ann swung her long legs off Smitty's desk and stood.

"And there's a party this weekend. You're more than welcome to come."

"I'll think on it." She walked to the door, stopped. "And which Van Holtz told you I was in town?"

Smitty glanced back at his monitor, an e-mail from Jessie Ann with a silly subject line making him smile. "Uh . . . one of the younger ones. Um, Ric? Ulrich? He's a friend of—"

Staring at the empty doorway, Smitty let out a breath. How his cousin always did that whenever the mood struck her, he'd never know.

Gwen pulled open the door to her office and stepped inside. Only to get slammed back into the wall by a five-eleven wolfdog.

"*Paaaaaarrrrrrrttttttyyyyyy!*"

Not entirely in the mood for this, Gwen snapped, "What?"

"*Party! Party! Party!*"

"I'm not going to any party." Gwen pushed past Blayne and headed toward her office, but she was yanked back by her hair and a thick envelope held up in front of her.

"*Party! Party! Party!*"

"Would you stop saying that!" Gwen snatched the envelope from her. Both their names were on the front, the letters raised, the paper thick and high quality. Opening it, Gwen pulled out the card inside.

*You are viciously invited to the most bloodthirsty party
of the century. Dress as the most ghoulish,
most frightening, or most terrifying fiend of the
known world and dance the night away with other
like-minded terrors. Costumes are mandatory.
Drinks are free. And chocolate! Chocolate! Chocolate!*

—The Kuznetsovs

"Is it really hard for them to be normal?"

Blayne yanked the invite from her. "We're going."

Again pushing past Blayne, Gwen at least this time made it in to the office. "You're going. I'm not."

"Why not?"

"Not in the mood." Why would she go to some goofy Halloween party with a bunch of goofy dogs? Her life was too short and getting shorter every day. She didn't plan to spend a minute of it bored out of her mind, if she could help it. "But go. Have a good time."

Gwen slipped off the straps of her backpack and she was pulling out her chair to sit down and get her paperwork together before they headed out to the snake farm, when Blayne tossed in, "Your mother's going."

Gwen froze in midsit. "What?"

Blayne shrugged. "She was invited and you know how she—"

"Dammit!" Gwen dropped into her chair. Now she *had* to go. Her mother at a party filled with predators and an open bar . . . Gwen couldn't even stand to think about the damage the woman could do. And the damage would be around all of Lock's friends.

"If you're really not going to go, let me know now because I have to R.S.V.—"

"I'll be there," Gwen snarled, opening drawers as if she was looking for something, but really it was simply so she could slam them shut again.

"Okay."

Blayne stepped into the hallway and walked around the big pillar that blocked the view of their office from people wandering through the lobby. Jess stood at the front desk with the receptionist, Mindy. When she saw Blayne, Jess faced her.

She gave Jess a thumbs-up, then raised her brows in silent question.

Jess lifted her hand, her thumb and forefinger in a circle, her three other fingers raised, letting her know that Lock was . . . well . . . a lock.

They grinned at each other like goofballs and then Blayne headed back to the office. She'd only opened the door when she heard Gwen roar, "*Where the fuck are the receipts from the construction site?*"

When it came to the task of babysitting her mother, Gwen would have only one volume level until it was all over. Thankfully, Blayne only had to put up with it until Saturday night.

Jay Ross reached into his girlfriend's car and yanked the keys out of the ignition. He quickly stepped away as the car door flew open and Donna stumbled out. She might be drunk off her ass, but that didn't make her any less strong.

"Give me my fuckin' keys!" Normally he would, never in the mood to bother with her when she got like this, but he had something else in mind. The timing was perfect.

He held the keys over her head. "Okay, so your mother popped you in the face—" *again* "—but why go storming off when I got a better idea of how to get even with the one who is really to blame for this?"

Trying to reach her keys, "I ain't goin' into Philly to get into it with a whole Pride. I ain't stupid." He wasn't so sure about that, but she gave a hell of a blow job, so he was willing to overlook her major flaws.

"You wanna hurt the mother . . . you hurt the kid."

Donna slowly lowered her arms and stared at him through the eye that wasn't swollen shut, although it was pretty glassy from all the Jack Daniel's she'd guzzled. "What are you talking about? Beatin' her up? We already did that."

"Nah. I'm talking about something a little more . . . permanent."

She turned away from him. Donna tried to pretend she didn't know what he did for cash, but she knew. They all knew, they just liked to pretend they didn't.

"Both?" she finally asked, no longer sounding nearly as drunk.

"Yeah. Both." He could practically feel the money in his hands. And Christ, it felt good.

Jay put his arms around her shoulders and nuzzled her ear. "Trust me, baby. They'll both get what they got comin'."

"How? The bitch isn't stupid. It's not like we can call her up and tell her to meet us somewhere."

"Gotta start thinkin' different, baby. Gotta start thinkin' a little more human."

Donna's lip turned up a little at that, but then she asked, "When?"

He smiled, his mind already turning. "Soon. Real soon."

She felt wonderful against him, all sweaty and soft, her exhausted body pressing down on his. He dragged his hand down her spine and across the curve of her ass.

"Use your claws," she murmured, snuggling closer.

He did, carefully dragging them down her back and up again. He didn't know if she realized she fell asleep like that, with his claws caressing her back while they lay on his kitchen floor.

They'd just arrived home after she'd met him at the training rink and he'd taken her to the diner down the block. They'd eaten dinner but decided to have dessert back at the apartment. He'd been heading for the ice cream in his freezer when she'd wrapped her arms around his waist from behind. She had his jeans unzipped and her hand inside his boxer briefs in less than five seconds. After that their clothes went flying and they ended up abusing his kitchen floor.

She only slept twenty minutes before she lifted her head from his chest, pretty eyes blinking as she looked around the room.

"Ice cream?" she asked.

"Freezer. I'll get it."

"No. I'll get it." Placing her palms flat on his chest, she levered herself up and scratched her head. Then she stretched, arms above her head, chest pushed out. Lock grew hard again and reached for her.

"Ice cream," she insisted, pushing his grasping hands away. "And don't pout," she ordered before she got up and walked to his freezer.

Gwen stared into Lock's freezer. *How much ice cream did the man eat on a daily basis?* The top three shelves were filled with pints of ice cream, from the expensive brand names to the cheap store-brand versions. He had every flavor possible.

While holding the door open, Gwen turned to ask Lock what kind he wanted, but he had his legs up in the air, his hands gripping his toes.

"Enjoying yourself?"

He grinned, nodded.

Did he really have to be so cute? Was that really fair to her *at all*?

"Which ice cream do you want?"

"Rum raisin."

She glanced in the freezer. "Any particular brand? You've got like ten rum raisins in here."

"Doesn't matter."

She grabbed the rum raisin at the front and dug around until she found butter pecan for herself.

"Where are the spoons again?"

"Second drawer to the . . ." he pointed with one leg ". . . left."

"That is *not* an attractive position for any man to put himself in."

He laughed and went back to playing grabby toes or whatever he called it.

Ice cream, spoons, and paper towels in hand, Gwen walked back over to Lock and sat down on the floor.

"We can go into the living room if you want."

"Nah." She took off the top to the rum raisin and stuck the spoon in it. "I'm getting a perverse enjoyment out of sitting naked in your kitchen, something my aunts would never allow because 'That's just nasty.' So, I want to savor that." Lock sat up, his back against the thick wood breakfast-table leg. But instead of taking the ice cream from her, he first pulled her over until she sat between his legs.

"Comfortable?"

Surprisingly, she was. Who knew she'd like having his thick cock pressing into her back like a lead pipe? "Yep."

Long arms reaching around her, he took hold of his ice cream and scooped spoonfuls out of the carton without Gwen worrying about him touching her with the cold container. His legs were so long, his toes kept pushing the swinging door open that led to the dining room. She felt completely dwarfed by him.

After a few spoonfuls of her ice cream, she finally had to ask, "Are you uncomfortable with your size?"

"No. I'm uncomfortable with how uncomfortable everyone else is about my size." He dipped his spoon into her butter pecan, which annoyingly left rum raisin residue behind. "There's only so many times you can hear, 'Holy shit, look at the size of that guy' before it gets old."

After scraping any rum raisin out and dumping it into a paper towel, Gwen said, "So Blayne and I were invited to this party on Saturday."

"It's Halloween."

She was waiting for more to that statement but it didn't seem like more would be coming. "Yeah. It's Halloween."

His spoon came in for another pass at her ice cream and she moved the container. "At least clean your spoon off better." She scrunched up her face. "I hate rum raisin."

"Blasphemer."

"Like I've never been called that before." And by actual men of God, too.

She took another scoop of her ice cream and offered it to Lock. Smiling, he cleaned off the spoon, and Gwen took a spoonful for herself. "Anyway, the party." She cleared her throat. "Blayne and I can bring someone with us, if we want, and I thought I'd see if you wanted to come with me. Although I should warn you that my mother's coming and I'll most likely spend a good portion of the evening stopping her from getting others drunk so she can make them do things they'll regret in the morning."

"I'll be working in my workshop on Saturday."

"Oh. Right. No problem. I mean, it was just a—"

"So I'll meet you there, if that's okay. Ric's gonna pick me up in his limo." He gulped down another mouthful of ice cream. "Afterward we can come home together like we did tonight."

"Okay. Sounds good." She scooped up another spoonful of ice cream but didn't eat it, instead placing the spoon back in the container. "You were already going?"

"Yeah."

"You hate parties."

"I know. But Jess threatened me with tears. It was either go or endure the crying. I hate when she cries."

"Right." Gwen picked up the spoon but ended up shoving it back into the ice cream. "So what is your attachment to her?"

"Jess is my friend," he explained while he continued eating.

"And?"

"And what?"

"Did you date her or something?"

"Jess?"

"Yeah. Jess. She of the weepy eyes and the excessively clingy hold on you. That Jess."

"She doesn't have a clingy hold on me."

"So if she told you to jump off a bridge . . . ?"

"It would depend on what she wanted me to jump off the bridge for."

Glaring at the bear over her shoulder, "*What kind of answer is that?*"

"Look, if she asked me to jump off the bridge because she was bored and wanted to see if I would die a painful death in the Atlantic, then no, I wouldn't. If one of her pups had fallen in or it was Jess or one of her Pack, then of course I would go in and try to get them. Because it's Jess."

"Oh, my God," Gwen blurted, feeling incredibly stupid for not seeing it before. "You're in love with her."

Lock's head snapped up, the spoon hanging out of his mouth like a lollipop. "*What?*"

"You heard me!" She tried to pull away from him, but he gripped her around the waist, holding her against his chest. "Why don't you just admit you're in love with her?" she demanded when he wouldn't let her go.

"Because I'm not in love with her."

"Bullshit."

"Gwen . . ." He took the spoon out of his mouth and stuck it in what was left of his ice cream, took hold of her container, and placed them both aside. He then turned her around and lifted her into his lap so they could look directly at each other.

"I love Jess," he said. "But I'm not in love with her."

"Then—"

"Let me finish, because this is not an easy story to tell." He took a breath and went on. "Jess talked to me when no one else would. She gave me a job when no one else would. She has my loyalty."

"Fresh out of the Marines, advanced college education, and

you were having trouble getting work?" She did try to keep the disbelief out of her voice but she failed.

"I wasn't simply fresh out of the Marines, Gwen. I was fresh out of the Unit."

In anger she'd forgotten, but she did know there was a difference. A large one. "Right."

"I was specifically recruited to be in the Unit. All my training, every year I was in . . . always with the Unit. After eight years I was honorably discharged with a substantial bonus and a year of mandatory, five-times-a-week therapy."

Five times a week?

"I met Jess in a coffee shop near her office. I was using my mother's laptop to try and hack into my service records to see if I could find out why they cut me loose. At the time I wasn't ready to face why they sent me home two years before I should have been, but I knew why. Everyone knew why. Anyway, I hadn't shaved in about ten weeks. Hadn't had a haircut since I'd been discharged. Was still wearing my uniform . . . I definitely looked like the guy who was about to go up to the roof of some building and start picking people off with a bolt-action rifle. So I'm sitting there, doing something I know I shouldn't be doing, and when I looked up—" he shrugged "—she was standing there. Holding two big cups of coffee. Staring at me. I expected her to run. If not from a general fear of the grizzly, then at least from my stench— since it had been a few days since I'd showered. But she didn't run."

"What did she do?"

His smile was warm, and Gwen felt that pang of jealousy again. She hated feeling it, hated knowing she even had it. "She handed me one of those cups of coffee, along with six honey buns, sat down next to me and . . . and she talked to me. I don't even remember for how long or what was said. And, in the beginning, she did most of the talking. For a week, though, I came back to the same coffee shop around the same time and every day she was there or she'd show up a few minutes later, and we'd talk some more. Before I knew it, she'd hired me to write code for some of her company's software and when that went well, they hired me to do more. I started shaving again, showering every day, and I put all my military stuff in my trunk and put it in the back of my closet. Soon I had goals and plans for my future that were months or years ahead rather than days or hours. She helped me move on . . . well, her and the therapy. And that's not something I can ever forget. So, yeah, if Jess told me to jump off a bridge, and there was a good reason to do it, I probably would."

Gwen swallowed, torn between feeling grateful to Jess for helping Lock when he needed it most and resenting her for being closer to Lock then Gwen might ever be. "So you do love her," she said softly, determined to face the truth.

"Yeah, I love her. But I'm not in love with her. I'm not in love with anybody."

Gwen felt her heart drop at Lock's words, but she wouldn't come down on him for being honest. She'd rather that now than later.

Nodding, Gwen reached for her ice cream and said, "I understand."

"I mean," he went on, unwittingly turning the knife, "not in love with anybody but you." He thought a moment and added, "God, I'm crazy in love with *you*. But yeah, I love Jess. Wait . . . what's wrong?"

He was probably asking that because her hand was frozen in the action of reaching for her ice cream, but she'd been so stunned, she left it dangling there. Staring at her nails, she asked, "You're in love with me?"

"*Crazy* in love with you. You know, that whole 'can't imagine my life without you' crazy in love with you."

She dropped her hand back in her lap and gazed up at him in astonishment. "How do you just toss that into a conversation?"

"Not tossing, clarifying."

"You see, this is what I've been talking about with you. It's like the whittling—"

"I never said I whittled. I said it was a hobby. *You* thought it was whittling and there would be birdhouses."

"But the way you described it to me—in your quiet, understated way—made it sound like whittling. Instead you're like the Ansel Adams of wood!"

"And that's a problem?"

"No. *That's* not the problem, your way of telling me things is. You do this constantly."

"I do what constantly?"

Using her most calm, relaxed, "surfer dude" voice, Gwen replied, "Hey, just want you to know . . . sky's falling. Hey, nothing to worry about but . . . uh . . . tsunami."

"Oh, come on!"

"Hey," she went on casually even as her heart slammed hard against her ribs as she realized the grizzly loved her, "I invited this old buddy of mine over for dinner. He's president of the United States of America, and he's bringing about three hundred people with him, but no problem, I'm sure we have something in the freezer."

Lock pouted. "I'm not *that* bad."

"Yeah, ya are. You're lucky I can overlook it."

Then Gwen reached up, her fingers stroking his cheek, his jaw; her eyes focused on his beautiful face.

"It's okay, Gwen." He gave her that sweet smile. "Say it when you're ready."

"Okay. I will." She slid her hands into his hair and tugged so he would move closer. She sat tall in his lap, raising her mouth to his. When they were barely a breath apart, Gwen said, "I love you." She smiled, shrugged. "I was ready."

Lock's hands bracketed her face, long fingers stroking her skin. He studied her like he wanted to absorb every part of her, take in every detail. No one had ever looked at her like that and, if they had, it clearly hadn't meant as much.

Lock's lips met hers and, as his tongue slipped inside her mouth, she leaned back onto the kitchen floor, taking Lock with her.

* * *

"Table Six up," Ric called out as he placed the two large and expertly roasted and plated slabs of venison on the counter. The server grabbed both plates and walked out.

Grabbing a bottle of water out of the fridge, Ric said to his sous chef, "I'll be back. Taking a break."

He walked out without waiting for an answer and headed into the alley behind the restaurant. Drinking water, he stared up at the sky. It was a nice night. A beautiful night.

"Planning to run away?" a voice asked.

Ric's grin was wide and real as he threw his arms around the man's shoulders. "Uncle Van! It's so good to see you."

"Hello, cousin." Niles Van Holtz, Uncle Van to the younger cousins of the Pack, stepped back and studied him closely. "Busy night?"

Ric let out an exhausted sigh. "You have no idea." He gestured with his water bottle. "So what brings you to this coast?" His shoulders slumped. "Do I need to involve my father?"

"Oh, God, no. I'm still recovering from Memorial Day weekend."

Ric cringed, remembering the family event that had turned ugly rather quickly. "I sent Aunt Irene flowers." Complete with groveling apology. "She said she liked them."

"She loved them. Although I had to hear, yet again, how it's my fault that we didn't take you from that, and I'm quoting here, 'Visigoth' when you were five and realized your IQ was higher than your parents' and brother's combined."

Laughing and appreciating the compliment from a bona fide genius like Irene Conridge-Van Holtz, Ph.D., Ric shrugged. "So what do you need?"

"The information you sent me a few days ago?"

"Yes?"

Van held out something and Ric took it. It was made of studded leather and when he unraveled the pieces, he realized it was a very large muzzle. A very large, blood-encrusted muzzle.

"I think it's time, cousin," the older wolf said and, sadly studying the piece of equipment in his hands, Ric had to agree.

Chapter 25

Alla Baranova-MacRyrie watched her son lift her husband's old and extremely heavy desk up and out of the way and put in the new one.

"I thought your father just wanted you to fix the old desk."

"I know." Lock shifted the new desk back, forth, back, trying to make sure it was perfectly situated. "But after examining it, I decided he needed a new desk."

"He likes the old one because his son made it."

"I was thirteen. It's flawed."

Alla rolled her eyes. Some things would never change. "Yes. Horribly flawed. It only managed to last eighteen years in perfectly acceptable condition. At your father's dangerous hands, no less. Must be a huge disappointment to you."

Stepping back until he stood beside her, Lock observed the desk and the surrounding area. "Think he'll like it?"

"He'll adore it."

Lock glanced at her. "Why are you wearing a witch's hat?"

"It's Halloween."

"Yes. I know. I'm going to a party later tonight."

"You? Going to a party? With people?"

"Cute."

Arms crossed over her chest, Alla said, "That desk is really beautiful, Lachlan."

"Thank you." Lock cleared his throat. "I'm . . . uh . . ." He cleared his throat again. "I'm probably going to be doing this as a business."

"Building desks?"

"Yes. No. I mean, building desks, chairs, tables, whatever."

"Like an assembly line?"

"No, not at all. I'm talking handmade pieces."

"Art."

"It depends who you talk to."

Alla nodded. "That fits you."

Lock gave her a sidelong glance. "You're not . . ."

"Disappointed?"

"Since I've been back you've been pushing school, teaching—"

"Lachlan, you're very good at many things, but I want you to do what makes you happy. The military didn't make you happy. Software—" she rolled her eyes "—honestly. Where's your joy in that? But this?" She held her hands out, gesturing to the desk. "This brings you joy. That's all I've ever cared about."

Alla turned to face him and placed her hands on both his cheeks. "I want my son happy. Because when you're happy, you shine."

Lock kissed her cheek. "Thanks, Mom."

"Now you've got a party to go to. And I hope you're not going alone."

"Nope. I'm going with Ric."

Alla let out an annoyed sigh. "I did not mean Ulrich."

Lock grinned. "I'm meeting Gwen there."

"Excellent."

"You like her."

"I like her for *you.*" After a moment, she shrugged and added, "And I like her." *Because she makes you shine.*

"Children are beginning to show up," Brody said as he walked into the room. "I can't terrify them from the bushes if you're not manning the door, Alla."

"Of course. Because that's what makes this dreadful holiday so entertaining."

Brody walked over to his new desk. "This is gorgeous!"

"I'm glad you like it, Dad."

"And a rolltop." He pushed the rolltop up and then twisted around and under to see inside. "I've always wondered how these types of desk work."

"Dad. Don't take my desk apart."

"Of course not!" Brody pursed his lips. "But if I were just to—"

"No!" Mother and son barked in unison.

Brody pouted and Alla had no idea why when he did that it always made her love him a little more. "There's no need to get testy," he grouched.

Gwen opened the door and stared at her best friend. "I can't believe you still have that costume."

"I can't believe I still fit in it." Blayne twirled once in the hallway. "Isn't it great?"

"Yep. It's great." And very, *very* Blayne. Her idea of a 1950s Satan's Cheerleader, complete with a full-length red poodle skirt— only the poodle was a snarling Doberman pinscher—a black V-necked sweater, saddle shoes, short black socks, black and red pom-poms, an inverted-cross necklace in black, and her long hair blown out straight and in a high pony tail with bangs combed over her forehead. Plus the "blood"-covered rosarys hanging off her hip was a nice and recent touch.

Blayne studied Gwen. "You and your sixties obsession."

"Best era for clothes and music."

"You look like you should be in an Andy Warhol movie." Blayne's eyes narrowed. "Is that a wig?"

"Nah." Gwen ran her hands through her freshly shorn locks. "I cut it."

"Lemme see."

Gwen lowered her hand and shook out her hair. She'd kept the front ends a little longer and cut the back shorter. It had been a whim after studying some old photos online when she was pulling her costume together. Blayne dropped her pom-poms and circled Gwen, playing with the ends of her hair.

"It's perfect."

"You like it?"

"I love it." Blayne dug her hands into Gwen's hair and scrubbed like crazy. Laughing, Gwen batted her off.

"Let's go!" Blayne cheered, doing a forward cartwheel back into the hallway—and almost popping Gwen in the face with those long legs. "I'm so ready to go. It's gonna be a blast!"

"Yeah," Gwen agreed. It'll be a blast—for Blayne. Gwen, however, would spend the whole evening keeping track of her mother and brother and making the peace when it was necessary. But Lock promised he'd meet her there, and she had no doubts he'd come through. If nothing else, she had a great after-party party to look forward to.

Hell, if she had her way, she'd forgo the stupid costume party altogether and hook up with Lock. But her mother . . .

"You ready or what?" Blayne asked eagerly.

"Uh . . . hold on." Gwen went to the coffee table and grabbed a pack of gum, a tube of lipstick, her ID, and cash. She placed those inside her boots. Then she grabbed the closed straight razor she'd carried with her everywhere in Philly and now New York and slid it into the small holder sewn into the inside of her pants. Having claws, she didn't need the weapon with other shifters, but when she dealt with humans, a lot of them carrying those damn cell phones with cameras around, she found it necessary. She'd rather be arrested for having an illegal weapon than end up on the cover of the *Daily News* as evidence of werewolves or something.

Gwen walked back to the front door and headed out with Blayne, closing the hotel door behind her.

She was glad to see that Blayne had had the cab wait for them. Halloween was a busy night in Manhattan, and she had no desire to get on the subway.

Traffic was thick, but they made it to the party in good time. The entire club had been rented out for the Kuznetsov Pack, and they could already tell tons of people had shown up. They found themselves stuck in line for a bit before reaching the front door.

While they waited, Gwen glanced over and watched as a too-young-for-those-tiny-shorts Assault and Battery Park Babe rolled up to them.

Gwen shook her head at Kristan's outfit and laughed. "Your mother is going to snap her leash when she sees you, girly-girl."

"Can I help it if I look really good in this?" Kristan said as she gave Gwen a warm hug and then Blayne.

"She does look good," Blayne agreed.

"Too good, if you ask me." Gwen glared at the three cougars standing behind them, checking out the young wolfdog. She hissed and they hissed back, so she tossed in, "Jailbait." *That* got them to look away, but her gaze quickly scanned the street, feeling like someone else's eyes were on them. "Who you looking so good for?" she asked Kristan as she turned back to them.

"Nobody."

Gwen snorted. "Liar."

"Total liar," Blayne laughed.

"Come on, kid. Fess up."

"Okay. There's a guy at school." She shrugged, looking adorably sweet. "He may swing by tonight."

"You bringing him in?"

"Are you kidding? He's full-human. My father will have a fit."

"Don't do anything stupid," Gwen warned her, unable to help herself.

"I'll work on that." Kristan pointed at the crowd. "Why are you two standing in line?"

"Because the last time we cut a line, Blayne got stabbed in the arm."

"I can't believe you're still blaming me for that."

"You shouldn't have cut the line."

"Oh, my God. You two are like bickering old women." Kristan grabbed an arm from each and skated forward, dragging them with her. "They're with me," she told security, who immediately let them in.

"Power of the pups," she explained happily before skating off down another corridor.

"We're going to have to keep an eye on her tonight, too," Gwen sighed.

"Why?"

"Look at her in that outfit." They did.

"Okay. Maybe you have a point." Then Blayne grinned. "You're so sweet, though."

"Huh?"

"Watching out for Kristan."

"In those shorts?" she murmured, watching some male walk by the entrance they'd just come through, his gaze slowly moving from Kristan and back to Blayne and Gwen before one of the security guards motioned him away. "Someone has to."

They went down a long hallway dressed up with jack-o'-lanterns, skeletons, and bubbling cauldrons. When they reached another set of doors, the phrase "Enter at your own risk" was scrawled across it in red paint. When Gwen grabbed the handle and pulled the door open, one of her favorite sixties songs, "Denise," was playing. She and Blayne grinned at each other, immediately feeling at home. At least where the music was concerned. Gwen loved anything from the sixties, but for Blayne it was the fifties, although they overlapped eras to keep their friendship intact.

They walked in, and Gwen admired the job the wild dogs had done, going for the high school gym look rather than the standard haunted house. An even nicer touch was all the "bodies" lying around.

"Carrie," Blayne blurted out.

"Who?"

"Not who, what. This is the prom scene from the movie *Carrie*. See over there? That's where one character gets slammed by water from a fire hose. And that's Carrie getting dumped with blood, and over there is the teacher who was nice to her and got cut in half. Brilliant," Blayne sighed.

Gwen had to agree. One could get a lot of things when they had the money to buy them, but something told Gwen that the Kuznetsov Pack lived for these kinds of details and, rich or poor, they'd always create entertainment at this level. They didn't do it to impress anyone but themselves and their intense geekiness. Gwen admired that.

Shame she wouldn't be able to fully enjoy it. "I better find my mother."

"There's Mitch," Blayne pointed out. Gwen nodded and walked over to the table her brother was sitting at.

"Nice costume," she mocked.

"Hey, hey. Watch what you say." Mitch glanced over his Roman soldier outfit. "I'll have you know I'm a legionnaire."

"A common foot soldier," she threw back at him. "You couldn't even make yourself a captain or a general?"

"What?" he asked as she dropped in to the seat beside him and Blayne sat across from them. "You think I have Roman soldier costumes lying around for my use? I got this from the wild dogs. Everyone's in costume tonight, according to wild dog law." He looked his sister over. "So you better change."

"I *am* in costume, you cretin."

Mitch leaned back, took another look. "Really?"

"White go-go boots? You see me wear these every day?"

"Don't get snappy. You look cute. The mole's a nice touch."

"It's a beauty mark."

"Whatever."

"Aren't you going to say 'hi' to me?" Blayne asked.

Mitch glared. "No."

Determined to deal with her burden now rather than later, Gwen demanded, "Where's Ma?"

Mitch shrugged. "I don't know."

"What do you mean you don't know?" Gwen kneeled on her chair and studied the crowd closely. "Where is she? Who is she talking to? She didn't corner anybody yet, did she?"

"What are you doing?"

"Looking for our mother. Why aren't you?"

"Because she's not here."

"What do you mean she's not here? You said you didn't know where she was."

· "I don't know where she is in the big cosmic scheme of life at this very second. But I do know she's not here."

"How do you know that?"

" 'Cause I talked to her ten minutes ago on the phone and she was screaming about how she was running late and the god-damn neighborhood kids were already ringing her doorbell and how she hated giving the goddamn neighborhood kids goddamn chocolate, but she didn't want them egging her goddamn house. And she hated this goddamn time of year, and why was I calling her on this goddamn night when she had to take the goddamn kids trick-or-treating?"

Blayne fell back in her chair laughing, while Gwen could only shake her head.

"So unless she's planning to sprint from Philly to Manhattan in the next few hours," Mitch added, "I think you're off the hook."

"Except I've gotta watch out for you."

"Nope. I'm sticking to two beers tonight."

"Since when?"

"Since I've gotta keep an eye on my woman. More than four shots of tequila and someone's going to jail . . . and it's usually Ronnie, which means Bren will be pissed and I gotta hear about it." Her brother looked at her. "So it looks like you'll be taking care of yourself tonight, baby sister."

Gwen sat in her chair, dropping her legs to the floor. "I've still gotta watch Blayne."

"Nope. I don't drink." Gwen and Mitch laughed at Blayne. "What?"

"Thank *God* you don't drink," Mitch said. "I can't imagine the level of trouble you'd get into if you weren't constantly sober."

"Yeah, but unlike you and your mother, I don't actively look for trouble. It finds me." She smiled at Gwen. "But I'm safe in a completely controlled environment, so you should just relax and have a good time."

Gwen nodded, sure things wouldn't go that easy. "I'll work on that."

Blayne glanced around. "When's he getting here?"

Mitch sneered. "That bear? *Ow!*" He glared across the table at Blayne. "What did you kick me for?"

"Because you should mind your own business," Blayne snapped.

"I don't want my baby sister settling on some flea-bitten honey-lover! Ow! Stop kicking me!"

"Then leave your sister alone or I swear by all that's holy—"

Sissy walked up and dropped into Mitch's lap, forcing Blayne to cut off the rest of her threat. Gwen didn't know what was going on between Mitch and Blayne, but then again . . . she didn't really care.

"Where's Bren and Ronnie?" Mitch asked Sissy while he still glared at Blayne.

At the mention of the canine's name, Gwen hissed and arched her back.

"Calm down, vicious kitty, they're off somewhere across the room." Sissy scrutinized Gwen. "You gonna tell me what happened between you and Ronnie?"

"Nothing," Gwen lied. "Why?"

Mitch stared down at his mate's T-shirt, jeans, and cowboy boots. "Why are you not in costume?"

"I am in costume. I told them I'm a killer of wild dogs who annoy the fuck out of me. Needless to say they backed off the whole costume thing."

"How is that fair?"

"We're predators, darlin'. There is no fair among predators."

"I keep forgetting." Mitch focused back on Gwen and Blayne. "Now you two need to understand something. I've got a reputation that must be maintained at all times. These wild dogs love me, so don't embarrass me."

Gwen and Blayne shrugged easily and said in unison, "Yeah. Okay."

* * *

Mitch had never noticed it before, but as soon as he'd told Gwen their mother wasn't coming to the party, all the tension she'd walked in with seemed to evaporate. Now she and Blayne were bopping their heads to the music and . . . Christ, was his sister smiling?

The whole thing was probably something he should look into but . . . eh. Why bother?

"Great music," Gwen said, and that was not an easy compliment to get out of her. She was as finicky about her music as she was about her food.

"It's all that oldies crap you like. According to Phil, that's what they're mostly playing tonight." The music on the sound system changed and he added, "And the eighties, because apparently a wild dog party isn't a wild dog party without Adam and the Ants."

Blayne grinned. "I love this song!"

" 'Prince Charming' circa 1981," Gwen announced.

"How little I care," Mitch said dryly. He pointed at his face. "This is my 'How little I care' face. Can you see that?"

"Really?" Gwen asked, just as dryly. " 'Cause this is my 'Beat the shit outta my brother' face. Do you like this face? Do you wanna see what I can do with this face?"

"Y'all!" Sissy snapped. "Cut it out!"

"She started it."

Sissy glared down at him. "Leave your sister alone, Mitchell Shaw."

"You still don't understand, do you? I am not the Alpha Male to your Alpha Female," Mitch patiently explained to the woman he loved.

"Is that right?"

"That's right. I am the Lord High God Ruler to your Alpha Female. And the sooner you learn that, and bow down to my greatness, the sooner this relationship is running like a well-oiled machine."

"You've lost your ever-lovin' mind!" Sissy shouted out, laughing.

"It's true! And do you know why it's true? Because I am a lion male. Ruler over all I survey. Tell her, Gwenie . . . Gwenie?"

Mitch looked for his sister and gasped in horror. "Good God, what is she doing?"

Sissy gazed out at the dance floor, and her laughter turned downright hysterical. Not that he could blame her when his baby sister and her best friend were in the middle of a bunch of wild dogs dancing. But not mere dancing, because that he could tolerate. They were actually doing the moves from the original Adam and the Ants "Prince Charming" video. All of them, to-gether . . . in sync.

"Apparently my 'do not embarrass me' speech has been ig-nored!"

"You're lucky she didn't deck you again. Besides," Sissy gave him a quick kiss, "she looks like she's having fun for once. I didn't know the girl knew how."

"My sister has fun."

"Not from what I've seen. So why don't you leave her alone?"

"Yeah, but—"

"Not listening." Sissy stood up and announced to anyone in earshot, "Tequila for everybody!"

When Mitch glared up at her she leaned in and whispered, "Don't worry, darlin'. Open bar, so we don't have to pay a cent."

"That's not what I—" But she was already gone and Mitch had a feeling it was going to be a long night.

Lock and Ric walked through the double doors and all Lock could say was, "Definitely a wild dog party."

"Absolutely," Ric muttered.

Lock surveyed all the costumes. Some must have cost a small fortune and some were ridiculous. "Is that supposed to be a used condom?"

Ric's lip curled in distaste. "That's just vile."

Lock was glad he and Ric had gone with the all-black look— black jeans, long-sleeved tee, boots, and leather jackets. Simple and understated. When it came to his wardrobe, Lock liked understated.

"What do you want to do first?" Ric asked.

"Find Gwen," Lock answered, eager to see her. Gwen had spent every night with him the past week and it had gotten to the point where he didn't even want to think of her sleeping anywhere else but in his bed, with his arms around her.

"Sounds good," Ric replied, but they'd only managed to get a few feet when Jess stepped in front of them.

Pleasantly startled, Lock peered down at her. "My God, Jess . . . you look beautiful." Although he wouldn't mention the pointed ears.

"Thanks! I'm a wood elf of the royal family."

Lock and Ric glanced at each other and then said together, "Okay."

She motioned to the two of them. "And what are you two wearing?"

"Clothes," Lock answered, immediately worried.

"Where are your costumes?"

Panicked, Lock turned to Ric who said, after a moment, "These are our costumes, Jessica."

"Explain please."

"We're . . . uh . . . spies. I'm Double-O Seven." He motioned to Lock. "And this is Jaws."

Lock scowled at him. "That's not funny."

Jess glared at them a few seconds longer, then waved her arms in the air. Before he could take his next breath, Sabina and Maylin appeared on either side of her.

Ric scrutinized Sabina's entire costume but appeared most focused on the short red lines she'd drawn around her entire neck. "Uh . . . who are you?"

"Queen Marie Antoinette," Sabina immediately answered. "They took her head in the French Revolution, but then they sewed the head back on and now she is one of the undead searching for fresh blood. Preferably of innocent virgin boys."

Ric let out a breath. "Lovely." He motioned to Maylin. "And you're—"

"Bonnie!" She grinned. "To my Danny's Clyde."

"The bloody bullet holes are an . . . *interesting* touch."

"Thanks!"

"Lock and Ric are trying to tell me these are their costumes."

"No," Sabina stated flatly. "That will not do."

"We're comfortable in our costumes," Lock said, desperately trying to avoid where this was going.

"Those are not costumes," Maylin said, looking extremely disappointed in both of them.

Jess crossed her arms over her chest. "The invite said costumes a must. Did you not see that?"

"But Ric said—"

Throwing up her hands as if the weight of the world were placed on her shoulders, "Well, this will have to be fixed!"

"Or," Lock said quickly, "I can go home."

Turning quickly before he could see that first wild dog tear track down that pretty face, Lock took several steps but stopped when Jess tossed after him, "I'll tell Gwen you left."

Damn! He'd have to remember that he couldn't panic and leave his loved ones behind. Very bear-type behavior but rude.

"Where is she?"

She jerked her thumb at the enormous dance floor that was filled to capacity. "Out there with Blayne. Having a wonderful time in costume . . . without you."

Not just in a costume but in a costume that made her look freakin' adorable! And apparently the males surrounding her and Blayne thought so, too.

Lock's jaw popped and he took a step, but a small hand fell against his chest. "Don't even think about going out there without a costume."

He scowled down at the adorable little wild dog who was pissing him off. "You can't be serious."

"Serious as linoleum."

Not sure what that even meant, Lock sent Ric a questioning glance, but the wolf could only shake his head. Ric's logical brain had given up trying to make sense of wild dog thinking years ago.

"The men, they like Gwen, yes?" Sabina asked brightly.

He snarled at her, and Ric quickly stepped between the two.

"Jess, we're sorry about this. But it's so late and we can't get costumes now. All the stores will be out. And the ones that aren't won't have our size."

"We know that." Jess grinned. "And that's why we're providing costumes for those who don't have them!" She pointed at a room off in a corner. "We even have tailors standing around to help with fittings."

Ric glanced at Lock and immediately grimaced when he saw his face.

"*You walked right into that one!*" Lock bellowed, causing several nearby wild dogs and felines to take off running.

"Come, bear." Sabina grabbed his arm. "We dress you so you don't look more like fool than you usually do."

Jess took Lock's other arm and led him to the room. Ric tried to back out the door, but Maylin got a good grip on him and dragged him along behind them all.

"I so blame you for this, Van Holtz!" Lock snarled at his best friend.

"*Like I'm not also in hell?*"

The music changed from "Psychotic Reaction" to "Land of a Thousand Dances" and Blayne was immediately back by Gwen's side, the two of them doing each dance called out in the song, the wild dogs clapping and cheering around them. Yup! Great music. As one nun had told her—or hissed at her, depending on your perspective—"Your only saving grace is your excellent taste in music, Devil's Whore." Gwen appreciated the compliment but could have done without that damn nickname.

Laughing and impressing the wild dogs, the friends danced, while Gwen enjoyed herself more than she had in a very long time.

After a few minutes, Blayne's teammates ran up to them. There were a few moments of derby-girl squealing and hugging that for once, because she was having such a good time, Gwen didn't mind—even though she did think, *Didn't you people just see each other yesterday?*

Gwen didn't even mind when they squealed and hugged her, too.

"I didn't know you guys were coming," Blayne said, her arm around Suli, a.k.a. Our Lady of Pain and Suffering, who was dressed as a very hot Sailor Moon.

"Invited by Jess Ward-Smith herself. She's been at every bout we've had lately."

"I heard you guys made it into the championships next week." Gwen smiled at Blayne. "Congratulations."

"You'll have to be there," Suli said. "As our . . . what was it, Blayne?"

"Teammate in spirit!" And Blayne threw her arms up, cheerleader style.

"Right." Suli laughed. "But seriously, Gwen, you should join the team. We're up against the Furriers again."

Gwen shook her head. "No, thanks." She was more than happy to let that call for revenge go. "But I'll definitely be there to support you guys." And Blayne.

The music changed again, Martha Reeves and the Vandellas' "Heat Wave" blasting through the club. The two friends grinned at each other before letting out a scream and breaking into the Watusi, the wild dogs going right along with them.

Nope, Gwen thought as she and Blayne moved expertly around each other. *Nothing can make this night any better!*

Nothing can make this night any worse!

Lock held on to the marble pillar, using his four-inch claws, while nearly ten She-dogs tried to pry him loose and drag him out of the room.

"I'm not going!"

"Come on, Lock! You look fabulous!"

"I look like an idiot! And I'm not going out there!"

This was ridiculous. He was an apex predator! There was no predator big enough or strong enough to hunt a grizzly except, maybe, another grizzly or polar—and humans didn't count, since they had to use guns. But instead of batting these tiny She-dogs around like they deserved, he was holding on for dear life and hoping they'd grow bored.

Of course, he should know better. They were dogs! Dogs didn't grow bored. They could dig a hole for hours, chase their tails for hours, and apparently, they could tussle with a bear for hours!

Then Jess was there. The queen of the wild dogs. She personified doglike behavior. Like the brilliant poodle hanging out with all the dumb labs.

"You're going out there," she said.

"No. I'm not."

"Oh, yeah?" And she reached up, gripped his nipples, and twisted.

"*Ow!*" Lock released the pillar to protect his nipples and that's when one of them screamed, "*Heave!*"

The next second Lock MacRyrie was skidding to a halt outside that damn room.

A tiger male standing by looked at him and snorted. "Nice skirt, Gentle Ben."

Embarrassed, mortified, and pissed off in general about the nickname, Lock slammed the back of his fist into the tiger's nose.

The tiger flew back twenty feet, eventually hitting the floor, his hand over his face. "*Motherfucker! You broke my nose!*"

Not caring about the sobbing cat, Lock turned to the room, ready to retrieve his clothes and run home like a frightened cub, when the door slammed shut in his face. "Sorry!" the She-dogs yelled from the other side. "We're closed!"

"Open this door right now, or I'll—"

"Lock?" he heard from behind him. "Lock, is that you?"

Cringing, Lock slowly faced the She-wolf. "Hi, Adelle."

"Lock!" Hands covering her mouth, Adelle walked around him in a complete circle. She looked elegantly Van Holtz in a

Grecian gown, her hair done up on top of her head in a mass of curls, with plastic snakes sticking out. "You look . . ."

"Like an idiot?"

"No. No! Not at all." Adelle stopped in front of him. "You look—" she took his hands and lifted his arms, gawking at him "—amazingly, *deliciously* Scottish."

"Half-Scottish," he corrected.

"Uh-huh." Adelle dropped his arms and began to fan herself. "My, my. You have grown since I . . . uh . . . I last noticed."

"You mean since I was ten?" Because she'd always treated him like he was still ten . . . until this moment. At this moment, she wasn't treating him or looking at him like he was still ten.

This was becoming a nightmare!

"So, Lachlan," she said, her hand stroking her collarbone. "Would you like a drink? Or something?"

"No . . . no thank you." He sidestepped away from Adelle, disturbed that the woman he saw as one of his aunts watched him as if he were a wounded baby deer.

He had to find Ric, he had to get his clothes back. He couldn't walk around for the rest of the night like . . .

Lock stopped, stared down at the Pack of She-dogs gaping up at him. They weren't Jess's Pack, they were Asian wild dogs visiting from Japan and really pretty . . . and gaping.

He forced a smile, knowing he wouldn't be able to slap them around either. "Hi."

"Hi," they all sighed out and, shaken, Lock sidestepped around them. He spotted Ric at a bar across the room, and headed over to him. As he walked he heard distinctive She-wolf whistles, dropped glassware, and several "Oh, my dear God in heaven!" exclamations. If they were directed at him, he didn't know, didn't care, and wasn't going to ask. He wanted out. He hadn't felt this in danger since his military days when he had to sit around and patiently wait for full-humans to get him in their sights.

"We need to go," he said as soon as he was next to Ric.

"They have some of the most exquisite wine here tonight. And a sommelier to serve. Surprising as it may sound, the wild dogs are rife with class, my . . . *holy shit!* Look at you!" Laughing, Ric shook his head and examined his friend. "I thought it was bad when they made me wear this Jane Austen–suitor outfit, complete with cravat. But you! You look like you just escaped the set of *Braveheart*."

"Right. Yeah. We need to go."

"Why? You're already in costume, you might as well have a drink and relax."

"That will not be possible."

"Why not?"

Lock motioned behind him with a tilt of his head and Ric leaned over to get a look. His entire body jerked and he abruptly stood straight, facing the bar.

"Dear God, man. They're following you like you're the Pied Piper of Scottish sex."

"There were six behind me before."

"Well, now you have fourteen." He glanced again. "And the number is growing."

"What am I going to do?"

"If you try and make a run for it, they'll simply take you down. It's best to see if they lose interest."

"Think they will?"

"Maybe if you'd worn a shirt—"

"They said they didn't have a shirt!"

"Then I have nothing for you, my friend. You're trapped. I, however—"

"Take one step away from me, you Mr. Darcy wannabe, and I'll snap your spine."

Nodding, Ric settled back into place and picked up his wineglass. "Well, then, here's to an interesting evening."

"Gwenie?"

Dancing to "I'm the Face," Gwen barely heard her friend, but when she realized every female on the dance floor was staring off, Gwen looked over at Blayne. And, yep, her friend was staring in the same direction as all the other females.

"What's going on?"

"You need to see this," Blayne said, grabbing Gwen's arm and yanking her over.

Gwen expected to see that her mother *had* arrived or Mitch had decided to do something particularly stupid. But it wasn't either of those painfully atypical scenarios. Instead, it was Lock MacRyrie simply standing by the bar. Yet it wasn't that he was merely standing there, it was that he was wearing a kilt. And it was the "full kilt experience," as Roxy liked to put it—and one of the reasons Roxy and her sisters insisted they go to the Highland Games every year although they were Irish.

The pattern was a combination of dark green, blue, and white with the kilt reaching Lock's knees, a large brown belt around his waist, and a swath of material stretching from his waist and over one shoulder, held together by a big brooch with a coat of arms printed on it. He also had brown leather armbands on both wrists and fur boots with thick flannel socks . . . and that was it. No shirt.

And wow . . . was that a lot of perfection to look at. Seven feet and three hundred and fifty pounds of perfection.

While most guys—most guys being her brother, cousins, and uncles—would be lapping this up—pocketing numbers, getting girls to strip, and playing "who can get my kilt to rise"—Lock looked more like a bear cub cornered by hungry grizzly males. But what exactly did he expect in that outfit? She didn't want to imply he was asking for it but . . . *he kind of was!*

"What do you think?" Jess asked as she and Maylin stood next to them. "Doesn't he look great?"

Gwen pointed a finger in Lock's direction. "Who are those women?" Those women *all over him*!

"I'm going to guess they're fans of Scottish culture and that kilt I have him in is a perfect replica of the MacRyrie family kilt."

Fans of Scottish culture, my ass! "They're checking out his legs."

"He's got great legs," Jess said as one of the bouncers from the front whispered something in her ear and she walked off.

But that was no problem, because May quickly took her place and said, "He's got big strong thighs, huh? Like a Clydesdale."

"*My Clydesdale*," Gwen ground out between clenched teeth, making the dog jump back from her.

"Well, if you're going to get all upset," Maylin looked at the whores surrounding Lock, "then you better get over there and get him." Maylin reared back from the slashing claws. "And there's no call to get nasty!"

Gwen cracked her knuckles and said to Blayne, "Watch my back."

"Go get your man, Gwenie."

The friends banged fists, then Gwen took several steps, crouched, and leaped forward. The legs she'd inherited from her father launched her from the dance floor, landing her directly in front of Lock. She slammed down in front of him and spun around to face the whores crowding around him.

"Hey!" some She-wolf complained. "We were talkin' to him."

Great. More horny hillbillies.

"Fuck off."

"Why don't you make us?"

Gwen unleashed her hiss-roar and the wild dogs took off running, the felines sidled away, and the She-wolves snarled back.

"I don't see your name on him, feline," another hillbilly complained.

"How about I put my name on you?" Gwen slashed her claws across the female's upper chest to get her meaning across. "Would you like that, whore?"

Covering up the gushing wounds with her hands, the She-wolf backed off and the others did the same, easing back until they seemed to fade into the dancing, partying crowd.

Snarling around what suspiciously felt like a hairball, Gwen caught hold of Lock's arm and dragged him over to one of the tables. She looked at the three males taking up her space and snarled, "Move!" They snorted at her and went back to their conversation. That's when Lock quietly said, "Move." And they did.

Gwen pushed Lock into a chair, paced off, and, after two seconds, paced right back.

"Have you lost your mind?"

He gazed up at her, looking so cute and sweet and unbelievably sexy she could eat the bastard alive! "In what way?"

What kind of answer was *that* exactly?

She was about to ask him that question, too, when some She-jackal eased up to his side and asked Lock in what could only be described as a disgustingly forced baby voice, "So are you really Scottish?"

"*Oh, my God!*" Gwen bellowed, beyond fed up. "*Fuck off!*"

"If you're going to get so defensive," the She-jackal sniped, that baby voice miraculously disappearing, "you may want to mark him so we're all clear."

Gwen's head lowered, her eyes locked on the target in front of her, and she growled out, "I will kill you."

Lock quickly grabbed Gwen's arm and dragged her onto his lap while she watched the jackal practically sprint back into the crowd.

Yanking her arm out of Lock's grasp, Gwen faced away from him, her legs straddling his big thighs, and she scowled at any encroaching females. No one was getting near what was hers. Nobody.

"Hi, Gwen," Lock finally said to her back.

"Don't talk to me," she snapped, still good and pissed.

"Ever?"

Gwen looked at him over her shoulder. "What were you thinking, sashaying around here dressed in *that* outfit?"

"I didn't sashay. Although I might have swaggered a bit."

Turning her body around so she faced him, Gwen moved up on Lock's lap and said, "That doesn't answer my question."

"It's not my fault." He pointed at the crowd. "It's *their* fault."

Without turning her body again, Gwen's head snapped around until she could look behind her.

The wild dogs standing behind her screamed in horror and

ran off. All except two. Sabina, who looked as if she didn't run from anyone, no matter how terrified she may be. And Jess.

Gazing in fascination, Jess asked, "How do you do that? Is it a genetic deformity?"

Gwen pulled her gums over her fangs, and Sabina caught Jess's arm and dragged her off into the crowd.

"But I need to know!" Jess argued. "That is *not* normal! But, I mean, how cool!"

Feeling surprisingly better knowing that Lock didn't pick this costume himself, Gwen faced him again and said, "You can't wear outfits like this around predator females, Lachlan. They're worse than males. They descended on you like vultures at a lion kill."

"I think you're blaming the victim."

"Shut up." She pointed a finger. "And don't laugh," she added when she saw his lips tighten.

"Okay." He gazed over at the bar and she knew he was holding it in. "I won't laugh." A few seconds later, he looked back to her. "Can't I laugh a little?"

"No!"

She wasn't surprised when her answer made him laugh anyway.

"I should have known you let Jess 'Weepy Eyes' Ward-Smith talk you into this."

Lock reached up and tugged the ends of Gwen's hair. "You cut it."

"What?"

"Your hair." He ran his hands through her hair. It was much shorter and she'd blown out the curls but . . . "I like it."

"Thanks."

He sighed. "And they ganged up on me."

"Who?"

"The wild dogs. I didn't stand a chance."

"You're so weak."

"I know, I know.

"And something else—" Gwen began, but it wasn't movement that snagged Lock's attention away from her but a change in landscape from the corner of his eye. One second they had a nice ring of space around them, the next a She-wolf was standing beside them. Gwen hissed and bared her fangs, but unlike the others, canine or feline, this She-wolf didn't run.

"That's a very nice how-do-ya-do." The She-wolf smiled at Lock. "Hey, MacRyrie."

"Don't sneak up on me, Dee."

"Lord, when did you get so sloppy? There was a time nobody could sneak up on you. Now you've got your hippy hair—"

"Told you your hair is too long."

"Let it go, Gwen."

"—and your feline girlfriend and you have become one lazy bear."

Chuckling, Lock introduced them. "Gwen O'Neill, this is Dee-Ann Smith. Dee-Ann, this is Gwen. Dee and I were in the Unit together."

"This?" Gwen asked with a definite snarl. "*This* is your Marine buddy?"

"Why do you say it like that?"

"We both know why!"

"Hi, Dee-Ann." Ric smoothly stepped in and smiled at Dee. And with his glass of wine and his Jane Austen–inspired costume, he couldn't look more wrong for Dee-Ann Smith. Not that that particular fact, Lock knew, would stop a determined Van Holtz wolf. Especially such a wily one. "It's good to see you again."

"You, too." She slapped him on the shoulder and Ric kept his smile until he turned his face away and then Lock saw the poor guy's expression contort into one of surprised pain.

"What are you doing here, Dee?" Lock asked. "A wild dog party doesn't seem like your speed."

"Figured what the hell. They're family now and all. Nice costume, by the way."

"Don't start."

"Well . . ." Dee looked back and forth between Ric, Gwen, and Lock. "See ya." Then she walked off.

"Friendly girl," Gwen muttered.

"Leave her alone. She rescued me from a bear trap once."

Gwen threw her hands up. "*How can I compete with that?*"

"No one asked you to compete with anything—now let it go." Lock glanced over at his friend and couldn't help but smile. "And Ric, how's that shoulder?"

Ric sat down at the table. "Fine. Fine." He moved it around a bit. "And with some reconstructive surgery and ten to twelve months of physical therapy . . . I'm sure it will be perfect again."

The two friends laughed while Gwen just rolled her eyes.

"She's sitting on his lap," Jess said, while spying through the partially opened door of their temporary Ye Ol' Tailor Shoppe.

"Only so she can scare off other She-predators," Sabina complained while trying to push Jess out of the way to get a better look. "It means nothing."

"She's not just sittin' there," May noted. "They're talkin'. Looks deep."

"It looks like arguing." Sabina observed.

Blayne went up on her toes to see over all of them. "It is arguing, but that's not bad."

"It's not?"

"Not with Gwen. She doesn't argue unless she gives a shit about you."

"I have to admit—" Jess went up on her toes, trying to get a better look "—I never thought your plan would work, Blayne, but it seems that it has."

"Told you they were perfect together. All they needed was a little nudge in the right direction. And I have to say, ladies, excellent choice on Lock's costume."

"It wasn't us." Jess motioned behind them to their "Insider." "That was her idea."

"Lord knows," their Insider said, "there's something about a man in a kilt that just—"

"*Ahhhhhh-Haaaaa!*"

Screaming and slamming into the door, the wild dogs and hybrid spun around to see Mitch and Brendon Shaw standing behind them, having found the second doorway in the back of the room. Ronnie came in behind the two men and shrugged an apology. "Sorry, y'all. They got away from me."

"You *traitor!*" Mitch said, pointing an accusatory finger at Sissy Mae, a.k.a. their "Insider." "You've been helping them all this time! How could you?"

"Now, darlin'—"

"Don't 'darlin'' me! You're working with *her*." That accusatory finger moved over to poor Blayne and Jess cringed. "She's already tainted my innocent baby sister with her insanity, now she's gotten you."

Jess grabbed Blayne's arm before the wolfdog could start swinging. "You're being a drama king," Jess sighed.

"I'm protecting my baby sister!"

Blayne crossed her arms over her chest. "You know, this is so typical of you, Mitch Shaw. You're barely in Gwen's life until you get your ass shot, and then, now that you're no longer a cop and seem to have way too much time on your hands, you want to roar in and take over like you have a right."

"And you," Mitch snarled back, "wanna mind your own goddamn business!"

"I like to see you make me!"

"Y'all!" Sissy stepped between them. "I can't handle another slap fight. And maybe, Mitch, it's time you open your eyes and realize that the grizzly out there is perfect for a woman who does that freak thing with her neck. 'Cause let me tell ya, he doesn't blink an eye when she does it, but it makes me want to call up an exorcist!"

"That's my sister you're talking about!"

"And we only want what's best for her." Jess stood next to

Blayne now, both of them with their arms crossed over their chests. "I'm also telling you as your friend and worshipper of your karaoke skills that you need to give Lachlan MacRyrie a chance. It's the fair thing to do."

"Fair?" Mitch pointed at his face. "Lion male. Totally irrational, self-absorbed, all about me. There is no fair in my world. Wake up to the reality, ladies. This bullshit is *over*."

Gwen crossed her arms under her chest and Lock looked to Ric for help. "Tell her, Ric. I told her about Dee, so I didn't do anything wrong."

Ric was still moving his shoulder, wincing from whatever that She-wolf had done to him. What Gwen found a little scary was that she doubted Dee tried to purposely hurt him. "Actually," Ric admitted, "you do have a tendency to downplay things."

"Ha!" Gwen crowed, triumphant.

"Dude! Where's the Bro-love?"

"I'm not sure what that is . . . nor do I want to know. But remember in tenth grade, when I wanted to go out with that junior and you said, 'Eh. I don't think she's the right girl for you'?"

"She wasn't."

"Because she was setting things on fire!" Ric announced loudly, making Gwen burst out laughing and Lock roll his eyes. "I'm serious, Gwen." Ric went on. "And when I say setting things on fire, I mean entire buildings. Mostly schools. She'd been setting them on fire or trying to, for *weeks*. I didn't find out until the cops came and arrested her during gym class. But does he say to me, 'She's setting things on fire! She's crazy! Stay away from her!' No. He says, 'Eh. I don't think she's the right girl for you.' And he's all calm about it over our chocolate pudding in the cafeteria."

"I don't see the point of getting hysterical."

"I didn't need you to get hysterical. But a little more specificity when these types of issues arise would be greatly appreciated. I'm sure if you said to Gwen, 'My old Marine buddy, the heavy-handed but statuesque beauty with' "—Ric sighed and stared off—" 'perfect breasts, soft pink lips, and silky-soft hair,' Gwen would have been fine."

"I'm doubting it."

"You know," Gwen admitted, "I'd have to go with Lock on this one."

Smitty walked up to the coyote pair who headed security for the evening. He'd be the first to admit, he was never a fan of coyotes. Had no real reason for his dislike other than an instinctual need to wipe them off his territory, but when it came to business, Smitty put all that aside and even he had to admit that coyotes did a good job when it came to securing locations. He knew this when the male escorted him to the back room they held for any interlopers who may try and get into the party and found his cousin handcuffed to the table.

"We found her sneaking around the back of the building, trying to find a way in."

Dee-Ann pursed her lips and sneered a bit.

"Is that right?" Smitty said. "I swear, just any ol' raggedy thing can come wandering in here, huh?"

His cousin glared at him and he laughed. "Give us a minute, Chuck."

"You sure? She's mean. And was carrying this." He held up the leather holder with the bowie knife inside it. Smitty took it and slid the blade out. At least eight inches and probably a gift from her daddy.

"I'll take this," Smitty said about the blade. "And I'll be fine."

"Okay. Howl if you need us."

The coyote left and, rolling her eyes, Dee lifted up her foot and placed it on top of the opposite knee. She pulled a thin piece of metal from the heel of her boot and quickly removed the handcuff from her wrist.

"Damn cy-otes. Gettin' in my way."

"I can't believe they caught you."

She rubbed her newly freed wrist. "I was busy, didn't notice them sniffin' around."

"You know you had an invitation, darlin'. You could have come in the normal way."

"I *did* come in the normal way, and then I went back out again."

"What for?" Dee opened her mouth and Smitty quickly added, "And don't lie to me, Dee-Ann. I'm married to a woman who could convince Saint Michael himself that hell is heaven and heaven is Detroit if it would protect her Pack, so don't think I won't know if you're lyin'. Now tell me plain why you're at my mate's party if it's not to be social."

Dee stood and they met eye to eye. She wasn't the tallest of the Smith family females, but Lord knew she was the most dangerous.

"I've been followin' somebody and they led me here."

"Why?" When she only stared at him, he tossed in, "Tell me or I'm callin' your momma and telling her you broke into the party like some common stray."

"All right, all right." She let out a breath. "I may have found a new job."

"Is that right? A new job that has you huntin' our kind?" And he couldn't keep the snide tone out of his voice, which was something he should have thought about a little more so he didn't get that fist to his face.

Smitty briefly closed his eyes and let out a breath as pain tore through his jaw and bells rang in his head. He'd almost forgotten the kind of strength his cousin had.

"*Ow,*" he snarled.

"Watch what you say to me, Robert Ray Smith. I don't take shit from your daddy and ain't gonna take none from you. I protect my kind. Always have, always will. Just like my daddy before me. But sometimes our kind needs to be protected from within as well as without. Sometimes, there are a few who don't know what loyalty is."

Realizing that Dee was the last being on the planet—full-human or wolf—who would ever betray their own, Smitty dropped his head and nodded. "You're right. And I'm real sorry for what I said."

That's when Dee smiled a little and he wondered if she was going to kill him now. "You may look like your daddy, but you sure don't act like him. Never known that man to apologize 'bout a damn thing, no matter how wrong he is."

She patted Smitty's arm, sending him stumbling into the table. He had to remember to brace himself better when dealing with Dee.

He turned and watched her head toward the door. "Where you goin'?"

"To find what I came for before your mate's little party goes to shit." She glanced back at him and shrugged nonchalantly. "Although . . . it may already be too late to bother."

Mitch was trying his best to untangle the wild dog females and one wolfdog who'd wrapped themselves around him like boa constrictors—trying to prevent him from marching right outside and telling his sister that the whole thing with the bear had been a plot hatched by Blayne "I have no boundaries or sense" Thorpe—when his phone rang.

Snatching it off his sword belt, Mitch snapped, "What?"

He stood up straight, blinking, the words his cousin Trish were hurriedly telling him not quite making sense. Something about his mother and McNelly and revenge and Asiatic lions and . . . and . . . a hair salon?

"Mitch?" Sissy asked, the headlock she had Brendon in while Ronnie held on to the cat's waist, loosening as she watched him. "Darlin', what's wrong?"

With her chin resting on Lock's shoulder, she watched the wolf pup desperately searching for something. He kept trying to cast for a scent, but he was too young to even understand how to separate the hundreds of scents that were surrounding him. When he stopped near her, going on his toes to look over the crowd's collective head, she couldn't take it anymore.

"Johnny." She said his name low so she didn't get anyone else's attention. He blinked, startled by her, and tried to slip away. "Get over here," she snapped.

Letting out a sigh, the kid walked over to her and Gwen sat up straight, Lock looking over his shoulder at Jess's adopted son.

"Hey, Johnny."

"Hi, Lock."

"What's going on?" Gwen asked, although she already kind of knew.

He shrugged and said, "I'm looking for Kristan."

Of course he was.

"You two have a fight?"

"Sort of."

Gwen couldn't help but smile. "Let me guess . . . you scared off the full-human she was supposed to meet outside."

Growling, the kid arrogantly put his hands on narrow hips. "I don't know what she was thinking!" *She's thinking how can she torture you*, but Gwen wouldn't say that out loud. "I know that kid," he went on. "He's a complete scumbag."

"So she ran off mad."

"Not quite. She started talking to some wolf. I didn't know the guy and I told her that and—"

"She completely ignored you. Right. Go on."

Lock looked away but she could feel his chest move as he quietly chuckled.

"Then they were gone. And we all know the Pack's going to blame me. It'll be my fault if something happens to her." Gwen knew Johnny was more worried about what little Kristan may be up to with another wolf than he was about his mom's Pack, but why argue that with him now? In another few years, he'd learn that all on his own.

"I'll help you find her." Gwen patted Lock's chest. "I'll be back in a minute."

"Why don't you just get her mother?"

Shocked he'd even suggested it, Gwen said, "I'm not rattin' the girl out to her mother. I'll take care of it."

Lock caught her arm before she could walk off. "Because she's your responsibility? I thought you had the night off with your mother still in Philly?"

Gwen leaned in and said, "You have your wild dog loyalties, and I have mine." And Gwen wasn't about to let Kristan do something she'd regret in the morning just to get even with Johnny. If she could stop even one girl going down that road, she would. "Now stay here and I better not find any more swarms of females around you when I get back."

"I'm still not sure how that would be my fault."

She snorted in reply, took Johnny's hand, and went off into the crowd of partiers.

Ric watched Gwen disappear into the crowd before he turned back to his friend. "So are you going to be like your uncles and move your woman into your house to live in sin, or like you father and marry her in a proper wedding?"

Lock smiled like Ric hadn't seen him smile in years. "I'm thinking a combination."

"Always smart."

"Just one problem."

"Which is?"

Hands slammed down on the table in front of Lock. "Where's my sister?"

Lock sighed. "Them."

Ric stared up at the lion siblings. How Lock hadn't killed them already, he didn't know. If nothing else, Ric would have had them . . . *managed* by now. They'd be alive, but in Siberia.

"Where is she?" Mitch Shaw snapped again.

Lock shrugged.

"Aren't you keeping an eye on her?"

"Because she suddenly can't take care of herself?" the grizzly asked.

"No. Because my mother shaved McNelly's head!"

The two friends stared at each other across the table and then both burst out laughing at the same time.

Ric wished his family was *half* this interesting.

"This isn't funny," Brendon Shaw said, shaking his big lion head. "Not funny."

"It's a *little* funny," Lock argued.

"No. Not funny," Mitch snapped. "Because Dee-Ann just told us she followed Donna McNelly and her Pack to this club, then lost 'em."

Lock's laughter cut off instantly and he peered up at Mitch. "When was that?"

"I don't know. Sissy and Dee are trying to find out if they got in and I'm trying to find Gwen, because she doesn't know that our insane mother shaved a woman's head out of retaliation for Labor Day weekend!"

Ric stood up. "Everyone calm down. We'll figure this out. Let's just find Gwen and then . . ."

His words trailed off as he watched his friend slowly stand up, his head moving as he cast for a scent. Lock had always amazed Ric; he was able to pick up scents nearly twenty miles away.

Lock's large body faced the direction Gwen had gone off, his head lowering, his breathing becoming heavy, and the air around him filling with a tension Ric had never been able to name but understood all too well.

Lock started moving and Mitch went to grab him, but Ric caught his arm. "Don't get in front of him, don't cut him off, and *do not* touch him. Follow and keep your mouth shut."

When the brothers started to argue, Ric said, "Gentlemen, you need to trust me on this."

Johnny stopped midway on the stairs that led to the basement and picked up the skate he found lying there.

"She probably fell down the stairs," Gwen said behind him. "It takes a certain skill to learn to go down stairs in skates."

She took the skate out of his hand and kept moving, Johnny following.

He couldn't believe he'd been reduced to this. Most days Kristan Putowski made him crazy, but lately she'd been really getting on his nerves. To be honest, he couldn't wait until he graduated in June and headed off to college. He needed to get away from her, her constant chatter, her annoying personality, and her goddamn scent! It was beginning to drive him insane, and it was getting harder and harder to resist her.

Nope. Distance was good. In fact, he might be able to manage distance a little sooner if he could get into the summer music program in Ohio. Three months of practice, classes, private concerts, and lectures. But most importantly . . . no Kristan.

"Don't worry, kid," Gwen said. "We'll find her."

Once they were in the basement, Gwen sniffed the air and headed to a door a short way down the hall. She had her hand on the doorknob but stopped. She leaned in, sniffed again, and that's when she reached back.

She slammed her hand against Johnny's chest and shoved him away. "Go get—"

From the other side, the door was torn open and a frighteningly large female reached out and grabbed Gwen by the hair, yanking her inside the room. A male came out and reached for Johnny, but he scrambled back and took off down the hallway, grateful he'd gone with one of the Roman soldier costumes rather than the more complicated and heavier medieval armor costume. The male was closing in behind him as Johnny made it up the stairs. He slammed his hands against the unlocked door, shoving it open. Hands grabbed his shoulders, pulling him back. An arm went around his chest and Johnny's mouth was covered.

Desperate, he reached for the switchblade he'd had since he was twelve and living with a foster family that had made him extremely nervous. But before his hand could reach it, he looked up at a massive body wearing only a kilt . . . and rage. Forgetting his blade, he watched as the bear reached down and grabbed hold of the arm wrapped around Johnny. Lock took it and twisted until the arm snapped.

The wolf released Johnny and howled in pain as Lock dragged the unknown canine away, flinging him across the club.

When the bear looked back at him, Johnny pointed down the stairs and said, "They've got Gwen."

She hit the ground, the wind briefly knocked out of her, poor Kristan's skate flipping out of her hand and disappearing under one of the tables.

McNelly reached down and caught hold of her neck, lifting Gwen up. "Always the do-gooder, rushing down here to help the kid," she said.

One of the males had hold of Kristan, his hand over her mouth, his arm around her waist. She was struggling, tears pooling at her feet. Poor kid. She was one of those protected pups, not used to this kind of attack. But Gwen and McNelly? They were more than used to it.

Gwen shoved McNelly off her. "Let the kid go. This is between you and me."

" 'This is between you and me,'" McNelly imitated back to her in a high-pitched voice. "You're fucking pathetic. Just like the girl. She might as well get used to it now. Might as well realize she'll always be a mixed-breed loser." McNelly stepped in closer. "Alone and helpless . . . and a freak."

And that's when Gwen popped her in the mouth, the She-wolf stumbling to the side as her Pack came at Gwen.

Gwen unleashed her claws and lashed out, swiping at anything that got close to her, trying to work her way over to Kristan.

Someone grabbed her from behind, and Gwen lifted up her legs and kicked out at one of the wolves in front of her, sending him flying back. Then she brought her legs back down, keeping her knees tight. Her feet slammed into the femurs of whoever held her and she heard a scream of pain as bones in both legs broke and the wolf released her. More wolves came at her, so she dashed up onto the tables and shelves, knocking things off them as the wolves tried to get hold of her. She kept going until she landed in front of Kristan. That's when she pulled out her razor and flicked it open.

She cut the face of the wolf holding Kristan and yanked the girl away.

She saw the open window that the wolves must have come in through and she pushed Kristan up on the table beneath it. "Go! Now!" Gwen yelled, spinning back around and lashing out with the razor, slicing someone's hand and someone else's jaw.

McNelly came at her again, catching the hand that held Gwen's razor. She twisted Gwen's arm, all that brute strength nearly tearing Gwen's arm from the socket. And while she held her, Gwen desperately reaching out for something, anything, she could use as a weapon, another male came at her. He took the razor from her hand and held it in front of her face.

"Wanna know how this feels, bitch?" Gwen already knew. She'd gotten the damn thing from the person who'd used it on her during a street fight.

He raised the blade over her and Gwen felt something under her hand. A pair of scissors.

Gripping them tight, she swung them out as the razor came down toward her face. But she was falling, the grip on her other arm suddenly gone. She landed flat on her back and saw the big arms of Lock reaching out. But the razor was already in motion and the blade cut across his forearm.

Uh-oh was the last thing Gwen could think before Lock's boar-rage snapped and unleashed on every wolf in that room.

Blayne pushed past the crowd standing at the doorway and flew down the steps, Sissy, Ronnie, and Sissy's cousin right behind her. As she neared the last door down the hallway, she heard a roar that she now knew. Lock's roar. She pushed past Mitch and Bren, yanking her arm out of Mitch's grip when he tried to pull her back. But she ended up stopping at the doorway anyway as a human body spiraled across the room.

Lock lumbered after it, still in his human form, but for the first time since she'd met him she could see the hump between his shoulders. It had grown and was now a mass of muscle that only intensified his already incredible strength. And all that strength was slamming into the wolf trying to pick himself up off the floor.

Four-inch claws dragged across the wolf, tearing off flesh and hair and clothes. Then hands rammed into the wolf's back, with an untold amount of pressure pushing against his ribs. The wolf screamed and sobbed, unable to fight off the boar-rage raining down on him, but he'd gone after the wrong girl, hadn't he? He'd gone after Gwen.

Gwen flipped onto her hands and knees. The scissors she'd been about to use and had dropped had been picked up by Mc-Nelly. She was charging toward Lock's back, hoping to protect the male Lock had pinned to the floor.

Fangs unleashing, Gwen charged McNelly, but Blayne rammed into McNelly first, shoving her into the opposite wall. The scissors skittered away and Gwen picked them up, letting out a breath. Another She-wolf stood next to her, but she knew this one.

"I hear sirens," Dee-Ann said. "Someone must have panicked and called the cops."

Gwen nodded.

"Sissy's gonna grab her friend Dez. She's a cop and here somewhere. She'll control things as long as she can, but we need to—"

"I know."

Dee-Ann leaned down a bit to get a better look at her. "You want me to handle Lock for ya, darlin'?"

Gwen didn't even know why the She-wolf was asking that. "No." She handed over the scissors. "But you deal with the wolves."

Gwen moved up behind Lock. He was crouching on the wolf's back, one claw dug into what was left of the back of the wolf's skull, the other pawing his exposed and torn flesh. He was breathing hard, the air pounding out of him as he fought not to shift and finish the job. She could see his muscles rippling as he fought the change, fought that last step that would turn this into a moment of regret for him. He had too many of those, she knew. She wouldn't let these McNelly fuckers hang him up with any more.

She pressed against his back, let him feel her weight on him before she pressed her mouth to his ear. "Let him go, Lock."

His muscles rippled again, she felt them moving against her own. She kissed his ear, nuzzled the side of his head. "I just want you to take me home. Keep me safe."

Slowly, the bear stood, stepping off the battered mass beneath him. One blood-covered hand reached out for her, claws still unleashed—and Gwen took it, gripped it tight. He pulled her into his side, his arm tight around her.

"Gwenie? Maybe you should—"

At the sound of Mitch's worried voice, her big brother still trying to protect her, Lock's head snapped around, his gaze latching on to the crowd of concerned shifters blocking the doorway. He roared and Mitch shoved Bren forward. "Take him!"

"You *bastard*!" Bren shouted at his brother.

Lock roared again and everyone took off running, bolting up the hallway and back to the club. Once they were gone, Lock's arms went tight around Gwen and he lifted her up, lumbering out after the retreating shifters and carrying her home.

Chapter 26

Lock snapped awake and found himself naked in bed. Normally nothing to get worried over except he had no idea how he got there.

"You're awake. Good."

He looked over at the doorway and Gwen stood there wearing one of his T-shirts, her arms crossed over her chest.

Sitting up slowly, he studied her close until he nearly begged, "Please tell me I didn't hurt you."

"Of course you didn't."

"But I scared you?"

"No."

"Not even a little?"

Gwen shook her head. "No."

"Oh."

"You did terrify everyone else, though."

Lock's shoulders dropped a bit but he couldn't help it. "Oh."

"Do you even remember what happened?"

Sort of. Or maybe not. It was all a jumble right now, which only meant he'd really lost it. Boar-rage lost it.

"I don't—" Lock shrugged. "Bits and pieces."

"Well, no one's dead. If that's got you worried."

It did, and he let out a relieved breath.

"Although at least one will need massive reconstructive surgery."

Shit.

"Lock—"

"It's all right." He stretched his shoulders out, the flesh between his blades sore, which meant his grizzly hump had grown while he was still human. Rare and *not* good. "Really. It's all right. And I can understand if you're not comfortable staying here tonight." He looked up at her. "Or if you want some space or . . . if you . . . if you . . . why are you getting naked?"

Not that he minded, but still. Shouldn't she be trying to ease her way out the door or keeping a healthy distance between them instead of pulling off the T-shirt and crawling onto the bed?

"Why am I getting naked? Did you really just ask me that?"

"I did, but only because—" Lock closed his eyes, his entire body trembling as Gwen's skin brushed against his own. So much soft skin on such a lethal feline was making him crazy. He swallowed and tried again. "I'd understand if you feel . . . uh . . ." *Oh, God. She's purring.* "A little scared about what happened earlier."

"I don't feel scared. I'm actually kind of turned on." She licked his ear with the tip of her tongue. "Does that make me a kinky girl?"

"No, no. Of course not. It's just—" His eyes crossed as she dragged her nails across the mass of sore and ultrasensitive muscles between his shoulder blades.

"It's just what, Lock?" she purred into his ear. "Because if there's one thing we both know, baby, is that the one person who was safe in that room was me. I know you'll never hurt me. I know you'll always protect me. And I know I'll never stop loving you."

Did she know that was all he needed to hear? All he needed to *know*?

Wanting to show her, he turned fast, his hands digging into Gwen's hair and tilting her head back before he ruthlessly took her mouth with his own.

* * *

No one's hands had ever felt so good on her before. The way Lock stroked her, petted her, his hands gentle but firm.

She hadn't been lying when she told him she knew she'd never been safer. Everyone else was at risk from Lock's vicious boar-rage, but not Gwen, not his friends, not his family. He'd, in fact, been protecting her more than himself. It was the danger she was in that had sent him into battle mode. *Her* grizzly had felt the need to protect its mate.

Not smother her, *protect* her. There was a difference between those two things that a lot of guys never understood. Mitch sure didn't, which was why he had to find a female who fought him every step of the way. But Gwen had found Lock, who was there when she needed him to be, and backed off when she didn't.

At the moment, though, he needed *her.* The mighty bear might be comfortable with his power, but he wasn't comfortable losing control. Unlike most shifters, he got no enjoyment out of hurting others, and she could tell he'd never dismiss anyone or anything as merely "collateral damage."

How Gwen O'Neill found a man of integrity, she'd never know, but she would be eternally grateful.

Gwen pulled out of their kiss, her hands brushing Lock's shoulders, his chest. She made sure to involve her nails because, as much as he may complain about them, she could tell they drove him crazy in other ways.

"Lay back," she said, her hands flat against his shoulders. He did and Gwen slowly ran her nails down his chest, across his stomach, lingering over the tight abdominal muscles. He moaned and moved restlessly on the bed. She smiled at his reaction, en-joying his response to her touch.

She dragged her hands down his thighs, always amazed not merely at the size of them, but at the strength. Everything about his body illustrated pure, unadulterated power waiting to be un-leashed. Yet it was that constantly analyzing, rational brain that turned him into straight catnip for Gwen.

Taking the tip of her forefinger, she dragged her nail along the length of his cock. Hard and long, it jerked at her touch while Lock's hands dug into the bedding beneath him. It already stood up straight, the thick head weeping fluid. Like the cat she was, Gwen took a quick swipe of it with her tongue. His reaction was so strong, the heavy bed frame moved beneath them, and Gwen decided a little cleaning was in order. The feline in her did like things tidy.

She started at the tip and worked her way down, alternating between short and quick licks to long, drawn-out ones that went from base to tip. She lost track of time as she focused all her attention on Lock. He groaned her name and she could smell his sweat as he fought his desire to grab her and fuck the hell out of her. She admired his restraint and yet had no problem using it against him while they were in bed. What could she say? She enjoyed making him crazy, bringing out the grizzly inside.

By the time she took his cock in her mouth, relaxing her throat muscles so she could swallow the entire length of him, his claws were out, and he'd moved from groaning to a guttural grunting that should have made her nervous but didn't.

Already on the edge, Lock barely lasted for another two minutes before he came, his initial roar of release ending on a steady hum.

Gwen sat up, wiping her mouth with the back of her hand and staring at the humming male stretched out beside her. He had his face turned away, but his entire body was relaxed.

Still, she had to ask. "What is with the humming?"

Although she could only see part of his face, she did see the way the corner of his mouth curled into a smile even as his eyes stayed closed.

"Contentment, Gwen," he said softly before he turned his head and opened his eyes to gaze at her. "It means contentment."

She looked down at her hands, seemingly uncomfortable with his answer. He didn't know why. A bear couldn't pay a higher compliment. Contentment, like pure gold, was not easy to come by in this world.

Lock reached for her, taking her hand and tugging her close until he could slide his fingers into her hair, bringing her head down for a kiss. He tasted himself on her lips and in her mouth and he grew hard again knowing she'd taken all of him without backing off. Of course, Gwen never backed off. She might skirt around, climb over, or circle in, but she never backed off until she got what she wanted.

As they kissed, Lock used his free hand and slid it between her thighs. He needed to be inside her, but he didn't want to take her too soon. Yet his fingers glided inside her pussy and he could feel how wet and ready she was for him. Touching him, sucking him had turned her on, and his fingers inside her had her writhing on his hand.

He pulled away, and Gwen mewled, her brows drawing down. But he wasn't nearly done with her.

Pushing her back, Lock dragged himself up. She began to lie down, and he grunted at her, pulling her back up and moving her around until she was on all fours and facing away from him. He grabbed a condom and put it on before settling in behind her. He braced his arms in front of her, his forearms pressing into her shoulders to hold her in place as he positioned his hips behind her. With one hard thrust, he entered her, grunting hard as all that wet heat wrapped around his cock, her muscles flexing as she worked to take all of him in.

"Link your hands with mine," he whispered against her neck.

Gwen nodded and wrapped her arms around his forearms, her hands clutching his, their fingers interlacing.

"I love you, Gwenie," he said before he took her in long, hard strokes.

He wasn't gentle with her, his arms keeping her trapped where she was while he fucked her with everything he had in him. But Gwen didn't seem to mind. Her head rubbed against his arm while she begged him to go "harder, faster" and then "Don't stop. Don't ever stop."

He wouldn't. Even when they were too old to bother anymore, he'd still never stop showing her how much he loved her, needed her, wanted her in his life.

Claws dug into his arm and Lock nuzzled the back of her neck, dragging his mouth along her skin. It rippled where he touched her and she met each of his thrusts with her own, her breath choking as she cried out. Her muscles tightened around him so much, nothing could have stopped him from coming, his body shuddering around hers.

Lock caught her in his arms and turned on his side as he crashed to the bed. They stayed like that for long minutes, too tired to move.

"At some point," Gwen told him, her voice sounding moments from sleep, "we're going to have to find a way to get honey in on this because I'm almost positive it's like your ultimate fantasy, right?"

"Don't worry, Mr. Mittens," he laughed, kissing her neck and enjoying that her hair was currently so short he didn't have to push it out of the way. "We have lots of time, and I have *lots* of honey."

CHAPTER 27

Blayne would admit she hadn't had this much fun since she worked the Renaissance Faire one summer. True, the circumstances surrounding this event were despicable, but the aftermath was *way* entertaining!

Of course, it didn't turn into a free-for-all until Roxy O'Neill snatched that wig off Sharyn McNelly's head, revealing what Blayne could only call a monk-cut. A look that was not good on a man, much less a woman. And once that wig came off, all bets were off. It probably would have lasted a lot longer if they weren't in a hospital waiting room. A hospital run by shifters with orderlies who were bears. One bear roar and everyone backed up into their own corners, the O'Neills, Shaws, Kuznetsovs, and Smiths on one side and the McNellys on the other.

Funny thing was, the only ones who needed to be at the hospital were the McNellys. Several of their Pack were down, but two males had suffered the most. One with an arm the doctors didn't think would ever work right again since it had been completely pulled from its socket and broken in sixteen places. And the other who'd been mauled.

And while the McNellys waited at the hospital to see if Donna McNelly's boyfriend would even survive that mauling, Roxy O'Neill had found out what happened, gotten to New York in record time with her sisters and brothers in tow, and headed right over to confront Sharyn McNelly. The Shaws, Kuznetsovs, and Smiths showed up soon after.

Normally, Blayne would be trying to calm everyone down, but for once she could sit back and watch. Why? Because of the Van Holtzes! Well . . . two of them anyway. Ric and his cousin Niles Van Holtz. At the moment, it was down to them and the bear orderlies that kept this whole thing from spiraling out of control. But Blayne was more worried about tomorrow, and the next day, and the day after that. She couldn't help herself; it was in her nature to think about the "what ifs." Like what if Donna McNelly just kept coming for Gwenie and her? What if McNelly never stopped? What if Blayne had to make her stop? And Blayne could make the She-wolf stop—she could make her stop for good.

"There has to be a way we can all resolve this," Niles Van Holtz said in his low, dreamy voice. Blayne had never been one for older men but yowza! Was the entire Van Holtz Pack this good looking? It was possible if Niles and Ric were only cousins.

"Yeah, there's a way," Roxy said simply from her side of the waiting room. "The bitch dies. Right here, right now."

"Bring it, ya Philly whore!" Sharyn snarled back.

"This isn't helping," Niles said over the lion roars of the Shaw brothers.

Munching on Doritos and sipping from her Diet Coke can that she'd purchased from the gift shop, Blayne watched the drama until Ric nudged her with his elbow. She offered him some Doritos and then a sip of her soda. As he handed the can back to her, Roxy held up McNelly's wig, which she still had a good grip on, and began to shimmy in a circle. Blayne cringed, eternally grateful that Gwen wasn't here for any of this. She was home safe with her homicidal bear . . . *wait*. She glanced up, trying to figure out if that was a good thing, when Ric sighed and shook his head. She gave him a little smile and looked away just as Kristan rolled past them, still wearing her Babes uniform.

Blayne and Ric watched her roll over to Johnny and hand him his own soda and chips, then Blayne and Ric looked back at each other.

When they both smiled at the same time, Blayne knew things were about to get seriously out of control.

Gwen woke up before her alarm went off. That wasn't unusual for her, though. What was unusual was to find her mother on the other side of her bed, lifting the bedsheet so she could check out her bear's naked ass!

"*Ma!*" she roared and Roxy instantly dropped the sheet.

"Morning, baby-girl," she said while trying to pretend she wasn't doing what Gwen caught her doing.

Lock's head lifted from the pillow, his voice urgent. "What? What's wrong?"

Roxy grinned. "Morning, handsome."

Lock looked over at Roxy. "Uh . . . morning."

Roxy pressed her hand to her chest. "I'm Gwendolyn's mother, Roxy O'Neill. But you can call me Roxy."

"Morning, Roxy."

"And you're Lachlan MacRyrie. I know your uncles."

"Ma!"

"I said I *know* his uncles, baby-girl. I didn't say I *did* his uncles."

"Ma," Gwen said on a breath "why are you here?"

"I need to talk to you."

Gwen dropped back on the bed, her arm over her eyes. "Oh, please, Ma. Not this morning. Last night was—"

"I know what happened last night. And I need to talk to you. It's important, baby-girl." She smiled at Lock. "It was really nice meeting you."

"You, too."

Her mother walked out and Gwen grabbed one of Lock's T-shirts off the floor and followed after her.

"What's up?" Gwen asked as she went into Lock's kitchen. She needed some coffee and she needed it now.

"That young man has a *fine* ass, baby-girl."

"Ma," Gwen ground out between clenched teeth. "Why are you *here*?"

"Well, about last night . . ."

Gwen snorted. "I guess Mitch the rat told you."

"Don't call him that, and he wasn't the one who told me. I actually heard because—" She stopped speaking and Gwen turned to face her mother. Gwen could never remember a time when her mother couldn't find the words to express herself. Which is a real nice way of saying she never shut the fuck up. Until today. And there was only one reason Roxy O'Neill would suddenly be speechless.

"What did you do?"

Her mother chewed her lip before vaguely admitting, "I may have taken things up a notch."

"You may have . . ." Then Gwen understood. "*Ma!*"

"I know! I know! I'm so sorry, baby-girl! I just couldn't believe that bitch was taking out our old grudge on my baby-girl!"

"What did you do?"

"Why does that matter?"

"What did you do?"

She shrugged. "I . . . uh . . . shaved parts of McNelly's head."

"Parts?"

"You know . . . so she looked like a monk."

"Ma!" *What had she been thinking?*

"Don't be such a drama queen. It'll grow back."

"Oh, my God! What is wrong with you? Seriously? Is it a genetic defect that can be passed to me? To my children?"

"Baby-girl—"

"Don't baby-girl me! You start this shit and you never think about the consequences. Do you know they grabbed one of the wild dog pups to get me away from the party? Do you even care you put a kid in danger?"

"Of course I—"

Gwen held her hands up. "I don't want to hear it. I just want you to go."

"You're throwing me out?"

"I'm throwing you out. I need space right now. Space from *you*." She waved her mother out of Lock's kitchen and toward his front door. "Go."

"Well if you're going to be this way—"

"I'm going to be this way. Now get *out*!"

"*Fine!*" Roxy bellowed before she stormed out.

Gwen heard the front door close, and all she could think about was getting back into her warm bed with Lock and letting him soothe all her troubles away with his four-inch bear claws. But as she headed to the room, she heard the front doorbell.

"If she's back . . ." Gwen went back to the front door and snatched it open. She blinked in surprise. "Oh. Hi, Jess. Uh . . ."

Gwen stood in Lock's doorway with a wild dog now hanging off her neck and she had no idea why. Although she was grateful to see Blayne behind her.

"What is she doing?"

"Thanking you."

"For?"

Jess answered before Blayne could. "For what you did for Kristan and Johnny."

Oh, that. She'd completely forgotten about that, but she sensed it wouldn't be a good idea to say that out loud.

"No problem. It was—" She let out a breath and focused back on Blayne. "Okay, she's still hugging."

"You're part of our Pack now, Gwen," Jess said fiercely. "You're one of us." Jess stepped away from her and she had tears in her eyes. "You ever need us, you ever need *anything*. You or Lock . . . because he protected Johnny, too. *My* Johnny. My son. You two will *always* be one of us."

"Thanks."

Then she was being hugged again. Gwen stood there, waiting for the wild dog to release her. Blayne finally helped by gently taking Jess's shoulders and pulling her away. "Why don't you head on home and let me talk to Gwen? She's not good with her raw emotions and she needs some time to experience the love you're giving her."

Gwen rolled her eyes, but Jess had her back to her and didn't see.

"No problem." Jess walked to the door, stopped right outside, and looked straight at Gwen. "I love you, Gwenie."

Gwen blinked. "Okay."

Blayne walked to the door and waved at Jess until the elevator doors closed. Once the wild dog was gone, Blayne stepped back into the apartment and closed the door. Then she was on her knees, laughing so hysterically that Gwen walked away, snarling over her shoulder, "I can't believe you brought that shit here!"

Blayne rolled to her back, kicked her legs. That's when Gwen went and made coffee. By the time she walked out with two mugs, a grizzly with a sheet around his waist was stumbling out of the bedroom.

She pointed. "Coffee. Kitchen."

"Love you more and more."

Blayne was standing now and she dug into her backpack, pulling out a bakery bag. "Honey buns! I brought them for Lock."

"Smart move."

Gwen put the mugs down on the coffee table and sat on the couch. "So why are you here? Because it's not even nine yet, and unlike me, you're not a morning person."

"You're a morning person?"

"*Why are you here?*"

"Okay, okay." Blayne dropped on the couch. "As you can tell, there's been much drama since you and your honey bun left last night."

Gwen chuckled. "Honey bun."

"The McNellys are up in arms, mostly about what Lock did to their two—" Gwen shook her head, cutting her off. She didn't want that shit hanging over Lock's head and, thankfully, Blayne understood her immediately. "Your mother also arrived."

"She was just here."

"Yeah. She got here last night, along with your uncles and aunts."

Gwen put her coffee down on the table. "Oh, no."

"They were at the hospital, along with the Smiths, Mitch and Brendon, and the Kuznetsov Pack."

"Okay," Gwen said, wanting to cut to it as quickly as possible. "How bad is this?"

"The Smiths are calling for war."

Gwen held up a hand. "Wait. What?"

"The Smiths are calling for war, and Ric had to put in emergency calls to the Board—which, to be honest, I didn't know we had a Board—who sent over his cousin Niles, who happened to be in town for some reason, don't know why. And can I just say . . . hottie?"

"Ric?"

"Niles."

"Mated."

"I can look."

Gwen gestured with her hand. "Just get to it. Why are the *Smiths* calling for anything, much less war?" Packs always seemed to be getting into wars with someone. She didn't understand it. They were either fighting each other or some Pride or Clan. The wars could get really ugly, too, lasting for decades.

"Who's threatening war?" Lock asked as he walked out of the kitchen with a mug of coffee in one hand and the sheet still held around his waist with the other.

"The Smiths," Blayne answered.

He sat down hard on the couch, his eyes wide. "Why? Because of last night?"

"Yeah. But not because of you two. It seems they don't care about you two at all. Kristan and Johnny, however . . ."

"What about Kristan and Johnny?" Gwen demanded. "When I called Mitch last night he said they were fine."

"They're completely fine. But they were threatened, and they're still pups."

"And part of Jess's wild dog Pack," Lock answered, understanding the dynamics of the wild dogs better than Gwen.

Blayne grinned, obviously loving this. "But Jess is with Smitty now, which means she's family. If she's family, her Pack is family."

"Okay . . . and?"

Lock put down his coffee and buried his face in his hands. "I see where this is going."

"I know you do."

"I don't," Gwen snapped. "Neither pup was hurt."

"True," Blayne explained. "But they were traumatized."

"Traumatized, my ass. They're just overprotected and spoiled."

"And," the wolfdog happily went on, "the Smiths consider it a hate crime."

"Oh, *stop it!*"

Laughing, Blayne nodded. "I am so serious. Word is it's so bad that someone they call Uncle Eggie is, and I'm quoting Smitty here, 'Fixin' to come on up here and wipe the land clean as if the Lord himself had decided Staten Island was Sodom and Gomorrah.' "

"Nice accent imitation," Gwen sneered.

"I try."

"This isn't good," Lock said. "Uncle . . ." His chin lifted and his nostrils flared. "Honey buns?"

Gwen handed the bag to him. "Honey buns for my honey bun."

He stared at her. "You're going to start calling me that now, aren't you?"

"You going to keep calling me Mr. Mittens?"

Pulling a bun out of the bag, the bear shrugged. "I can live with being your honey bun."

"All I know," Blayne said, "is that Uncle Eggie must be some major badass, because everyone's in this rather hysterical tizzy, even Mr. Smooth Move Niles."

"Niles Van Holtz is here?" Lock demanded around his bun.

"Yes. And hot."

"Stop saying that!" Gwen snapped.

"Why is he here?"

"According to Ric, he was in town."

"For what?"

Not caring about Niles Van Holtz, Gwen cut in and asked, "This is all because my mother shaved McNelly's head?"

Lock choked on his bun. "I forgot about that."

"McNelly won't."

"Well," Blayne said, "this all goes deeper and further back than that. And it looked pretty much like war was coming."

Gwen studied Blayne. "It *looked* like war was coming?"

"I do believe I've come up with a satisfactory solution to resolve all this once and for all—and have managed to get everyone to agree. Now you just have to agree, Gwen."

Gwen stared at her best friend. "*I* have to agree? Why me? I thought I didn't matter and it was all Kuznetsovs and Smiths and pups."

"Right. And the Kuznetsovs, Smiths, O'Neills, and McNellys have all agreed to let all bad blood end here . . . if you're in."

Confused, Gwen shook her head. "If I'm in to . . ." Blayne gave Gwen her biggest grin and Gwen's confusion quickly turned into righteous anger. "*Oh, come on!*"

Laughing around Gwen's bellow of rage, Blayne said, "You and only you, Gwen O'Neill, can prevent this war."

Gwen rubbed her forehead. "And of course this is your *shitty* idea, Blayne Thorpe."

"Wait." Lock looked back and forth between the two friends. "I don't get it. What's Gwen going to have to do?"

CHAPTER 28

Gwen rolled around and around that little hallway about a hundred feet away from the locker rooms. She should stop, take a breath, but the fact she couldn't breathe was making at least one of those impossible.

With her hands clasped tightly together, Gwen kept focusing on trying to force herself to breathe and not vomit.

Vomit, bad. Breathing, good.

She couldn't do this. She couldn't. And she'd been a fool to agree to this. But now Gwen was in and couldn't get out.

Why? a sane person may ask.

Because, in the end, Gwen had been unable to pass up the chance to take the trophy out of McNelly's mannish grip. And that's exactly what Blayne had used to get Gwen to agree to this stupidity knowing that Gwen didn't give a fuck about Pack wars or Smiths or men named "Eggie." No, it was Gwen's ego that had gotten her here. And either this would go down in history as the bout that stopped a war or it would go down as the time an O'Neill vomited on the track.

What had never occurred to Gwen, what she hadn't thought about when she'd agreed to this, was her fear of facing the screaming crowd—again. That's what had gotten her nailed during her first bout all those years ago and it seemed that fear hadn't changed. And that's why she felt ready to vomit.

God, what if I do vomit on the track? There will be no coming back from that! she thought hysterically.

The door to the small hallway where she'd been hiding opened. "I'll be fine, Blayne," she said without looking up. And she knew it was Blayne, because the wolfdog had been trying to calm her down for the last two hours, but she'd only managed to make Gwen ten thousand times more nervous. "No need to worry. I'm fine."

"And you call me a lousy liar."

Gwen's head snapped up and she never thought there'd be a day where she'd be *ecstatic* to be startled by a grizzly.

He would have walked right by her if it hadn't been for her scent. That would never change—thank God—but the rest of her sure had. At least for the moment.

She had on thick black eyeliner and her naturally long lashes were even longer and thicker. She wore blush on her cheeks, and her lipstick was dark red and glossy. She had her curly hair pulled into two small ponytails and a black headband covered in skulls and crossbones tied around her forehead.

Lock had debated about coming back here, not wanting to make her any more nervous than he already knew she was, but then he'd gotten that text from Blayne. It had one word . . . "Help!"

Gwen rolled over to him and right into his arms. "Oh, my God! I'm so glad you're here!"

Rubbing her back, Lock decided not to be too freaked out about her wardrobe. He didn't mind the glittery, bright red four-wheel skates. They were cute. But Gwen was hot when she wore her cargo pants and an old Eagles sweatshirt. Now she was volcano-hot in black fishnet stockings with kneepads over them, a miniscule red pair of shorts, three layered tank tops with red on the bottom, black over that, and white on top, black elbow pads, and body glitter smeared on her biceps and neck that made the tattoos on her arms pop.

He was torn between wanting to show her off to everyone and covering her with his jacket.

But before he could worry about that, he had another concern at the moment . . .

"Why do you have Van Holtz on your ass?"

Startled, Gwen glanced at her ass as if expecting to find Ric there. Thankfully for the wolf, he wasn't. However, his name was there . . . right on Gwen's ass. Or, in this instance, her shorts. Her derby name—TastySkate—and her number "59" were on her tank top.

"According to Blayne, he's a sponsor."

"Does he know his family name is on the asses of a Roller Derby team?"

"Doubt it."

Okay, that was actually kind of funny. "And TastySkate?"

She let out a sigh. "You know . . . like Tastykake."

"You mean the fine makers of my favorite Krimpets?"

She glared up at him and hissed, "Yes. Like the Krimpets and cupcakes and the pies that we of the Tri-States all grew up loving. It was either that or Philly Killsteak." When Lock frowned, she added, "You know . . . like Philly *cheese*steak?"

When he laughed, she scowled, so he stopped.

"Gwen, you're going to be great. You shouldn't be worried."

"Oh, I know. I'm sure I'll be fine."

She was lying again. He knew that because Gwen was shaking. *His* Gwen. Fistfight with an entire derby team? Nothing. Taking his intimidating uncles at poker? Nothing. Getting in a vicious revenge fight with crazy wolves in the basement of a club? Eh.

Putting on derby skates and facing off against her mother's reputation? A mess.

"Gwenie?" He tightened his grip on her, hoping that talking would get it out of her. Although, Gwen wasn't much of a talker. "What is it? What's really bothering you?"

Gwen may not be much of a talker, but once she got going . . .

"What if I screw up? What if I blow it? What if I let the team down? What if I make a complete fucking idiot out of myself? In front of everybody? What if I lose to that humongous bitch? What if I get so injured I can never walk again? What if there's a war anyway? What if I embarrass my mother? What if I embarrass myself? What if your parents find out? What if your *sister* does? What if—"

"Okay, okay." He had a feeling she could run with the "what if" scenarios until the next millennium and he knew they didn't have that kind of time right now. So what should he do? Tragically, he knew what he had to do. As much as it appalled him, he knew there was only one thing he could do at this moment to snap his Gwen out of this.

So, taking a page from the Alla Baranova-MacRyrie handbook of motivational techniques, Lock said, "Hey, I totally understand if you can't do this."

"You do?"

"Sure. I mean . . . McNelly's good."

Gwen snorted. "She's brute force. That's different from being good."

"But she's bigger than you, weighs more than you, and you can't shift into cat or pull out that razor blade when you're on the track, so you have no real advantage over her. And . . . to be honest—" Oh and this would be the hardest part to say "—I don't want you out there. I want you home, safe . . . where I can protect you."

Gwen eased out of his arms, her body gliding away because of her skates, her gold eyes peering at him curiously. "What?"

"I said, go put your clothes back on and let me take you home. This is no place for you. You're mine now and I want you safe and preferably unmarred."

Her hands went on her waist, her red, white, and black nails tap-tap-tapping against her hips. "You don't think I can do it."

Lock shrugged. "Sweetie, she's gonna kick your ass."

"Did you just call me sweetie?"

"You rather I call you baby?"

Without another word, Gwen rolled past him and into the main hallway that led to the stadium.

"Good," he said behind her as the Babes rolled out of the locker room, Blayne moving in front of them. "I'll take you home and we can forget all about this. I'll always take care of you, Gwenie. You'll never have to worry about anything."

Blayne's eyes grew wide and her gaze bounced back and forth between Gwen and Lock.

Slowly Gwen faced him. "I don't need *anybody* to take care of me. Especially freakishly sized bears with kumquat heads." She held her hand out and one of the Babes slapped a helmet into her palm. "Now get the fuck out of my way."

She rolled toward the stadium entrance, where they'd wait to make their grand entrance, and the team followed right behind her.

Reaching out, Lock snagged Blayne by the forearm and pulled her back. "When this is over, she still better love me."

"Don't worry about anything," Blayne promised. She leaped up and kissed his cheek. "You're the bestest bear ever."

"Yeah, but I better not be the loneliest," he called after her.

Typical. Absolutely typical. Show a man a moment of weakness and he figures he can turn you into a barefoot breeder making him honey-soaked meals all day.

"You all right, Gwenie?" Blayne asked.

When all Gwen could manage was a growl, Blayne didn't say another word.

As they waited in the long hallway that led out to the stadium, the Furriers rolled in. Their uniforms were cute little plaid skirts and tiny pink and black tops to match. But it didn't matter. McNelly still looked like a big bitch in a cute-girl's outfit.

McNelly stopped in front of Gwen and stared down at her. What was happening between McNelly and Gwen was something that went back to their mothers' time when the derby queens wore a lot less makeup but lived the life of the true derby girl.

Now all that past shit was coming down to this and Gwen wouldn't back away. Yeah, her mother embarrassed the holy hell out of her, but she was still her mother and Gwen was still an O'Neill.

"See you out on the track, O'Neill."

McNelly followed after her team and Blayne muttered, "I hate her."

"Yeah . . . but I hate her *more*."

And that was why *if* Gwen went down tonight, she'd go down fighting—and she'd make sure to take McNelly with her.

Lock stood at one of the entrances to the VIP seats, searching for his parents and Ric. His father had insisted on coming. "How could I miss something so interesting?" Of course, his mother was no better. "Females in a battle of strength? Why would I miss that? Besides, it's our Gwenie!" Iona, however, had simply stared at him when he mentioned it to her. But she did promise to have the emergency room on alert should any of the players need medical care.

After a few moments, Lock saw Ric with Brody and Alla sitting behind him, but when he saw who surrounded them, he started to back away until two sets of strong hands grabbed him from behind.

"Oh, no you don't."

The two lion brothers hauled him toward Ric.

"You didn't really think we'd let you get out of this so easy, did you?" Brendon Shaw asked.

"You wanna be with my baby sister, then you'll have to get the *full* experience," Mitch said.

They dragged him to the section that had been taken over by the O'Neill Pride, the Smith Pack, and the Kuznetsov Pack. Several of them had banners, air horns, and superbly made T-shirts with Gwen's name on it.

"Lock!" they all cheered when he stood in front of them.

"I'm so sorry," Ric mouthed. He glanced at the female who had her arm around him. Roxy O'Neill.

"Lock! You sit right here, baby-boy." She nudged Ric. "Move handsome. I want this gorgeous grizzly to sit near me." Once Ric had moved over, she patted the empty spot beside her.

Mitch and Brendon pushed Lock and he snarled, snapping at them both.

Roxy O'Neill laughed and clapped her hands together. "And cranky just like a bear should be! I love it!"

Remembering well how his mother warned him falling in love often had unpleasant side effects, Lock stepped past several rows of Gwen's family and friends until he could drop down next to Gwen's mother. He held his hand out. "Hi, Miss O'Neill."

"Call me Roxy, Baby-boy. Everybody calls me Roxy." She ignored his hand and pulled his head down so she could kiss him on the cheek. "I've just been chattin' with your parents."

"It's been fascinating," his mother said, but when he looked back at her, she crossed her eyes in exasperation.

"But you and I will talk after the bout," Roxy threatened. "I want to know *all* about you."

Lock scowled at both lion males sitting one row back and over, and they gave him the finger. *Philly bastards.*

"I can't see past your giant melon head," a thick Southern accent complained.

Lock looked over his shoulder. "If I tear your head off that measly body, I can put you in my lap for a much better view."

"Or we can switch!" Jess said, stepping over her mate and forcing him to move one seat over so she was now next to Lock's parents. "Hi, Lock."

"Hi, Jess."

"I'll just lean on you like this." She leaned forward, wrapped her arms around his neck, and rested her chin against his shoulder. "Then I can see everything."

"Jessica Ann—"

"You started this, Smitty, and I'm comfortable."

"Jessica, I'm not letting you—"

"*Don't make me upset!*" Jess screamed in Smitty's face, shocking everyone but her fellow Packmates, who had to quickly look away so they could laugh in peace. "*I wanna rest on Lock!*"

"Okay! Okay! Calm down!"

Brody watched Jess as if she were a coiled snake ready to strike, but Alla only rubbed her nose and looked off, a little snort slipping by. Jess returned to her spot on Lock's shoulder, her cute face pressed against his. "I swear," she whispered against his ear, "I'm going to stay pregnant all the time. I totally have control when I'm pregnant."

"That innocent face attached to that ruthless heart."

She snickered until the lights shut completely off and that rough female voice from the first derby bout Lock had gone to came over the speakers.

"Ladies and gentlemen, you're about to experience a night you will always remember. A night of raw spectacle and unbridled brutality. Welcome, one and all . . . to the East Coast Roller Derby Finals!"

The crowd roared, but Gwen's mother was the one who could be heard above everybody else.

"You've been waiting all year for it. And now it's about to happen. Hold on to your seats and gird your loins for the battle of the century. The Staten Island Furriers versus The Assault and Battery Park Babes!"

More roaring, which could be barely heard above Gwen's mother.

"Now get ready, because this is the time. This is the place. Because these tough bitches are going to leave the track soaked in the blood of their enemies!"

Lock and Jess looked at each other, Jess's adorable face scrunched up in disgust. "What the hell kind of intro is that?"

"I bring you last year's regional and national champions . . . *The Staten Island Furriers!*"

The spotlights hit the track and the Furriers were spread out, their heads down, each one wearing a fur hoodie.

"What do you wanna bet those jackets are made from the fur of animals they've skinned themselves?" Jess joked.

Lock snorted as music came up and the player at the very end rolled across the track, moving around her teammates, a spotlight on her as she picked up speed. The wild dogs groaned in disgust and Jess shook her head.

"What?"

"'More Human Than Human' by Rob Zombie for their introduction music? How clichéd." And she sounded just like a 1980s Valley Girl when she said that, too.

When the music picked up, the lone skater passed the first player and the whole team took off, keeping time to the music and pulling the hoods of their jackets off as the announcer called out their team names. As before, they were perfectly in sync and did some very cool dance moves as they skated.

But apparently that wasn't good enough for her Ladyship of the Wild Dogs.

"Unimpressed," Jess muttered.

The Furriers finished their presentation, the crowd cheering wildly, especially the section directly across from where Lock and Gwen's supporters were sitting. There he could see Sharyn McNelly. She raised her hand in the air and gave the finger most likely to Roxy, who responded by giving both fingers with her sisters joining in.

Yeah, it was going to be a long bout.

As the Furriers rolled to the infield to get ready, the lights were lowered again and the announcer came back on.

"They began as the new predators on the block, but they've clawed their way to the top. They're tough, they're brutal, but they're always ladies. Let's hear it for the one, the only . . . *the Assault and Battery Park Babes!*"

The announcer screamed, the crowd screamed, and a guitar riff Lock hadn't heard in years blasted through the speakers. Joan Jett and the Blackheart's "Bad Reputation" played and the Assault and Battery Park Babes tore out on the track. They came out screaming, pumping their fists, and getting the crowd ready. As they did, the announcer called out the derby name of each teammate and the corresponding female did some stunt to get the crowd wild, including leaps, splits, and flips. When they called out "Evie Viserate!" Blayne sped forward, turned, and backflipped, landing on both feet. Unlike during the Furriers presentation, the wild dogs were standing, Jess resting her knees on Lock's shoulders and applauding like crazy.

But then the announcer called out Gwen.

"And new to the team tonight, let's welcome Number Fifty-Nine, the classic Philly treat—TastySkate!"

If there had been screaming and cheering before, no one would ever know it. Not when everyone in their section got to their feet, stomping and cheering—even Lock. But hell! This was his *woman*!

And because his woman rocked the universe, Gwen did a forward flip, her hands bracing her on the track and flipping her body over. She landed easily, but she wasn't done. Blayne caught hold of one of Gwen's hands and flipped Gwen forward again, this time using only the momentum of their matched speed.

The crowd loved it and, Lock had to admit, so did he.

The song ended and the Babes rolled into the infield. A bony elbow slammed into Lock's side and Roxy leaned over. "I taught my Gwenie that move."

He smiled appropriately, nodded and when Roxy looked away, he glared over at Mitch and Brendon—who gave him the finger.

But she's worth it, he reminded himself. Anybody who could look that good in those shorts was worth every second of this torture.

Gwen didn't go out for the first jam. They sent Pom-Pom Killer out for that, which gave Gwen ample time to stand around being nervous.

Tragically, Pom-Pom ended up eating track thirty seconds in, taken down by one of the knuckle-dragger She-wolves of the

Furriers, and although Pom-Pom got back up and kept going, she never could get through and past the pack to get even a chance to earn some points.

"You ready?" Cherry asked, shoving the black jammer helmet with big red stars on both sides at Gwen.

"Yeah," she said with way more confidence than she could ever hope to feel. "I'm ready."

"Good. Keep your eye on me and Blayne. And, Gwen," she motioned to the blockers and pivots who'd already moved out on the track for the next Jam, "she's out there. Be ready for her."

"I know."

"And don't forget the rules, because that's where she's gonna fuck with you. She's gonna push you to lose it. But remember, no claws, no fangs."

Gwen nodded and rolled out on the track, the crowd suddenly getting louder and she knew that was because of her family and friends.

Ignore them. Ignore them.

A hand fell on her shoulder and she looked up at Blayne. Even with that muzzle on her face, Blayne was obviously smiling. Gwen could see it by the way her eyes crinkled in the corners.

"Watch me, babe. Don't let anything stop you."

Again, Gwen nodded and moved over to stand by the Furriers' jammer. With her hands balled into fists and her arms bent at the elbow, Gwen crouched down, ready to take off.

The first whistle sounded and the pack took off, already jostling for position. She waited, holding her breath, and then she heard it; the second whistle sounded, and Gwen shot off, using the natural power of her legs to propel her forward. The crowd noise got louder, but she couldn't focus on any of it as her gaze sought out either Blayne or Cherry in the mass of pushing and shoving bodies ahead of her.

She saw Blayne first and Gwen picked up speed, heading for her and the hand that would grab hold of her and launch her through the pack. Her mind was so focused on reaching that gloved hand, she didn't see anything else. But she heard the scream of warning from the other Babes watching from the infield.

She looked in time to see McNelly coming right for her. Gwen jerked her body around, but for her size, McNelly was faster than Gwen realized, catching hold of Gwen around the waist and lifting her off the track. The She-wolf spun and used the momentum to launch Gwen right over the railing.

Gwen's small body slammed into the protective glass that was up between the track and the bleachers.

The entire section reared back—except Lock and the wild dogs who'd already been through this with Blayne—the cheers and clapping fading out as they sat there.

Brody tapped his finger against his chin, analytical as always. "Is that why there's protective glass? Because of all the body tossing they do during the bout?"

"And for the blood. See?" Jess pointed to several cute but young girls standing around with buckets, watching the action from the walkway between the track and the stands. "They're cleaners. You'll see them occasionally come by and clean the glass or track of blood or whatever."

Wincing, Lock rubbed his forehead. "Or whatever?" he asked Jess.

He felt her small body shrug against his. It seemed she still had no intention of moving away from his shoulders.

Next to Lock, Gwen's mother was craning her neck, trying to see what happened to her daughter as the Jam continued without her.

"Ma, look!" Mitch said, pointing halfway down the walkway that encircled the track. None had even seen Gwen move from where she'd landed.

But she'd dragged herself to her feet, and now she was moving, faster and faster.

"Uh-oh."

Lock didn't even look at Roxy. "Uh-oh? What uh-oh?"

"When it comes to business, baby-boy, my Gwenie takes after me. It's all about the ducats. But when it comes to suppressed rage that explodes when least expected, she definitely takes after her daddy." Wringing her hands as they watched Gwen pick up speed from outside the track, she added, "I just hope she doesn't get kicked from the game."

Yeah, he was afraid to know the answer, but he still had to ask the question. "How does one get kicked out of a game where rules seem to be few?"

"For my cousin Maureen, she had to snap a hyena's spine clean in half—of course, she did it on purpose. And if we hadn't pulled her off when we did, she would have ripped that spine right out along with that hyena's head."

"She's going!" Mitch warned and he was right.

"She's got her daddy's legs, too," Roxy added right as her daughter went airborne, the power of her legs taking her up and over the railing and into Donna McNelly. She hit her with such force, the two slammed into the ground and then kept rolling until they were deep in the infield. The referees and the two teams surged on them, trying to separate them, but even in that pile, Lock could still see Gwen's fist as it rose up again and again before slamming into whatever part of McNelly she had a hold of.

Sure, the Gwen cheering section went wild behind and around him—especially Alla, who seemed to be enjoying her first bout immensely—but then so did everyone else except for the growing-smaller-by-the-second Furrier fans across from them.

In that moment, TastySkate was the darling of most of the audience. And she probably didn't even know it.

It took most of her team to pull Gwen off McNelly, and most of the Furriers to hold McNelly back. But once they were separated, the referees put Gwen in the penalty box—actually a bench in the infield, but whatever—and only the Furriers' jammer on the track for the next jam. In other words, the jammer wouldn't have to worry about anything but getting through the pack and getting points in the next two minutes, because the Babes wouldn't have their own jammer out there.

Panting, Gwen sat on the bench and kept her head down, completely embarrassed. She didn't know what she'd been thinking.

Blayne dropped down next to her.

"What are you doing here?" Gwen asked.

"They suggested I may have slammed the Furriers' pivot in the back of the head with my knee—repeatedly—until I got to you. But I don't agree!" she yelled over at the refs, who ignored her.

Gwen bumped her forearm into Blayne's. "I'm sorry, Blaynie. I fucked up."

"Getting thrown out of the game would be fucked up. Mostly because you kind of have to kill somebody."

"Nice."

"I like the precise rules we have." She unhooked the right side of her muzzle.

"I let you guys down. I let her piss me off."

"Gwen . . . listen to the crowd."

"I hear them. It's Ma and Mitch and those insane wild dogs."

"No, sweetie. It's not just them."

Gwen finally lifted her head and looked around. Blayne was right. The entire crowd was chanting her name and screaming for her to be back on the track.

"Bitch, they love you."

"I don't . . ." Gwen shook her head. "I . . . I . . ."

Blayne put her hand on her knee. "All I want you to do, Gwen, is when you get back out there—you be the most diabolical, calculating, plotting bitch that you are in everyday life. You don't let anything get in your way. You don't let anything stop you."

"That's an interesting pep talk."

Blayne gave the grin. "You can thank Daddy."

Gwen glanced at the scoreboard. "We're already six points behind."

"So? This championship is still ours to take."

Gwen rested her arm against her knee and wiped blood from the open wound on her forehead. "You know, it was this sort of attitude that nearly got us expelled from St. Mary's of Perpetual Sorrow."

"I still say it was a fair question to ask."

"Not when the Pope is coming to visit."

Blayne held her hand out—after flicking the blood off—and Gwen clasped it with her own.

"Let's win this, Gwenie."

Gwen smiled. "You're on."

"Five bucks, though, you crack a nail."

Gwen glanced down at her hands while Blayne hooked her muzzle back on. "You are so *on*."

"I have to be honest," Ric admitted, looking away from Gwen and Blayne in the infield and at Lock. "I've never found a handshake so frightening before."

"I can't argue that observation."

"I do have a question for you."

"Sure."

"Why is my family name on the Babes' asses?"

"Because apparently you're a sponsor."

Ric let out a sigh. "I was afraid you were going to say something like that."

Gwen rolled out on the track, Blayne beside her. When they separated, they tapped fists and got into position. McNelly rolled by Gwen, winking at her. Lifting both hands, Gwen gave her the finger—twice.

The two teams laughed, as did the audience. But Gwen wasn't laughing and neither was McNelly.

As she'd done before, Gwen crouched and waited for the second whistle that would be her signal. The Furriers' jammer stood next to her. She remembered this one from Blayne's first bout. A superfast cheetah with a mean streak named Pussy-N-Boots.

"You sure you're up for this, Fresh Meat?" she asked, grinning at her.

Gwen shrugged shyly. "I hope so," she replied in a small voice.

She saw the cheetah's grin get wider. "You'll be fine, kid," she said.

The first whistle blew and the pack took off. A moment later, the second whistle. Pussy-N-Boots shot forward and Gwen came up after her . . . behind her. Reaching down, she caught hold of one of those long cheetah legs and gripped it with both her hands. Spinning around and using the upper-body strength she'd inherited from her mother, Gwen lifted the Furriers' jammer up and flung her out and over the railing. Without waiting to see where the female landed or if she'd cleared the railing, Gwen spun completely around and took off after the pack.

As she moved in closer, she saw McNelly waiting for her even as the She-wolf kept skating forward. So focused on Gwen and her desire to take her out, she didn't see the wolf-coyote, Lethal Lacey, until she'd slammed into her, forcing McNelly into the railing. At that point, Gwen picked up speed and took hold of the gloved hand held out for her. Blayne's fingers closed over Gwen's and she said, "Hold on, Gwenie!"

Gwen did, waiting as Blayne grabbed the neck of one of the Furrier blockers right in front of her and shoved her aside. Once she'd cleared the way, Blayne whipped Gwen through the cleared path through the pack.

Knowing she was the lead jammer, Gwen ripped around the track, passing the Furriers' jammer as she was climbing back over the railing. Gwen ignored her and kept going until she reached the pack again. The team needed the points, so Gwen pushed her way through the pack, unable to use Blayne this time since she was having a bit of a scuffle with two Furriers. That meant she had to get through on her own and McNelly was back and tearing across the track right for her. She kept going, hoping to pass one more Furrier before she stopped the jam or McNelly dropped her.

But she'd forgotten something important. For once, Gwen and Blayne weren't on their own. For once, they had someone else watching their backs.

McNelly was inches from her, snarling, her fangs beginning to show when a busty liger crashed into McNelly and dropped her right there on the track. Gwen passed the Furriers' other blockers and pivot for three more points and then quickly brought her hands to her hips twice to call off the jam.

Gwen rolled into the infield, Blayne coming up beside her. She threw her arm around Gwen's shoulders and said cheerily, "That went well, huh?"

"Yeah." Gwen glanced at her as they stopped. "Sweetie, what's wrong with your finger?"

Blayne shrugged, trying to be nonchalant. "Nothing."

"Your forefinger always points *back* at you that way?"

"It does now."

Gwen held out her hand. "Give it to me."

"Gwen—"

"Give it."

Growling, Blayne held her hand out. Gwen took hold, felt around a bit, and said, "Blayne, look. Mr. Squirrel."

Blayne looked across the track. "Where?"

Lock heard that bone snap back into place from where he was sitting and it took everything in him not to just get up and leave.

Jess barked out, "Holy shit!" before burying her face against Lock's neck while Ric dropped his face in his hands and visibly shuddered.

"War wounds!" Roxy cheered, her sisters laughing and clapping along with her.

When Roxy realized Lock was gawking at her, she patted his knee and promised, "She'll be fine, baby-boy."

"When you say 'fine' do you mean she'll be unharmed when this is all over, or do you mean that she bounces back really well from life-threatening injuries?" When Roxy opened her mouth to speak, Lock quickly added, "If you're not going to say something that will make me feel better, please don't say anything at all."

Roxy's mouth slowly closed and she looked back out over the track. "Oh, look, baby-boy. Next jam's starting. Why don't we watch?"

"Yeah," he sighed, trying not to panic. "Why don't we?"

CHAPTER 29

It happened every time Gwen rolled out on the track. They would chant her name . . . "Tasty!"

Okay, so it wasn't her name, but Lock felt it was close enough. And those from Philly who'd attended seemed to love it.

Lock had to wait until the cleaner had wiped off the glass in front of him before he could see Gwen getting in position on the track. She wiped off the blood leaking from her nose and then popped it back into position using both hands.

Ric let out a breath, quite pleased they'd had Heineken beer among all the Millers and Buds the roaming sellers were hawking. "You know how we always thought we were so much tougher than the football players because we play hockey?"

"Yeah."

"It's official. We're all pussies."

Lock laughed but absolutely agreed.

The ref blew the whistle and the pack took off. The "jostling" from earlier had turned into a "melee" Sun Tzu would have been afraid of.

The second whistle blew and Gwen moved. God, his woman was *so* fast. Between her lighter weight combined with those powerful tiger legs of hers, none of the other jammers could hope to get close to her. The only thing that helped them was whether Gwen could get through the pack. She tore up the track, catching up to the pack in seconds. One quick hyena slammed into her, but Gwen shoved her off, sending her spinning into her own teammate, both of them crashing into the railing and flipping over.

Gwen grabbed hold of Blayne's arm, and Blayne held her back, using her free hand to grab the blocker in front of her by the neck and yanking her out of the way. Once she had the opening, she flung Gwen through it. Free of the pack, Gwen took off, the ref tagging her as the lead jammer as she shot around the track.

Lock glanced at the scoreboard. They'd been ahead for a while, but now they were four points behind with thirty seconds left on the board. Gwen had to make it past the pack at least one more time to tie.

A hyena and a lioness went for her, but Cheeky Charming—a ligress who was bigger than Lock's mom—took them both out, allowing Gwen to zip past. McNelly went for her, but Pop-A-Cherry slammed into her from behind, sending the She-wolf spinning and landing in front of Gwen, but Lock's tigon went up and over. Unfortunately, because her skates weren't touching the track, McNelly wouldn't count for any points. But at least Gwen was able to keep going, shooting around the track for another pass. She'd passed another Furrier, tying the teams, but before she could go past the next Blocker, the Pivot hit her from the side and slammed her into the rails. The Furriers came at her and would probably tackle her to the ground. So, with only two seconds left on the clock, she called off the jam by putting her hands to her hips twice.

Then the Furriers took her down anyway, slamming her to the track.

The crowd cheered and booed with equal vigor and Lock let out a breath.

"You're worried about her," Roxy observed, although her eyes stayed focused on the track.

"Of course he's worried," his mother answered for him. "They're going after your daughter like a polar after a baby seal. He doesn't want her irreparably harmed."

Suddenly incredibly strong hands gripped Lock's face, squeezing his cheeks so hard his lips pursed out and it hurt.

"*You*," Roxy said, with what Lock would consider an inordinate amount of enthusiasm, "are a sweet, sweet grizzly." She squeezed harder. "I just adore you, baby-boy."

Struggling with his desire to knock Roxy out of the stands merely to get her hands off his face, Lock said, "T'ank you." Which was the best he could manage with her squeezing so hard.

"Mom approval," Jess whispered in his ear once Roxy had released her hold. "Check."

"Quiet."

Gwen waited in the infield with her team while the refs conferred with the coaches and captains.

"They're probably going to go into overtime. You up for that?"

Gwen nodded at Blayne's question and took the clean rag she handed her so she could wipe off some of the sweat and blood.

"What about your shoulder?"

"It'll hold up. I just need Ma to shove it back into place."

Cherry rolled over to them and stopped in front of Gwen. "This is the deal—their team has four girls out, we have about five." Only two from each team were out due to injuries. The others had been thrown out of the game during a particularly nasty melee, which led to the four game-ending injuries. "Plus, they called a personal foul on Gwenie."

"Which means what?" Blayne asked.

"They've suggested a two-lap duel with Gwen."

The Babes rolled their eyes, threw up their hands, and made all sorts of noises suggesting annoyance, but Gwen didn't. Yet she could understand their annoyance. If she made it around the track twice, she'd get two automatic points and they'd win the East Coast championship. But she wouldn't be out on that track alone. One player from the other team would be out there with her and there were even fewer rules in the two-lap duel than there were in general. That player could cut through the infield, use the bodies of other teammates to slow Gwen down, or stomp on Gwen with her skates. A no-holds-barred event.

"Who suggested it?" Gwen asked while her teammates grumbled.

Cherry smirked. "McNelly."

"Forget it," Blayne said.

"I'm in."

Blayne grabbed her arm. "Excuse us." She dragged Gwen a bit away from the team and asked, "Have you lost your damn mind?"

"I'm in, Blayne. I'm doing this. Just me and her."

"I love you, Gwen. I really do. But you've lost your fucking mind. That bitch could care less whether you get any points out there. All she cares about is killing you. Killing you *a lot.*"

"I'm doing it."

"Why?"

"Because she needs to learn there are liabilities to being a prick."

"Good plan if she weren't a sociopath."

"I'm doing it." She looked over at Cherry. "I'm in."

"You sure?"

"No!" Blayne barked.

"Yeah. I'm sure." She focused back on Blayne. "I'm doing this."

"You're an idiot."

She leaned against her friend. "You sweet talker you. Now shove my shoulder back, I can't wait for Ma."

"That's right, folks!" the announcer gleefully intoned. "It's going to be a two-lap duel. Two minutes have been put on the clock. If the jammer makes it around the track twice, the Assault and Battery Park Babes win. If the blocker keeps her from getting around the track in those two minutes, the Staten Island Furriers win!"

"Oooh!" Brody MacRyrie applauded behind Ric. "A two-lap duel! How exciting!"

But when Ric looked at his friend, all he could see was panic in the bear's eyes and he worried that the grizzly was about to do something stupid.

"I'm sure it's fine," Ric tried to assure him, using his most calming voice. Always best to keep the grizzlies calm and rational. Did these people have any concept what a crazed bear could do to their precious stadium? "Right, Roxy? It's going to be fine, right?"

Roxy was busy chewing her lip until she realized both men were staring at her, waiting for their fears to be assuaged. She stopped, forced a smile, and said, "I'm sure she'll be fine."

"You are *lying to me!*" Lock growled, making Smitty tense up since Jess was still resting around the bear's shoulders like a mink stole.

"Baby-boy, now calm down." Roxy took Lock's hand in hers and patted it. "My Gwenie knows what she's doing."

"Your Gwenie will do anything to make sure her team wins, because she hates that woman so much. And although your daughter is, on most days, a little psychotic, Donna McNelly is a *sociopath*. She just wants to kill her."

Roxy let out a sigh. "I know." Wait. How was *that* helpful?

"She'll be fine," Ric said again, hoping he was right. Of course, as he watched the battered, bruised, and weary-looking Gwen roll onto the track and then the barely bruised, much bigger, and wide-awake She-wolf roll on after her, Ric realized that he definitely had his doubts.

Panting, Gwen rested one hand on the railing and one hand on her waist.

"How ya doin', little kitty?" McNelly taunted. "You sure you're up for this? I don't know, you took some bad hits during that last jam. And you look so tired. You tired? People never realize how long two minutes can be, huh? But we know, don't we, little kitty?"

While McNelly kept going on, Gwen looked down at the hand on her waist. Her eyes narrowed. Was her nail polish chipped or had she cracked her nail? She leaned in a bit, examining it a little more. Letting out a sigh, she relaxed back. *Nail polish chipped.* That was good. She had no desire to pay Blayne five bucks.

The ref stood diagonally from her but still in the infield. "Just a reminder," he said. "To make two complete laps your feet have to mostly be on the track. Any leaps over ten feet—whether vertical or horizontal—won't be counted, understand?"

Gwen nodded.

"She can come at you from any direction and in any way. Fangs and claws are now *allowed.* Whatever you do, don't stop. You've got two minutes, hon." He briefly glanced at McNelly before adding, "And good luck."

He clamped the whistle between his lips, pointed his arm at her, and blew. Gwen took off, but McNelly wasn't behind her. As the game had progressed, Gwen had become really good at sensing where the blockers were coming from. And this time McNelly had cut through the infield and was going to meet her on the other side.

Gwen ignored the sound of the screaming crowd, focusing instead on just McNelly, the track, what was in or near her space, and Blayne's voice. As she made it halfway around, McNelly was there, coming right at Gwen.

Twisting her body, Gwen spun out of her reach, McNelly slamming into the rails so hard she almost went over. Gwen kept going, not even looking back. The crowd got louder, but she could still hear Blayne over them all.

"Five feet, Gwen! Five feet!"

Gwen took a breath and waited until she heard Blayne yell, "Hard left!"

She jerked to the left and McNelly flew by a second after, landing hard on the track, her body splayed out.

Again, she kept moving, never looking back. She heard the announcer scream, "Lap one!" And she knew she'd have to get through this next lap to win.

"Head-on, Gwen!" Blayne screamed. "Head-on!"

Gwen looked up and there NcNelly was, coming right at her, fangs and claws out, her long arms open wide.

Gwen could leap over her, but anything more than ten feet, she was screwed. And she'd have to go at least that high because she had no doubts the big bitch would jump with her and catch her legs.

No. She couldn't leap up and over her, but she could go off the track into the infield to run away. Yet she'd have to push through all those Furriers who'd be beating the shit out of her to stop her. So that left her with one option . . .

When Gwen's fangs and claws came out, Lock sat up straight.

"*What the hell is she doing?*" he snarled, barely realizing Mitch Shaw asked the same question at the same time.

"Now this," Roxy sighed, "this is going to be ugly."

"I'm right there with you, Rox," Alla sighed behind him.

But Lock didn't dare look away from the track to glare at either Gwen's mother or his own. Not when the action was moving so fast.

They were about five feet from each other, McNelly about to scoop Gwen up in those massive arms of hers, when Gwen finally went airborne. But instead of leaping over McNelly, which was what Lock had assumed she'd do, she went right into her.

She hit McNelly full force, her mouth open and wrapping around the She-wolf's face. Gwen clamped down, her claws digging into McNelly's shoulders. They hit the ground in a bloody, violent mess, McNelly's claws slashing at Gwen's shoulders and arms as the female desperately tried to get Gwen off her.

Gwen sat up, spitting out the blood that wasn't already running down her chin and neck and twice slammed her fist into McNelly's face.

"Thirty-five seconds!" Blayne yelled from the infield.

Gwen scrambled over McNelly and started to get to her feet. But McNelly caught hold of her ankle, flipping over on her stomach to drag Gwen back.

"Twenty-five, Gwen! Twenty-five!"

Gwen yanked her foot away from McNelly, but the She-wolf took hold of the other one.

"Twenty! Twenty!"

Lock watched as the two friends looked at each other and he thought exactly what Roxy had said, *This is going to be ugly.*

"House cat her, Gwen!" Blayne yelled. "*House cat the bitch!*"

And Lock finally found out what it meant to "house cat" someone as Gwen turned so fast, if he'd been more human he would have missed it. She turned and using both hands, raked her unleashed claws down McNelly's face three . . . oh. Nope. Four times.

It definitely reminded him of a house cat fighting off the family dog.

McNelly screamed, her hands covering her face and what was left of her nose, lips, and cheeks. And maybe her eyes.

The crowd jumped to their collective feet, the wild dogs howling louder than anyone.

Flicking something red and pulpy from her claws, Gwen sprung to her feet and took off, Blayne right with her from the infield, counting the time down as she did.

Lock didn't know when he'd gotten to his feet, but like everyone else in that stadium he was up and cheering, screaming for Gwen to make it as the counter went down.

"Eight! Seven!" Blayne's voice counted as Gwen flew around the last turn. Her friend's voice the only thing she was focusing on at the moment. "Six! Five!" She saw where another ref stood, his arm out, marking where Gwen would have to be by zero to win. She wanted to leap for it but knew she couldn't. So she kept moving. Her eyes focused on the last ref and how close she was getting. "Four! Three!"

Just a little more, baby-girl. She could hear her mother's voice in her head, coaxing her on like she used to do when she was only five and had put on Gwen's first pair of skates. *I know you can do it.*

"Two! One!" Gwen went past the ref, but Blayne's voice was

drowned out by the crowd and she didn't know if she'd made it in time. Then Blayne was on the track, her arms open. The way they used to do when they played field hockey and had just knee-capped one of the rich girls from the local private school. Gwen dived right at her best friend and threw her arms and legs around Blayne's body.

Blayne spun her around, screaming, "*You did it, Gwenie! You did it!*"

At least that's what it sounded like she said. Hard to tell with the crowd going crazy. All that roaring, howling, cackling, and foot stomping made it impossible to hear much of anything.

The rest of the team surrounded her and Blayne, hoisting Gwen up, carrying her on their shoulders around the track. The howls, roars, etc., lowered as one chant rose above everything else . . .

"Tasty! Tasty! Tasty!"

As they passed the section filled with her family and friends, she could see her mother applauding like crazy, tears streaming down her face, the Drs. MacRyrie clapping and waving at her, while Mitch and Brendon pumped their fists in the air and screamed her name like they were at a Bon Jovi concert. Hell, everyone in that section was going a little crazy.

Except for one lone grizzly. He stood there, a center of calm with a wild dog sitting on his shoulders, howling with her Pack, and his best friend beside him calling out "Bravo!" But the bear was breathing, slowly, in and out, until he finally looked up, knowing her eyes were on him and him alone. And then he smiled. A smile filled with pride and love. She only saw it for a moment before her team marched her away to get their trophy, but it was enough.

Hell, it was damn near everything.

CHAPTER 30

What started off as a big multiderby team party at one of the coolest clubs downtown quickly morphed into a Babes and friends–only party at a karaoke bar near wild dog territory.

Lock would be eternally grateful, too. He'd always hated clubs and club people, while a karaoke bar was much more his speed as long as no one tried to make him sing.

Wandering away from the table he pulled out his vibrating cell phone. "Hello?"

"Hey. It's Dee."

"Hey. You missed a great game."

"I saw it. It was great."

"You were there?"

"Sitting three rows behind you. Didn't you see me?"

No. He hadn't seen her there because she hadn't been there, but Lock knew what Dee was doing. "Barely. I was busy, you know."

"Yeah, I noticed."

"Where are you now?" he asked.

"Roaming."

"We moved locations, in case you plan on stopping by. We're at a bar called Caleb's Corner . . . or Caleb's Deck . . . or Caleb's something. It's a karaoke bar."

The pause was long. "And you expect me to show up?"

"Not really."

"Smart bear. But I'll check in with you later."

"Okay." Lock disconnected the call and put his phone back in his pocket. He turned around and stared down at the tiny kittens glaring up at him. "What?"

"Who was that on the phone?" Mitch demanded.

"Uh . . . Dee-Ann."

"You're calling other women when you're hooked up with *my* baby sister?"

"But Dee-Ann's my—"

"I don't care! You're with my sister now, scumbag. And I may have promised Sissy I'd back off, but—" he motioned between him and Brendon "—don't think for a second we're going to let you get away with *anything* when it comes to our baby sister."

Dee shut off her phone completely and put it back into her front jean pocket. She took another glance around and popped the trunk on the old Ford she'd taken from a junkyard and managed to get running. She pulled the wolf out and placed him over her shoulder. Slamming the trunk closed, she headed to the nondescript door in the middle of the alley. She'd already picked the lock and now she went down the stairs deep into the bowels of the tunnels.

Once she'd traveled as far down as she could, Dee stepped away from the stairs and lowered the body onto the floor. She crouched beside him.

The wolf opened his eyes, glared up at her.

"Names," she said. The last one she'd said that to, the bar owner, he'd given her names of the dealers he got his product from. Of the ten names he listed, only one had been shifter. Only one had been Dee's concern. The rest would be handled by others.

Funny, this hadn't been how this was supposed to go down, but in her line of work it was all about rolling with the unexpected. Like Lock MacRyrie. She'd been surprised when the road to Ross had led to one of the best friends she'd had in the military. For a brief moment, she'd thought about bringing him back into this life. They'd always been an excellent team. But, no. That wouldn't do for the bear. He'd done his service to his country and his kind. Now he deserved exactly what he wanted: a deadly feline who liked to skate.

And what did Dee deserve? Doing what she did best: Protecting her own and fixing problems. She was real good at fixing problems.

"Names," Dee said again when Jay didn't answer her.

He told her one name. It wasn't easy for him. The doctors had had to wire his jaw shut and his head was covered in bandages from what Lock had done to him Halloween night. His face . . . not much better. Those were scars that wouldn't fade. But he told her one name because he'd only sold one. One that had yet to be picked up. And that night at the party Ross was about to move from selling names to handling the product himself. Amazing what desperation would make a man forget—like how hard it was to capture and keep shifter females.

"Thank you kindly," Dee said when he finished. She stood, her mind already turning with what she should do next. She'd have to call in some help because that one . . . that one whose name he sold would be a problem.

"What . . . about . . . me?" she heard him ask.

Dee looked at him over her shoulder. For days she'd watched the man and Donna McNelly. For days she'd watched those two argue, fuck . . . fuck, argue until Dee had seriously considered removing her own eyes. For that torture alone, he should suffer, but there were bigger issues. Bigger mistakes he'd made. "You betray your kind? What do you think should happen?"

"Just . . . names. Just—"

"I know. Just crossbreeds. They're still us. But don't you worry none . . . you'll be gettin' what you deserve."

She walked back to the stairs, but before heading up, she stopped. She listened. The hyenas who ruled these tunnels crept closer. She could hear them, smell them. And they could smell her . . . and Ross's blood. She looked back at him one more time and smiled. "It won't last long," she promised.

Then, before she went up those stairs, she yelled out, "*Dinner!*"

She made her way out on to the street, closing the alley door, the screams and hyena howls left long behind. She headed down the street, but stopped at the corner when a limo pulled up in front of her. After a moment's hesitation, she got in.

"Well?"

She stared across the seat at the man who'd hired her. Who'd offered her a chance to continue doing what she did best. She loved her cousin, but working security? Getting a regular paycheck and clocking in and clocking out every damn day? Not exactly her style. "You were right," she said. "He did sell her name before he tried to grab the other one."

"I'm guessing he needed the cash. Besides, after meeting her I can see why he tried to bring in the feline instead. The other would have been much more of a challenge." Niles Van Holtz, Alpha Male of the entire Van Holtz Pack and head of the simply named Group, the protective arm of the Board, took a sip of bottled water.

"Want me to bring her in?" she asked.

"No. We'll use her as bait instead."

"She's a wild card. Never know what she's gonna do next."

"I could say the same about you."

Dee grinned. "Look at you. Tryin' to sweet-talk me."

The wolf smirked, glancing out the limo window. "Why did you bring Ross here? You could have expired him at the hospital." And she had to fight real hard not to laugh at the fancy way he'd put that rather than just saying "killing" like any self-respecting predator. "It would have appeared that he died from his injuries."

And Lock MacRyrie would have spent the rest of his life thinking he'd killed that wolf in an ugly fit of grizzly boar-rage. No. Dee-Ann wouldn't do that to the man who'd saved her life more than once. She wouldn't let that rest on his giant shoulders.

Seeing him happy and in love was a wonderful thing. Dee wouldn't be the one to take that away from him now.

She didn't, however, mention any of that to Van Holtz. "Figured it was better he disappeared, since he was healin' up and all. Scumbag dealer disappearing, no one will think much about it."

Van Holtz shrugged. "As you like. I was just curious."

Reaching into a small fridge, he pulled out another bottled water and handed it to her.

She took it, nodded. "Thank ya kindly."

"And what about that girl you picked up? Abby something?"

"She's safe."

"She's a coyote-wolf and barely sixteen."

"And she's safe." And, in a few years, sly little Abby would be the one in the back of this fancy limo, haggling for this job. But until then, she needed to be cared for like any pup, no matter the breed . . . or the mix.

"So are you in, Miss Smith?" he asked.

"Not sure. Don't much like feelin' hemmed in."

"We're not the military. And, as a boss, I'm quite hands off."

"Except the Unit's been keepin' an eye on me. Even following my friends around. I don't like it."

"You won't have to worry about them once you're with us. They just want to make sure you haven't snapped your bolt."

"Who would be my contact here?" Dee asked, doubting Van Holtz himself, who hailed from the West Coast, would do that job.

"You've already met him."

Dee thought a moment, then couldn't help but give a little sniff. "That *kid*?"

"Ulrich is hardly a kid. Actually, I think he's only three years younger than you."

And a little too damn pretty for her to trust her life with. "He's the best you can do?"

"He's the best. So are you in or out?"

She shrugged. "In."

He grinned. "Are you always this enthusiastic?"

"Pretty much. Like my daddy."

"He was one of our best."

"He still is."

Van Holtz nodded and said, "Welcome to the Group, Dee-Ann."

Dee-Ann looked out the window to watch the city move by. She didn't know if it would be her home forever, but it would do for now.

Gwen grabbed her mother's purse and dug around until she found the aspirin. Roxy never needed headache medication for herself, but she usually kept a small bottle in her bag for Gwen.

She poured two in her hand, glanced at her mother, who was "yoo-hooing" over at Lock's uncles, and went ahead and poured out another three.

Blayne placed a bottled water in front of her and climbed over the back of the booth to get into the seat.

"Figured you could use this."

"Thanks." Gwen downed the five pills in one swallow and chased them with the water. "Between the singing and my mother . . ."

"I know, I know. Still . . . better than the club."

"Only because my mother yelled more while we were there."

Gwen closed her eyes and waited for the pills to take effect, but that was when she heard Blayne fidgeting.

"What, Blayne?"

"What what?"

"Your leg is bouncing, so I know it's something."

"I don't know what you—"

Gwen put her hand on Blayne's knee, forcing her leg to stop bouncing up and down on the ball of her foot. It was a habit she'd had for years.

"Spit it out, Thorpe."

And she did, in one long sentence: "Cherry wants you to stay on the team and she definitely wants you to stay with us through Nationals because we'll be going up against the Texas Long Fangs and I heard they're really mean and I know you said you were only doing this for one bout, but you were so in it, and it was so you and you and me are the most rockin' team ever and . . . and . . . and you're not saying anything."

"I didn't think you'd notice."

"Come on, Gwenie!"

"You already know what I'm going to say."

Blayne's face scrunched up as she squeaked out, "You'll say . . . yes?"

Gwen shrugged. "Yeah, all right."

The squeak turned to a loud squeal and she hugged Gwen while the wolves and felines glared at Blayne and the dogs barked.

Putting her knees on the booth seat, Blayne looked over at her teammates, now Gwen's teammates. "She's in!"

The Babes clapped and cheered and Gwen couldn't help but smile until she saw her mother leering at her from the other end of the booth. At the moment, her mother sported a lovely black eye courtesy of Sharyn McNelly. It was a black eye that Roxy deserved, too, since she'd snatched off McNelly's wig in front of everybody outside the stadium.

"Just wipe that look off your face," she told her mother. "I still haven't forgiven you."

"Why can't you simply admit you're blessed to be the daughter of Roxy 'The Rocker' O'Neill?"

"When did this become about you? *How* did this become about you? This is about me." Gwen pointed at her chest. "Me, me, me. For once . . . me."

"Selfish," her mother muttered, turning away from her to hit on Lock's Uncle Hamish.

Gwen's mouth dropped open that her mother *dared* toss that word at her when Blayne elbowed her.

Still glaring, Gwen faced forward and blinked up at Lock. "Uh . . . Lock?"

"What did I miss?" her bear asked. "I heard applauding."

"Gwen's joined the Babes," Blayne cheered, hugging Gwen again.

Lock grinned. "I had a feeling that was coming. You looked way too happy out there."

"Yeah, but Lock—"

"I know, I know. And believe me, I didn't mean *any* of the stuff I said to you in the hallway. But based on your family dynamic, I knew coddling wouldn't work, so I gave you the proverbial kick in the pants you needed. Don't be mad at me."

"I'm not mad, it's just . . . look at your hands."

Frowning, Lock looked down at his hands. "Oh, gosh!" He dropped the Shaw brothers, both lion males grunting when they hit the floor. "I did it again."

"Again?" Blayne asked.

"Remember? Bears beat up their prey, then drag them into the bushes to feed," Gwen explained.

"Ohhh. That's why Daddy always said never let them take you to a secondary location."

"I think he was talking about serial killers, sweetie."

"Oh . . . it still sorta applies, though." Blayne jumped up and over the back of the booth. "I'm going to circulate." She kissed Gwen on the cheek. "You're totally, like, the best friend *ever*," Blayne teased.

"You say that now, but you won't when I kick your ass in training, heifer."

Head down, Blayne walked away but Gwen yelled after her, "None of that sloppy skating when we go to Nationals!"

Lock took Blayne's seat and asked, "How long before you're cocaptain?"

"I give it six months."

Picking up her hand from the table, Lock kissed her bruised and bloody knuckles. "I was really proud of you tonight. I have the toughest girlfriend *ever*," he finished, mimicking Blayne.

"You do. And I have the sweetest, most cuddliest, most adorable bear *ever*."

Grinning, they rubbed noses, moving in closer to kiss, but abruptly stopping when that hand slammed onto the table and Mitch lifted his head from the floor.

"Dying," he gasped. "Internal bleeding. Call. Ambulance."

"Ma," Gwen whined, not in the mood to stop flirting with her boyfriend.

Roxy slammed her hand down on the table and snapped, "Jesus Christ on a cross, Mitchell O'Neill Shaw! Get off your lazy ass and stop acting like a baby! You're embarrassing me!"

"Dying! Painful death!"

Roxy pointed a finger at her son. "Don't make me get the staple gun out of the back of my car. I *will* use it."

"But will it stop the bleeding?"

Ignoring her brother and mother, Gwen leaned into Lock and said, "Any interest in getting out of here?"

"And miss Phil's rendition of 'Rawhide'?"

They glanced up at the stage. The wild dog even had a whip.

"Tell me you're being sarcastic," Gwen said.

"I actually have to *say* I'm being sarcastic?"

Lock eased out of the booth, stood, and held his hand out for her. Gwen took it and let Lock lift her up and over her brothers' bodies. With their fingers twined together and mostly oblivious to the rowdy crowd of shifters all around them, they headed toward the exit and home.

EPILOGUE

Gwen jumped out of the cab and tossed money at the driver. "Come on!" she ordered Blayne. "We're late."

"I know." Blayne handed off the bags she'd held throughout the trip to Gwen and slid across the seat and out the door. "Merry Christmas!" she said to the driver, who looked at her in surprise.

"Aren't you bubbly?"

"It's Christmas!" Blayne cheered, taking one of the heavy bags from Gwen.

"It's Christmas Eve, so don't annoy me." Together they ran up the stairs to the front door.

Gwen rang the doorbell and followed with a knock, not sure she could be heard over the Christmas music. Out of the corner of her eye, she saw Blayne look over her shoulder again.

"What's with you?"

"Ever feel like you're being followed?"

"No."

"I do."

"Sure it's not just her?"

Blayne turned her head to look at Gwen, but caught sight of Dee-Ann standing behind them.

"Ahh! Where the hell did you come from?"

"Momma says from the love she shares with my daddy," Dee calmly replied.

Blayne said, "Awwww," and Gwen desperately stabbed at the doorbell again until it opened.

"You are late, feline."

"Don't you have a cold war to start?" Gwen asked as she walked past Sabina.

"And where is my chair?"

"He's an artist," Gwen gleefully reminded the wild dog. "He won't be rushed." She shoved the bag at Sabina. "Here's your damn chocolate cakes."

Sabina took the bags from Gwen and Blayne and then looked them over.

"What are you wearing?"

Blayne glanced down at the tiny velvet green minidress she wore. "Jess asked us to be Santa's helpers tonight."

"You look like Santa's whores. And has Santa been pimp-slapping you all over New York?"

Gwen took a step toward the mouthy wild dog, but Blayne caught her arm. "We came right from practice. We'll wipe the blood off."

"Do that," the Russian ordered before heading off to the kitchen with the cakes.

"And happy fucking holidays to you, too."

"Ignore her." Blayne shook off the rudeness like she always did and grabbed Gwen's hand, dragging her into the party.

"Blayne!" the crowd called out as soon as she walked in.

Gwen pushed Blayne toward her waiting friends and cut through the crowd. She saw Ric and said, "Where's my honey bun?"

He laughed. "Upstairs, I think. And was that the lovely Dee-Ann I just saw come in with you?"

"Yeah. And if you can find her again, more power to you." She kissed his cheek and kept moving through the crowd until she saw Mitch and Sissy kissing on the stairs.

"Find a room," she teased, stepping over them.

"Don't begrudge us our forbidden love," her brother playfully chastised.

Laughing, Gwen jogged up the stairs. "Hey, Bren."

"Hey, Gwenie. You look cute."

"Thanks." As Gwen went past him, she saw Ronnie Lee, slammed back into the wall, and bared her fangs at her while hissing.

"Hey, darlin'," Ronnie Lee said with that big smile. "Have a wonderful holiday!"

Still hissing in very clear warning, Gwen went down the hall, keeping her back to the wall until Ronnie and Bren disappeared down the stairs. She turned and kept moving until she reached another set of stairs. She ran up those, passing others she knew, wishing some a happy holiday, ignoring others she didn't really like.

She caught sight of Jess coming out of a room. She slowed down and stopped in front of her. "How ya doin', sweetie?"

"Everybody gets morning sickness in the *first* trimester. Leave it to me to get it in the second."

"At least two of my aunts got it in the second. You have Saltines?"

She held up the packet. "But it's Christmas. I should be gorging, not purging."

"Now you're like all those Hollywood stars."

She smirked. "Thanks."

"Have you seen my honey bun?"

Jess nodded. "See those stairs at the end of the hall? Go all the way up and the door at the end will take you to the roof. He's been up there for like an hour."

"You know how he is about crowds." Gwen headed toward the stairs. "How long before you need me?"

"Another ten, fifteen . . . I . . . I . . ." Hearing retching noises, Gwen spun around to see Jess dashing back into the bedroom with her hand over her mouth. Gwen started to head toward her, but she saw Smitty.

"She needs you."

"I know." He held up a soda can. "I got her some ginger ale."

He winked and disappeared into the bedroom, closing the door behind him.

Following Jess's directions, Gwen found Lock right where Jess had said he'd be. On the roof.

Gwen sat across from him, her legs straddling the roof's ledge. It was a healthy drop if either of them fell, but hell . . . they'd survived going over a mountain, they could survive this.

Lock smiled. "Hey."

"Hey. Sorry I'm late."

"No problem." He leaned in and kissed her and like always she lost herself in that kiss. Hard not to when he had those damn lips that did something to her every time.

Lock was the first to pull back, but he nuzzled his nose against hers, and Gwen ended up giggling.

"I'm glad you're here," he sighed.

"I'm glad I'm here, too." She took his hand between her own. "You ready for tomorrow?"

His eyes crossed, making Gwen giggle more.

"Breakfast at my parents' and dinner at your mom's? Can't wait."

"Let's get through tomorrow and then for New Year's Eve it'll just be you, me, champagne, Chinese food from down the block, and your favorite honey."

"You promise?"

"Absolutely. We'll need the break."

"You sure you want to miss out on the yearly Shaw extravaganza at his hotel?" When Gwen only stared at him, he said, "I'll take that as a yes."

"Good. Now let's get downstairs." She started to get up, but Lock tugged her back down.

"Wait."

"I want to give you something," Lock said, digging deep for the balls to do this.

"I thought we were going to wait until Christmas . . . especially important since I haven't actually finished wrapping."

"This can't wait." Lock took a deep breath and quickly placed his gift into her palm. "Here."

Gwen opened her hand, gazing down at it until she said, "It's an engagement ring."

"Yeah. It had a box. Two, actually, including one of those blue Tiffany ones."

Slowly Gwen's gaze lifted to his. "It *had* a box?"

"Yeah. I was holding it, trying to think of the best way to ask you to marry me and I . . . uh . . . accidentally crushed it."

"I see."

"The ring's fine, though. Right?" He leaned in, trying to look. "Isn't it?"

"It's . . ." Gwen suddenly looked up at him. "Are you asking me to marry you?"

"Badly but . . . yes."

"Why?"

"What do you mean why?"

"Mitch still calls you 'that bastard' and Bren won't even speak to you and I'm almost positive something is going on between my mother and one, if not *all*, of your uncles and Blayne is well . . . Blayne, and my Uncle Cally is still talking about taking a two-by-four to the back of your head and—"

"Gwen. They're not you. I love *you*. I want to marry *you*."

"You're sure?"

Lock laughed. "Of course I'm sure. You're the best thing that's ever happened to me. But . . . I don't want to rush you into anything. So if you feel more comfortable—"

Gwen slipped the ring on her left index finger. "It fits. And it's perfect."

"I went for subtle. Hope that was okay."

"Perfect."

She looked up at him and Lock was reaching for her, knowing what her answer would be from the love in her eyes, when the roof door slammed opened and Blayne walked out. "Hey. They want to start giving out the gifts so . . ."

Lock didn't know what Blayne saw or if the friends had some nonverbal communication that passed between them but suddenly Blayne shot forward and grabbed Gwen's hand.

"Oh, my God! *Oh, my God!*"

"Blayne," Gwen warned. "Don't do anything stup— *Blayne!*"

Lock watched as Blayne dragged his fiancée off the roof.

He charged after them, but the pair moved like lightning, their derby skills allowing Blayne to drag Gwen through the crowd of people in the wild dog house, dodging bodies and kids and *stuff* with amazing ease.

As Lock made it down the stairs to the first floor, people instantly moving out of his way while the wild dog pups followed behind him as they always did, hoping he'd roar at them, Blayne jumped up on a coffee table in the middle of the room, holding Gwen's hand up.

"*They're engaged!*" the wolfdog screamed out.

There was a long shocked pause, and then the room erupted into hysterical cheers, the wild dogs rushing forward while Ric smiled, the Smith wolves appeared confused, and the Shaw brothers scowled at Lock.

He shrugged at them and said, "At least I'm marrying mine."

"Bastard," Mitch snarled.

"Son of a bitch," Bren snapped before both brothers stormed off.

As the crowd of well-wishers surged, Gwen was suddenly spit out of the group and right into Lock's arms.

"Are you okay?" He put her on her feet but kept his arms around her.

"Yeah, but . . ." She motioned to the crowd around Blayne, Ric, and a rather unwell-looking Jess. "Shouldn't they be congratulating *us?*"

"That's usually the protocol, but they're wild dogs, which automatically translates to weird."

"I guess, but still."

Not caring about any of that, Lock lifted Gwen into his arms and held her close, her legs around his waist and her arms around his neck.

"So," he said, rubbing his nose against hers, "I'm assuming when we were on the roof you were about to say yes."

Gwen laughed. "Yeah. I was about to." She kissed him. "And yes. I'll marry you."

Pulling her closer, Lock went in to kiss Gwen again, but she pulled back.

"You should know that an O'Neill female getting married? That hasn't happened since the druids ruled Ireland. So you should be prepared for me and Blayne to be doing a little cousin torturing."

"If you're going to do that, Mr. Mittens, then we should really have some fun and think about a big wedding."

Gwen's face scrunched up in clear disapproval.

"Big wedding? You, who hates being the center of attention and me who hates . . . everything else?"

"Think about it. Your mother forced to work with mine—who has huge moral issues over large weddings—while your brothers are forced to help them by your mother. In the meantime you, me, Blayne, Ric, Jess, and Dee, if we can actually find her, are in Hawaii. By the time we get back, we'll be married, and the wedding will only be a nightmare party we have to get through."

"Diabolical."

"I am my mother's son."

Gwen brushed her hand across his chest and shoulders, before slipping her arms around his neck, and Lock hiked her up a bit so they could look each other in the eye.

Kissing his cheek, Gwen asked, "And, baby?"

Lock sighed as she kissed his neck. "Uh-huh?"

"For the wedding night—" kissed his jaw "—when we're alone . . ."

"Uh-huh?" he asked again seconds before he started humming, his eyes crossing as her tongue traced his ear and those damn nails dragged along the corded muscles of his neck.

"You'll wear the kilt, right?" And Lock burst out laughing, the amazing feline in his arms grinning and snuggling closer, her body fitting perfectly against his. "Ya know? Just for me?"

Every girl could use
A GREAT KISSER,
so pick up Donna Kauffman's latest today!

The man holding her elbow tugged her in out of the rain.

"Thank you," she gasped. "I'm so sorry—my umbrella—"

"Marco picked it up," came a very deep voice with a bit of a rough edge to it, like maybe he'd just woken up.

She was still blinking water out of her eyes and he still had a hold on her elbow. Her other hand was clutching her purse and laptop bag to her side in a death grip. Everything was just a blur. "Marco?"

"Ground crew. Here, let me take those."

Her elbow was abruptly released, which sent her a bit off balance, then her bags were suddenly lifted from her shoulder and slipped out of her death grip as if her hands were made from putty, sending her staggering a step in the other direction. Both her feet slipped a little as the smooth soles of her shoes were not made for . . . well, any of this. And then his hands were on her again, both elbows this time, and, and . . . well, the entire last sixty seconds had been so discombobulating, for a person who was never discombobulated, that she didn't know quite what to do. She blinked at him through wet ropes of hair and fogged glasses, arms still akimbo as he wrestled her to a balanced position.

"Bad day?"

It was the dry amusement lacing his tone that gave her the focus she so mercifully needed. She tugged her elbows from his grip, as if all this was suddenly very much his fault, but instead of being the liberating, independence-returning move she was so desperately seeking, the action only served to send her wheeling backward. Which resulted in being caught, once again, even more humiliatingly than before, by his very big, very strong, and very steadying hands.

"Thank you," she managed through gritted teeth. She carefully removed one elbow from his grip, not chancing leaving his steadying powers all at once, and scraped her hair from her forehead and removed her fogged glasses from her face. Finally able to see, she looked up . . . only to be thrown completely off balance all over again. But, this time, her feet were totally flat and stable, on hard, steady ground. "You can let me go now," she managed in a choked whisper.

He was just above average height, probably not even six feet, but given she topped the height chart at five-foot-six, and that was in three-inch heels, he was very tall to her. But it wasn't the height part that commanded the attention. Nor was it really the square jaw, the thick neck, broad shoulders, very nicely muscled arms and chest that were obvious even through the old sweatshirt and T-shirt he wore. The thick, sun-bleached brown hair might have been a teensy part of it, but mostly it was the piercing blue eyes—truly, they pierced—staring at her from his weathered, deeply tanned face.

Crinkles fanned from the corners of those eyes, and there were grooves bracketing either side of his mouth, but she didn't know if that was from squinting into the sun or smiling a lot. He wasn't smiling now, so it was hard to tell. But he was still holding on to her, and it was that, plus those look-right-through-you eyes, that were keeping her from reclaiming the rest of her much-needed balance.

"I'm—fine. Really. Thank you. Again."

He held her gaze for another seemingly endless moment, then gently let her go. "No worries."

"I, uh, need to rent a car." She was normally calm and cool under fire. It was why Todd had been so impressed and promoted her up the ranks of his campaign staff so quickly. It was also why she'd been one of the first ones the senator had hired to his permanent staff when he'd won his bid for office. If he could see her now, he wouldn't even recognize her. She didn't recognize her. Of course, the fact that she probably looked like a drowned cat didn't help matters. "If you could just point me in the right direction—" *I will slink off and pretend we never met.*

"You don't need a car."

She looked up at him again, and though she'd never particularly thought of herself as vain, she'd have given large sums for the use of a comb, a tissue, and a handheld mirror. Okay, so a full salon makeover probably wouldn't have hurt at that moment, but her pride wouldn't have minded at least a brief attempt at restoration. "Where I'm headed is about two and a half hours from here, and though it's probably not all that far-fetched to think they probably rent horses here, I'm thinking the locals, not to mention the horse, will be a lot safer if I get a nice SUV instead."

His lips quirked a little then, and her pulse actually did this zippy jumpy thing. And it felt kind of good—in a somewhat startling, disconcerting kind of way. However—reality check—she hadn't forgotten that her appearance was highly unlikely to provoke the same reaction in him. Besides, she was not here on vacation. She was here on a very serious mission that had absolutely nothing to do with having a vacation fling of any kind. Not that she was the fling type. Or that men ever flung themselves at her, vacation or otherwise, for her to know. But, still.

"Given the weather, it would probably be as uncomfortable for the horse, but that's not why I said you don't need a ride. You don't need one, because I'm your ride."

God help her, she looked him up and down before she could stop herself. *He* was her ride?

Try Dianne Castell's newest book,
HOT AND IRRESISTIBLE,
in stores now from Brava . . .

"**W**ho the hell was that?" McCabe said from behind her. "And this day just keeps getting better and better." Bebe turned to face Donovan. "Dara's none of your business, so forget her."

"Dara who?" He had his cop stare firmly in place. She hated being on the receiving end of cop stares, because it meant the cop wasn't budging till he got an answer.

"Dara is my mother-of-the-year. Make that foster mother. There, now you know. Happy? And what are you doing here anyway? Thought we were meeting at the station?"

Donovan's eyes widened and he let out a soft whistle, his gaze on Dara retreating down the street. "How the hell did that happen?"

"You're not letting this go, are you?"

"What do you think?"

"I think you're a pain in the ass." But the crack wasn't as sarcastic as she intended because he wasn't all pain and he certainly had a nice ass. And right now he was all yummy with his black hair damp from a recent shower and a soft navy shirt and worn jeans hugging lean hips. "I'll give you the ten-cent version to shut you up. Best I can figure, Dara was paid to take me, and no, I don't know why, and no, I don't intend to find out, because my real parents must be total scum to sell a kid. And yes, I did change my name and don't you dare go feeling sorry for me, because I sure as hell don't need a pity party, and now you want to tell me what you're doing on my front stoop at this hour?"

Her gaze met his and she braced herself for the *Oh, you poor thing* look, but instead Donovan bent his head and kissed her. She started to protest, but her lips were busy and suddenly her tongue was, too, and then her arms got into the act and then her insides melted into hot goo, which had acid beat all to hell and back. This kiss was all wrong on every level except one . . . Donovan McCabe felt so darn good when she was feeling crappy as hell.

And don't miss Terri Brisbin's first book for Brava,
A STORM OF PASSION,
coming next month!

Whatever the Seer wanted, the Seer got, be it for his comfort of his whim or his pleasure.

She stood staring at the chair on the raised dais at one end of the chamber, the chair where he sat when the visions came. From the expression that filled her green eyes, she knew it as well.

Had she witnessed his power? Had she watched as the magic within him exploded into a vision of what was or what would yet be? As he influenced the high and the mighty of the surrounding lands and clans with the truth of his gift? Walking over to stand behind her, he placed his hands on her shoulders and drew her back to his body.

"I have not seen you before, sweetling," he whispered into her ear. Leaning down, he smoothed the hair from the side of her face with his own and then touched his tongue to the edge of her ear. "What is your name?"

He felt the shivers travel through her as his mouth tickled her ear. Smiling, he bent down and kissed her neck, tracing the muscle there down to her shoulder with tip of his tongue. Connor bit the spot gently, teasing it with his teeth and soothing it with his tongue. "Your name?" he asked again.

She arched then, clearly enjoying his touch and ready for more. Her head fell back against his shoulder and he moved his mouth to the soft skin there, kissing and licking his way down and back to her ear. Still she had not spoken.

"When I call out my pleasure, sweetling, what name will I speak?"

He released her shoulders and slid his hands down her arms and then over her stomach to hold her in complete contact with him. Covering her stomach and pressing her to him, he rubbed against her back, letting her feel the extent of his erection—hard and large and ready to pleasure her. Connor moved his hands up to take her breasts in his grasp. Rubbing his thumbs over their tips and teasing them to tightness, he no longer asked, he demanded.

"Tell me your name."

He felt her breasts swell in his hands and he tugged now on the distended nipples, enjoying the feel and imagining them in his mouth, as he sucked hard on them and as she screamed out her pleasure But nothing cold have pleased him more in that moment then the way she gasped at each stroke he made, over and over until she moaned out her name to him.

"Moira."

"Moira," he repeated slowly, drawing her name out until it was a wish in the air around them. "Moira," he said again as he untied the laces on her bodice and slid it down her shoulders until he could touch her skin. "Moira," he now moaned as the heat and the scent of her enticed him as much as his own scent was pulling her under this control.

Connor paused for a moment, releasing her long enough to drag his tunic over his head and then turning her into his embrace. He inhaled sharply as her skin touched his, the heat of it seared into his soul as the tightened peaks of her breasts pressed against his chest. Her added height brought her hips level almost to his and he rubbed his hardened cock against her stomach, letting her feel the extent of his arousal.

As he pushed her hair back off her shoulders, he realized that in addition to the raging lust in his blood, there was something else there, teasing him with its presence.

Anticipation.

For the first time in years, this felt like more than the mindless rutting that happened between him and the countless, nameless women there for his needs. For the first time in too long, this was not simply scratching an itch, for the hint of something more seemed to stand off in the distance, something tantalizing and unknown and something tied to this woman.

He lifted her chin with his finger, forcing her gaze off the blasted chair and onto his face. Instead of the compliant gaze he that usually met him, the clarity of her gold-flecked green eyes startled him. Connor did something he'd not done before, something he never needed to do—he asked her permission.

"I want you, Moira," he whispered, dipping to touch and taste her lips for the first time. Connor slid his hand down to gather up her skirts, baring her legs and the treasure between them to his touch and his sight. "Let me?"